BANE

BRIAR BLACK

Copyright © 2024 Briar Black

All rights reserved.

No part of this book may be reproduced, distributed, or transmitted in any form or by any means, including photocopying, recording, or other electronic or mechanical methods, without the prior written permission of the publisher, except in the case of brief quotations embodied in critical reviews and certain other non-commercial uses permitted by copyright law.

This is a work of fiction. Names, characters, places, and incidents are either the product of the author's imagination or used fictitiously. Any resemblance to actual persons, living or dead, events, or locales is entirely coincidental.

Cover design by Tim Faulkner
Editing by Sarah Ridding
Formatting by Rebel Wolf Marketing

Paperback ISBN: 9798345606964

For the geeks, freaks, weirdos, Trekkies, Whovians, Potterheads, Gamers, Otakus, Ringers, and Browncoats. Never settle for anything less than someone who truly sees you, appreciates you in all your quirky oddness—and loves you unconditionally.

ACKNOWLEDGMENTS

This novel started out as a silly way to pass the time. Good friends talked me into actually doing something with it, and I'm very glad they did; you know who you are. You know I love you. Thanks also to Hazel, Simon, and the whole team at Rebel Wolf Marketing for project managing all my fiction efforts, creating my website, and being so patient with me as I navigate the murky waters of social media and marketing. If only I had Amelia's drive and Suzie's fearless confidence, I'd be a bestselling author!

A huge thanks to Tim Faulkner for his fantastic artwork. It's really made my characters come to life, and so perfectly matches my aesthetic it's better than I ever imagined. Very special thanks also go to Sarah Ridding for her hard work and patience editing my silly stories.

This tale is set in the fictional town of Ashfordby. This is not a real place, nor is White Deer Park! Rather, they are creations inspired by various towns, villages, and country parks in Cheshire. Please don't waste your time trying to figure out where they are—they don't exist!

Trigger Warning: While they do not take place on the page, this book references the beating and attempted sexual assault of a child. It also mentions other violent activities.

CHAPTER 1

In the unspoken language of small-town life, a prodigal daughter's return is either a triumphant success or a scandalous failure. Which side I'd landed when I moved back home had yet to be determined. Local gossip was leaning in the direction of the former. But I was perched (uncomfortably) on the fence.

Cautiously optimistic yet realistically sceptical.

Anxiety had gripped me by the throat every morning since I returned. Those first few days had been crippling. Now, the panic only maintained its stranglehold briefly each morning. Considerable progress, but it had taken considerable effort. Beginning with a morning run.

Endorphins, or some shit.

Which explained why I found myself pounding the pavement in the wee small hours, rain flying horizontally into my face. The sun was struggling to rise from its bed beneath the horizon, spilling a faint orange glow over the world. Night had birthed a cold mist. The grass was spiked into endless ranks of tiny soldiers, each sporting a little coat of ice. Frost had powdered the path as I left the house, leaving it on the cusp of being too slippery to run. With rain clearly brewing in the skies, I'd left Echo at home.

Now, soaked to the bone, I was starting to wish I'd stayed there myself. Alas, I still had a couple of miles to go.

A buzzing vibration in my ear told me someone was ringing, and I tapped to answer, grateful for the distraction. "You're up early," I said by way of greeting.

"I knew you'd be awake. And I wanted to remind you about the weekend."

"Still not coming, Suzie."

I heard the whistle of a familiar kettle, thrifted on my first trip to visit Suzie after she'd moved, and now the pride of her kitchen. Some miles away, in a small basement flat, beneath an aged Victorian building a short walk from Bangor University, my best friend sighed. "You can't be working *another* weekend."

"And yet, somehow, I am. You're more than welcome to come attack my garden again."

She sighed so dramatically I felt sure her neighbours would be banging on their floor to shut her up. "But I'm only back in Manchester for the weekend, I told you. And I promised Tom a night on the lash."

"Please," I huffed, picking up my pace to get out of the rain sooner, "you've never needed me to give Tom a good lashing."

"Ah, now, you know we've stopped all that. He was getting too—"

"Loved up."

"—*invested*, I was going to say." She paused.

Not for the first time, I sensed that she was panicking at the thought Tom had real, genuine feelings for her. She had none for him. I was sure of that, though she'd become very fond of him as a friend. Whatever part of Suzie's brain allowed love had shut down years ago.

"Why don't you bring him here?" I ducked my head and powered up a short rise, knowing trees lay beyond and some small amount of shelter. "Night out in Ashfordby, darling of Cheshire, he'll love it."

"But it's so…pedestrian."

"Hardly. Besides, it might help me meet some new people."

That gave her pause. We'd both grown up in town, but unlike me, Suzie had never expressed the slightest interest in returning. She came to visit her parents, that was it. Neither of us had kept in touch with anyone from school save each other, and I was beginning to seriously regret that.

"I'll speak to Tom. Should I invite anyone else?"

"Like who?" I pawed rainwater out of my eyes. "Most of my city friends lost interest when I quit my 'real' job, and I didn't have many to begin with."

"There's Johnny, I'm sure he'd—"

"No."

"You're still friends," she protested.

"Of a sort. Stop meddling, woman; that ship sank. Johnny was—"

"Pleasant."

"*Pedestrian*," I corrected.

Suzie didn't answer. She wouldn't contradict me; she knew it was true. Johnny was a lovely bloke. Kind, sweet, reliable, loyal.

Uninspired.

Unambitious.

Utterly vanilla.

Had I dipped him in magnolia, he couldn't have been more beige.

I swear I could hear her shrug down the phone. "Speaking of men you shouldn't settle for, any further sightings of His Godliness?"

"He just goes by Adonis these days," I said, trying to sound casual.

"*And?*"

"And I'll be running into him any minute," I chuckled, "so I have to go."

In the last few weeks, I'd come to live for the brief, heart-racing moments our paths collided each day. Though I'd never admitted it to Suzie, she'd rapidly figured it out.

"I think today's the day," Suzie said.

"Today is not the day."

"You haven't seen him in over 15 years, Aimee. You're not the same people. Just talk to him. He might not even recognise you."

"Thanks," I scowled at the rain.

"No, I just mean... You look so different now. I doubt he'd connect the platinum blonde queen you are with the girl who dedicated a dance to him in year nine, and fell on her arse doing it."

I cringed. "Good times."

"Just start a conversation. Ask him for coffee. Let him get to know you. He might like you."

"He might not."

"Well, what's the alternative?" she snapped. "At least you'd know it's a no-go and could stop mooning over him."

I was, I knew, dangerously close to burning out her patience on this topic. Hell, I'd been close to that when we'd moved away for uni, let alone now. Nobody wanted to hear about my crush anymore. Even I was sick of thinking about it. Not that it would stop me.

"Fine," I relented, "I'll ask him for coffee."

❖

My breath clouded the air. The tip of my nose was numb and the rest tingled unpleasantly. I was so focused on keeping my footing that I hadn't even noticed him approaching until he shot from the mist a few metres to my left. Our eyes locked. A brief nod, reciprocated. And I continued forwards to join the path just ahead of him. Just like every day since the morning after I'd moved back here. I almost stumbled, catching my balance at the last second, grateful I hadn't fallen flat on my arse because he was now running directly behind me.

His route collided with mine about a half mile into White Deer Park. We trotted along the same path for another mile or so before parting ways just past the end of the mere. For a few breathtaking, aching moments, we shared a path. Some days, we met here, where the less-used path that started near my house branched into the main thoroughfare bisecting the park. It meandered past both lakes to the beautiful old hall and ended on the farthest outskirts of Ashfordby. Some days, we ran into each other further down. But, most days, he was a little way behind me as I hit the main path. He'd catch up, and we'd briefly run in tandem before his pace took him beyond me.

After about a week of daily encounters, we'd silently accepted that we were on the same clock. Words never passed between us, only a nod, and his silent smirk as he overtook me.

Which was problematic today. It was cold, and pissing rain, and I wasn't in the mood to slow my pace and let him get ahead of me.

Sure, it made him feel all manly and superior, but a girl has to draw the line somewhere. There are times to pander to the male ego and times to force them to watch your arse as you surpass them.

Michael Bane expected to catch me up shortly after I joined his path, then slowly pull ahead. That was our usual routine, and I swear, as I watched his blond, tousled hair bobbing away from me each day, I could feel the testosterone wafting back towards me.

So, it didn't surprise me when I heard him pick up the pace as I trudged along, fifty yards or so ahead of him.

I could have let him go.

Maybe it was the cold. Maybe the rain. Maybe it was the conversation I'd had with Suzie. I just wasn't in the mood.

My feet picked it up a beat.

He followed suit.

Followed was the operative word; for all his effort, he couldn't quite catch up.

I might have let it go; I'd proved my point. But the sky took a sudden, drastic turn. The warm glow of sunrise slowly seeping towards us was struggling in the face of furious clouds. Thunder rolled, the sky cracked with light too angry to hang around and brighten the day, and the rain that had been rhythmically pounding me suddenly turned to frozen bullets pelting me from every which way.

My feet slapped the path as my eyes roved the surroundings, looking for shelter. Winter was stingy when it came to coverage, even if we were edging towards spring. But I'd been coming to this park my whole life. I might follow the same rigid path every day now, but as a kid I'd been a roamer. We were coming to the end of the water. If I strayed from my usual route and followed the bank around instead, I'd come to a small hide, still used by local twitchers, but originally created as a permanent duck blind, back in the days when hunting unsuspecting waterfowl was considered great sport.

Hail pelted me as I turned my feet from the path and crushed the icy grass soldiers. I'd almost been running at full speed, now I did in earnest, storming down the bank. Rounding a bend, my feet skidded in the mud, arms flailing to catch my balance, but the hut was in sight. An old stone structure, sneakily camouflaged with overgrown ivy and moss, nestled quietly at the edge of the mere. You'd never spot it if you didn't know it was there. As hail stung my face, I'd never been so glad to be a native Ashfordbian in my life. With one final burst of speed, I skidded into it through the empty doorway, what was left of the door rattling on its hinges as I thundered past.

In my haste to evade the weather, I'd forgotten to factor in the need to slow down. I only just got my arms up in time to brace myself as I collided with the opposite wall.

Rain dripped down the cold stone from my soaked hands. More pooled at my feet. A laugh escaped my lips, only slightly tinged with hysteria.

Turning, I leant my back against the wall, just in time to see Michael hurtle through the door and run straight into me. One of his hands shot out to the wall beside my head, steadying himself, while his other arm wrapped around my waist, pulling me against him. As we collided, he grunted with the effort of shielding me from the impact as he lost the battle with momentum and his shoulder hit the wall. I tried to step back and give Michael some space, but his arm was still curled around my waist, and I didn't get very far. He stepped forward, closing the gap I'd created between us. Gently brushing wet hair from my face, he tucked it up under my beanie. His fingers traced a line down my cheek as his thumb slicked across my chin, tilting it so I looked up at him. His touch sent sparks shooting down the length of my body, tightening everything in their wake.

The shock of him thrummed through every inch of me.

Smoky blue eyes bore into me. His breath misted the air between us for a brief instant before he bent, his lips finding mine.

They were slick with rain, pressing gently, parting my own slightly to allow the lightest touch from his tongue. Heat flooded my body, my eyes closed. I leant hard into the kiss, only to find him pulling away.

My eyes snapped open. Michael was gazing at me, a silent inquiry; *Is this okay?*

God, yes.

My fingers slid up his chest, clenching his hoodie and pulling him back towards me. A smile quirked his lip into a lopsided grin, and then those lips were on me again. Harder this time. Hot, insistent, as he expertly entwined his tongue around my own.

The arm around my waist tightened, his hand cupping my bum and lifting me, crushing me into him. His cock was rock hard between us, pressing almost painfully against my hip. I wriggled against him slightly, repositioning it to a more pleasing location, and he broke our kiss as a moan escaped his lips. His other hand snaked up the back of my neck, cushioning my head as his arm released my waist, and he twisted me back into the wall.

He kissed me again. Long, languid, his body pressing against me the whole time, heat radiating between us despite the chill in the air. His free hand burrowed under my fleece, under my vest top, until he found what he wanted; flesh. His thumb stroked my stomach, fingertips inching their way up until they hit the curve of my breast. He cupped it, squeezing gently until his fingers grazed my nipple, and it was my turn to gasp.

Michael's face pulled back for a second, another questioning look; I answered by running a hand down his stomach, slipping it inside the waist of his joggers and stroking the length of his cock. His gaze intensified, fingers tightening around my breast, squeezing my nipple hard before abruptly abandoning it. He thrust his hand into my shorts, parting my legs, parting my lower lips, and running his thumb up and down their length on each side as he resumed kissing me. Hard now, fierce.

As his touch found my clit, I arched into his fingers. The angle, coupled with the tight fit of my shorts, made it awkward, and I released him long enough to peel them and my knickers halfway down my thighs. For an instant, his hand found the perfect angle, the perfect spot, and my legs spasmed, twitching uncontrollably as pleasure built within me. I was right on the edge of an orgasm when he stopped. Stepped back. A small noise of disappointment escaped my lips, but I needn't have worried. His hands tore my shorts the rest of the way down my legs. I stepped out of them as I yanked his joggers down. He lifted me up, my legs wrapped around his waist. There was an instant of awkward repositioning as he pressed me back into the wall. Reaching up, I grabbed a heavy beam overhead and pulled myself up a little, sliding down over the tip of him.

Michael's hands tightened around my arse, cold palms pulling me to him as he thrust further inside me. I gasped, that first shock of pleasure as the length of him stroked inside me. He pulled back and thrust harder, deeper. I gasped louder. His lips found my neck, nuzzling and kissing along my jaw as a rhythm built between us. The ribbed edge of his hoodie was wedged against my clit, and every thrust of his hips roughed it up. Pressure was building inside and out, mounting inside me as a wave of pleasure crested externally and crashed over me. I cried out, and he groaned into my neck as my cum washed his cock. His pace quickened, satisfied now that I'd been satisfied, seeking his own release. My breath rasped in my throat as aftershocks of the orgasm rippled through me, but that pressure within was still building, with every stroke of him against my insides. As his own pleasure overtook him, Michael sank into me, groans becoming cries, and I felt every inch of him pulsing with pleasure.

We came together, the intensity making me lose my grip on the beam. I thought I'd fall, but he had me, keeping me snug against him, firmly held between his body and the wall. I wrapped my arms around his neck and kissed him as he rocked his hips into me, savouring the last vestiges of pleasure. He returned the kiss, but softer now. The urgency was gone, heat replaced with something else.

Gently, Michael lifted me down and set me back on my feet. I swayed slightly, legs wobbling. He chuckled, turning away from me and roughly pulling his joggers back up. In an instant, I went from elation to mortification.

The fuck just happened?

I was, suddenly, alarmingly self-conscious. And freezing cold. As Michael stretched and walked towards the door, I scrabbled on the floor to retrieve my soaked clothes, struggling to get my knickers back on. Eventually, I gave up, stuffing them in a pocket with my phone as I jerked my shorts up.

Michael was leaning out of the door. I took a step towards him. "So—"

His raised hand silenced me as his other went to his lips in a silent, *'Shh.'*

I was about to tell him I wasn't a toddler to be shushed when he slowly leaned back into the room, slipped a hand through mine, and gently pulled me to the doorway. He wrapped both arms around me and hugged me to him, hands rubbing me up and down, trying to keep me warm.

Turning me to face out across the water, Michael bent and whispered in my ear, "Look up the hill."

The hail had stopped, as had the rain, storm clouds rolling away and leaving a crisp, pale blue sky in their wake. Mist still coiled around our ankles, but it was washed through with the warm amber of the rising sun. Frost sparkled wherever the light touched it, and away over the water on the far side of the bank, where the ground rose in a small hill topped with a smattering of trees, a great white stag stood at the summit.

Regally, he surveyed the morning, almost silhouetted against the sunrise, antlers towering above alert ears.

He was looking right at us.

I stared out over the water as the mist coiled around the beautiful creature's legs, and the golden glow of morning drenched his snowy white fur. We remained that way for a few long, perfect moments, Michael's breath hot on my neck, his arms gently crushing me into the solid wall of his chest. The deer's ears twitched, his head snapped around, and he strolled purposefully over the top of the hill and out of sight.

"Beautiful," Michael breathed. Then, with absolutely zero hesitation, he said, "Dinner tonight?" Without waiting for an answer, he kissed my temple, gave me a quick squeeze and said, "I'll call to arrange it. Where do you work?"

"Kobayashi Maru, in town."

A nod, then he jogged off down the path.

I stepped out of the hide, staring after him as he disappeared into the mist.

I guess that saves me asking him for coffee.

CHAPTER 2

"Well." A loaded pause. "That escalated quickly."

"Right?" Switching my mobile to speaker, I tossed it on the sofa. Echo leapt up to follow it. She spun in a swift circle and settled, head on paws, so she might observe my day in comfort. It was a three-seater sofa. If I was lucky, she might let me squeeze on with her. It was also white, as was the fluffy rug, her other favourite place to sleep. In hindsight, the colour choice might have been impractical.

I let my office door swing shut behind me as the light flickered on overhead. I'd made it three steps across the office before a knock at the door forced me to turn back.

"Yeah?"

The door swung open and a slim, pale face appeared. "Hillary for you."

"I'll call back."

"Says it's urgent."

"I'll call back. Soon."

Isla's mouth started to open in reply, but she clicked it shut when I fixed her with an uncompromising stare. She vanished. There was a pause. I waited. The door reopened, and she reappeared, offering a steaming mug of coffee.

"Thanks." I took the mug and wedged myself into the

remaining space beside Echo on the sofa.

"Is that Hillary of the mind-numbing doohickey?" Suzie's voice asked from the other side of the sofa.

"Plant food spikes, and yes. The woman is the bane of my existence."

Suzie snorted, "Not anymore she's not." She descended into fits of hysterical giggles at her own pun.

"Michael Bane is less a cause of annoyance, more a—" I dropped my voice to a whisper in case Isla was still outside the door, "—source of multiple orgasms. And he won't stick around long enough to be a regular feature."

I took a sip of coffee and sighed. Echo lifted her head and shuffled around to thump it back down on my knee. I scratched her between the ears as she stared up at me with sympathetic eyes. "Maybe I should just get another dog."

"He asked you for dinner."

I winced. "That was an instruction, not an invite, and I doubt he'll follow through."

Echo whined. I sipped my coffee contemplatively.

"You're so pessimistic."

"Realistic."

"Whatever. I say he calls."

I'd just begun to consider what the consequences of him actually calling would be when Isla knocked on the door again.

"I gotta scoot," I sighed.

"Places to go, doohicks to market, childhood crushes to fuck."

"Yeah, ya know…the usual."

I hung up and called Isla, who was still loitering outside the office door. "What?"

The door inched open. "I'm sorry, but Hillary's on again—"

"Yeah, put her through." Gulping down the last of my coffee, I braced myself for another round of '*Why haven't I sold a million products yet?*'.

It was after I'd finished my *fifth* call with Hilary, and shortly before I'd managed to take a sip of the cinnamon latte (two extra espresso shots) Isla had brought to help me recover, that *the* call came. The poor girl had barely left my office after delivering my drink before she was back to tell me that *a man* was on the phone. A man named *Michael*. And that I'd know who he was. She was decidedly arch as she relayed this information, as if it was somehow cryptic and intriguing.

I stared at the phone in confusion for the first couple of rings, genuinely flummoxed that he'd called. Pushing the speaker button I said, "Hey," then winced because I sounded like a div.

"So, when you said you worked at Kobayashi Maru, you actually meant you *own* Kobayashi Maru."

"Yeah."

"You could have led with that."

I shrugged, then realised he couldn't see me. "And spoil the surprise?"

Michael laughed. "Preserving your mystique?"

"Something like that."

"Might you and your mystique be free for dinner? Say, Giuliano's? Seven?"

I paused, pretending to consider the question. "Sure. See you there."

❖

Tugging self-consciously at the cowl neck of my dress, I fidgeted as I waited for a server to seat me, then adjusted my belt for the tenth time. I'd dressed for work that morning, not a date. There hadn't been time to go home and change, and I wasn't sure over-knee boots and a knit dress were quite *the look* for Giuliano's. The hostess came over to greet me by name, with a beauteous smile and a reassurance that Michael was waiting for me. She took my coat, and I followed her to our table.

You look fabulous, darling. Stop being a melt.

Michael stood as he saw me approach, pulling out my chair

and smiling as I sat down. He looked far better than he had a reasonable right to; a tailored suit was definitely a change from the running gear I was used to seeing him wear. It was blue, too. Not navy or anything predictable, but a striking shade of periwinkle, the modern cut accentuating his physique with a touch of unconventional elegance.

I'd never been more grateful that I'd become a fashion fanatic in recent years and prided myself on looking put together and à la mode. Still, a party dress would have been nice right now. Something daring and asymmetric.

And red.

A waitress handed me a menu, and I smiled a thank you.

"Shall we have a bottle of wine?" Michael asked.

"Sounds good."

"What's your preference?"

I glanced at the waitress. "Do you have a good Pinot Noir?"

"We have a lovely 2016 Domaine Leroy Pinot Noir from Burgundy. It's exquisite."

I raised a questioning eyebrow at Michael.

"Sounds perfect," he said. Though I got the impression that, had I asked for yak milk, he'd have said the same thing out of politeness.

The waitress left us to study the menu.

"I'm glad you could make it," Michael said.

I looked up to find a smile on his face that appeared genuine.

The waitress returned, popped the wine cork, poured me a taste, and then waited patiently as I sampled it.

"That's delicious, thank you."

She smiled, poured us both a glass, then departed. I took another sip.

"I'm glad you called," I said. Not adding that I'd never expected him to. "Anything to take my mind off Hilary's infernal tits."

Michael was an inch away from snorting his wine. He recovered, swallowed hard, and said, "What?"

"Oh, a client. She's invented a little plastic doohickey that holds water and plant food. Shaped like a blue tit. Thinks it's going to change the world, and, of course, it's my fault that's not happened yet."

Michael's left eyebrow arched. "How will it change the world?"

I laughed. "It really won't. But every budding entrepreneur, startup and inventor thinks their thing is *the thing*." I slapped the palms on my hands dramatically on the table and fixed him with the most intense stare I could muster. "'It's *Ground. Breaking. Amelia.* It will *Change. Lives. Amelia.* All it needs is the right marketing message and it will *Sell. Millions. Amelia.*'"

A knowing smile crept across Michael's face. "And of course, it's down to you to find that magical million-making message."

"Natch."

He snorted a laugh. "How's that going then? You sold a million tits yet?"

I sipped my wine and smiled. "Not yet, but we only launched last week. Give me to the end of the quarter."

Both eyebrows shot up this time. "Confidence. I like it."

I shrugged. "The damn things will be all over Plantstagram by the end of the week, viral on TikTok by the end of the month, and because I'm not a moron, her website's already ranking for every conceivable search term relating to plant feeders and watering doohickeys. They're cute, they're cheap, they're an easy impulse buy."

"I'm sorry…Plantstagram?"

"There's a 'gram for everything. A Tok too."

Michael sat back in his chair and took a slow sip of wine. My stomach tightened as I remembered those lips on mine, his hand in my hair, the solid weight of him pressing me into that wall.

"You make it sound so simple," he said.

I swallowed. Hard.

What were we talking about? Oh, right.
Tits.

Michael shook his head. "Our marketing department doesn't seem to know how to do anything but push out crap PDF brochures."

I winced. "It's not simple. But certainly not rocket science. You can sell anything these days with the right influencers and a solid long-term organic strategy." I waved my glass at him. "*Although*, selling a service isn't the same as selling a product. It's easy to sell a £10 thingy that makes your life easier. Considerably harder to sell a finance package that requires an investment of thousands." I took a sip of wine. "Still, the whole PDF thing is pretty much done. Nobody reads them anymore; they all want video."

Michael considered that as the waitress returned and took our order. I was half expecting him to order for me after the way he'd delivered the dinner invite, but he was the perfect gentleman, gesturing at me when the waitress naturally looked to him first, and stoically studying the menu while she tried her best to flirt with him as he told her what he wanted.

Not so much as a sideways glance at her very shapely butt as she sashayed away from us.

You know the bar isn't terribly high when you're impressed by a guy who doesn't openly leer at other women on your first date.

"So," he said, drawing my attention back to the conversation, "if marketing is so easy, how come so many new businesses fail?"

He seemed genuinely interested. Another point in his favour. I held up a hand and checked off the big three with my thumb and fingers. "Impatience. Fear. Lack of funds. Getting any marketing campaign off the ground takes time. You need a good 6-12 months to do things properly. We may have just launched the infernal blue tits, but work started eight or nine months ago building the website, creating a platform, building a list of plant fanatics, raising the brand profile, lining up influencers. That's months of work and money spent where you're seeing zero return. Most people either get impatient and rush it, are too afraid to risk that much money without having any coming in, or don't have the capital to do it in the first place."

Michael was nodding. "I can see that being an issue. Especially when you have no guarantee it will work at all. Maybe your product flops. Maybe someone else beats you to it and you end up looking like a cheap knockoff."

"Exactly. A lot of my job is keeping clients on track when they panic. Reminding them, repeatedly, what we talked about at the start, the timescales we laid out, the reasons for doing everything the way we have. Mid-launch - which is where the plant feeder currently is - that's the worst. You often have a slow start, and the client panics. All that work, all that investment, and they're only selling a few measly items a day. They want to shake things up, change the plan, throw a ton of money at ads or, worse, blame you for the fact it wasn't an instant success and demand you foot the bill for all those ads."

Michael made a face. "That doesn't seem reasonable."

I shrugged. "Nobody's reasonable when money's involved."

He chuckled, and my stomach seemed to fall right through me and hit the floor beneath my chair. It was unreasonable for a man to be that attractive. Dangerous. Like, how could I ever drive a car with him in the passenger seat? One sideways glance while he was smiling like that, and we'd be straight off a cliff.

Something of my thoughts must have shown on my face as he gave me a questioning look. Heat rose in my cheeks. I looked away. Thankfully, the waitress returned with our starters, and I deflected by thanking her and nibbling on my pomegranate salad.

Michael chivalrously allowed me to avoid embarrassment and pretended to be captivated by his calamari, but I caught the little smile that quirked the corner of his mouth.

He might not have known exactly what I was thinking, but he was damn sure I was thinking he was hot.

For a moment, I was lost in a wave of nostalgic embarrassment. He never used to appreciate my appreciation of him. Far from it. He'd always been mortified and furious whenever I'd said or done anything to reveal the monumental crush I had on him.

He'd been one of the cool kids; I had most definitely not been. He'd hated me for crushing on him. And I'd hated myself for being inexplicably incapable of keeping that crush to myself.

What I'd hoped to achieve was anyone's guess; it had been clear to anyone with half a brain he'd never be remotely interested in me.

Yet here we were, sitting across a table at a nice restaurant, as he not only showed every interest in me and my life but found it cute that I was still floored by his annoyingly perfect face. The chiselled line of his jaw sported a stubbly beard that was just scruffy enough to be sexy but not so unkempt it looked unprofessional. The taut lines of his muscles were clearly visible across his shoulders and down his arms. His tailor was an artist. And yes, he most definitely had a tailor; there was no way that was off the rack. I suspected he'd worn a tie for work, but that had been discarded and the top buttons undone and loosened for dinner. His cufflinks were tiny silver footballs, which surprised me not at all, though the cartoon design did. They looked ever-so-slightly out of place in his otherwise immaculate outfit.

"So." He took a sip of wine and looked back up at me. "How do you keep them on track?"

I blinked. It took me a second to remember what we'd been talking about. I pretended to be considering the question while my brain scrambled for a semi-intelligent answer.

"Balance," I said finally. "They need to have enough faith in their offering to counteract the fear. They need enough capital to sustain them through their impatience. And they need a realistic understanding of how long things will take, what things will cost, and when they will start seeing a return. They need to be grounded enough to remember that reality throughout. And they need a product that can genuinely be profitable even after you've factored in all the expense of marketing it."

"What happens if a client doesn't have the right balance?"

I shrugged. "I don't take them on to begin with. I'm quite discerning about my clients. A lot of them give me the ick."

He finished chewing his mouthful of calamari with a frown. "The ick?"

"Yeah, that gut feeling when your mate sets you up on a blind date and makes you promise to give the guy a fair shake. And you know, the entire date, they're all kinds of wrong, but you go on a second date anyway."

Michael smiled. "Because you convince yourself you're being unfair and you should get to know them before writing them off completely."

I waved a fork at him. "Exactly. Second date rolls around, and it's worse than the first. Now they think they're a shoo-in."

His smile became a grin. "Now they're not even trying to tone down the crazy."

"Now they let it all spill out on the table, and when you excuse yourself and leave early, they don't take the hint."

He winced, nodding his head. "They call, text and just flood your voicemail. You politely decline, ignore them, and finally outright tell them to fuck off; they don't take the hint."

I grinned. "Every time you think they've gone, they just pop right back up. Like the mother of all floaters bobbing back up again no matter how many times you hit the flusher." I made direct eye contact with him. "Ick." Last time I used this analogy to explain work to a guy, he made a face, changed the subject, and never called again.

"I get it," Michael smirked. "You knew they were going to be a pain in the arse. Gut instinct. You ignored it, and got kicked in the balls."

"Exactly. When clients give you the ick, and you ignore it and take them on anyway, they expect the earth but aren't willing to invest what's necessary to achieve their goals. Or they lack the funds to do what's needed but aren't willing or able to compensate for that by learning to do some of it themselves and investing their own time instead of money."

Michael paused mid chew, seemed to think for a moment then finished his mouthful and swallowed. "I'm surprised to hear you advocate for people doing their own marketing. Doesn't that put you out of a job?"

"Not really. I run an eCourse that teaches those who can't pay me to do it how to do it all themselves. A lot of them end up coming to me once their businesses can support outsourcing their campaigns."

"And in the interim, you've got a nice source of passive income." He nodded approvingly, giving me a thoughtful look as he sipped more wine. "You'd be amazed how many business owners refuse to see the potential of passive income streams. That is one of *my* constant challenges; convincing people to implement them."

"You're in finance?" A casual question. As if I hadn't stalked him incognito on LinkedIn already.

"For my sins." He smirked again. "But you know that already."

I stared at him, rabbit in headlights.

"You pointed out it's harder to sell a high-ticket investment package than a low-price product."

Shit. "Busted."

He laughed. Not a quiet, polite laugh, but a full-on belly laugh. "It's okay, I stalked you on your website too. But since you asked, yes, I run a wealth management firm with two of the lads I was at uni with. We work mostly with businesses, helping them maximise their profits, make wise investments, run pension funds etc." Michael sounded like he was reciting an elevator pitch and was utterly bored of it.

He paused to nod to the waitress as she returned once again to clear our plates, assure her everything was delicious, and order a second bottle of wine.

"Why do I get the impression you're less than enthused about your work?" I asked when she'd left.

A slight lift of his eyebrows suggested I'd surprised him, and he paused before answering. "I suppose, because I am.

Finance isn't exactly my passion." His eyes sparked on the final word.

"Oh? And what is?" I couldn't help a soft chuckle, anticipating a dirty answer.

"To be honest, I only went into finance for the money." He waved a hand. "Predictable, I know. When I was a kid, I was convinced I'd be a pro footballer..."

I smiled, remembering many an afternoon watching him from afar as he booted a ball round a muddy field.

"...but I was injured early on and suddenly that wasn't an option."

Shit. How did I not know that?

He rubbed a hand over his jaw and looked down. "I had thought about becoming a coach, but..."

"But?" I prompted, ducking my head slightly to meet his eyes and smiling.

He startled and lifted his head back up. "Sorry. People don't usually ask, it caught me off guard."

I said nothing, giving him space to answer, or not, as he wanted. The waitress returned with our wine, and he took it from her without meeting her gaze, topping up both our glasses himself. She looked stricken with disappointment for an instant before she retreated to gossip with the bartender, who shot me an appraising look and shrugged. I wondered if he was dismissing her irritation, as it was inevitable Michael would ignore her while seated opposite a goddess such as myself, or if he was baffled as to why a guy like *that* was out to dinner with *me*.

Probably the latter.

I was certainly confounded by the turn of events.

"*But*," Michael finally continued, "my sister fell pregnant while she was still in school. It was a friend of mine who knocked her up, and he did a runner as soon as he found out." Michael shook his head. "My parents weren't in a position to support her and I didn't want..." He looked up at me, a slight frown creasing his brow, and for the first time, I noticed that age had touched him after all. Not a lot, and not in an unattractive way, but there were lines where there hadn't been before. Just a hint of them between the brows, at the corner of his eyes.

In every other respect, he was the same boy I'd adored as a child. He'd just grown more substantial in time, his body hardened by muscle where once he'd been quite scrawny. The line of his jaw lacked any trace of puppy fat and was now squared off and strong. I wondered if the posturing tough guy still lurked within him, ready to raise both arms out and beckon with outstretched fingers yelling, *'Come and have a go, if you think you're hard enough!'*

He'd had so much anger. I'd never wondered where it had come from. Thoughts like that simply hadn't occurred to me as a teen. His eyes had lost the juvenile delinquency I'd once found so appealing, yet this morning they'd still danced with mischief and just an edge of danger. Now, they frowned at me, clearly contemplating whether he should finish his sentence or not.

Finally, he said, "I didn't want her or the kid growing up like we did. So, when I was offered a chance to make more for myself, my family, I took it."

Wow. That was unexpected.

"I don't normally talk about it." He frowned again. "There's something about you, though. Like you might actually get it. I underestimated you. When I looked up where you worked to call earlier, I assumed you were a graphic designer or something. I wasn't expecting to find you owned the business. Much less that you're the sole owner."

"Why?" I bristled. "Because I'm a woman?"

"Partly." He shrugged an apology. "But mostly because I don't know many people our age who work for themselves. Who refused to settle for the hand life dealt them and spun the wheel. Who…" His mouth moved around words he didn't seem happy enough with to voice.

"Broke the cycle?" I offered.

"Yes. That's it, exactly. My niece is thirteen now and in the best private school in Cheshire." The smile that lit his face was a whole other kind of attractive. This was a side to Michael I'd never expected to see. Certainly a million miles from the rough and ready bad boy of our youth. "I did that," he added softly, almost to himself.

Had he not fucked me in a duck blind that morning, I'd have thought the boy I'd known was gone completely. Michael shook himself and snorted. "Well. That made me sound horrendously egotistical."

"Not at all. It's not easy creating success on your own terms. You've done it. And you're not a total dick about it either; you're spending it on your family, not Ferraris."

A sketchy expression passed across his face, and I laughed. "You totally have a Ferrari!"

"Lotus, actually."

"No way!"

"What's wrong with that?" He was getting defensive, which only made me laugh more.

Defensiveness turned to irritation, and I quickly explained, "I have an Elise."

The wariness in his face dissolved into laughter.

"The only thing that costs me more," I added, "is footing the bill for my brother's kids to go to private school."

"No. Serious?" He laughed some more. "Which one?"

"The best in Cheshire," I smirked. "Of course, they're only seven and ten, so still in the Primary."

"Boys or girls?"

"One of each; Aaron's the eldest, and an absolute tearaway. Sasha's a lot quieter, a classic Belle."

Michael frowned and shook his head slightly.

"You know, from *Beauty and the Beast*, nose permanently stuck in a book, everyone thinks she's rather odd. Kinda like me as a kid, I guess."

He smiled, as if that was cute, and he hadn't despised me for all my bookish oddness back then. I couldn't decide if it was nice that he was just ignoring all that, or a little offensive he'd chosen to avoid addressing it.

I was about to ask, but then, I might not have liked the

answer. And why spoil a good meal? Instead, I switched subjects. "So, do you still play?"

"Play?"

"Football."

"Ah. No, not so much. But Becca, my niece, she's a nut for it. Probably my fault, that. She's been playing since she was a kid. I coach the school team, and I may be biased, but I reckon she's the best player we have."

"I didn't know they had a girls football team."

Michael nodded.

"How very progressive."

"Well, to be honest, it's very new. She played for a local under 10s when she was in primary school, but once she switched to high school she wanted to play for her school." A look I took to be pure irritation crossed his face. "They refused to let her play for the boys' team, even though she is far better than most of them. So, I kicked up a fuss until they agreed to create a girls' team. In the end, the only way to get them to agree was to coach it myself."

"You poor thing," I chuckled, "such a hardship."

"Yeah…fairly sure they expected me to drop it when they made that a condition. They still haven't realised I care more about coaching that team than running my business."

I shrugged. "It's a different world for most of them. When you come from money, it seems to be all you care about."

He nodded. "True words."

We sat in companionable silence for a time as our main courses arrived and we both tucked in. Another glass of wine later and we found ourselves at the end of our meal. He called for the bill, and didn't irritate me by arguing when I paid my own half.

"Shall we share a taxi?" he asked, as we headed for the door, and the hostess returned our coats.

"I need to swing past the office and get Echo. We usually walk home."

"That's your dog? She often runs with you."

I nod. "When the weather isn't too cruel."

He smiled. "In that case, may I walk you both home?"

My office was nestled in a row of charming 17th and 18th-century Georgian shops, bars and restaurants that had been meticulously groomed. They were all old buildings here, on old streets, each with its own unique character, their façades ranging from warm brick to smooth, painted stucco, accented with traditional wooden signs and great expansive shop fronts. Windows boasted flower boxes overflowing with colourful blooms, while the pavement was occasionally littered with small tables and chairs perched outside cafés, or tiered wooden stalls laden with goods and wares. At this hour, the latter had been packed away, but the bars and some of the cafés remained open, warm light spilling from their windows and the heaters nestled in umbrellas and awnings sheltering the tables outside.

I'd left Echo sleeping on my sofa. We walked through the shop front that acted as an open-plan office for my team, with huge glass windows looking out onto one of the main roads through town. Michael stepped inside, glancing around with open curiosity, taking in the sleek modern desks, the open breakout spots and quiet nooks.

"You just have the downstairs?" he asked.

I glanced back to find him studying the mural of a starship, zipping through space, that covered one of the walls.

"No, upstairs too. There's a kitchen, toilets, and we've been building out media areas; a podcast studio, filming sets and the like."

"Very impressive," he murmured, then pointed at the words next to the spaceship. *We don't believe in the no-win scenario.* "I don't get it?"

I smiled. "It's from *Star Trek*. The Kobayashi Maru is a test, a no-win scenario that's meant to gauge a cadet's reactions to impossible situations, see how they act under the pressure of an unwinnable battle. Kirk famously passed the unpassable test by reprogramming the scenario so he won."

Michael had raised a sceptical eyebrow at my mention of *Star Trek,* but now he smiled. "Because he didn't believe in no-win scenarios."

I nodded. "Sometimes, the rules of the game are what need changing, not the players or their strategies. When you're marketing a brand or selling a product or service, there's always a way to win. Even if your competition massively outstrips you on budget, or you have something that is exactly the same as a million other brands out there. There is nothing that can't be successfully marketed as long as you're willing to think creatively, push boundaries, and sometimes redefine what success means. Kirk didn't accept the scenario as it was; he transformed it into something he could conquer." I shrugged. "When I set up on my own, that's exactly what I wanted to do. Change the script. Flip the experiences I had elsewhere on their head. Do things differently. Everyone kept telling me I was crazy for leaving a stable corporate job."

Okay, so mostly just my mother.

And Johnny.

"I argued it was stifling, demeaning, not what I wanted to do with my life. They were all 'It's a no-win scenario; you can either have stability and drudgery, or freedom and poverty, *choose your hard*.' So I said, fuck that"—I shrugged again—"you want me to play by those rules, I'll change the rules so I can win."

Michael nodded. I couldn't be sure, but he was looking at me like he was impressed. "So... you're the Kirk of the marketing world?"

I laughed. "Something like that. It's a gimmick, a brand, but it means something. It's also a good barometer; clients who don't like the sentiment aren't a good fit for us, we know not to take them on."

"The ick."

I smiled. "Precisely." I turned and walked towards my personal office, which sat at the back of the room, stretching across the full width of the place. Floor-to-ceiling, wall-to-wall glass prevented it from feeling too segregated from everyone, yet I had the option to close the blinds and shut them out when I needed some quiet time. I pushed the door open.

Echo lifted her head lazily at the noise, realised it was me, and went from sleep to excitement in a blink. She jumped down from the sofa and shot across the room to collect her lead. I took it from her and clipped it to her collar. In all honesty, she didn't need it, but the walk back involved roads and no matter how well-behaved she was, I wasn't inclined to risk it.

Besides, people see a big dog off the leash and freak the fuck out.

Wankers.

"She's a beauty." Michael stepped into the room behind me, crouched and held out a hand, palm up, letting Echo approach and give it a good sniff before he touched her. Even then, he gave her chin scratches instead of going straight for the top of her head too soon.

Smart.

The nice way to greet a dog so you don't make them anxious.

"Doberman, right?"

"Yep."

"You had her from a pup?"

"Almost. Six months old. A friend of my brother's got her and rapidly realised they were out of their depth. She needed a new home. I'd been waiting until I settled into a house to get a dog and had just moved into my new house here. Good timing. They'd done well with her training but didn't have the time to exercise her as much as she needed. She's the best."

Echo momentarily detached her attention from her new friend to respond to the tone of my voice, stand on her back legs and nuzzle into my neck. Say what you will about dogs; you'll never convince me they don't understand what we're talking about.

"Do you live far?"

"Over on Pine Crescent."

"That explains the morning runs in the park." He caught my eye and smirked.

"It's a good spot for running."

"A good spot for a lot of things, it would seem." He leaned

in towards me but Echo chose that moment to head out of the door, dragging me along with her. I locked up the office, and we meandered down the road in the direction of home.

Cobbles rang out a serenade under my heels as a chill wind whipped around us. I shivered, shrugging deeper into my coat. Michael glanced over at me, hesitated half a breath, then looped an arm around my waist and pulled me close, tucking me neatly into his side as Echo fell in at my other heel.

"I take it you live near the park too?" I said, leaning into his warmth and trying to ignore the flips my stomach was doing at being so close to him.

"Just down the road from the main entrance. You come in through the little gate in the wall at the end of the woods?"

"Yeah." Every breath brought me the smell of him. Musky with just a hint of spice. "Down to the lake, around past the big house, and back to the woods. Same route every day." I shrugged. "I'm a creature of habit."

"What's that"—he sounded slightly surprised—"about five miles round?"

"More like five and a half, I think." *Why are you trying to sound less impressive? Dumbass.* "I've been debating adding in a loop around the old mill, get it up to 10K."

He fell silent. We crossed the road, rounded the corner onto my lane and headed towards the winding driveway that led to my house. It sat quite a way back from the road. I loved that.

Land. Privacy.

I loved it almost as much as the rustic look of my cottage, which I was slowly modernising inside. When we reached the entrance, I let Echo off her lead, and she bolted ahead of us through the trees flanking the drive, chasing an unsuspecting squirrel up an oak, before sniffing every inch of the place to check what else had happened in her absence.

As we neared my front door, Michael's gaze lingered on the ground, his brow furrowing. I reluctantly detached myself from him and fished my keys from my pocket, pausing and glancing up at him before opening the door. "You fancy a coffee?"

His eyes met mine, and he opened his mouth to reply but didn't quite manage it. I took a step back towards him. "I have tea if you prefer?"

"I do, actually. But that's not why I hesitated. Much as I want to say yes." He paused, winced, and looked away. "I'm going to say no."

Huh. I tried not to let the disappointment reach my face.

Fairly sure I failed.

"Or rather, I'm going to say, raincheck?"

Mustering as much nonchalance as I could manage, I asked, "You got somewhere else to be?"

He held my gaze. "No. But the more I get to know you, the more I regret going about everything so…backwardly."

I frowned.

"This morning… I'm not in the habit of…"

I snorted. "Neither am I."

"It's just, we kept running into each other…"

Literally.

"…and I'd been meaning to ask you for a drink."

Huh.

"But I hadn't really thought much of it beyond that."

Probably shouldn't mention I imagined our first, second and fiftieth dates in immaculate detail.

"Then it rained this morning and…"

"What? You can't resist a girl that looks like a drowned rat?" I laughed, but he was making me nervous. The kind of stomach fluttering, I'm about to embarrassingly need the toilet very urgently kind of nervous.

"You outpaced me."

I stared at him. Somewhere in the darkness, an owl hooted from one of the trees. I wondered if it was the same oak that squirrel was in, and if they were as perplexed as me.

"I…outpaced you?"

"You're a faster runner than me."

I stared at him for a long moment, blinking a couple of times, trying to make sure I was still awake and hadn't slipped into some bizarre dream. Now that I thought about it, the whole day could have been nothing more than that.

Did I oversleep?

"Are you joking?" I asked.

But then, he'd got oddly quiet when I'd mentioned running further each day. Could it possibly be that the mighty Michael Bane was *intimidated* by little ol' me?

"I underestimated you." He shook his head. "I'll hold my hands up on this and say I was shocked you could outrun me. And it was…"

What? Annoying? Emasculating? Frustrating? What?

"So fucking hot."

Huh.

"I ran my hardest trying to catch you. Seriously, I think I pulled a hammy."

I swallowed a snort of laughter. It didn't seem appropriate.

"But I couldn't catch up. You ran right past me and just kept on going. And by the time I caught up, you were breathless, and your hair was all curly from the rain, and I didn't think, I just…kissed you."

I waited, afraid to speak in case I stopped him from speaking.

"Then the kiss just kind of…escalated…and I realised we'd never even had a conversation let alone a date and…I thought I'd fix it. Take you to dinner. Maybe we'd see each other again, maybe not. Either way, hopefully, you wouldn't think I was a total dick."

But what a dick you have…

"And then, I find you don't just *work* at a marketing agency, you *own* one. And…I keep underestimating you." He sucked in a breath and looked at me, eyebrows raised in, what? Expectation? Hope?

I had no idea how to respond, though some stupid part of me seemed to think apologising was the move.

I clamped my teeth shut to stop me from saying the word.

"You're already far more interesting than I anticipated,"

Michael continued, slightly breathless now. "And, I'm sure, I've barely scratched the surface. So. Can we have a do-over?"

I blinked. "A do-over?"

"Can we pretend I didn't let my dick run away with my head this morning? That we've just enjoyed a very pleasant first date, which will now end with a titillating kiss, the promise of a second date, and considerably more chivalrous behaviour on my part?"

Disappointment that I wouldn't be getting a repeat of this morning's orgasm warred with a sinking feeling.

If he continued to act like this and turned out *not* to be the fuck boy I'd assumed he was, then I was in deep shit.

But then, he'd given me the option of kissing him, and whatever else it led to, I wasn't about to let that opportunity pass. Closing the gap between us, I snaked both hands up his chest, my fingers tingling as the wool of his coat scratched them slightly. Wrapping my arms around his neck, I clasped my hands together and pulled him down towards me. He obeyed without question, wrapping both arms around me and lifting me onto my tiptoes slightly so he didn't have to bend down too far. His lips closed on mine, hot and firm, and tasting ever so slightly of the wine we'd shared. My eyes closed as his tongue teased open a gap and slipped into my mouth, wrapping around my own. It was a long, lingering kiss. When I finally pulled away, we were both slightly breathless.

"A do-over," I agreed, and the grin that spread across his face was like sunrise.

"Good." He pulled me tighter and squeezed, kissing me again. "At the risk of pushing my luck, are you busy tomorrow night?"

I stared at him for a moment. "I see. So, you want to wait, but you don't want to wait long."

"Something like that, although if you're expecting a repeat of this morning, that seems more like a third date event."

I swallowed. Hard.

Deep, *deep* shit.

"I'm busy tomorrow."

His disappointment was palpable.

"I might be able to rearrange though. What did you have in mind?"

"Honestly, it's kinda lame, but I have this charity ball I have to go to and…well it would be good to take a date for once."

For once. So, he usually went stag. There was really only one reason to do that.

"You're quite the contradiction, Michael Bane." I considered the kiss. The heat of it still lingered on my lips. His hips were still pressed against mine from our embrace, and I could feel exactly how much he wanted to take things further right now. Yet he was asking me to wait. "Yes, Michael, I'll be your date."

CHAPTER 3

"Well, that was unexpected."

"*Right?*" I half screeched down the phone.

A kerfuffle in the background distracted Suzie's attention, and I finished curling my hair as she navigated her way out of the university cafeteria.

"So, you're going out with him again *tonight*." She paused. "Gotta say, wasn't expecting that."

"Me neither. But, getting ready as we speak." I bit a hairpin open, twirled a few locks into place and secured them to the back of my head. "But I don't get it. Is it a trick?"

"A trick?" Suzie laughed. "What kind of a trick?"

"I don't know." I frowned at my reflection. *Why does my hair never look as good as in the tutorials?* "Like, he's already had his wicked way with me and didn't want a repeat performance. But he didn't know how to tell me, so he told me this instead?" I grabbed another pin and twirled some more hair, stabbing it into place.

"That makes no sense," Suzie scoffed. "Why take you out to dinner if he was already done? Why ask you out on a second date at all?"

"Maybe it's a gotcha moment." Grabbing a tiny glob of gel, I smoothed some flyaways down and surveyed my efforts.

"Huh?"

"We'll get there. I'll be in my gown and my heels, and I'll walk in the room, and there's everyone we ever went to school with in their regular clothes, pointing and laughing at me for being so fucking stupid as to think *Michael Bane* would take me anywhere. Let alone a ball."

Silence permeated the air. It went on so long I actually picked my phone up to check we were still connected. Suzie finally snapped out of whatever stupor had muted her. "You're so much more fucked up than you let on."

"What?"

"Aimee, we're not in high school anymore. You're not the same girl you were as a teenager. I'm sure he's not the same guy. From the sounds of it, he's a successful player…"

"Thanks for that."

"…who is used to the women in his life being frail, *come rescue me* airheads. He's finally met someone he can have a conversation with, and he doesn't want to blow it."

I stared at my reflection. *Okay, I'll admit it: the tutorial worked out.* My hair was artfully up and tumbling in a cascade down one side, pretty little curls peeking out in seemingly random but actually very strategic places.

It would do.

"That all sounds very mature and put together," I said. "It's never going to work if he's that good at adulting."

Suzie laughed. "Girl, you're building an empire singlehanded. You're pretty damn good at adulting yourself."

"That's different." I fiddled with a curl, then wished I hadn't. "That's work. This is…"

"Michael Bane," Suzie finished. She knew. Of all people, she understood.

This guy had been my obsession from year seven right the way through sixth form. I'd daydreamed about him. I'd dreamed about him. I'd spent more time thinking about him and the blissful life we'd have together than I'd dedicated to any other single thing in my life save my business. Eight years.

And not only had he never had a kind word for me, he'd

been cruel.

"Shit." I slammed my hand down on the desk. Everything on it bounced.

Echo jumped, fell off the sofa, spun about in confusion and shot me a look of pure, unadulterated irritation.

"Sorry, girl."

She huffed at me, then returned to her spot.

"Aimee, you've got nothing to apologise for."

"I wasn't speaking to you."

"Oh." Silence for a beat. "I swear, you like that dog more than me."

I didn't answer. No point lying to her. "What am I doing?" I demanded, by way of changing the subject.

"You'll be fine. Just don't get drunk."

I winced. Drunk Amelia was a hussy. "Good plan."

There was a knock at the door. "I gotta go," I said. "Speak tomorrow."

"Okay, good luck!"

I hung up and called out, "Yeah?"

Isla pushed the door open with her foot and walked in, catching it with her bum before it shut. One hand held a coffee, the other a strapless, scarlet cocktail dress. It had a full, tulle skirt with a feathery hem. Black satin crisscrossed the sweetheart neckline, and a black lace overlay came down to the waist.

"Isla, you little legend." I stood up from my desk and strode over to meet her as she walked fully into the room. The door swung shut behind her. I took the dress and held it up, surveying it. "Wherever did you find it?"

"That little boutique on Chivalry Lane."

I raised an eyebrow at her.

"What? I didn't name the damn road."

"Well, remind me to send them a thank-you card."

"Already in the post." Isla smiled at me. She'd been with me a relatively short time but already knew my ways so well. It frightened me a little; I'd be lost without her. "With your Louboutin heels?" She paused, thinking. "Can you dance in those?"

"Not comfortably, but I'll battle through." I paused, stricken. "I still don't have a mask. Oh god, I can't go to a masquerade without a mask."

Isla set my coffee on my desk, reached inside the dress and pulled out a delicate lace mask. "As if I'd forget the mask." She rolled her eyes at me dramatically, then glanced at Echo. "You want me to drop her at your house on my way home?"

"Would you mind?" I held the mask up to my face and peered at myself in the mirror. "That's really going above and beyond."

"No problem," Isla said. "Or…maybe you want me to babysit for the night?" She smirked.

"No need."

"Likes an audience, does he?" She cackled, and I blushed. "I'm only teasing. I'll drop her at your house."

I retrieved my spare key from the desk and passed it to her. "You're a star."

"Please, it's nice to see you doing something fun for once."

That took me aback. "I have fun."

"You have work, running and a dog."

Echo lifted her head indignantly, and Isla paused on her way out to give her pets by way of an apology.

"All of those things are fun, to me," I said. She'd hit a nerve. I knew she meant well, but I really didn't need reminding I was the world's most boring nerd.

Isla shrugged. "Doesn't mean there's no room in life for other fun."

I inclined my head. She wasn't wrong.

"I know you're super busy today, but do you have time for a chat next week?"

Panic seized me. If she quit I was so fucked. "Are you okay?"

"Fine." She smiled, but it didn't quite reach her eyes. "I just wanted to run something by you."

"Sure, stick some time in my diary."

"Thanks." She smiled, and this time it filled her whole face.

"Have fun tonight."

"I'll do my best," I said dryly, flicking the blinds shut on my office windows so I could change.

It's fine. You'll be fine.

❖

Elaborately carved double doors stretched several feet above our heads, gliding open as we approached. I almost made a joke about *Star Trek* doors, but caught myself. As we entered the ballroom, a pair of immaculately dressed doormen in waistcoats and dicky bows revealed themselves to be operating the doors. I nodded my thanks, wondering how on earth they knew when to open them, then clocked the FBI-style earpieces and smirked.

Smart.

As we moved past them, my eyes were drawn up, up, impossibly far up to an ornate ceiling, a masterpiece adorned with frescoes of ancient myth and legend. This side of the room depicted Artemis and the Golden Stag. The Greek goddess of the wilderness and the wild hunt, Artemis took centre stage, her posture all power and grace, bow in hand, quiver of arrows slung across her back. Ethereal stags surrounded her, ranging from the more common shades of brown to brilliant white, and in their midst a magnificent golden beauty. He stood, resplendent in his majesty, and I knew my attention should have been commanded by him or the goddess, but instead, my focus lingered on a lone white stag nestled among the lush forest surrounding them.

Michael followed my gaze, and I glanced at him in time to see a small smile curve his lips. The midnight blue and gold mask he wore covered only half his face. It was full across one eye and his nose, but only arched over the other eyebrow, making it easy to still read his expression. A sidelong, lingering glance told me he was thinking exactly the same as me, and my pulse quickened, pounding against my ribs.

He took my hand, lacing my fingers through his, and we

stepped further into the room.

I'd been in the ballroom at White Deer Hall precisely three times before, all as a child, all during the day as part of a tour. The atmosphere at night, with the place dressed for the occasion it was made for, was quite different.

Soft, golden light flickered from crystal chandeliers, each of which was probably worth more than my house. At my feet, the floor was a highly polished expanse of dark mahogany, reflecting a shadow version of the room. It was too early yet for much dancing, and the floor lay waiting to be animated by the swirl of gowns and the graceful steps of dancers.

Massive, arched windows punctuated walls of dark oak panelling, draped in heavy brocade curtains and offering a glimpse of serene, moonlit gardens beyond. In one corner, a small orchestra played a melody I didn't recognise, classical notes weaving through the chatter and laughter, the clink of glasses.

A woman swept towards us, her face partly obscured by a Venetian-style mask, elegantly studded with gems and in the same forest green hue as her velvet gown. Its mermaid tail trailed the floor as she reached her arms out and embraced Michael with a kiss to either cheek.

"Michael," she exclaimed, "delightful to see you."

He returned her embrace politely. "And you, looking radiant as ever."

She blushed, fawning over him slightly, and only then seemed to notice me.

"Amelia, this is Eleanor, she spearheads the event every year." He glanced around the room. "You've excelled yourself as always."

I wracked my brain for everything I knew about the charity running this shindig. "Eleanor Hughes?"

She smiled, and I extended a hand in greeting, which she took politely, although the way she barely looked at me indicated her disinterest.

"I was hoping to meet you. I've been following your work

with the new women's shelter; it's wonderful to see."

Eleanor's eyebrow arched a fraction of an inch, and she turned to look at me properly, ushering us further into the room. "How lovely, at least someone is aware of our efforts."

"It's such an important venture"—my enthusiasm was genuine—"I'd love to help out if I can?" Out of the corner of my eye, I saw Michael blink, pulling his head back slightly as if surprised, though whether it was at my interest or the fact I was aware of the shelter at all, I couldn't tell.

Eleanor glanced at Michael, then back to me. "Certainly, that would be splendid. Michael, you have my number, be sure…"

"Amelia," I supplied.

"Amelia gets it." She paused, *really* looking at me now, then turned her attention back to Michael. "You remember Marcus and Don?" She gestured at a pair of chaps in a cluster of chattering, bemasked guests.

Michael nodded to them, and they smiled in greeting. "Yes, we've crossed paths before."

"Excellent, I'll leave you to enjoy the event then. Amelia—" She extended her hand to me and shook it again, in earnest this time. "Lovely to meet you." And away she swept.

Michael's arm wrapped around my waist and he whispered in my ear, "I do believe you impressed her; that's not easily done." Then he turned his attention to the assembled collection of peacocks before us.

"…yes, precisely—" a tall chap was saying, "—this is why embracing sustainability is so critical. Ah, Mike, good to see you."

"Marcus." Michael smiled in reply, then nodded to the man next to him. "Don, this is Amelia."

The pair bobbed their heads at me in unison. Given that one wore what appeared to be a Phantom of the Opera mask and the other a Renaissance jester, the effect was slightly eerie.

"Amelia, welcome." The jester, Don, smiled at me. "We were just discussing the new urban development project in Ashfordby."

"I've heard about that," I said absently, trying to ignore the way most of the women in the room were craning their necks to get a look at me. "A struggle to achieve the right balance between modernisation and preserving the town's character, I would think?"

Okay, most is an exaggeration. It's only a few. Actually, just one. And she's probably not even looking at me. Fuck, calm down, would you?

"Exactly. We don't want ugly modern monstrosities, but at the same time we need affordable housing the younger generations have a hope of actually affording on their own."

I smiled politely, wondering if his idea of 'affordable' was under half a mil.

"I'm telling you it's all about sustainability," Marcus reiterated. "If we build them right, they'll not only fuel themselves but generate power for the rest of the town. Growth can no longer be a drain, it should *sustain*."

To my left, a lady in a stunning black satin gown and feathered raven mask chuckled. "You'll have to forgive Marcus." She laid a hand on his arm and patted it affectionately. "He does get over-enthusiastic. But, speaking of growth, the new policy changes are bound to impact local businesses. It's not just residential builds that need to shift towards sustainability."

"Helen is one of our local councillors," Michael said by way of introduction, "and I couldn't agree more. We've been looking at installing solar panelling in the spring."

Marcus nodded. "A good start, but adaptation is key. The bother with solar is retaining the power generated during daylight; the grid can't hold it."

Helen caught my eye and chuckled silently. I smiled back, suppressing a laugh.

"We've just finished getting EV charge points installed for our company cars," I commented. "Charge the cars with solar during the day, they can then top up the grid during peak times and overnight."

"Wonderful." Marcus nodded enthusiastically. "Nice to see

your boss is forward-thinking."

Michael snorted. "Ah, Marcus, living with your foot in your mouth as usual."

Marcus blinked, looking at Helen, "What did I say?"

"You assumed it wasn't Amelia's idea," Helen said, "even though she clearly has a good grasp of it."

"Worse," Michael snorted. "You assumed she had a boss; it's Amelia's company."

Helen, Don and the two other women nearby burst out laughing.

"Priceless," Don said. "Trust Marc to bang on about forward-thinking bullshit while forgetting women have brains too."

Marcus' face reddened, and he gave his jacket a sharp tug, glancing about as if unsure what to do.

"Don't worry about it, mate." I smiled. "At least you didn't mansplain solar power to me and repeatedly try to find a more senior man to speak to instead of me."

"Ouch." A younger woman, appearing closer to my age in a mask so delicate it barely concealed her eyes, laughed. "Was that before or after you explained you were the decision maker?"

"After." I shrugged. "Honestly, it happens all the time. My landlord still directs all his questions and comments to my PR guy whenever he comes in."

"Let me guess," Helen said, "he's the most alpha man in the office."

I nodded, and beside me, Michael snorted. "You'd think we'd be past all that." As an afterthought, he introduced the other guests. "Amelia, this is Isabel, she runs the gallery on Northgate Street, Robert has the wine shop out towards the football fields, and Vanessa—"

"I thought I recognised you," I interrupted, "sorry, Michael, but Vanessa saved my life today."

He frowned, eyebrow arching in a silent question.

"It suits you." Vanessa gestured at my dress. "Your assistant said it was for the ball; I was keeping an eye out for it."

"Well, Haute Harmony is officially my new favourite place. Expect to see me often." I laughed.

Michael glanced back and forth between me and Vanessa, brow creased.

"You asked me to attend a masquerade ball with less than twenty-four hours' notice," I chucked. "What? You think I just had this outfit hanging in my wardrobe?"

"I didn't really think about it, to be honest." He shrugged. "Sorry?"

Marcus chuckled. "But you're so *insightful* about women, Michael, how could you?"

That got him a laugh. A waistcoated waiter passed with a laden tray, and the aroma of gourmet hors d'oeuvres mingled with the expensive perfume already lingering in the air.

"I must say, Michael," Don said, swiping a glass of champagne from the tray as it passed, "it's nice to see you bringing a guest for once."

Michael shifted his weight back and forth between his feet the way I did when my shoes hurt, which, if the tingling on the balls of my feet was anything to go by, wouldn't take long. "Well, I—"

"Mike!"

My head whipped around. I'd know that voice anywhere. *Shit.*

A tall woman, slender to the point of being bony, who could only be described as *unnaturally* buxom, barrelled towards us. On the increasingly crowded dance floor, several people swerved to avoid colliding with her as she made an unconcerned beeline for Michael. A luxurious, deep crimson ball gown hugged her figure, from the fake boobs all the way to the floor, where it flared out in a dramatic poofle that forced everyone around her to watch their step. Her face was half obscured by a lace mask, not unlike my own. As she drew closer, I realised the pattern on it was an intricate web, like a spider's, threaded with what appeared to be actual diamonds.

Typical Gemma.

In her wake trailed three other women who put me firmly in mind of the Pipettes. I half expected them to start snapping their fingers and lyrically echoing her words.

"Mike, there you are."

I almost thought I heard him sigh, before he turned and was enveloped by a hug that went on just a second too long.

"You look ravishing." She smoothed the lines of his brocade jacket and waistcoat, both black and the same navy blue as his mask. Her fingertips lingered on his biceps.

It was tough to blame her for that. He had phenomenal biceps.

But then she reached up and adjusted the high collar of his shirt, straightening his tie, and he smiled, reaching up and taking her hands in his. My stomach roiled at the sight. I felt sick. He gave her hands a quick squeeze and quite deliberately moved them back towards her before letting go.

"Good to see you, Gemma." He nodded at the assembly behind her. "Nikki, Miranda." He frowned and peered closer at the remaining girl in the trio, whose face was entirely obscured by an elaborate swan mask. "Is that you, Jessie?"

The poor thing didn't get a chance to answer, nor did any of them have time to speak, before Gemma was taking Michael's arm and moving back towards the dance floor. "I thought you'd never arrive. I've been waiting for a dance."

He disentangled himself from her grip as politely as possible. "Maybe later, Gem, I've not even danced with my date yet." He turned back to me and held out a hand. "Now we mention it, that seems very remiss of me. Care to dance?"

I smiled, taking his hand. "I'd love to."

He drew me away onto the dance floor, and I caught Gemma's expression as we passed—her mouth hung open in a most undignified 'oh', though whether it was surprise or jealousy I had no clue. Either way, Don wasn't the only one shocked he'd brought someone with him.

"Sorry about that," Michael said. "She means well."

That would be a first.

The world around us became a blur of colours and sounds,

the orchestra's symphony rising and falling like a melodious tide.

His hand was firm on my waist, guiding me effortlessly through the steps of the dance. The warmth of his touch seeped through the fabric of my dress, sending shivers of delight up my spine. Our movements were synchronised, as if we'd danced together for years rather than minutes. His body carried the subtle scent of his aftershave, earthy with a tang of citrus. It was both comforting and intoxicating.

Looking up into Michael's eyes, I noticed the subtle lift of his lips, a playful glimmer in his gaze, even behind the mask. Doubtless, my own expression betrayed disbelief at the situation. Apparently, this was funny to him. It still seemed utterly impossible to me that I was somehow here, dancing, with *him*. There was something deeper there too, more tender. Unexpected. His gaze held mine, and the rest of the ballroom faded into insignificance.

The music swelled around us, other couples parting to make room as he twirled us through each beat. Michael's fingers teased tiny circles on my back, a silent promise of sorts, and I felt a familiar tightening in my stomach, and further down, a longing for him so deep and so strong it was almost painful.

Maybe I should have let Isla take Echo for the night after all. What if he wants to go back to his place?

I took a deep breath to steady my nerves. An instant later, both his hands wrapped around my waist and he was lifting me from the floor, spinning me effortlessly above, setting me down, then sweeping me on with the dance. We moved with the music, our bodies close, the soft rustle of my gown melding with the rhythm of the orchestra.

As the music reached its crescendo, Michael pulled me closer, our steps becoming more intimate and fluid. The final notes of the tune lingered in the air, and we slowed to a stop, still holding each other. For a moment, we stood there, surrounded by the grandeur of the ballroom, lost in each other's eyes.

Then, as the applause around us broke the spell, Michael leaned in, his breath warm against my ear. "You're an incredible dancer," he whispered, his lips brushing my neck.

I blushed at the compliment.

"Shall we get a drink?" He held his arm out, crooked at the elbow.

I took it as he led me to a table. The pristinely pressed linens dressing it were threaded with shimmering gold that flickered in the light of a giant candelabra. Flowers cascaded down a centrepiece twined with ivy and jasmine, bringing a touch of the outdoors in. They carried a subtle scent and added a delicate undercurrent to the room's heady atmosphere.

After pulling out a pair of chairs and facing them towards each other, Michael flagged down a waiter, passed me a glass of perfectly chilled champagne, and sat opposite me. "Well," he said, "I can honestly say I've never enjoyed one of these things quite so much." He smiled at me. "Thank you."

"For what?" I took a sip of champagne, resisting the urge to immediately have another. It was so good.

Don't get drunk, Amelia. Not a good call.

"Agreeing to accompany me to an incredibly dull event, on very short notice." He eyed me slowly from the curls pinned to the top of my head all the way down to the tips of my very tall heels. His gaze then worked its way back up, lingered on my legs, neatly perched in a Duchess Slant, and paused again as they traversed the modest peaks of my breasts.

My blushes deepened. Ferociously.

"And not only that," he continued, "but showing up looking absolutely ravishing."

I turned my face away as the blush reached flame-level heat and engulfed my entire face. But he wouldn't let me go. His finger hooked my chin and turned me back to face him. He'd leant forward slightly in his chair and was now mere inches from me.

"Thanks for making me look good in front of people who are not easily impressed," he whispered. "For making me laugh, genuinely, not politely." He leant even further forwards. "And thank you for a dance so hot it didn't just turn heads and part crowds; it scorched the dance floor." He closed the gap between us and kissed me, slowly. It wasn't the passionate promise of the night before, but a chaste reminder of that promise. Somehow, it carried just as much heat.

"Talk about scorching," I murmured as he pulled away.

Michael chuckled and opened his mouth to speak, but whatever he was about to say was swallowed by the loud arrival of Gemma, Double, Toil, and Trouble. The four of them clattered into the remaining chairs at the table.

"Well, Michael Bane," Gemma exclaimed loudly. "You've kept this one quiet."

Michael's sigh was clearly audible this time as he turned to Gemma, who had taken the seat that would have been beside him had he not twisted his chair to make conversation with me more intimate. "It's our second date, and we're in a very public place. Hardly quiet."

Gemma's mouth pursed. "Rather a lot of PDA going on for a second date, Mike."

An expression crossed his face, half frown, half huff, but it was tough to pinpoint it when he was twisted back towards her, and he quickly smoothed it away. "Is there a new Rules edition out that I'm unaware of? One dance and a brief kiss barely qualify as PDA. And in either case, neither are any of your business." He turned his back on her, returning his full attention to me.

He should have known better.

So should I.

"I'm proud of you, Mike. Setting aside her years of pathetic stalking. All the times she embarrassed you."

A different kind of frown creased Michael's brow, and he turned back to her.

"Don't get me wrong," Gemma continued, "nobody's more surprised than me that she managed such a spec*ta*cular glow up." She sneered at me. "But have you really forgotten that time she recited a love poem for you in *Klangon*."

I shook my head, looking to Michael for backup, but he was still staring at Gemma, the frown on his face deepening.

Urgh, fine, I'll stand up for myself. It's about bloody time.

"It was Klingon, Gemma," I said with a sigh, "and we were just kids."

Slowly, painfully slowly, Michael's head turned back to me and his eyes met mine. The frown dissolved, his jaw going slack, eyes wide. Realisation stole across Michael's face like a thief.

Oh, my god.

The air left my lungs.

He didn't know.

How was that even possible?

He cleared his throat. Stood.

"Well," he said. "I've had quite enough *charity* for one night." Without another word, he strode from the room, and I lurched to my feet, struggling to keep up in heels that were rapidly becoming instruments of torture.

How the fuck did he not know?

And to think, a couple of days ago, I'd thought Hillary and her tits were going to be the worst of my problems this week.

CHAPTER 4

"Wait, *what?*" Suzie's voice screeched from the phone, making Echo jump.

I patted her head reassuringly, and she settled back down on the bed beside me.

"He. Didn't. Know," I repeated slowly, so my meaning was crystal clear and I didn't have to cop to the mortifying revelation yet again. I drained the rest of the wine in my glass, picked up the bottle from the bedside table, and poured more. I nearly put it back on the bedside table, but that seemed pointless.

I'd only have to pick it up again in two minutes when my glass was mysteriously empty once more.

I upended the bottle into the glass, sloshing Malbec over the rim. It spattered my snowy white duvet cover, but I didn't care.

"How could he not know?" Suzie demanded.

"Fucked if I know," I said, taking another big swig. "He stalked me online. He's been to my office. He got the *whole* Kobayashi Maru speech and *liked it*."

"He must have known then. We went to school together for eight years; there's no way he didn't recognise your name."

I made an indiscernible noise that might have been a sob.

"Well, apparently, he didn't."

"Even so, what's so wrong with... Wait, he *liked* it?" Suzie's voice went alarmingly high-pitched. She sounded more shocked by that than the revelation Gemma had instantly recognised and humiliated me. "Aimee, nobody likes that speech."

"Well, he did!" I yelled at the phone, then burst into tears.

Suzie made soothing noises. "Okay, I'm sorry, it's alright. I just... I don't know what to say here. I'm shook."

I calmed down, sniffling. "You and me both." Another swig of wine and I realised that, despite my efforts, the glass would soon be empty after all.

And now the bottle was also empty.

Spectacular.

"I knew it was too good to be true." *Why didn't I listen to myself?* "As if Michael Bane could ever be interested in me. How is this a lesson I'm still learning? How is this happening *again*?"

"Aimee, sweetie, this isn't a *you* problem. I promise. This is a *'why the hell does he give a damn if you were a nerd in high school'* problem. He's a grown arse man. You're a beautiful, successful, and utterly charming woman. Who gives a shit if you like *Star Trek*?"

"He didn't!" I exploded. "That's what I'm saying. He got it. He understood the whole thing. He was *impressed* by it. He thought I was *hot*," I whimpered. "He fucked me in a duck blind because I was so hot. Then he found out who I used to be, and suddenly he turned into a total. Fucking. *Arsehole*!"

Suzie was silent for a moment. "Is it possible that he was *always* a total fucking arsehole? He was just hiding it because he wanted to date you?"

"What? He suddenly stopped wanting to date me the second he discovered my sordid past as a sci-fi-loving bookworm who wasn't in with the popular clique - who, by the way, are all exactly the same as they used to be. They're more botoxed and less youthful these days, but they're the same. Gemma's still the queen fucking bee, and those three follow her around like the loyal coven sisters they are."

"But this isn't about them either. I'm sorry to say it—" She paused. "Actually, scratch that, I'm really not. This conversation has been a long time coming. The problem with you and Michael was never you. It was always him. He was a twat in high school. And it sounds like he, the coven of Gemma, and probably the rest of that godforsaken town haven't changed one bit. And how could they? They stayed there. They've been fully indoctrinated into *the greater good*."

She intoned that last part like she was suddenly staring in *Hot Fuzz* and trying to explain village life to the clueless London copper who just would not get with the programme.

"This is why you left," she continued, "why *we* left, why everyone with half a brain got the hell out of dodge, the second university beckoned and never looked back."

"But I love this town," I said. "It's home." It sounded pathetic, even to me.

"I know, hon," she soothed, "but you spent time away and grew. Not everyone did. And those who didn't, never moved on from the high-school bullshit. They still have their cliques and petty dramas. Now it's just on the PTA instead of the hockey team."

I fell silent. She was right, in some ways. There was certainly a very high-schoolesque mentality afflicting certain circles in the town. "There are good people here too. It's just the bored housewives who've never done anything other than be in school, have kids, and send them to school. Is it any wonder they're stuck in that high-school way of thinking? They never really left."

Suzie scoffed. "It's no excuse. There was no need to treat people like shit when we were in school, and there still isn't now. Besides, Gemma's no housewife. She's never married. No kids. No excuse."

"I guess," I said. "I just…I really didn't think Michael was like that."

"He was always like that," Suzie snapped. "Sorry." She sighed. "You've always been a bit delusional where he is concerned, Aimee. He was never a good guy. He was a *good-looking* guy, and he knew it. He was a popular guy, and he used it. He's always been a user and a cad. The fact he's older doesn't mean he's suddenly had a personality transplant. He's proved it to you now, and I'm glad."

I said nothing, silently seething at her words.

"I don't mean I'm glad he upset you tonight," she clarified. "I mean, I'm glad you're realising what he's truly like *now*, and not six months from now when you're head over heels in love with him again and planning the wedding."

My face twitched. "I'm not *quite* that pathetic."

"You are where he's concerned. You always have been. Your hormones fell for his pheromones when your brain wasn't fully developed, and you didn't know any better. Now you know better."

I snorted. "Much good it'll do me. I doubt I'll hear from him again now."

"Good." Suzie sighed. "Sorry. Again. I'm just so angry he's done this to you. That she's done this to you. Again."

My glass remained annoyingly empty. I debated getting up for another bottle but thought better of it. "I think I should just go to sleep. I'm so done with today."

"Good idea. Speak tomorrow."

I sighed. "Sure."

❖

Chill January air stole my breath the second I opened the front door. My feet crunched in frost as they hit the step, and Echo hesitated for an instant before following me out. As if unsure it was worth it. I shared her sentiment, rubbing the sleep from my eyes and stretching. "Come on, girl," I said. "It will make us feel better."

She trotted out, snuffing the air curiously, and set off ahead of me down the driveway. My final stretches done, I took off at a nice, slow jog after her, crossing the wide courtyard in front of my house. Rounding the edge of the trees ringing it, I headed down the winding stretch to the road. Bare branches waved at me forlornly in the morning breeze. It was still mostly dark, though the sun had started her steep climb for the day.

Frosted dirt crunched beneath my feet and, starting to feel slightly more like myself, I picked up the pace, rounded another bend in the drive and collided with a solid, muscular chest.

"Jesus," I exclaimed, rebounding off the dark figure. I stumbled backwards, heart pounding, instinctively trying to remember my self-defence training. Trying *not* to think of fat sausage fingers sliming all over me, forcing me back into a table as I struggled to break free. The solid weight of Echo pressed against my leg, and a low growl erupted from deep in her belly. I got my wits about me, took another step back, this time into a defensive pose, and raised my arms to fend off whatever fresh hell the world had decided to deliver to my doorstep.

Echo stepped in front of me, the growl intensifying to a warning bark.

Reassured by my canine bodyguard, I squinted against the rising sun, looking up at his face.

Shit.

"*Michael?*" I said. "What the fuck are you doing skulking about in the dark?" I peered at him more closely.

His face was ashen, skin sallow, aside from one side that was caked in dirt. I frowned, stepping closer again to get a better look.

That's blood.

"Amelia?"

"Well, who else would it be?" I snapped. "This is my driveway." My frown deepened as he looked around in confusion. "You're disorientated." I peered at his head more closely, taking in the split just about hidden in his hairline.

That's where the blood was coming from.

"You hit your head," I said. "How long have you been out here?" I was so confused. Last I'd seen him, he'd been in the taxi that had unceremoniously dumped me home after Gemma's little revelation cut our evening short.

He hadn't said a word to me the whole ride back. I'd awkwardly attempted to ask if he wanted to come in and talk when we got here, but he'd just shaken his head and said, "Not tonight." Then reached over me and opened the door on my side of the taxi.

Had he shoved me out of it, he couldn't have made it more plain he'd wanted to be rid of me.

"I…" He stumbled, and I instinctively caught his arm to steady him. "Amelia." He leant heavily on me. "I'm in trouble."

Echo whined, snuffing at Michael's clothes. He glanced at her, a small smile crossing his lips, and he absently patted her on the head.

For some reason, that decided me.

"Come on." I looped my arm under his shoulder and let him lean on me, turning back to the house.

We went in through the mud room. A small utility room housing the washer and dryer, it was also kitted out on one side with a waist-height shower and tiled area so I could hose Echo down before she went back in the house.

Given how filthy she was wont to get on any given day, it was a lifesaver. I shoved Michael in and over to the laundry side of the room, where he leant heavily on the counter. As the light flared overhead, I gasped.

"Your hands." I moved towards him, reaching out to take them, but he winced and pulled away.

"I shouldn't have come here." He looked me in the eye for the first time since Gemma had told him who I was. "I'm sorry, this is…" He glanced down at his hands. "I'll go." He moved to the door to leave, but I blocked him.

"Who'd you punch?" I said.

His eyes widened momentarily, and he paused, apparently taken aback that I'd realised what he'd been up to. Or perhaps more so that I didn't appear to be bothered by it.

"My brother's been in a few fights; I recognise a pair of

hands that have beaten the shit out of someone. So"—I crossed my arms over my chest and stared at him—"who'd you hit?"

"Amelia—"

"You acted like a colossal arse last night, Michael Bane."

He winced but didn't contradict me.

"You dumped me back here like I was something unpleasant you scraped off your shoe. Now you turn up, covered in blood, probably with a concussion, and tell me you're in trouble. You think you're walking out of here without any kind of explanation?"

"This isn't your concern."

"You made it my concern when you wandered down my drive for help," I snapped. "Now"—I gestured at the bench by the door—"sit down and let me clean you up."

"It's not—"

"*Sit!*"

"Please"—he held his hands up—"you don't understand. This is trouble you don't need. I shouldn't have come here."

I stared at him. "Why did you?"

"I needed..." He huffed out a long breath. "...help." He dropped his arms, defeated. "I know, I've no right to ask for it. Not from you."

"You're damn right you don't." I softened. He really did look rough. "Let's get you cleaned up." I pointed at the bench, and for a mercy he sat. I started with his face, dampening a cloth in warm water and cleaning the dry, cakey blood away. The wound appeared to have stopped bleeding. I cleaned it up as best I could, wary of making it bleed again.

"I don't think you need stitches," I said, glancing down at him.

He was trying very hard not to stare at my boobs, which were pretty much pressed into his face, thanks to where I'd had to stand to get at his head. I cleared my throat, suddenly feeling awkward, and took a step back.

The harsh light above gave me a clearer look at him than I'd had outside. "Michael," I whispered. "Take your coat off."

He stood, removing it slowly, painfully. Like someone had got a really good shot in on his ribs. The front of his navy coat was spattered with blood. The heavy wool disguised it pretty well, but not well enough. With it safely removed, I was relieved to see no blood on his waistcoat or the front of his jacket. Someone had bled on him; he wasn't bleeding anywhere other than his head.

And his hands.

I helped him out of his suit jacket and waistcoat. He went to roll the sleeves of his shirt up, but I stopped him. "Just take it off," I said, gesturing at the cuffs. "I'll wash it." He stared at his hands and the blood that had seeped down them, staining the previously pristine white of the shirt.

He swallowed. Hard. And for a second, I thought he might throw up. Instead, he went to undo his buttons, then paused, realising he was just going to get more blood on his shirt.

"Here." I reached under his arms and undid the buttons for him.

He held his arms wide so he didn't touch me with bloodied hands.

"What happened?" I asked, trying not to think about the fact this was the first time I'd actually seen him shirtless as I removed the garment and placed it on the side.

He took a deep, shuddering breath. "My sister called last night," he said. "There was an…incident."

I frowned. "Is she okay?"

"No," he choked, and it was clear he wasn't either. "She's not hurt, but Becca…"

My stomach twisted. "Your niece?"

He nodded.

"She was attacked," his voice broke. "She was…" he trailed off, unable to verbalise it.

"Oh god." I sat down heavily on the bench beside him. "Is she…?"

"She's at the hospital. She'll be fine. Physically. But he tried to… She stopped him." His voice dropped to a hollow whisper, and he repeated, as if to reassure himself, "She stopped him."

I shut my eyes. *Jesus.*

"The whole thing was caught on CCTV. The police arrested the guy. My sister didn't want to tell me until they had. She was afraid I'd..." He didn't need to finish that sentence. "But it seems this guy has the right friends. A fancy lawyer, and a few hours later, he was out. Didn't even hold him twenty-four hours, can you believe that? She knew I'd find out come morning; she wanted me to hear it from her."

"Michael," I said, "whose blood is this?"

"The guy," he said simply.

I closed my eyes. "Is he?"

"He's still alive." Michael sniffed. "But I fucked him up, Aimee," he sobbed, and I started. He hadn't called me Aimee since we'd been kids. Even then, it had never been said kindly.

"Did he see you?" I asked.

He looked up at me, head tilting to one side in apparent confusion.

"The guy? Did he see you? Can he identify you?"

Michael thought about it. "No, I don't think so. It was dark. He was on his driveway, walking towards his house. I came up behind him and..." He took a deep breath. "I don't think he'd have seen my face."

I gave him a hard look. "You're sure he's not—"

"Certain," he said. "I thought about it." He looked away from me. "But then Becca would have lost an uncle as well as all this. And my sister would have blamed herself..." His face scrunched up, and he rubbed at his eyes with both hands. I was fairly sure he was scrubbing away tears. And I was inordinately grateful he'd at least stopped himself before doing something infinitely worse.

An idea formed in my head.

A really, really bad one.

"When did she call?"

Michael looked up and frowned. "Who?"

"Your sister. When did she call to tell you? Was it before or after you dropped me back here?"

He looked at me for a long moment, then lowered his head. "After," he said softly.

I swallowed. Not the answer I'd hoped for, but the answer I'd needed. An honest one.

"So, your behaviour was because of what Gemma said."

"I was angry," he said.

"About what? The fact I like *Star Trek*."

He scoffed. "Of course not! You lied to me." He finally looked back up at me. "You let me…feel things."

I stared at him. "Heaven forbid you experience an emotion."

"I never asked for this." Michael gestured back and forth between us. "I never intended it to be anything more than it was."

"A quick fuck in a duck blind."

He winced. "That was shitty of me. I felt shitty. I figured the least I could do was buy you dinner. But then we got to talking, and I liked you." He rubbed his eyes, suddenly looking as exhausted as this conversation was making me. "I liked you."

"Sure. Until you realised I used to be a geek. Then suddenly, I became persona non grata."

He snorted. "You think I give a shit you like *Star Trek*? I'm not in high school anymore, Aimee."

"Well, you're not acting like it."

His mouth clamped shut on whatever he was about to say. He took a deep breath. "You lied to me. Why, I've no idea, but did you seriously think that wouldn't hurt my feelings?"

"I never lied to you!"

"You didn't tell me we already knew each other!"

"I thought you knew!" I shrieked, going a little too high-pitched and making Echo whine. I patted her head reassuringly. "Or are you in the habit of screwing complete strangers without ever exchanging more than two words with them?"

He had the decency to blush.

Jesus.

"You really didn't know it was me?" I stared at him, replaying the entirety of the last few days in my head. "You looked me up online, you went on the website. Was I so insignificant in high school that you couldn't figure out it was me even while you were *reading my name*?"

"Well, maybe if you put your *last name* on the bloody site, I might have! We could have saved ourselves a lot of bother."

Wait...shit. He was right. I'd debated back and forth whether to use full names or not and had decided against it. First names only; it was more modern.

Shit.

"I thought you knew," I said simply. What else was there to say?

He nodded. "I see that now," he conceded. "But I didn't know that last night. I'm sorry I was an arse. I was hurt."

I considered him. He could have lied just now and said he'd got the call as we were at the table. That he'd rushed out to phone her back. That, by the time I caught up in my ridiculous heels, he'd already got off the phone and was lost in a rage mist. That he'd dropped me right back at my house so as not to involve me. That his actions were all due to receiving *that* news.

I probably wouldn't have believed him, but most guys I knew would have given it a shot. Instead, he'd done the hard thing; copped to being a dick, and had the argument, even though today was already probably one of the worst days of his life.

Call me delusional, but it says something about a person when they have a choice between doing what is right and doing what is easy, and they choose the former.

Even when they don't have to.

Even when doing it is actually bloody tough.

I could kick him out, leave him to clean up his own mess.

That would be easy.

"Okay, strip."

Michael gave me a withering look. "I'm not exactly in the mood, *darling*."

"Nor do you have a shot in hell, *pookie*. You're still going to strip. In here, and wash off as best you can. Leave all your clothes on the floor. Go upstairs, take a proper shower."

"Amelia—"

"You weren't there," I said, "you were nowhere near him. Do you hear me?"

"Amelia, you can't—"

"Don't tell me what I can't do," I snapped. "This guy is a piece of shit. He got what was coming to him. He should be in a jail cell right now, facing a long, *long* stretch inside, at the tender mercy of some humongous colossus. Some tattooed brute who'd make him hold onto his turned-out pocket, and bend over quietly so he could wreck him a new arsehole every night. That would be *right*. Come on, Bane, *think*. You've made some money and connections for yourself, but you're not *connected*. You think some fancy lawyer can waltz in there and get *you* off the hook?"

He dropped his head, staring at his bloodied hands. "Maybe that's for the best."

I considered him for a moment. "Maybe. But I don't want to watch it happen. So, strip." I opened the door and ushered Echo out through it. "I'll see if I can get them clean while you're in the shower."

"It won't help," he said. "I have no alibi and every motive."

Don't do it.

"You do have an alibi," I said.

Amelia, for fuck's sake, do not do it.

"You were here, with me, making passionate love, all night." I ignored the look on his face and shut the door.

Fuck. Great going, Amelia. Bloody brilliant.

CHAPTER 5

Echo stood in the doorway, fixing me with a baleful stare. I endured it for as long as possible before I cracked.

"What?" I demanded. "What else would you have me do?"

Echo's ears flattened against her head, and she whined.

"We'll be fine," I said firmly, turning back to the thick salt paste I'd been mixing and slathering over the cuffs of Michael's shirt. "It'll be fine," I repeated, more for myself than Echo's benefit, and dabbed gently at the stained cuff. I left it to sit, turning my attention back to his coat. I'd blotted it as best I could, removing all the visible staining. It was the invisible ones that worried me.

Staring at the coat, I considered my options. If he was ever arrested, they'd want the clothes he was wearing last night. Destroying them didn't seem like an option; there was no reasonable explanation for why he would destroy a three-grand Gucci coat. I kind of wanted to cry at what I'd already done to it.

"I could get it dry cleaned," I said to Echo, "but they're trained to report blood stains to the police, and I'm not convinced you can't still see those." I looked down at Echo. "Even if they didn't, the cleaning probably wouldn't remove all forensic traces." I wiped the sweat from my forehead with the back of my hand, belatedly realising I should have put on gloves before doing this.

I sighed. "Better late than never," I said, donning a pair of disposable plastic gloves I kept for Echo-induced poonamis. "Okay," I stood up again, "one problem at a time."

Rinsing the salt out of his shirt, I was relieved to see most of it had gone. I covered the stains in bleach, plunking myself down on the bench and staring at Echo.

"What the fuck am I doing?"

Echo gave me a look as if to say, *'That's what I've been wondering.'*

I stared at the shirt for a long moment, trying to scrub the image of the blood stains from my memory as I had from the fabric. Trying to ignore the disturbing similarity with the wine stains I'd left on my duvet cover last night, while I'd sobbed over the dickish behaviour of Michael fucking Bane.

I glanced back down at my trusty hound. "Why am I helping him?"

Echo tilted her head and whined in reply.

"Should have left him out in the fucking rain," I grumbled.

Echo let out a disapproving whine.

"Don't you dare," I warned. "You do not get to be on his side. Or did you forget him dumping me back here because I had the audacity to be myself?"

Echo snorted and tilted her head back the other way. I slumped against the wall, resting my head for a moment. My gaze landed on Michael's still-bloody coat.

"Fuck. I did not think this through."

Echo's head appeared on my knee, and I scratched her ears.

"He doesn't deserve my help." I sighed. Seeing him hurt and offering basic first aid was one thing. This was something else.

Unfortunately, it was something else I'd already dived head-first into, and leaving it half-done wasn't going to help anything.

Why am I scrubbing his sins like a fucking martyr?

Because you're a fucking moron. Just get it done. Then never speak to him again.

Except you just offered to be his fucking alibi, you utter twat. If that gets out, everything you've built here could vanish overnight. For what? Michael fucking Bane and his stupid fucking chiselled jaw and glorious cock? Little good it will do you now he knows you're you.

"Fuck's sake," I muttered.

And yet, dumb as it had been, I was already doing it. For some reason, it seemed harder to explain why I'd started covering up a crime and stopped halfway through than it did to just finish cleaning up the mess he'd made.

"Okay, let's Spock this bitch." I stood up, pacing the utility room. "That's a wool coat. I can't wash it. I can't bleach it. Sending it for dry cleaning is very risky and might not work anyway. Logically, I should destroy it." I stopped pacing. *Think.* Total destruction that left no remains whatsoever was the only way to go here.

"Where's a herd of pigs when you need them?" I asked Echo, who sneezed. "Sorry, girl, these fumes are a bitch." I cracked the window, shivering at the gust of cold that blasted me. "Go sit in the kitchen."

Another baleful stare. She wouldn't leave me.

"Okay...total annihilation," I thought. I thought some more. Somewhere in the recesses of my brain, in the insane amount of seemingly worthless information I had amassed over years of writing for clients in all walks of life, watching countless hours of police procedural dramas and apparently endless seasons of *Midsomer Murders*, was an answer.

Eventually, Michael came padding back downstairs. He wore the clothes I'd dug out for him while he was in the shower. A pair of oversized joggers I wore on period days when I didn't give a fuck about anything but comfort hugged his hips. They were a tad too tight and about a foot too short. Teamed with the Mandalorian oodie my brother had bought me last Christmas, he looked more than a little ridiculous.

His bare feet on the tile floor made me cold.

"There are wellie socks in that basket." I pointed at a woven drawer under the bench. "They should fit you."

"Thanks." He sat, pulled out the drawer, plucked out a pair of mottled purple socks, then kicked the draw shut again. When he looked up, he finally seemed to see me and frowned, standing.

I finished clipping the previously beautiful coat into small pieces and dropping them in a plastic tub.

Michael stood, walking over to me, and very slowly picked up the empty bottle beside me. "Everclear?"

He took another step towards me, and I recoiled slightly.

Blinking, he glared at me. "I wasn't going to hurt you," he snapped. Then his face softened. "Though I can't blame you for—"

"I wasn't scared, Michael. I was repulsed."

He glared.

"You were a total arsehole last night, even before you did this." I nodded at the box. "And it's 185 proof," I said. As if that explained everything. The washing machine beeped. I flipped the door open, pulled out his shirt and surveyed it. The thing looked pristine, but looks could be deceiving. Still, I'd soaked it, then washed it in bleach on the highest heat I thought I could risk. If that didn't do it, nothing would.

"If I'm such an arse, why are you helping me?" he growled.

I popped his shirt in the dryer, left it to spin, picked up my Really Useful Box (currently filled with the shredded, Everclear-soaked remnants of what had once been a beautiful Gucci coat), and padded towards the back door.

"Amelia?" he snapped. Then took a breath and tried again more softly. "Amelia, please speak to me.

Ignoring him, I stomped outside, only to glance back as Echo whined. Michael stood at the back door, my dog at his feet. She looked up at him and then out to me, clearly torn. Slowly, hesitantly, Michael peered out after me. Echo snorted, impatient with his indecision, and shot out past him as I continued on my merry way. At the back of the house, the burn bin was happily consuming the garden prunings that were no good for the compost heap. I picked up the kitchen barbecue tongs I'd brought out earlier and carefully transferred the alcohol-soaked cloth from the tub to the bin, standing well back and reaching as far as I could to drop them in.

The flames engulfed them greedily. When the lot had been added to the burn bin, I stoked it with some leaves, pulled the disposable gloves off with a snap, deposited them in the bin, popped the lid on, and left it to do its work. Trudging back to the house, I passed Michael, who was staring at me wide-eyed. Unceremoniously, I dumped out the contents of the plastic box in the sink. Picking up the empty Everclear bottle, I took both into the kitchen, opened the dishwasher, loaded them in with last night's wine glass, and left them to wash.

A knock on the front door reverberated down the hall. Michael whipped around. "Oh god," he said.

I walked past him, opened the front door and greeted the affable brunette lady standing on my doorstep. "Morning, Judy"—I smiled—"just let me grab the basket." I turned back into the hall and picked up my washing basket as Echo trotted out onto the step to say hello.

"Good night, was it?" She fussed Echo's head, smiling, then paused as she looked up and caught sight of Michael. "Oh, my, a very good night." She winked at me.

My blush wasn't faked. I handed over the basket. "You're a star, as always."

"Any stains?"

I winced and answered truthfully, "Champagne on my dress."

"Ah"—Judy waved a dismissive hand—"that won't be an issue." She glanced in the basket. "I see we're looking after the Mr's getup too?" She chuckled. "I'll have these back to you by morning."

"Thanks," I said, waving her off and closing the door behind her.

"Amelia." Michael's voice was steady but strained. "What.

The *fuck*. Is going. On?"

"That was Judy," I said, "she does my dry cleaning."

"You sent my clothes to the dry cleaners?"

"Except your shirt," I said. "And coat."

"But that was the worst!" he exclaimed.

"Exactly. No saving it." I shrugged by way of an apology.

He frowned, glanced at the sink, then the back door. Realisation dawned slowly.

"That was a very expensive—"

"Yes, yes," I said, "super-posh coat for a super fashionable finance god. We are all suitably awed."

"Amelia!"

I took a very deep breath and let it out slowly. "Sorry. I get bitchy when I'm stressed."

He surveyed me as I walked back into the utility room. "You don't seem stressed."

"Appearances can be deceiving," I said, picking up his shoes.

Behind me, Michael yelped, lunged forward, and snatched them off me.

"Not my shoes," he snapped.

"They're covered in blood," I remarked.

He dropped them. Echo started at the sound, snorted, and trotted off into the living room, heartily sick of my antics.

Retrieving the shoes from the floor, I placed them on the counter, donned a fresh pair of poonami gloves, and picked up the bottle of urine remover I'd been using on them earlier. Carefully, methodically, I cleaned every millimetre of each shoe as Michael stood in the doorway and watched me. When I was finally satisfied, I wiped them down with a damp cloth several times, then set about cleaning them with a leather cleaner.

By the time I was done, they were pristine.

Michael watched, transfixed, as I took the shoes I'd meticulously cleaned out through the back door, stuck my hands in them, stomped them through the mud, and carefully set them in a sunny spot by the step. I repositioned them twice before deciding they looked like he'd taken them off there before he'd come into the house.

Then I walked over to the burn bin, peeled off my second pair of gloves, and lifted the lid, tossing them in and checking everything was properly incinerating.

Suddenly, I was exhausted. I put the lid back on the bin and walked back into the house to scrub down the countertop I'd been working on.

"Amelia." Michael reached out for me as I passed him in the utility room, but paused just shy of touching me. "Are you okay?"

I looked at him. Really looked at him. So much of his face was still the boy I'd known. Yes, there was a beard where there had been none before. He'd filled out a bit, but certainly not in a bad way. I could have cracked nuts on that jaw now, had I been so inclined. His body had filled out, too. He'd always been fit, but he'd been rangy. Now, he was stacked. But his eyes. They were unchanged.

And in pain.

I'd heard the anguish in his voice when he'd told me what had happened to his niece. I'd seen the pride, the animation there at dinner the other night when he'd spoken of her. And I knew, probably better than he realised, how the system was skewed to protect those who hurt the innocent and vilify the victim.

"I'll be fine," I said. "I just need a shower. And a coffee."

He craned his neck back towards the kitchen. "Well, I think I can do the coffee"—he managed a weak smile—"while you get your shower."

I nodded. "Thanks."

"Please"—for a second, I thought he might be about to cry—"don't thank me."

Without another word, I went upstairs and sat in the shower, hugging my knees under scalding water for as long as I could bear the heat. Drying off, I cocooned myself in a towel and stood staring into my wardrobe. Echo's nose bumped into my hand. I looked down at her. "Hey, girl."

She shoved her nose under my hand again and up. I scratched her head. "Why am I standing here worrying about what to wear?"

She tilted her head to one side and gave me a look that said, "*Cause you're dumb.'*

I sighed. "You're right." I pulled on clean underwear, leggings, and a Ralph Lauren cable knit dress that always did a great job of making me look more put together than I was. I shoved my feet into my slippers. "Fuck it."

We went back downstairs, and I found Michael in the kitchen with two steaming mugs of coffee. I picked mine up, went into the lounge, and curled myself into the nook of the corner sofa. Michael trailed after me and perched on the edge.

"I won't bite," I said.

He smirked. "That's disappointing."

I saw the exact instant he remembered we weren't on flirting terms anymore. Had the sofa opened up a great toothy maw and swallowed him, I think he'd have been eternally grateful. "I'm sorry, I…" He shook his head. "I wasn't thinking."

Unsure how to take that, I opted to ignore it and was relieved when Echo jumped up and settled herself between us. I sipped my coffee and picked up the remote.

"Amelia, what are we doing?"

I scrolled through Netflix, sipped my coffee, and didn't answer.

"Aimee?"

I sighed. "We're watching TV after a wonderfully romantic evening was interrupted by terrible news that has upset you greatly. I invited you to stay the weekend with me to keep your mind off things and make sure you weren't alone. We've been tidying the garden since early this morning. Now we're going to Netflix and chill."

I scrolled past all the suggestions that we watch *Star Trek*, then stopped.

Fuck it.

I'd been binge-watching *Deep Space Nine* at night while I

caught up on admin and other crap I never had time for in the day. 'Flix picked up where I'd left off with the opening notes of 'Improbable Cause'. I listened to the amiable banter of Doctor Bashir and Garak as Michael's lips parted slightly. His brow furrowed as he looked at me, his expression incredulous.

"Are we really not going to talk about this?"

I looked at him and took a sip of coffee. "Which part would you like to discuss?"

"I—" he trailed off.

I stared at him, arching my eyebrows in silent query.

"I don't get you. Why are you doing this?"

Why am I doing this?

It's not going to make him love me. Clearly, nothing will. That was a pipe dream. A ridiculous, childish fantasy.

You know that. So why are *you doing this?*

"Why did you come back here this morning?"

He frowned. "Honestly? I don't know."

I shrugged. "There you are then."

I drained the last of my coffee and set the mug on the table beside me. Unfolding my legs, I pulled a bottle of arnica gel out of my pocket and held it out to him.

He stared at it blankly.

"It will help with the bruising on your hands."

He took it, clumsily attempting to squeeze some out. Impatient, I took it back off him, squirted a generous helping onto the back of one of his hands and methodically rubbed it in, ignoring his winces of pain. I did the other hand next, surveying the damage on both as I did.

His skin was scraped over his knuckles, but it wasn't too visible. Now he'd washed all the blood off they didn't look that bad. I put the gel away and passed him some ibuprofen.

"I'm fine."

"You're swollen; just take it."

The briefest flicker of something passed through his eyes. I strongly suspected some part of his brain had made a pun about swelling, and he'd caught himself just before saying it.

Just as well, my heart couldn't handle him flirting with me

anymore. It was too cruel.

I finished the careful application of some concealer to his hands just as Garak's shop blew up. Michael jumped, tearing his eyes away from me and paying attention to the TV for the first time since it had started playing.

He glanced back at me, then down at his hands, which could now pass a cursory inspection without anyone knowing what he'd done. "I'm really struggling to figure you out, you know."

"Well," I said, "if you ever do, I'd *love* an explanation."

❖

"Oh, it's clearly a trap!" Michael exclaimed. "That Romulan is well dodgy. And why do they need to destroy the entire surface of the planet? It's not like they're going to be hiding in the fucking magma." He grunted as the Romulan he was so suspicious of did something else suspicious. "He's a shapeshifter, isn't he?" He turned to me, pointing at the TV. "He is, isn't he?"

I chuckled, "I can neither confirm nor deny."

Echo lifted her head and looked at me. I shrugged.

"I knew it!" He leapt out of his seat. "'*So much for the Dominion',* my arse. Arrogant—"

A knock at the door interrupted him. He sat back down again. "Your dry-cleaning lady is very quick."

I slid off the sofa. "That's not my dry cleaning. Echo." Her name held an edge of command, and she leapt down from the sofa, running to the door and barking. She knew not to bark at visitors.

Unless, of course, I wanted her to.

Opening the door, I snapped my fingers at her, and she obediently sat beside me. I looked out expectantly at two individuals standing on my doorstep, who I assumed to be police.

"Amelia Thornbridge?"

I glanced at the speaker, a woman a few years younger

than me with reddish brown hair.

"Yes?"

She flashed a warrant card at me. "I'm Detective Sergeant Brown, this is Detective Inspector Rowan." She gestured at the older woman beside her. "We're looking for a Mr Michael Bane. We believe you were with him last night?"

"Yes, what's this about?"

"Is he here, ma'am?"

As she spoke, Michael appeared behind me, pulling the door open further to reveal himself.

"Yes, I'm here. Is this about Becca?"

"After a fashion," the DI spoke. "May we come in?"

"Of course," I said, stepping aside to let them in. "Echo, basket."

She gave the intruders a glance that seemed to say, *'I'll be watching you from the kitchen. Don't try anything'* and loped off to sit in her basket.

"Please, come through," I said, gesturing to the lounge. They walked in and took in the rucked-up blanket on the sofa I'd been snuggled up under, the assorted half-eaten snacks and empty mugs on the coffee table.

"Sorry to interrupt your weekend," the DI said, "we won't keep you long."

At my gesture, they seated themselves on the sofa. I sat on the cuddle chair in the bay window, Michael perching on the arm of the chair.

"Is Becca okay?" Michael asked, and I knew he wasn't faking the fear in his voice. "Has something happened?"

"Your niece is—" The DS seemed to catch herself. "—still at the hospital. As far as I know, there's been no change in her condition."

Michael breathed a sigh of relief. "How can we help you?"

"Where were you last night, Mr Bane?"

"We attended a charity ball at White Deer Hall," he said.

"And what time did that finish?"

Michael considered. "I'm not sure; we left early, about…" He glanced at me for confirmation. "nineish, was it?"

I nodded. "Sounds about right. We caught a taxi back here."

"I see," DS Brown said, "and then?"

"I stayed the night," Michael said. "What's this about?"

"You were here all night?"

"Yes," Michael said.

"Well, pretty much." I looked at them. "We had a bit of a spat, and he left, but thought better of it and came back."

"I see." The sergeant was taking notes. "What time did he return?"

"Oh, it wasn't long after." I glanced at Michael.

He paused, thinking about it. "We didn't get far. I had the taxi let me out at the end of the road and walked back."

"And this would have been what time?"

Michael shrugged. "Can't have been much after nine, nine-thirty maybe."

"And you remained here after that?"

He nodded. "Yes."

They both looked at me. "You're happy to confirm Mr Bane was here with you, from—" The sergeant consulted her notes. "About nine-thirty until now?"

I nodded. "Yes. What's this about?"

"He hasn't left? Not nipped home for a change of clothes."

Michael gestured at my Mandaloiran oodie and the far-too-small joggers. "You think I've been to pick up clothes?"

The sergeant smirked. "Fair point."

"Apologies for the questions, Mr Bane," the DI said. "I'm afraid there was an incident last night involving Eric Hale."

Michael's fists clenched at the name. I moved a hand to his leg and squeezed it reassuringly.

"The man who...attacked your niece. We simply needed to ascertain your whereabouts."

"I was here," he said.

"So I see." The DI smiled. Perhaps it was paranoia, but I didn't think it reached her eyes. "I assume you're aware of what happened to your niece?"

Michael nodded. "My sister called last night."

The DI nodded. "What time was that?"

"Er." Michael frowned and reached for his phone from the coffee table. "I'll check, ah shit." He waved the phone at them. "Battery's dead. Ah, it must have been about nine-forty-five, maybe ten?"

He glanced at me. I shrugged. "Sounds about right," I said, keeping it vague. I didn't actually know what time she'd called. I suspected he was telling the truth when he'd said he'd got out of the taxi just after it had left. But if she didn't call until ten, that meant it wasn't the reason he'd waved off the taxi.

Had he actually been coming back here? Was that when she'd called? As he'd been walking back?

"And where were you at that point?"

"Here," he said, "with Amelia. I was… Well, obviously, I was livid." He stood and paced the room before stopping abruptly and looking back at me. "She's been amazing."

My breath caught in my throat.

He meant that.

"Yes, it wouldn't be good to be alone when you received that news, I imagine." The DI stood. "Well, we've kept you long enough, thanks for your help. We'll be in touch if we need anything else." She nodded at his phone. "You might want to charge that."

"I will," he said.

She stood, passing Michael a card. "In case you need me."

He nodded his thanks, and I showed them to the door.

"What happened to him?" I said suddenly.

Stupid, stupid, shut your dumb mouth.

The DI turned and looked back at us both. "Eric Hale was murdered last night."

CHAPTER 6

The loaded pause on the phone line was palpable. Finally, Suzie said, "You did *what?*"

I sucked in a breath and thanked whatever was in control of these things that she wasn't in the room. "I didn't do anything. The police asked me questions, I answered them."

"Right." Another loaded pause. "Am I missing something here? Like...the plot?"

"I don't see what's confusing."

Suzie's exasperated sigh was the only sound she made for a long moment. Then, "Last we spoke, you were in bed, drunk, furious with him, and very much *alone.*"

"He came back."

"After that."

"Yes."

"Where was he in the middle?"

"There was no middle."

"Sure there was, a whole middle. We were talking all the way through it."

"No, you weren't," I snapped. "Just...Suze, please, I know what I'm doing."

Honestly, she was making an art of silence at this point. At length, she replied, "Do you?"

"Yes."

"This can't be one of those times you run away with yourself and do what you think's best for someone else. Like launching me a TikTok channel without telling me or even letting on you'd been filming me. Did you even *ask* him before you did this?"

"I didn't *do* anything," I repeated.

"You bloody well did," she snapped. "I don't know what exactly, but I know you did. And I'd wager it was against all reason and sanity. A man is *dead*, Amelia."

"A *paedophile* is dead. He lost his rights the second he hurt a thirteen-year-old girl."

Suzie sighed. "I get that. But it doesn't mean you can just rewrite what happened last night and expect everyone else to roll with it."

I didn't do that. Did I?

"And it doesn't make what *he* did right," she said.

"*He* didn't kill him," I said flatly. Zero room for disagreements.

Somewhere in the background, a muffled voice queried if everything was okay. "Ah, just Aims pulling another Aimee," Suzie said absently, and I heard Tom chuckle.

She lowered her voice and said, "You don't *know* that."

Okay, maybe more room to disagree than I'd realised.

"I do know that." *Do I?*

"Do you?"

I stared at the phone and fiddled with the dressing gown hanging on the back of the bathroom door. I'd never lied to Suzie. "Yes."

"Amelia?" Michael's voice floated to me down the hall.

"I've got to go."

"Aimee—"

"It's fine, Suze. Honestly. Speak to you later. Say hi to Tom!"

I hung up, praying I hadn't just lied to her twice in the space of a minute.

❖

Michael called for me again before I finally emerged from the bathroom, quietly closing the door behind me. I took a step across the landing, uncertain where he was. Then I saw him, slumped on the floor at the top of the stairs, staring vacantly at nothing in particular. The ridiculous combination of my too-small joggers and huge oodie made him look younger, but his face… There was a slightly haunted look about him. Beside him lay Echo, her head and one protective paw across his lap.

She'd never been a poor judge of character before.

I padded across the landing. "Michael?"

He startled, looked up, saw me, then struggled to his feet. His mouth opened to speak, but no words came out. Dragging one hand down his face, he stared at me, eyes huge, glistening, as if he'd been fighting back tears.

Finally, he asked in a hoarse whisper, "Did I do this?" And for some reason, the question made me less inclined to think he had. "Oh God." He sagged against the wall. "Aimee, did I kill him?"

Every inch of me wanted to reach out and comfort him at that moment. But every inch of me was a moronic schoolgirl when it came to Michael Bane.

It's not like he was here, comforting you last night, after Gemma fucking Foster beat the emotional crap out of you yet again. Nope. He was off beating the literal crap out of someone.

But killing him?

"I don't know," I said, trying to keep my voice neutral. "Did you? I mean, could what you did have…"

"I didn't think so, but…" Michael shook his head. "I mean, yeah, I beat the shit out of the guy, but he was conscious and talking when I left."

"Talking?"

"Well…" He shifted, twisting his hands in his lap. "More

moaning…in pain," he admitted reluctantly. "I did…I really did hurt him, but I didn't think… But could I have?"

I stared at him for a while. "I don't know. Maybe. But if you did." I patted him on the arm gently. "I do believe it was an accident." My voice hardened. "And he had it coming."

Michael started, surprised by the tone of my voice. "You don't even know Becca."

"I don't have to," I said. "She's a child. It would have been unforgivable to do that to a grown woman, but a child…"

He nodded slowly, and I got the impression the full impact of what had happened to his niece was occurring to him all over again. Or perhaps not. Perhaps it was like grief, hitting you in waves; every time you thought you understood the true horror of it, the whole thing would wash over you again, drowning you, pulling you under.

"I think—" His hand went to his mouth, and he shot across the landing into the bathroom.

At my feet, Echo whined as the bathroom door slammed and the sound of Michael's muffled puking reached us.

My hand dropped to her head, petting it reassuringly. "It's okay, girl. It'll be okay."

Shit.

What was it with me and lying to my friends today?

I had no clue what was going to happen, let alone if everything would be alright.

More information. That's what I needed. Context.

I left Michael to throw up in peace and went downstairs, pushing open the door to my study and booting up my laptop. Some Googling, several calls to local journalists and a chat with a friend in the local police force later, and I was feeling…something. Relief?

Somehow, that seemed inappropriate.

"Aimee?"

"In here," I called, and Michael wandered in, glancing around at the room. I'd forgotten he hadn't really seen most of the house yet. So strange. His presence felt so familiar and…comforting, despite the bizarre circumstances.

He stepped towards me, and I looked up from my laptop, only realising after I'd done it that I'd pushed my chair back to maintain the distance between us.

He frowned, though whether I'd hurt his feelings or pissed him off with the move, I couldn't tell.

"Are you okay?" he asked.

"I was about to ask you the same."

He looked pale and exhausted. He shrugged. "I'll be fine. More worried about you. Look, you didn't ask for any of this, I know what we told the police, but that was before... Well, I'm sure there's a way we can walk it back. I'll call my lawyer, we'll get you out of this and—"

"It wasn't you, Michael," I said, getting up from the desk, walking around to the front and perching on the edge of it.

"You don't know—"

"I do. I've spoken to a few people. Eric Hale was stabbed to death; he died from exsanguination."

Michael frowned.

"He bled out," I clarified.

Michael stumbled backwards, catching himself on the wall. "I didn't do that," he said. "Amelia, I did *not* do that! I hit him, I didn't... I didn't do that." He stared at me. "I didn't do that."

"No, you didn't."

He blinked. "How do you know that? I mean, I didn't, but you sound certain."

"I am." I gave a small smile. "I cleaned your clothes, remember? Stabbing him would have left castoff stains."

He stared at me. "How—"

I shrugged. "I ghostwrite a series of crime novels. The main character is a forensics expert. You learn the weirdest things in my line of work."

He blinked. "You just casually drop that in conversation? Like, *Yeah, sure, I'm a successful marketeer, but on the side, I also write multiple novels!*"

I shrugged. "Loads of people I know write novels. I guess it doesn't seem strange to me."

"Oh, so you're also friends with a load of novelists?" He

snorted a laugh. "Like that in itself isn't cool."

"They're just people, Michael." I shrugged again. Irritated for some reason.

"Whatever," he sniffed. "You're still basing everything on my word and...blood patterns? You're taking a lot of faith."

Am I?

"Maybe. But I remember your drama class performances; you're not that good an actor."

A ghost of a smile crossed his face, but it faltered. "Aimee, about school—"

His mobile rang, interrupting whatever mortifyingly embarrassing thing was about to come out of his mouth. I'd had enough of a rerun of what school had been like last night. I didn't need any further reminder of how much he hated me.

"I put it on charge for you," I said, nodding to the side table in the corner.

He crossed the room without a word. "Hello?"

A pause, a female voice, but I couldn't make out what she was saying.

"I'll be right there," he said. "What ward are you on?" He frowned, glancing around.

I handed him a pen and a Post-it pad. He took it without looking at me, scribbling something down. "Do you need anything?" More chatter on the other end, and he jotted down a few more things. "Okay, I'll be there soon as I can." He hung up, moved to the door, remembered where he was and glanced down at his clothes.

"Aimee." He looked back at me. "I'm sorry, but I need another favour."

❖

My Jeep rolled around the corner of the hospital, the EV engine near silent as we approached. It gave us a second to take in the sea of reporters, news crews, and general carnage going on outside the main entrance.

I should have expected this.

"Shit," Michael said, "what are they all doing here?"

"Small-town murder, the victim beat a young girl; everyone knows he's guilty, but it seemed he was going to get off scot-free? We're talking about police corruption. Come on, Bane, this isn't just local news. This is a national scandal."

"I—" Words failed him.

"It's okay, take a breath," I said. "They're loud, obnoxious, and tenacious as hell, but they're still just people. I'm going to park. We're going to get out and walk in right past them."

"I can't—"

"Yes, you can," I said firmly. "And you have to. You're the uncle of the true victim in all this. As far as they know, you've done nothing wrong, and I'm the proof of that. So, get out of the car, get your bag, take my hand like you're actually dating me, and walk right on in there."

"Amelia—"

"I know, I know, I'm ruining your street cred." I rolled my eyes and cast a sidelong look his way. "But if I leave, they'll ask why. They'll dig. And I'd rather people didn't question why I wasn't supporting you in this. Or have any cause to start picking your alibi apart because, honestly, it's not that great."

He looked back at the crowd of press as I turned into a spot and killed the engine. They'd seen us.

"They'll swarm," I warned him. "Just keep your head down, keep walking, and pretend they're not asking you anything. Whatever they say, *do not answer*." I grabbed his arm and squeezed. "I mean it, Michael. They have a way of twisting things out of context, and they won't hesitate if it gives them more air time or higher ratings. So, you don't speak. Not one word."

He nodded, glancing back at me. "Okay. We'll do it your way," he sighed. "It's the least I owe you."

I moved to open my door. Before I could, he said, "For the record—"

I paused so nobody overheard him

"—I don't give a shit about my *street cred* and haven't since I was about nineteen." Swinging out of the car, he let the door

shut behind him. He didn't *exactly* slam it, but it was close.
Huh.

Climbing out, I rounded the car. Michael hoisted a holdall out of the boot and shut it. We'd made a brief stop at his house so he could change. The tell-tale signs of a teenage occupant were evident in the driveway. The abandoned bike on the lawn, the footie goals set up at each end of the garden. We walked past them and down the side of the house, where Michael retrieved a football. Pink, clearly well used. Michael scooped it up and held it tight to his chest, head bowed over it for a moment. He shook himself, shoved through the side gate and let himself in the back door, stowing the football safely in a basket inside.

I was about to follow when I noticed the clothesline stretching across the back garden was laden with soaked items. Pink tops vied for space amidst cropped hoodies and women's underwear. For some reason, having heard him speak about his sister and niece, I was thoroughly unsurprised to find they shared a house with him.

Silently, I gathered in the washing that had clearly been hanging on the line since the day before, and followed Michael into the house. While he changed and gathered some things for his family, I rewashed the clothes and tried not to be too nosy, peering at the photographs lining the hall wall in a gallery of happy memories. A teenage Michael grinned out at me, his arm slung around a much younger girl's shoulder, as he pointed the camera back at them. A selfie from the days before selfies. In the absence of a screen to show him what he was pointing at, he'd caught more of the beach behind them than he had of them.

I had no idea where they'd been, but they'd been drawing in the sand. Lexi's name was scrawled beside a love heart pierced with an arrow. On the other side, the name of a boy I assume she'd had a crush on.

Had that boy grown up to be her boyfriend? Was that Becca's father?

Michael's reappearance at the top of the stairs prevented

me from snooping any further. He looked considerably more like himself in jeans, shirt and jumper, but I'd kinda liked the sight of him in my clothes.

Why are you such a weirdo?

There was no time to contemplate that particular question. We turned towards the hospital, and I took a deep breath, my stomach roiling alarmingly.

Like I might vomit.

Michael's hand slid around mine, his fingers lacing through my own, and he squeezed, pulling me close so he could whisper in my ear, "You don't have to do this."

But I did. And it wasn't even for him anymore. I'd lied to the police. If that lie unravelled, I was in serious shit.

Probably should have considered that *a little more before doing it.*

"It's okay," I murmured. "We'll be okay."

And we strode past the tangled, eager, rabid media circus. I didn't breathe again until we were inside the lobby. It felt so strange, walking in on his arm in full view of everyone. Like we were together. Like I was his, and he was mine. Like everything that had happened between us since I'd moved back hadn't been one colossal misunderstanding. Like the proverbial wool hadn't been pulled from his eyes, and he actually would still want to be seen with me.

He's using you.

Just like he was using you when he fancied a quick fuck the other morning.

The thought made me angry and I stomped through the lobby. A local hospital, it wasn't huge, but we still had to ask for directions from a porter and it took a full ten minutes to navigate the rabbit warren and find the right ward. A nurse showed us to Becca's room. She paused as we reached the door.

"Brace yourselves," she warned us, "it looks a lot worse than it is."

Beside me, Michael sucked in a breath. His hand tightened around mine. This time, no show was involved. Just a man about to be confronted by anyone's worst nightmare. I squeezed back. Hell, this was my worst nightmare. If my niece was lying in that room, I'd be apoplectic.

Michael's hand moved to the door handle, then froze. Beside me, I felt an uneven shudder run through him, a ragged breath, and the slightest sound escaped him. It wasn't a whimper, but it was damn close.

"Deep breath," I said softly.

He took one, then another. By the third, he'd stopped the rising panic. He pushed the door open and stepped inside, drawing me behind him.

"Mike!" A woman flew across the room, and he dropped my hand to catch her up in his arms.

"Oh, my god." Michael's voice was hoarse as he took in the pale, bruised form of Becca, prone in the bed. Her eyes were closed, but whether that was from swelling or sleep, I couldn't tell. Her face was a tapestry of purples and reds, one eye so swollen you couldn't even see it. Michael's arms tightened around his sister, who sobbed into his chest. Great, heaving, gasping sobs.

My own eyes filled with tears. I remembered Lexi, vaguely, as a scrawny girl trailing at her brother's heels, always eager for his attention and the attention of his friends. She'd started first year the year we finished our A Levels, so I hadn't known her well. Yet here she stood, a grown woman with a daughter older than she'd been last time I'd seen her.

When she finally pulled back, tears stained her face and she struggled to control the snot trying to stream from her nose. Feeling utterly useless, I fished in my pocket and pulled out a packet of tissues, holding them out to her.

She took them gratefully, blowing her nose and dabbing her eyes. It took her a second to realise she didn't know who'd given them to her. Confusion clouded her eyes, and she looked at her brother. "Who—"

"You remember Amelia? She was in my year at school?"

Lexi's frown deepened, either because she couldn't remember me, or she remembered me all too well and couldn't fathom how the hell we were in the same room. I couldn't tell which.

"I'm sorry to intrude," I said awkwardly. "Michael didn't have his car."

Panicked, she turned back to him. "What happened?"

"Nothing," he soothed, "I'm fine. I was still at Amelia's when you called, and didn't want to wait for a taxi. She gave me a lift."

"Still..." Lexi struggled to process his words. I could hardly blame her for that. The implication that we'd spent the night together was confounding enough, without adding in her emotional state and what I imagined had been a completely sleepless night.

"How is she?" Michael asked, smoothly changing the subject.

Lexi returned to a chair pulled up close to her daughter's bed. I glanced around the room, which was surprisingly empty of other relatives. I wondered where their parents were, or Becca's father. Michael had said he'd been supporting them, I hadn't realised he'd meant he was the *only* one doing so.

I frowned.

What kind of parent didn't show up for their daughter and grandchild through *this*? What kind of father didn't come for *this*?

Undomesticated equines wouldn't have kept my parents from this room if it were me and my daughter.

Not that I had a daughter.

"She woke up earlier, but they mostly have her sedated," Lexi said. "I'd rather she slept through this anyway." Lexi smoothed a stray hair out of her daughter's face.

"Is she..." Michael paused, took a breath, tried again. "Is there any permanent damage?"

Lexi shook her head. "Not that they can tell. Physically, she will heal, thank god, but until she's fully regained consciousness, they can't say for sure there's been no cognitive damage. And mentally..." Lexi sobbed. "*Oh god, how will she ever get over this?*"

Michael crouched beside his sister, wrapping both arms

around her and hugging her to him. He kissed the top of her head. "She's a strong kid. We'll get her the best physio, a great shrink. Whatever therapy she needs. She'll get through it, Lex."

"She shouldn't have to!" Lexi snapped. "It's not fair!" Her voice broke, and she descended into sobs again.

Silently, I left the room, sliding out into the hall and closing the door behind them, giving them privacy. A man walking towards the door nodded to me, and I stepped aside to let him pass, assuming he was hospital staff and noticing the camera half hidden behind his back only as he drew level with me.

My arm went up, palm slamming into the door frame, shoulder slamming into him and knocking him back just before he pushed the door open. "What the *fuck* is wrong with you?" I demanded.

"I'm just doing my job, lady," the guy protested, trying to push past me.

I wasn't having any of it. "There's a girl in there going through a hell you will never know. And you want the world to see her in the worst moment of her life?"

He scoffed, but his attempts to get past me wavered. Like he hadn't thought of it like that before.

"Look, if it's not me, it will just be someone else," he tried to reason.

"It will be nobody," I said, rather too savagely. "Press gets in this room over my rotting corpse. Do you hear me? And if they tried then, I'd come back and fucking bite them for their trouble. Get the fuck out of here."

Without moving from the door, I shoved him back, hard.

He rocked back on his feet slightly but didn't budge. "I'll be quick," he said, "just one shot and—"

The door opened behind me and Michael stepped out, one arm wrapping my waist and gently moving me out of the way. The photographer, to his credit, tried to stand his ground, but Michael had a good three inches on him and he was fucking furious.

I pulled the door shut behind him just as the arsehole managed to get his camera around to chance a side snap.

"Try that again," Michael said, his voice low but surprisingly calm, "and that camera won't live to see another scandal."

The guy considered him, glanced at me, and sagged slightly. "Fair enough," he said. "No harm meant."

Michael didn't answer, just took two deliberate steps forwards, forcing the photographer to back up. The guy nodded, turned, and walked away.

I let out a breath, sucked in another, and released the fistfuls I'd taken from the back of Michael's jumper. He leant back into me. "I wasn't going to hit him," he said.

"Not sure I'd have blamed you if you'd tried."

He snorted. "Tried?"

"I wasn't about to let you."

Another snort. For a second, I thought he'd tell me to get over myself, but instead, he simply said, "Thanks." He turned back to look at me. "I can't believe he just did that."

"I can," I said. "Look, I know it's the last thing you want to think about right now, but honestly, you're best putting out a statement. Give them something to chew on so they stop trying to take chunks out of you."

He stared at me. "You think that's the best thing to do?"

I nodded. "The press can be relentless, especially with a story like this. Whether you like it or not, you, your sister, Becca, are part of their narrative. You can either have a say in that narrative, or you can let them decide how they spin it." I shrugged. "If it were my family, I'd want a say."

He nodded, thinking. "I'll speak to Lexi. I... What would we say?"

"We handle the press for clients all the time." I shrugged. "Not for stuff like this, but still. I can call my PR Manager and get him to work up a statement, help you figure out what's best to say and how you want to say it?"

"Make the call," he said. "Lexi may not be up to it, but I can talk to him for her."

I nodded, pulling out my phone and stepping aside so he could get back in the room.

"What happened," I heard Lexi ask before the door swung shut after him.

"Isla?" I said into my phone. "Are you in the office?"

"Yeah," Isla's voice cracked down the phone. "I figured you'd be otherwise occupied today," she chuckled. "What do you need?"

"Is Brennan in?"

"One sec."

I heard the whistle of the coffee machine fade as Isla stepped out of the kitchen and went down into the main office. We kept the office open on a Saturday to catch the weekend foot traffic. Flexi-time meant people often had days off in the week and worked Saturday instead, or left early one night and came in a few hours over the weekend. I didn't really care much when they worked or how many hours, as long as they finished their shit.

"Yeah, he's here," Isla said. "Working on stuff for Hilary. You want him?"

"Please." I waited as Isla handed the phone over.

"Hey, boss," Brennan's cheerful voice greeted me. Had I been working on Hilary's campaign, I'm not sure I could have mustered that much enthusiasm. Although, perhaps, he was grateful for the distraction. "What's up? If she's moaning already, I've not even—"

"Hilary can wait, mate, how fast can you get down to the infirmary?"

"Are you hurt?" Concern sharpened his usually affable voice.

"Not me, but I'm here with a friend, and they could do with some help."

"Sure, but it might take me a while to get in, there's a frickin' circus over there today. Have you seen the news? Some guy got wasted after attacking a local girl."

"Yeah," I sighed, "that friend I mentioned? He's the girl's uncle."

There was a loaded pause as Brennan processed the implications of that statement and what he was walking into. "I'll be right there."

CHAPTER 7

Wind howled in the eaves, making me shiver despite the crackling flames of the fire, the blanket I'd cocooned myself in, and the comforting weight of Echo spread down the length of my legs. Her head rested on my belly, nose pointing towards my face. She was dozing, but opened her eyes questioningly every now and then when she heard me sigh.

I'd been sighing a great deal this evening. Shrugging further into the blanket, I tried to focus on Brennan's clear voice drifting through the room from the TV. I'd always been impressed by Brennan's professionalism and media savvy, but I'd never tested it in an environment like this before.

Marketing campaigns were a far cry from *this*. The worst he'd faced in his time with me was helping manage some backlash after the locals in the village where our client was building a new abattoir took issue with them and kicked up a fuss. The company's reputation had been dragged through the mud, and the new venture had become a financial failure before it was even built.

Brennan had handled it well; there was no turning the locals around, and we'd known that going in. Damage control was the name of the game, and walking back as much damage as we could in the hopes the company could salvage the situation.

Which they had.

So, I knew he could handle himself. But still, *this* was nothing like *that*.

"We would like to thank everyone for their well-wishes and support," Brennan continued. *"We request the media respect our privacy during this incredibly difficult time, and give Rebecca the time and space needed to heal."* Brennan looked up to deliver the last line, enunciating each word to perfection so there was no room for misinterpretation. *"We would also like to express our condolences at this time to Eric Hale's friends and family."*

A collective murmur rippled through the crowd.

"While we remain devastated that the justice system failed Rebecca so completely, Mr Hale's actions were his own. It saddens us to know that another family is now grieving."

Brennan disappeared from the screen as the newsreader reappeared to say, *"That was the scene earlier this evening at Elizabeth Infirmary in Ashfordby, where thirteen-year-old Rebecca Bane is recovering after a brutal assault on her way to school yesterday morning. In the wake of the arrest and subsequent release of the man believed to be responsible for the assault, questions were raised regarding the merits of a justice system that allowed Hale to be released under investigation despite damning CCTV footage clearly showing him committing the crime. Why were charges not immediately filed? Why, given the evidence, was he released at all, without charges and the constraints of bail conditions? While those questions linger, another investigation is now underway, as police hunt for the person or persons responsible for murdering Mr Hale in the early hours of this morning."*

I shivered again, switching over to Netflix and looking for something animated and wholesome to distract me.

My phone rang. I slid right and hit the speaker button without picking it up.

"Hey," I said.

"I just saw the news," Suzie said. She paused, as if considering her words with care. "Are you okay?"

I didn't answer immediately. Then, "No." Because I wasn't,

and I was quite exhausted from telling people everything was going to be fine when I wasn't at all sure it was.

For Becca, in many ways, it never would be again.

She would recover, in time. But her life would never be what it would have been. Should have been. She would carry this with her forever. Even if she made a full physical recovery.

"Brennan did good," Suzie said. "I'm glad it was him reading it and not you."

So was I. Selfish of me, I knew, for dragging him into the situation and then placing the burden of speaking those words on him, but I couldn't face it, and it had never even occurred to him that I might.

"I'm surprised Michael didn't want to read it himself," Suzie said.

"He did. We squashed that right away."

"Good call," Suzie sighed. "I know what I said before. I don't want to argue or add to your worry, but—"

"It wasn't him, Suze," I said flatly. "Whatever he did, he didn't do this."

"Is he still there?" she asked, clearly unconvinced but unwilling to press it.

"No, I left him at the hospital with his family. I came home once Brennan had done his thing."

"Brennan did a good job," she said again. "Will *he* be back later?"

She didn't mean Brennan. "I don't know."

"Is—"

"You know what? I'd really appreciate it if we could talk about something else. Anything else. I feel like my entire life has suddenly been overrun by Michael fucking Bane."

"Suddenly?" Suze said dryly. "Girl, that happened when you were eleven years old."

"Not like this, it didn't. I mean, seriously? When did we start talking about nothing but *boys*."

"Fair point. Okay, I'll change the subject, but before I do, I just want you to know that whatever you've done, it's not too late to undo it."

"Now you sound like him."

"Really?" She didn't even try to hide the surprise in her voice.

"Whatever you may think of him, Suzie, he's not a bad guy. He tried to talk me out of it before I ever did it, and since it got...more complicated, he's tried again. Several times."

"He's right. This isn't your problem. You're risking your reputation, your business, your livelihood, possibly even your freedom, and for what? Some fuck boy."

"It's not about him," I countered.

Echo opened her eyes, lifted her head and gave a sceptical rumble.

"Okay, it *was* about him at the start. But that was before I knew the whole situation. If you'd been at that hospital, Suzie. If you'd seen that girl. And that's just the physical stuff I could see. What she'll go through when she wakes...assuming she's still all there at all, I—"

"Easy," Suzie soothed, "I'm not a monster, I do understand the wider issue. And that had to hit close to home given...well..."

"There but for the grace of god," I said.

"Exactly." She paused. "You got out of a similar situation without any physical damage. Can't have been easy to see."

"They let him go," I said, disbelief draining all feeling from my voice. "They had him dead to rights, and he walked without even being charged." I shook my head. "It's not just about Michael anymore. It's about Becca and every other girl, woman and, yes, man who has had something like this happen and been too afraid to speak. Who finally mustered the courage to come forward, only to be told they're overreacting, or being dramatic, that it was their fault, they were asking for it."

I fell silent. The fire crackled merrily beside me, and the opening beats of *Howl's Moving Castle* danced across my giant flatscreen.

"Guess what I did today," Suzie said.

I blinked, staring at the phone. Even for Suzie, that was an abrupt change of subject.

"Thrifting for more vintage chairs to upcycle into planters?"

"Nope."

"Cycling around searching for new graffiti walls to use as photo-shoot backdrops?"

"No, but that's definitely something I need to do tomorrow before I go home, huh—" She paused. "When did I stop thinking of Manchester as home? When did Bangor become home?"

"I think," I said, shuffling around on the sofa, "it was that week we spent there over the summer between your first and second year. There was so much you wanted to do and show me, people you wanted me to meet. I had a rare week off, and you didn't want to spend it back at your flat in Manchester."

"I guess," Suzie sighed. "I'm halfway through my degree, though. What will I do when I finish?"

"Knowing you, something completely unexpected. You've plenty of time to figure that out. Are you still enjoying it?"

"Love it!" she enthused. "We went out to survey the winter habitats of red squirrels last week and tracked their feeding patterns. It was freezing, but seeing them in their natural environment was incredible. I got some *amazing* footage. And we even spotted some signs of pine martens in the area—they're starting to make a comeback."

I laughed. "Is that what you were doing today then? Hunting for squirrels in Manchester?" Given the litany of random activities Suzie might engage in on any given day, it honestly wouldn't surprise me.

"I wish. The best wildlife we get around here are rotund pigeons so fat from stealing chips they've forgotten how to fly. And they're hardly documentary material. Okay, I'll tell you what happened, but only because you begged."

Echo whined indignantly at the phone, and I smiled despite myself.

"You were half right," she said. "I was thrifting. I found a glorious old monstrosity of a skirt and decided to transform it into a chic, stylish dress."

"Uhu." I frowned. Never in my life would I pair the words chic, stylish, and old skirt, but Suzie's fashion sense was edgier than a razor blade and twice as cutting.

"So, there I was, scissors in hand, thinking I'm about to revolutionise sustainable fashion with this genius new design…" She paused for dramatic effect. Michael might have been terrible in drama class, but Suzie always excelled. "I mean, this is viral content *in the making*, right?"

I chuckled. "Sure." I'd seen more than enough of Suze's viral content *in the making* mishaps to know this was about to go horribly wrong.

"Long story short, what was supposed to be an asymmetrical hem turned into... Well, let's just say I didn't realise the extent of my error until I turned the camera on to capture the big reveal, only to find I'm revealing *far* more than I intended."

"Oh God." I covered my eyes with one hand. As if that could stop me from seeing the mental image. "You weren't live were you?"

"Yep." She sighed. "Which is great. The last thing I need is a ban."

I made an indiscernible noise. "Eh, there's always OnlyFans."

"Don't even joke about that," Suzie said. "I've a recurring nightmare that everything goes tits up with the eco stuff, and nobody will hire me for a real job again, and I'm forced to film hobbit porn with that weird Irish guy who packs bags at Tesco Express."

I laughed, and something in my chest that had been clutching at me all day eased. Snuggling down into my blanket and Echo's hug, I listened to Suzie give me every minute detail of her week from start to finish, no boys included.

❖

It was well after 2am by the time Suzie finally conceded she needed sleep and hung up, with strict instructions I should go straight to bed.

I did not.

Without the distracting chatter of my best friend, or the chaotic, vexing presence of Michael Bane, the reality of the day's events finally dawned on me. I hadn't been joking when I'd told Suzie it felt like I'd not spoken about anything but him all week. Truthfully, work aside, I hadn't thought about anything but him since that first morning after moving back here. I'd headed out for a run, all ready for a new chapter, and he'd flashed me that killer smile, a quick nod of hello, and suddenly I had been thirteen again.

I sighed and resumed my *Deep Space Nine* marathon. Even that wasn't enough to dispel the balloon of anxiety growing in my chest, making it hard to breathe. Making it *hurt* to breathe. Cleaning the already pristine kitchen brought me little respite. I hoovered. It didn't help. In the course of wandering the house, furiously pushing the vacuum back and forth as Echo watched me from a safe distance, I found myself in my office. Work beckoned, but after several frustrating hours of trying to edit one of Leah's whitepapers, I realised I was just making it crap and gave up.

The house was closing in on me. I needed to move, and wasn't waiting for the sun to make an appearance. Echo followed in my wake as I powered around my run far faster than normal, headlamp firmly in place to dispel the last vestiges of night. By the time the sun deigned to suggest an appearance, I was almost back home already. Realising I felt no better, we went on a random extra leg just to try and burn off the anxiety. I finally arrived home feeling slightly sick, breathless and flushed, despite the chill damp covering my skin from a misting rain.

A sneeze at my heel informed me Echo was heartily tired of both the weather and my funk, and I towelled her off, fed her breakfast, and left her chomping on a new buffalo horn while I slid into a hot bath and tried (without success) to read a novel.

My phone sat silently on the side of the tub, mocking me with its lack of messages. I kept picking it up and checking my WhatsApp in case I had somehow failed to hear it ping.

Nothing.

He's probably sleeping.

He'll check in when he wakes up.

The water went cold. I read the same page four or five times and still had no idea how Felicity, the somewhat feckless heroine, had wound up stuck in a mineshaft. Or why she thought her strapping, on-again-off-again cowboy lover would come and save her. Not when he was, clearly, off on another inexplicable time-travelling jaunt. One that crossed centuries and oceans and had deposited him in Victorian London.

He's not coming, you dumb bint.

He doesn't even know you need him.

I checked my phone again, nothing.

Cold air stealing across the cooling water on my skin set every hair on my arms on end, and I shivered. It was gone elevenses; surely he must be awake by now? I caved, opened WhatsApp and checked when he'd last been online.

Seven fucking minutes ago.

That rat bastard.

I stared at the phone. It was in no way shocking, yet somehow I was shook.

Morning! I fired it off before I could stop myself, then agonised for several minutes over whether to unsend it, or if that would seem even more cringe. Before I'd made a decision, Michael's status switched to online and a double tick told me he'd already read it.

Fuck.

And then he was gone again.

He left me on read!

I slammed my phone down on the side of the bath and returned to my novel. This only served to vex me further as, contrary to all logic or sanity, Clayton Rider, the beefy cowboy, turned up just in time—

How could he possibly have known she was in danger when he was in 19th-century London?

—Clayton proceeded to single-handedly kill off a trio of cowboys who were, quite clearly, evil. It was evident from the fact they each sported an elaborate moustache—

Oh, come on, guys, there are three of you. If you all attack him at once instead of waiting patiently while he kills your... Wait, aren't they your brothers? And you're just standing there waiting your turn?

—Having effortlessly, if somewhat inexplicably, dispatched the bad guys, Clayton swept Felicity up in his arms and carried her from the mineshaft—

Wasn't that tunnel caved in a minute ago?

—they paused for a quick victory shag in the prairie grass before he whisked her off to Victorian London, to buy her some elaborately corseted gown and escort her to a ball—

At that point, I threw the book into the bathwater, spraying the room with cold water and the forlorn remnants of my bubbles.

I bet she got more than one dance and a grumpy taxi ride home. He probably gave her a triple orgasm in the hansom cab on the way back, before singing her another love sonnet and playing his fucking harmonica like he's Max bloody McNown.

The phone was only spared the same fate as the book because it pinged right as I was about to drown it.

Michael!

But no.

It was Just Eat trying to cajole me into ordering lunch.

I checked my WhatsApp.

Still on read.

I watched my novel succumb to the water. The pages curled in disdain at my treatment, warping the glossy cover image of a shirtless, ripped, delicious man bareback riding a humongous horse. It reared before a settling sun. Sprawled on the ground before him lay a woman, legs spread, either waiting for him to dismount and take her, or recovering after being thrown from the horse as he rode off and left her in the dust.

I couldn't figure out which.

Fucking arsehole cowboys.

Hauling myself out of the bath, I fished the novel from the bubbly water, belatedly realising I would now never discover who'd killed the wife of the mysterious Lord Featherstonehaugh or whether Felicity would ever return to the present day and win the fricking chilli cook-off.

How she'd manage that when she doesn't even use chorizo is beyond *me.*

I dressed. Threw the novel in the bin. Ordered a new copy on Amazon (because, honestly, I just had to know), and went in search of coffee.

All the while, he left me on fucking read.

❖

"Sooooo, you threw the book in the bath?" Suzie asked, sometime later, as I lay listlessly on the rug before the fire in the lounge, Echo flanking me, as we both soaked in the heat.

"Yes."

"Why?"

"It enraged me."

"But you love cowboy romances."

"It was completely unrealistic!"

Echo lifted her head at the sharp squeal of my voice, presumably realised I was just being overly dramatic again, and flopped back down with a huff.

"She's just a simpering fool, waiting around for him to come save her, instead of saving her own damn self. And like he's all that anyway, with his rock-hard abs and chiselled jaw and cock the size of a fucking shotgun barrel."

"Sure, because who wouldn't want a double tap from a Winchester."

"Don't think you can distract me with *Supernatural* references. I'm talking about the stupidity of cowboy romance."

"And here I thought we were talking about your unrealistic

expectations of Michael Bane and the crushing realisation that reality does not, in fact, match the world in your head."

"That is not what's happening here."

"Sure, sure. And Jensen Ackles isn't hotter than hell."

"You take that back!"

"Ah, you're right, that was sacrilege. We all know he's a snack."

"Veritable smoke show."

"Wouldn't kick him out of bed."

"Maybe tie him to it."

"Maybe he'd wear a cowboy hat for you."

"Eurgh, what's the point? He's just riding off into the sunset without me in the end."

"That's a pretty shitty end to a romance novel. Isn't the stud supposed to get his geek in the end?"

"Felicity Snuffington isn't a geek," I said sharply. "She's a waitress."

"Girl, I wasn't talking about the book. I was... Wait... *Flick Snuffington*? You can't be serious."

"Yep. Cooking up a storm with her spicy chilli con carne."

"Talk about flicking the bean."

"You just summed up the entire point of the genre."

"It wasn't me!" Suzie cried. "It was that name!"

"Sure, sure, keep telling yourself that."

We waffled on at each other a while longer, until Suzie had to go beautify herself for a date with some undoubtedly handsome, earthy chap she'd met while trekking through the wilderness in search of red squirrels. Apparently, he was a ranger, which, to my mind, was dangerously close to being a cowboy, but whatever.

Shit...She's right. I love a cowboy romance. I'm not actually mad at Clayton Rider at all.

Now Bane's ruining my fantasy life as well as my real life. Fucking brilliant.

If I was honest, however, it really wasn't new. I'd been fixating on a fantasy life revolving around Michael fucking Bane and his perfect fucking everything since the moment I'd clapped eyes on him in the park.

Moving back here was meant to be about me. My dreams. My company. Proof I could stand on my own feet, that I was *good* at what I did, good enough to succeed. To help others succeed. And to do it without pulling the shit I'd endured in other agencies I'd worked at since I'd graduated uni. Yet somehow, within a day of setting foot in town, I'd been consumed by a teenage obsession that, back then, had never had a chance at becoming reality.

But then there he was. And he'd smiled at me. I was no longer a pariah, an untouchable, sullied by the dirty audacity to have intelligence, and like things I *liked* instead of what everyone else told me was cool.

But it was all a lie. He hadn't recognised me. Hadn't realised he'd always been wrong about me. The grand and, I have to say, highly *elaborate* narrative I'd constructed in my head. How we'd get together. How he'd fall hopelessly in love with me. How I'd shock and awe the cunts from high school by being the girl that actually bagged Michael Bane *for real* and not just a night or three… It was all gone.

I'd lost something.

Truly, gut-wrenchingly lost something.

The fantasy I had cocooned myself in like a cosy blanket over the last few weeks, no, months, was gone. Its absence was hollowing. A sudden vanishing. Like a bad breakup.

I'd fallen in love with the version of Michael that lived in my head. Confronting the reality of him was thoroughly unpleasant. The fact he hadn't even bothered to call today, couldn't even be arsed replying to a message, was just salt in the wound. It confirmed the lingering suspicion that, had he not needed some sucker to provide him with an alibi, I'd never have seen him again after the debacle at the ball.

Yet he'd got out of the taxi to come back to me before his sister had called.

As if he were coming back to me.

A flicker of hope sparked in my belly, warming me for just an instant before I realised the obvious.

If he's so into you, where the fuck is he now?
Idiot, fucking girl. Grow up.

CHAPTER 8

"You didn't have to walk me to work."

Michael scuffed his feet on the floor slightly as we rounded the corner onto the main road. It was a move I'd seen him do a thousand times, usually in football boots on a field or the Astroturf, not Horsebit loafers on cobblestones.

"It's the least I can do," he said, not lifting his head or looking at me.

"You'll get no argument from me there."

He paused, head snapping up to look at me. I glanced at him for a moment. He rubbed his jaw and frowned, as if trying to puzzle out my meaning, then carried on walking.

"I'm not quite sure how to thank you," he said. "For all you've done the last couple of days, I mean."

"Then don't," I sighed. I risked a sideways look at his face. It was clouded with some emotion I couldn't identify, some expectation I couldn't meet lurking in stormy blue eyes.

Eurgh. What do you want from me?

"I still can't figure you out," he said.

His arm came up, and he pulled me to a stop. Ahead of us, Echo wheeled before her leash went taut to give us a questioning stare. He held out his hand to her absently. She nuzzled at it and let him scratch her head in compensation for the abrupt stop. "At first, I thought this was your way of…" He pursed his lips, seemingly searching for words.

"Forcing you into a relationship."

He winced, but fair play to him; he didn't deny it. "I wouldn't have put it quite like that, but yes. I was…appallingly rude to you. And…" He blushed. Actually blushed.

The great Michael Bane. The aloof Adonis. Could it be he's human after all?

And why can't I resist a man who blushes?

"I know you have…" Again, he appeared to grope about for words. This time, I wasn't helping him out.

Make him squirm.

"You've always…" He looked at Echo. She gave him no quarter. "You always had a crush on me."

There, he said it.

"If you thought I'd recognised you before our…" He turned a shade closer to chartreuse "…encounter, I assume you believed the subsequent date, the ball, were leading to…something." He dropped his gaze and scuffed at the poor cobbles once again.

I stared at him.

Was he expecting me to contradict that statement? Tell him it was all okay, and I hadn't been mortally crushed by disappointment when I'd realised he had no idea who I was. When the revelation of who I *am* caused him to become so…disgusted by me.

Fuck you, Michael Bane.

Residual anger bubbled up in my belly. With everything else going on, I'd quite firmly shoved that aspect of our relationship aside while I'd dealt with more pressing concerns. But over the course of yesterday, all my own feelings suddenly had space to flourish. Now, here we were, on a perfectly nice walk into work, ahead of what I imagined would be a perfectly normal day.

And he had the nerve to humiliate me even further by stating the blindingly fucking obvious.

"When you first offered to…"

Lie for you. Cover up your violent outburst. Risk my career and freedom for you. Entangle myself in a murder investigation for you. Get caught up with the national press for you.

No, scratch that thought. *That* I'd done for Rebecca.

"…help me," he finally managed, "I wasn't sure why. I figured maybe it was a way to keep seeing me. Maybe so I'd give you another chance, and—"

"So *you'd* give *me* another chance?"

A passing couple startled at the sound of my voice. I smiled politely at them and shuffled out of their way. They gave Echo and me a wary glance as they passed.

Great. Now random strangers think I'm crazy.

"Please"—Michael held both hands up—"just let me finish."

I clamped my jaw shut on the *Fuck you, Michael Bane,* that I'd been about to verbalise and waved a hand to indicate he should continue.

"I thought, *foolishly*," he emphasised, "that you were helping me because you wanted us to be together."

I snorted.

He glared at me. "*Clearly*, I was mistaken." He pinched the bridge of his nose, a crease deepening between his eyebrows, his mouth a tight line as he struggled to meet my gaze. "You're far more…complex than I realised—"

"When you thought I was a stranger, good for a quick fuck in a duck blind? Or when we were kids, and you hated me for daring to have a crush on you when I was so *unpopular*."

"Amelia," he snapped, then checked himself, took a deep breath, then another. "You said you'd let me finish."

"I changed my mind." I turned on my heel and continued towards my office.

"Aimee—"

"Don't *Aimee* me," I said, turning back to face him and stomping my foot before I could stop myself.

He glanced down at my boot, raised his eyebrows, opened his mouth to say something, and then clearly thought better of it.

Argh!

"In case you're still labouring under the delusion that I would entertain any kind of relationship with you, Michael Bane, let me be clear. I thought our tryst in the park was the culmination of *weeks* of low-key flirting and sexual tension built on the back of knowing each other for *years*. I am not in the habit of fucking random people in the park without ever speaking a word to them. Clearly, the same cannot be said of you. Now, why on earth would I want to have any kind of relationship with a man like *that*?"

He shifted awkwardly from one foot to another, stuffed his hands in his pockets and scuffed the cobbles some more. His contrition appeared genuine. But then, there were a lot of things about him I'd thought were genuine since we'd hooked up. I was no longer convinced of any of them.

"We're not friends, Michael. We've never been friends." I turned and walked away from him, Echo trotting at my heel.

A moment passed, and I heard the soft falls of his feet as he jogged to catch up. "Could we not *become* friends?" He caught my arm and pulled me to a stop again. "*Are* we not friends now?" He searched my face. Whatever he saw there pissed him off. "Fucking hell, if we're not friends after the last couple of days, what the fuck are we?"

"Absolutely nothing."

His face fell, and for half a second, I could swear he was…disappointed.

"Like I said"—he released my arm and carried on walking—"I don't get you."

I matched his pace, Echo falling in between us. Whether it was to act as my buffer, or because she didn't want to offend me when she walked next to him, I couldn't tell.

"Everything you're putting yourself through, and you don't even… Why then?"

I swerved abruptly to avoid a mother and pushchair careening towards me. Echo danced neatly ahead, out of the way. I, on the other hand, lumbered right into Michael. He caught me and pulled me into him while the woman passed. She nodded her thanks, and I tried to pretend the heat of his breath on the back of my neck wasn't making me want to turn my face just a little to the left, tilt it up just a fraction of an inch, and...

Oh, what's the point?

"If you don't get it, I'm not sure explaining will help." I continued walking.

"Aimee," he said.

But we'd reached my office, and I had no inclination to continue this conversation. I pushed open the door, letting go of Echo's lead. She bounded in, straight to Isla, who bent to greet her affectionately.

"Morning," I said cheerily. Too cheerily.

Isla visibly winced at the forced cheer.

"Sorry," I said, "rough weekend."

Isla's gaze slid to Michael, then back to me. "I bet. I'm so sorry." She turned her attention back to Michael. "About your niece, it's just...shocking. And wrong." She looked away quickly, her grip tightening visibly on Echo's collar as if she needed the reassurance of the hound's indelible presence. "So very wrong, what happened to her, and...everything."

I gave her a closer look and frowned. Isla was a lovely girl, but not prone to becoming overly emotional. The most I'd ever seen her upset before was when a client had yelled at her. And she'd delivered that news with a kind of stoic neutrality that had caused me to wonder if she was even being serious or not.

Having got to know her considerably better since then, I knew she had been perfectly serious, but still...she looked like she was tearing up.

And she didn't even know the people involved.

On impulse, I gave her a quick hug. She stiffened in my arms, seeming confused for a moment, before awkwardly returning the embrace with one arm.

"You okay?" I asked.

She nodded, pulling away and opening her mouth to say

something.

"Ah, Brennan," Michael said as Mr PR himself sauntered down from the kitchen upstairs with a steaming mug of tea in his hand. "I was hoping to see you." Michael crossed the room and extended a hand.

Brennan shook it, smiling affably.

"I wanted to thank you for all your help. It was…" Michael shook his head. "Honestly, I don't know how I'd have done that without you."

"All part of the service." Brennan shrugged.

"Well, you can be sure I'll be calling on your services the next time we need PR at work." He smiled, and Brennan nodded. The pair parted ways as one went to his desk and the other saw himself into my office, my dog on his heels.

Fucking Michael Bane.

Why couldn't he just leave? I gritted my teeth. My day was going to be full enough without *that* conversation continuing any longer. Through the window, I saw him flopping down onto my sofa, just making himself comfortable.

"Right," I said, striding towards my office door.

"Amelia."

I paused, glancing back at Isla.

"We had that time scheduled to talk this morning."

"Ah, shit." I rubbed the bridge of my nose. "We did, yes. Just give me a minute to get rid of this clown and I'll be with you."

I turned and shoved my office door open, just catching a glimpse of Isla's confused face. Too late, I remembered we were supposed to be pretending to be the happy couple.

How long did that need to last before we could reasonably break up without endangering his ill-conceived alibi?

"Will you sit with me?" he said as the door clicked shut behind me.

I stared at him as he patted the seat next to him like he fucking owned it.

"No," I said.

"Fine." He scowled. "At least listen. I owe you an

apology."

I waited.

And waited.

"And?" I said.

"I was waiting for you to contradict me."

"Why would I? You do. Probably more than one."

He winced. "That's fair."

I saw Isla walking over with my morning coffee, and I opened the door before she reached it. Smiling, I took it off her. "Thanks."

She looked at Michael. "Would you like a—"

"No, thank you," I said, "he's not stopping long." I shut the door on her gawking face. I'd apologise later. I returned my attention to Michael. "I have a very busy day, Michael. I can't sit here waiting for you to say two very simple words all day."

His scowl deepened, and he stood, pacing the room. His foot lifted off the floor a fraction of an inch—

"Don't scuff my rug."

He plonked his foot back down with a thunk.

"I'm sorry," he said.

I took a sip of my coffee and waited.

"You have every right to be angry. I was a dick to you in high school. For no real reason. I was popular, you weren't." He shrugged. "It's how it was back then. It's not how I am now." He paused, seeming to consider this. "At least, I hope it isn't. My reaction the other night wasn't... I didn't react like that because I was embarrassed by you."

"How sweet. But how do you expect me to believe you're sincere? You have every reason to butter me up, and showed zero remorse prior to that need arising."

He glared at me. "I was angry! I thought you lied to me. Or tricked me. Or...something. I'm not really sure what I thought. I hadn't had chance to sort my feelings out on the subject."

"Rather convenient that you suddenly decided you don't care who I am now you need me."

He growled. "I wasn't angry because Gemma said you were a…geek in high school. I certainly wasn't embarrassed to be out with you. If anything, I was…" He trailed off without finishing the thought, met my eyes and shook his head. "That's a tough crowd, and they loved you. You were smart, clued up on all they were talking about, insightful, not to mention…" He blushed without finishing that thought either. "I was just the oaf who usually lumbers in and cops off with the fittest waitress."

I snorted.

"Point is, they know me, they know what I'm like. But that night, they saw me differently because I was with you. And I was enjoying that. And when I realised who you were, I thought it meant everything wasn't real. That you'd tricked me—"

"I didn't trick you!" I yelled, then winced as Derek stumbled as he walked past my window and shot me a concerned look. I waved him off with a forced smile.

Michael crossed the room, took my coffee mug off me and set it on the bookcase beside him. "I am now painfully aware that you were nothing but completely open and honest with me. While I, somehow, completely failed to realise we already knew each other. That's on me. My behaviour that night, how rude I was. That's on me. And I apologise. It was unfair and idiotic of me to ever think so little of you."

I stared at him. Part of me wanted to believe him. But the majority of me wasn't that dumb.

"But for all I know, you're just saying that because you can't afford people seeing me yell at you." I gestured out to the office, where Derek had wandered over to Brennan's desk and the pair of them were talking, glancing back towards my office and frowning. "You can't have people questioning."

He took my hands in his, rubbing circles around my palms with his thumbs. The gentlest of tugs, and he'd pulled me a step further towards him. I swallowed, hard, thinking he'd finally run out of words, but then, "I didn't mean to hurt you."

And the spell broke, and it all came crashing in again. "But you did." I pulled my hands from his, retrieved my coffee, and retreated to sit behind my desk with it. When I looked up at him again, his head was bowed and he was studying his shoes.

"I'm sorry," he said again. "Truly."

I sipped my coffee, considering him for a long moment. I wanted to tell him I accepted. That all was forgiven. But it wasn't. I could still feel the sting of it, the acid in my stomach, when I remembered the look on his face as he'd realised who I was. The way he'd hightailed it out of the ballroom without so much as a backward glance. The stony, frozen silence of the taxi ride back, and how he'd all but dumped me out on the drive when we'd got there.

Contrasting that night with our kiss the night before. How he'd so eloquently asked for a do-over.

How many do-overs could we possibly have?

I sipped my coffee, but it tasted bitter.

Even if I forgave him, it wouldn't restore the fairytale I'd been living in. Wouldn't undo the damage done to the dream I'd been harbouring of what life with him could be.

"Are you going to say anything?" he asked.

I took another swig, despite the bitter twang. "What can I say? I appreciate your apology. I'm glad you've realised you were mistaken." I shrugged. "It doesn't undo it."

He sniffed, looking away, then nodded slowly. "Okay then. Well. We're stuck together for a while until all this blows over."

"Yes. But I think we can both agree that some clear boundaries are needed."

He straightened. "Fine. I'm due at a function tonight, I was going to cancel and stay with Lexi and Becca, but the doctor said if Lex hasn't slept by evening he'll give her a sedative so she can rest. I know my sister"—he looked up at me—"she won't be sleeping today. So, do I go to the thing, or do I cancel?"

I blinked. "You're asking me?"

He snorted a laugh. "Yes, Amelia, I'm asking you. I don't want to do anything that seems…suspicious. But I have no idea which would be more suspicious, going to an event two nights after my niece is attacked, or cancelling the damn thing."

I thought about it. "If you hadn't done what you did, what would you do?"

He huffed out a breath. "Go, I guess. If Lexi and Becca didn't need me with them, I'd need the distraction."

"Then that's what you should do." I finished my coffee.

"Okay, thanks. In that case"—he winced—"go with me?"

You've got to be kidding me.

"Why?"

"Because if I hadn't done what I did, I'd have sobered up, realised I was a colossal twat, and come to you to apologise."

Was that why he got out of the taxi? To walk through the cold night and sort his head out? To come back to me?

"I'd have grovelled, sent flowers, and when that didn't work, turned up on your doorstep with one of those Beanie Babies you used to love, and asked you to come with me tonight so I could make it up to you."

I stared at him.

What?

He smirked. "My, my, could it be I've finally got one up on the mind of the great Amelia Thornbridge?" The smirk became a grin. "You think I found out who you really were, and I was just done with you? Think because I didn't recognise you that I didn't remember anything about you?"

A small noise escaped my throat. Fairly sure I was trying to say *'Kinda'*, but it came out more of a squeak.

"You weren't getting rid of me that easily. The question is, would you have given me another chance?"

I stared at him, swallowed, and forced my vocal cords to function. "Honest answer?"

"Always."

"No."

His head jerked back slightly, and he blinked.

"I get it," I continued. "You weren't embarrassed. Well done. You're not a completely shallow dick after all. But whatever the reason for your reaction, that was still your reaction. And knowing you didn't realise it was me recolours everything that came before. We *didn't* have a connection. It *wasn't* special. You didn't see the woman I'd become and reassess your opinion of me. You didn't spend weeks plucking up the courage to eat your former oaths to date me over your own rotting corpse. You fucked me without a word because your dick twinged at being out-run, then you felt bad for using me, so you asked me out to dinner."

"Aimee—"

"Am I wrong?"

He signed. "No."

"You're a couple of years late for my risky sex era." I lifted my chin, a little defiant. "You may have been what I wanted in a teenage boy, but you are not what I want in a man."

He stared at me for a long moment, and I stared back, unblinking, watching the morning light streaming in through the window and play across his perfectly sculpted jaw, remembering the feel of his tongue in my mouth, the strength of his arms as he held me, as he buried himself inside me, and how perfectly he seemed to fit. The gush of pleasure rushing through me as he'd so effortlessly brought me to such exquisite climax. The mere thought of him inside me seemed like it could be enough to get me there again. If he touched me now, if he slid so much as a finger inside me, I might just come on the spot.

He's not what I want in a man. He's not.

I swallowed. Hard.

His jaw tightened, and those stormy blue eyes narrowed as he glared at me, the tension radiating off him like that storm was about to break. For a long moment, he stood there, colour rising in his face as if the temperature within was steadily peaking, and he'd boil over at any moment. He took several deep, deliberate breaths.

They were the kind I'd learned to take to manage anxiety attacks; apparently, they also worked on anger issues.

When he had composed himself, Michael finally spoke.

"Could you come with me regardless?" He considered his words. "Please."

"Why?"

"You may be *done* with this, but we're supposed to be dating. If we actually were, I'd be taking you with me. So. Do you think you could *pretend*, for an evening, that I *am* what you want in a man?" He ground out the final words, and for a second, I saw something else lurking beneath the anger.

I'd hurt his feelings.

Well, shit. Karma's really a bitch.

"Okay," I said.

"Good." He nodded. "I'll see you later then. Pick you up here? Say seven?"

"Sure." *Why are you agreeing to this?* "It would be better to meet me at home, though, so I can change." *Seriously?* "What's the event, anyway?"

"Oh, some god-awful networking thing."

I raised an eyebrow at him. "If you hate networking, why do you do it so much?"

"Why do you?" he countered.

"I don't," I said. "Never go to shit like that, can't be doing with it."

He glanced about. "Where do they come from then? Your clients?"

I gave him a withering look. "That would be the *marketing*." I gestured at a collection of awards sitting on the shelf beside the desk, which clearly read things like Kobayashi Maru, Best Marketing Agency 2023, and Amelia Thornbridge, Rising Star in Marketing 2020. "The clue is in the word."

"Oh." He nodded like that made perfect sense, turned to leave, then turned back. "Wait, so you're telling me I can have clients *without* doing all the nonsense?"

His confusion seemed genuine and was utterly adorable.

"Sure," I said. "But given the circles you move in, there's a definite benefit to doing *all the nonsense*. It was good for me to be at that ball the other night, get my face out there, meet people in person." I shrugged. "Digital is great, but it doesn't beat a handshake. Not when you're dealing with an old-school crowd, at least."

"Well"—he shifted uncomfortably—"I'll make sure you shake the right hands later then," he said. "Seven?"

"Seven."

The door swung shut behind him as he left, and I took a few long, deep breaths before hitting the intercom button on my desk phone. "Isla, come in when you're ready. I'm sorry I kept you waiting."

But Isla was already at the door, pushing it open.

"I'm so sorry." The look on her face stopped me. She was white. Snowflakes on a raven white.

A man stepped into the room behind her, and I swear I saw her cower away from him slightly.

"Isla?"

"I'm sorry," she whispered, "he insisted."

I took the guy in. He was tall. Bulky, not muscular. Fit, but not in the svelte way that Michael was; he was *built*. A barrel chest, thick arms, a wide stump of a neck. His head was shaved smooth, and he sported a worn leather jacket and faded jeans, putting me very much in mind of a Mitchell brother but uglier.

Easy, Aimee. You've no idea who he is, play nice.

But I didn't want to. Everything about his demeanour and appearance put me on edge. I couldn't blame Isla for looking so sheepish.

Here be monsters.

"Don't worry about it," I reassured Isla, nodding to the door. "Could you get me another coffee?"

She nodded, seemingly grateful for the chance to escape, and fled.

The man stepped fully into the room, the door swinging shut behind him. "Ms Thornbridge." It wasn't a question.

"Yes. How can I help you?"

"My name is Clark. I'm investigating the murder of Eric Hale."

"Can I see some ID?"

He smiled but made no move to show me a damn thing. "I'm a private investigator."

"I see."

"I was wondering if you could answer a few questions."

"No." I stood up, strode across the room and pushed my office door open. "You are, however, welcome to leave."

He blinked, and tilted his head, considering me carefully. Clearly, he'd expected me to fall over myself answering whatever he asked. "It will only take a few moments of your time."

"It won't take any of my time. I have zero interest in speaking with you."

"It would be in your best interests to—"

"Call the police and notify them that an unidentified man who won't even tell me his full name is poking around asking questions? Yes, I do believe you're right. Isla—" I raised my voice to carry across the office. "Could you please call the police station and tell Detective Inspector Rowan there's a man here with information about the murder of Eric Hale."

The private dick smiled coyly. "I'm collecting information, not offering it, Ms Thornbridge. I merely wish to ascertain your whereabouts at the time of the murder."

"Why?" I lifted my chin and gave him a hard stare. "Who are you working for? What's your interest in this case?"

His smile broadened. "Let's just say I'm a friend of the family."

"Well, *friend*, I'm not obliged to speak with you or answer your questions. And quite frankly, my whereabouts, on any day, are no concern of yours."

"Oh, but they are, Ms Thornbridge." He stepped closer to me and lowered his voice. "Particularly when they coincide with the whereabouts of one Michael Bane. You'd do well to stay away from him."

"And why might that be?"

"He's a murderer."

I smiled in a manner I usually reserved for my brother's children when they told me something particularly absurd, and

I didn't want to make them cry by pointing out their stupidity. "We both know that's not true."

"Do we?"

"Yes."

"Truth, as they say, is in the eye of the beholder. And since you weren't with Michael Bane at the time Eric Hale was killed, seems to me you'd have a hard time knowing whether he killed him or not."

There wasn't a trace of uncertainty in his voice. Not a drop of consideration that Michael and I had actually been together at the time the guy died.

Interesting.

"Given the public interest in this case and considering your"—he glanced around—"*business*"—he somehow managed to make that sound like an insult—"you would do well to consider how…vocal you are in support of a man you don't know to be innocent."

"And you would do well to consider who you're threatening before barging into their place of work and trying to be intimidating." I closed the gap between us and got right in his face, grateful for the extra height afforded by my heels. "Dick swinging is a risky business when you've got little to work with."

Clark grunted but didn't reply. Instead, he stepped away from me and stalked out of the office, past Isla, who was on the phone to, I assumed, the local police station. I followed the PI out slowly, ensuring he actually left, and took the phone from Isla when she motioned to indicate I should take it.

"Ms Thornbridge?" The light voice of the DI who had come to my house floated down the phone.

"You said to call if we had any further information? Well, I've just had a rather odd visit." I relayed the encounter, took down an email address and promised to send over the CCTV so they could get a look at him. When I hung up, I stood for a long moment, poised over Isla's desk. A moment stretched to three, then five.

"Amelia?"

I startled.

Brennan had a tentative hand on my arm. "Are you okay?"

"Yes, sorry, just thinking." I forced a smile. "Did you need something?"

Brennan gave me a concerned frown. "I was about to ask you the same thing."

"No." I shook my head. "All good, just... it's been a couple of days, ya know?"

He nodded, eyes creasing in sympathy I knew was genuine. He'd been at the hospital. He'd seen Becca. "Yeah. I know. You want coffee?"

"Please." I meandered back towards my office, Echo in my wake, belatedly realising that I'd asked Isla for a coffee when the PI had appeared and she'd not brought me one. Unlike her. I really needed to find time for that talk she wanted, but the appearance of a mysterious investigator looking into this case had made me realise something.

I needed to call in one of my own.

CHAPTER 9

Charlie Ross strolled into Kobayashi Maru with a nonchalance born of years of experience on the police force, decades of exemplary service to the public, culminating in the crushing realisation that it meant fuck all at the end of the day. No matter how many cases he closed, how many bad guys and dolls he caught, there would always be more. Late nights, missed dinners, forgotten anniversaries, cut-short birthdays, unseen milestones with a child who had eventually gone and been replaced with divorce papers.

That was Charlie's reward for being a really fucking great detective.

Six feet and change, fit but stocky. He sported sandy brown hair kept in a sensible, professional crop that was impressively thick, considering his march toward fifty was almost done. When he'd turned forty, he'd reassessed his career and concluded - quite rightly - that if he was going to sacrifice his whole life for the pursuit of justice, he should at least be well recompensed for his troubles.

The pension beckoning him at the end of his thirty-year stint just wasn't going to cut it. He'd quit the force and gone private.

Now, he walked with the air of a man who ruled his little

corner of the world exactly to his liking. Charlie now slept soundly at night, knowing his kid might never reconnect with him, but at least she'd have a monster trust fund at her disposal. She could pursue her passions and dreams and never have to worry about the pay cheque.

I'd met him by accident a few years ago. He'd come to the agency I used to work for in Manchester looking for a new website. Charlie had good instincts, and one sit-down meeting with my former bosses had been quite enough to tell him he needed to look elsewhere.

This had been during my wallflower era when I'd yet to fully realise just how much of a shithole I was working in. I was still taking crap from all and sundry while shouldering most of the work.

Charlie had passed my desk on his way out, caught sight of a website I was working on, and paused. He watched me code for a moment, watched me flit between three different monitors as I got images formatted and uploaded on one, previewed on another, and tweaked everything to perfection on a third. I couldn't remember whose site it had been now, but whatever it was, he'd liked the look of it.

And, for whatever reason, he'd liked the look of me. In a purely professional capacity. Hadn't even glanced at my breasts, a refreshing change in that particular environment.

He'd asked me to create what the agency was trying to sell him freelance, offered me £30K to do it, and then walked out. I'd practically fallen over myself chasing after him, finally catching up outside and, after a brief exchange, he'd shoved a business card into my hand and I ran back upstairs without another word.

His chuckles had echoed after me, and it was the start of a beautiful friendship. I'd built him a website, got it ranking in the top spots for all the towns he covered, and ensured a steady stream of clients flowed his way. People loved his blog, couldn't get enough of his YouTube channel, and his current day rate put the one I'd quoted him back then to shame.

I didn't personally write his blog anymore (I'd handed that

one off to Leah as soon as I hired her, and she did a cracking job of it), but he remained a dedicated client.

He'd also helped me out when I'd first broken away from Rick fucking Sandford and his hellhole of an agency, walking me through my legal obligations, the non-compete clause that was part of my contract, and helping me figure out that I needed to wait at least 12 months before setting up an agency of my own. Charlie was the one who gave me the idea to come home in the first place; Ashfordby was close enough to Manchester to still catch outlying clients from the city, but far enough that it didn't sit within the no-go zone.

Turned out Rick really hadn't wanted anyone stepping on their toes after leaving, and I couldn't set up shop within a fifteen-mile radius of their office. When things got nasty and I finally left, Charlie was the one who hand-delivered my resignation, ensuring I didn't have to set foot in the place again. He made damn sure Rick knew there'd be hell to pay if he pulled anything after I'd left.

When they found out I'd rented space in Ashfordby - and I'd no idea how they'd even known that - they still tried to block me by opening a new office of their own down the road.

Charlie shut that shit down faster than Rick hit on hot new hires. A few well-placed calls, some legal wrangling with the aid of my lawyers (now clients, who technically speaking I poached from Rick), and he'd demonstrated the new office they were trying to open was in violation of local competition laws. Somehow, Charlie managed to show Rick's planned expansion into the area wasn't to serve Ashfordby's needs but to purposefully block my enterprise. Apparently this—along with the fact I was a local girl trying to come home—swayed the local business council against them. Charlie had obtained an injunction preventing them from opening an office of their own in Ashfordby or within a fifteen-mile buffer zone around the town. It effectively ensured any new locations they opened couldn't activate the non-compete clause and shut me down.

The whole thing was so complicated that thinking about it

still gave me a headache. But I'd never have got this far without Charlie. I trusted him to help, despite the mess I was in.

Ushering him upstairs to the kitchen, I stuck the kettle on and made a teapot of Pu-erh. Charlie picked up the packet after I'd spooned some into the pot and sniffed at it appreciatively. I added water to the pot.

"This is authentic stuff." He scrutinised the label, which was entirely in Chinese. "You have to special order this in?"

I shook my head, nodding through to the open kitchen door to the petite form of Daiyu, who was frantically typing away from the comfort of a hammock, swinging in one corner. Her curly, chocolate brown hair was tugged up into a messy high bun, and her heart-shaped face was tilted to one side, lips pursed in concentration as she worked on a new book for one of our finance clients.

She'd been at it for a few days, bashing books about and talking to herself as she dictated notes into her headphones. Now, she was in the thick of the writing fugue and wouldn't come up for air until she was done.

"I'd introduce you," I said, "but she's in the zone."

Charlie followed my eyes and chuckled. "Chinese?"

"English born, Chinese parents," I said. "She noticed the box of supermarket stuff I'd got in for you, pulled a face, and threw it right in the bin. The next day this appeared." I stuck the teapot on a tray with cups and a small pot of honey, and walked Charlie down to my office. He opened the door for me, strode through behind me, and immediately sat on the floor to accept Echo's enthusiastic welcome.

I poured the tea, adding the most minuscule amount of honey to Charlie's cup and a far more generous spoon to my own. He joined me at my desk, took the cup, and wafted it under his nose appreciatively before taking a tentative sip. For a long moment, his eyes slid closed as he savoured the taste. "Well, that really is quite something," he said. "Remind me to thank—"

"Daiyu," I supplied.

"Daiyu," he repeated with a smile, "on my way out."

"I'd say an invitation to drinks would do nicely."

Charlie quirked an eyebrow at me. "Amelia, don't start."

"What?" I sipped my tea and feigned innocence.

"I don't need you fixing me up on blind dates."

"It's hardly blind; you've seen her already, and she knows your favourite tea." I shrugged. "You'd get on is all."

He stared at me for a beat. "I'll consider it. Now, walk me through the mess you've got yourself in."

Pouring more tea, I stalled. I'd known when I called him that this was going to be a tough choice to make. To level with him, and trust him with the truth, or attempt to leave out the less than savoury parts and hope he didn't walk out of the door and never come back when he realised I'd lied to him.

"It's bad, Charlie," I said quietly.

He didn't speak, just sipped his tea and waited.

"I may have really fucked up this time."

His eyes softened. I couldn't lie to him. Even if I'd been a good enough liar to convince him — and I really wasn't — I *wouldn't* lie to him. So, I laid it all out, start to finish, sparing no detail, pulling no punches.

"Well," he said when I was finally done, "shit."

Two hours later, we had a plan. The teapot sat cold and long empty on my desk as Charlie pored over his notes and all the details I had given him. He wrote in shorthand, illegible and indecipherable, like a private language only he could read. When he was done, he huffed out a breath and leaned back in his chair.

"First things first," Charlie said, his voice taking on a *'don't even try to disagree with me'* edge, "you need legal cover."

I opened my mouth to say no, but he silenced me with a raised hand and a look. "Amelia. You just confessed to the destruction of evidence and the provision of a false alibi. If I were still in my former career, I'd be arresting you right now."

I swallowed.

"Fortunately for you, I have a far more flexible approach these days." He shook his head, closing his eyes briefly.

"You're a fucking moron."

I winced. "I know."

"No, really." He opened his eyes and looked at me again. "All this over a *boy*?"

"No." My turn for a firm stare. "Over a little girl who was left beaten, bloody and comatose in a hospital bed while the man who beat her walked free. A girl who had to fight tooth and nail to stop him from doing far worse, and paid for it. She still hasn't woken up, Charlie. She may never see out of one eye again. I went to school with him, I knew his sister when she was younger than Becca is now." My throat closed painfully, and my voice squeaked to a stop.

"And that," he said softly, "is why I'm giving you the number of a lawyer and not escorting you to the station. Janet's sharp and used to handling messy cases like this. I'll give her a call, see what she can do. You need her advice, but I don't want you meeting with her or speaking to her directly. Not yet. People will wonder why, and you don't want them wondering."

"Can't I just use Lewis or Paul? They know me, they—"

"Exactly," he interrupted. "They know you. You might not realise it right now, but you don't want people to know you did this. It's not... This isn't a thing rational people do, Amelia. They're your clients. Your friends even. And while they would fully understand why you did it given your history, you'd be putting them in a bloody awkward position. Besides, this isn't their speciality. You need someone used to navigating this shit."

I nodded, my stomach knotting.

Had I put him *in a bloody awkward position?*

The tea sloshed about my insides uncomfortably, and I was starting to regret drinking it, polite as it might be. Coffee wouldn't upset my stomach like this.

"What about the PI snooping around?" I asked. My voice held a twang of anxiety even I could hear.

Get a grip!

"We'll handle him next," Charlie said. "I'll see what he's

dug up so far. Sometimes, these guys get overzealous, step over the line. If he's done that, we can use it. If he's clean"—Charlie shrugged, as if that was highly unlikely—"we'll still keep an eye on him. Make sure he doesn't interfere or distort what we find."

"And Michael?"

Charlie paused, considering his words carefully. "I'll look into the original case myself—the assault on Michael's niece, the CCTV footage, everything. If Michael's telling the truth—"

"He is."

Charlie gave me a withering look. "*If* Michael's telling the truth, we may struggle to prove it *wasn't* him who escalated things to murder. Proving a negative is bloody tough. Our best bet is finding who *did* kill the guy, and working on proving *that*."

He stood up, walking over to the window, staring out into the dim light of late afternoon. "If the news coverage is to be believed, the town's divided on this. We could use that."

I thought for a moment. "Everyone was already outraged over the attack on Becca. Michael has sympathy. There's some talk of him being a vigilante hero, so a lot of the people assuming he did it think it was justified. He's well-known, well-liked, and well-respected in town. It might not be hard to find people willing to speak up, maybe even provide us with more information."

Charlie sucked in a breath. "That's good." He turned back to face me.

I could see the *but* coming a mile off.

"Amelia, this is going to be tough. Tougher than you think. You need to brace yourself here, kid. Are you prepared for him to be arrested? For getting dragged in and questioned at the station? Not just him, you as well; you're on record as his alibi now." He shook his head, like I was the dumbest creature ever to walk the earth. "I know, when you did it, you didn't think it was this bad. But you still did it. There's no way to walk that back and come away clean. You understand?"

I nodded, but my heart sank. Somehow, somewhere, I'd been secretly hoping he was going to swoop in and just fix it. Pop down to the station, have a quick chat with the DCI, explain it all away and extricate me from this mess.

"Fuck," I said.

He crossed the room, pulled me out of my chair, and surprised me with a swift but hard hug. When he stepped back, he held my shoulders in his hands and squeezed gently. "We got this," he said. "But you need to buckle up and brace, you hear me?"

Breath quivered out of me, and for one awful second, I thought I might cry. Instead, I swallowed, huffed out a few deep breaths, straightened, and nodded.

"Good." He smiled. "Go to the thing tonight. Act like the happy couple. Concerned for Becca, yes, but nothing else." He walked to the door, and I followed to see him out. "And, Aimee"—he glanced back over his shoulder—"if it turns out he did it—"

"I know." The fear that gripped me at the thought almost made me faint. "I'll have to tell the truth."

Charlie inclined his head, gave me a quick smile, and pushed out of my office. The door swung shut after him. Echo whined.

"Yep," I told her, "couldn't have put it better myself."

❖

Echo gave a sharp bark and pawed at the door.

"I know, I'm late." I stood from my desk, still typing a hasty reply to one of a million emails I'd missed today. Stuffing my feet into my heels, I wobbled, leant awkwardly over the desk, signed off, smashed send, and slammed the laptop shut with more force than necessary. Wincing, I dashed towards Echo and the door, realised I'd forgotten my phone and scooted back, the wide legs of my palazzo trousers wrapping awkwardly around my ankles, leaving me stumbling over the rug. I snatched my mobile and bolted, snagging my jacket on the way out.

Isla collided with me as I made a bid for freedom.

"Sorry"—I ducked around her—"horrifically late."

"You're leaving?"

The tone in her voice halted my feet, turning them back to her. Disappointment creased her eyes and furrowed her brow. No, not disappointed, something deeper. Her hands wrung each other out. Nails, usually perfectly manicured, were torn and tatty. As if she'd been biting them.

Not good. Not like her at all. "Isla?"

"You said we could talk…" She trailed off, not mentioning the obvious.

I kept blowing her off.

"Shit." I skidded to a stop, teetering precariously on my Knife Mules. "I'm so sorry, please don't think you're unimportant. I will, one hundred per cent, make time first thing tomorrow."

I struggled into my jacket, the soft fabric of the lining snagging awkwardly on the lace of my bodysuit. It was an Alexander McQueen affair: black, double-breasted, padded shoulders, adorable peplum, but the big shiny buttons weren't half a bitch to fasten.

I was all black today, like a Victorian widow had fallen through time.

Isla hadn't responded, and guilt twisted my stomach. "Normally, I'd stay late, no problem. But Michael's picking me up in, like, an hour and I have to get home, get Echo sorted, change—"

Isla silenced me with a single raised palm, an understanding smile, and a nod. "It's fine, Aimee. Honestly. But tomorrow?"

"Definitely," I told her, flashing her a quick grin, and rushing out of the door, Echo hot on my Balenciaga heels.

Michael ended up waiting while I finished squeezing myself into a sleek, emerald-green cocktail dress. The velvet clung to every curve. I'd been avoiding in-person networking since I'd left Manchester. It was different here, strange. Back in my hometown, where nobody had known my name when I'd left, but everyone was learning to associate it with marketing savvy on my return. There would be people there I knew, had known, who had never thought much of me before. Gemma's reaction the other night was exactly what I'd been avoiding.

Oh, look, you dyed your hair blonde. Remember what it used to look like? That fringe*!*

Wow, you've lost so much weight. Do you remember what a frump you were?

You own your own business? Who bought that for you? And how many times did you have to ride him for it?

Small town. Small minds.

It wasn't fair; not everyone was like that. In truth, most people here wouldn't even remember a girl named Amelia Thornbridge. I'd left for university at eighteen and had seldom returned since. Most wouldn't even recall the girl, let alone her name. I'd never been present enough in people's lives for them to take note. I wasn't even sure my teachers would remember me.

But it was the ones that did remember, who judged me on my former merits and marvelled at how I'd possibly become a person fit to rub shoulders with the illustrious Cheshire Set, the Gemmas of the world.

They were the ones I dreaded.

So, I needed to dazzle.

The dress, a stark departure from my daytime black, featured a daring backless design with criss-cross straps that added a hint of allure. I swapped the Knife Mules for a pair of Saint Laurent Cassandra sandals, the silver YSL logos catching the light with every step, elevating the outfit from corporate to cocktail.

A quick makeup check later, and I was heading downstairs.

Michael was to be found perched on a high-backed Victorian-style armchair by the fire in the lounge. Silence permeated the room, but it was the comfortable kind one sought when pensive and wishing to be alone in your thoughts for a while. His gaze took in the garden in the gathering dusk, the flutter of a blackbird worrying at the hedgerow, and beyond, fields rolling out to the horizon, where the sun was starting to set in a searing gash of orange.

On his lap, Echo's great head rested quietly. Huge eyes stared up at him with rapture, and one of his big hands absently scratched her behind the ears. She glanced at me as I appeared in the doorway and let out a tiny, almost inaudible whine.

'He hurts,' she seemed to tell me. *'Make him better.'*

I wish I knew how.

Unfortunately, I was too distracted by thoughts of how our last social outing had ended and did not have much bandwidth for his feelings.

"Michael?" I said.

It took a long moment for my words to penetrate whatever thoughts had been clouding his mind. Time lapsed between when I'd spoken and when he startled at the sound, taking a deep breath, rousing himself from the stupor.

"Are you ready?" He dropped his gaze to Echo, gave her a double-handed pet, and gently moved her off his legs so he could stand. His gaze rose as he did, and his eyes widened at the sight of me, darkening with…something.

Desire?

We're so past that.

The potential of our relationship was a smouldering wreck in our wake, the bridge not burned so much as decimated. Michael's lips parted a fraction, and I heard his breath catch in his throat. He swallowed, hard. Took a step towards me. A tiny smile pulled at one side of his mouth, and he moved as if to hug me, pausing at the last.

"You look amazing." His voice had thickened, taking on a husky edge that put me firmly in mind of a wolf, standing ready to devour me.

I was sorely tempted to let him.

Heat flooded my face, and I knew I was blushing like an imbecile. My mind spun, trying to think of a clever answer, a little witty repartee, something I could say that would keep him looking at me like that.

Nothing came to mind.

Michael shook himself and stepped away. "Well"—his voice was back to normal—"we should get going."

"Sure." I clamped a vice grip around my disappointment, squeezed, and shoved it down, down, deep down, where the residual hope that we might actually be something couldn't cripple me. "Hold the fort, hound," I told Echo, then turned and stalked out into the night.

Behind me, Echo snorted her disappointment that her newly acquired human had abandoned her.

I knew the feeling.

❖

As the cold night air hit me, a brief shiver ran down my spine. The drive had been quiet, filled with the kind of charged silence that made my skin itch. Orange light dimmed to a bloody red and washed over us as the sun died in the distance. Michael's Lotus had meandered through the winding country lanes leading out of town to the sprawling grounds of Davenport Manor. A golf resort and spa, the manor has once housed the younger, female child of White Deer Hall. Unable to inherit on her father's death due to complicated Victorian rules, she had watched as her brother had taken on the family title, family fortune, family home, and all the prestige that came with it.

Fortunately, she had been in possession of enough fortitude to forge her own path, even in the face of overbearing Victorian standards. A secret career as a novelist publishing under an assumed (male) name, and a couple of strategic (though by all accounts loveless) marriages later, and she'd found herself here.

Not quite as grand as the home she'd grown up in, and lacking the sprawling grounds and mythical blessing of those elusive silvery white deer, but stunning regardless.

Now, the manor stood as a testament to opulence and exclusivity, its grand facade illuminated by elegantly placed lights that highlighted its architectural beauty. The long driveway was lined with ancient oaks, whispering stories of old, leading us to the stately entrance where uniformed staff awaited to greet each guest with discreet professionalism.

We were ushered inside, where rich wood panelling adorned walls accented with artwork so modern it was almost painful. Michael offered me his arm and flashed a devastating smile as I took it. The smell of him and the sight of that smile, the knowledge it was aimed at me, made my stomach do uncomfortable things.

It took me a minute to remember he was faking it and quash my internal, fluttering, teenage idiot self. He leant in and whispered, "Get your game face on."

"Please," I purred, leaning into him and synchronising our steps effortlessly, "it's never off."

My peripheral vision caught the brief flash of something in his eyes, the slight lift of an eyebrow; that hadn't been the answer he'd expected. Michael bobbed his head, nodding to himself, and snorted a quiet, incredulous laugh, squeezing my hand. "Let's go then."

The vast lobby opened up to a spectacular view of the meticulously maintained golf course, serenely languishing under the twilit sky. The air was perfumed with a subtle blend of potted citrus trees, dotted through the space, and the fresh, crisp outdoor breeze.

Expensive watches twinkled under the lobby's grand chandeliers as folk exchanged greetings that were as much about subtle business negotiations as they were about maintaining social ties. Here, everyone played their part with a polished ease that spoke of long-held privilege. Their interactions were a carefully choreographed dance, their laughs measured, their smiles calculated. In their midst, I felt the weight of my own narrative—the local girl made good, now threading her way into the fabric of this elite community.

Did I feel like strutting, or puking?

I couldn't tell.

As Michael and I made our way through the crowd, I felt the curious glances thrown our way. I tightened my grip on his arm, reminding myself to keep my game face on—not just for them, but for me. This was my arena too, now. These gatherings, these faces, this subtle dance of power and prestige… I was part of it, whether they were ready for me or not.

We stepped inside, and a wave of familiar faces greeted us, their eyes darting between us with poorly masked curiosity. Logic told me it wasn't all a silent question of me. Who is she? Does she belong here? What's Michael Bane doing with her?

No.

Some of it, most of it, was the swirling questions surrounding the attack on Becca, the scandal of the police's monumental mishandling of her case, and the fact Eric Hale was now dead.

And common gossip had it that the uncle of the girl he'd attacked had done it.

Murder wasn't exactly a common occurrence in Ashfordby. Not these days, at least. Though this house, I knew, could tell as many stories as its former mistress had written. I wondered if she'd faced such scrutiny.

Probably.

Probably worse.

The weight of the gathered stares almost made me turn around and run for the door, but beside me, I felt Michael tense. He had enough, right now, without me acting like a fruit loop. Inhaling slowly, I rolled my neck, smiling sweetly at a passing couple eyeballing Michael with something approaching disdain.

The lady blinked, taken aback, glanced from me to Michael and back, then evidently decided if I was okay being seen with him, it couldn't be that bad.

"Michael." She smiled, hesitantly.

"Camilla, how are you?" He gave a tight smile in response.

"You've not met my partner." Camilla detached herself

from the taller lady beside her. "Lara, this is Michael Bane; he's a financial adviser who handles some of our business investments."

Michael extended a hand. Lara took it, smiled, released it. "Lovely to meet you." She turned to me. "I'll save him the embarrassment of forgetting to introduce you." She held her hand out to me. I shook it with a laugh.

"Amelia," I said. "I run Kobayashi Maru."

Interest sparked in her eyes. "The new marketing agency on Regent Street. I've been hearing good things." She dug in her clutch and tugged out a card. "I liked the work you did on the new website for Steeped Slopes. Very innovative."

"Thank you." I smiled. "That's the first site we took on when the new office opened, and we're very proud of it."

"I can see why," she said, handing the card over. "I hate our website. Give me a call, we'll talk."

I took the card. "Thanks."

"Steeped Slopes…" Camilla frowned. "Isn't that the weird tea you love?"

Lara nodded enthusiastically. "Yeah, it's grown locally. Some budding botanist figured out he had a microclimate on the south slope of some otherwise useless land his family owned. He kitted it out with greenhouses, terracing, and protective windbreaks to enhance the natural warmth and light. They even added reflective panels to extend the daylight hours during the winter. It's pretty ingenious."

Michael chuckled, glancing at me. "Tea farmers in Cheshire? How do you find these people?"

I shrugged. "They find me. I'm telling you, it's all about the SEO."

That got Camilla's attention. "You're telling me you landed a new client immediately after opening an office in Ashfordby, and they found you through search? There has to be…what a dozen or so agencies in the area?"

I nodded. "Fourteen, including me."

Camilla gave me an appraising look and handed over a card of her own. "We don't rank for shit," she confided. "And our SEO guy talks out of his arse. Call my office, have them set up a meeting." She leaned into Michael and spoke so quietly that even I struggled to hear her. "Whatever's gone on, Mike, don't let them see it get to you. Send my love to your sister and niece, they're both in all our prayers." She squeezed his arm, nodded at me, then continued on her way, Lara on her arm.

The pair both wore sleek, tailored dresses embellished with elegant ruffles that cascaded down the back. The layers of fabric, falling gracefully down their skirts, coupled with the gentle swaying of their hips, put me firmly in mind of a pair of peacocks.

"That went well."

"Too well," Michael said.

I glanced at him, eyebrow raised.

"What if we used up all our goodwill at the door?"

I cupped his ridiculously chiselled and annoyingly handsome jaw in my hand and squished it. As if I truly were an adoring girlfriend and he truly was my man. "This face buys a hell of a lot more than that, trust me."

I swung us back towards the main room and started towards the circling sharks. Tonight, Davenport Manor welcomed the local glitterati. The Cheshire Set. That elusive, exclusive enclave of the wealthy and influential residents of Ashfordby and other well-to-do areas in the county. Like gossamer butterflies, they floated through the venue with the kind of grace that can only be born of too many years of attending too many similar events.

These weren't my people. Not naturally.

And they weren't Michael's either.

Even without everything going on at the moment, this would have been an awkward transition. Well, for me at least. Michael had done it already. He'd earned a place at this particular table through hard work and clever thinking. And now, so had I. Sort of. I didn't for a second think either of us had the wealth to fully compete on this level. Sure, we both owned a nice house, nice car, designer clothes. We could pass.

New money, obviously, but still members of the club.

But if I attended more than three or four of these events, I'd run out of things to wear. Sharply dressed entrepreneurs whose disruptive businesses kept the local economy buzzing mingled with footballers. Ethan Shaw played for Everton, Liam Connolly for Liverpool, and at the far side of the room, I caught a flash of the bright red Mohawk that was the trademark of Manchester United's very own Mason Wilder.

He caught sight of Michael and nodded across the room.

I nearly swooned.

Michael turned into me, his hand sliding around my back. I tensed, and he felt it, releasing his touch and leaving his hand hovering just off my back instead. I felt him silently sigh, and I relented, leaning back into his touch. "You know *Wilder*?" I whispered. "And you reprimanded me for just casually dropping impressive things in conversation?"

He pulled me to him and leant down, lips a hair's breadth from my ear and whispered back, "Just because I'm impressed by you, Thornbridge, doesn't mean I'm not impressive myself. I know all the ballers. Want to meet him?"

"No! I'd faint!"

He chuckled, and for a moment I forgot how mad I was at him, savouring the warmth of his touch on my bare back.

"He's just a guy, Aimee. Normal guy. Just fucking good with a ball. He grew up on fish-finger butties, clothes from M&S, day trips to Blackpool, just like you and me."

"Yeah, well." I tilted my head back to look into his face, and spoke without thinking, "Sometimes you make me want to faint."

He gave me a wicked grin, chuckled again, and kissed my neck right below my ear. His free hand grabbed mine, and he twirled me unexpectedly in Mason Wilder's direction. Stepping close to my back, he dropped both hands to my hips and sashayed us through the throngs of business owners, socialites, media personalities and B-list actors. They navigated the crowd with the ease of those used to being out in public, while I shrank back, willing myself to be as small and unnoticeable as possible.

My shrinking violet efforts collided with the hard, muscular wall of Michael's chest, his arms pressed intimately close to my own, fingertips gently applying pressure to the bones of my hips, thumbs countering on my back, lightning bolts of electricity dancing back and forth between them, right through me.

Tiny hairs rose on the back of my neck as his hot breath hit me, and I resisted the urge to arch my back into him. To turn my head and kiss the soft spot where his neck and chin met. To guide his hands lower and press those fingers to the suddenly throbbing nub of my clit.

I swallowed, hard. Took a deep, steadying breath, and focused on not making a total tit of myself.

"Michael Bane, as I live and breathe!" Mason Wilder reached an arm out towards us in greeting, and the weight and warmth at my back suddenly vanished.

Michael stepped out, and I almost sagged in relief that he was no longer touching me. It was too confusing. He took Mason's outstretched hand and shook it, clapping him on the shoulder in greeting just as Wilder's other hand smacked into Michael's other arm.

"Good to see you, mate." Mason's face softened, and his voice lowered. "I've seen the news." He frowned, and Michael's jaw tensed. "How's Becca?"

Michael shook his head slowly, eyes closing for a second. When they opened again, the pain had vanished, replaced by a society-safe mask of seeming indifference.

"She's…resting," Michael managed.

"Fucking shameful," Mason said. "To let a man like that go. You need anything"—he leant in—"anything at all. You let me know." He turned to me. "You I've not met. I'd remember."

My tongue had tied itself in knots, and it took me a moment to remember my name. "Amelia," I finally managed.

He took my hand, which I'd haphazardly waved in front of myself in a feeble attempt to extend it, and kissed it.

"Charmed."

"Fucking hell, Wilder," Michael growled, though a grin tugged at the corner of his mouth. "I'm hoping to keep hold of this one. Give a man a chance."

Wilder raised both hands in supplication and took a step back. "My mistake. Still, you can hardly blame me, the lady is exquisite. Well done, old boy."

He hit Michael with a genuinely playful punch on the arm just as a harem of ladies in various brightly coloured and expertly tailored cocktail dresses swarmed him in a gaggle of perfectly coiffed hair, sprayed and lacquered to within an inch of its life.

You struck a match in the vicinity of this lot, the whole place would go up.

"Mike, darling!" a voice rang out through the throng of giggling women.

I winced, as if someone had just screeched their nails down a chalkboard. Irritation flared as I tried to mask my reaction with a polite smile.

"Gemma." Michael greeted the harpy with far more politeness than I'd have managed.

"I came to check on you after the ball the other night, you left in such a hurry! And then I heard the *awful* news. I knew you'd just be in *pieces*. But you weren't home." Her voice was chiding, and it cut right through me. "You should have called. I'd have been there to take care of you."

Don't speak. Don't rise to it. Don't acknowledge. Don't even fucking look at her.

I chanced a glance at Michael. He wasn't staring at Gemma with rapt attention. He didn't seem overly bothered by her presence at all, in fact. If anything, he seemed…bored.

Interesting.

"Thank you." Michael smiled. "I was with Amelia, and well taken care of."

A frisson rippled through me as Gemma bristled. And even though I knew it wasn't real. And even though I really didn't want it to be real anymore, I couldn't help but delight in the sight of her irate expression. She straightened, squaring her shoulder and needlessly smoothing down the chiffon fabric of her already immaculate burgundy dress. Her eyes ticked my way, and her top lip twitched in what might have been the start of a sneer, swiftly masked. The comment (and its implication) clearly irked her. And Michael knew. And didn't care.

It seemed he'd done it quite deliberately.

More interesting.

"I don't know about you"—Michael turned to me—"but I need a drink. Shall we?"

He drew me away towards the bar. "Nice seeing you, Gemma."

I couldn't see her glowering at me as we walked off, but I swear, I could feel it. Fury, emanating from her in waves.

"Sorry about that," he said, dipping his head down to me. "She really is a bitch to you, isn't she?"

"Always has been."

He glanced over his shoulder, back to where Gemma stood, struggling to hold a conversation with Mason Wilder. The footballer nodded with polite disinterest, then caught the eye of someone else across the room and unceremoniously excused himself.

He practically ran away from her.

No matter how much money I made or how successful I became, certain people would never accept me as one of them. Gemma was top of that list. But, it seemed, she wasn't entirely accepted in this crowd herself. On the other hand, humble beginnings had never held Michael back from being one of the boys in *this* circle. He'd been popular with these people when they were children; they were happy to accept him once he was grown.

Unlike most of her peers, Gemma had attended Ashfordby's state school with Michael, me, Suzie, and all the other children of the middle-class and reasonably well-off residents of town who, nevertheless, could not afford the posh school.

Rumours had swirled about Gemma's father's unpaid tax bills and struggling stocks. This was, supposedly, the reason he'd failed to send her to the illustrious independent school I was now so proud my niece and nephew attended. But the official line was that her father had wanted to avoid Gemma becoming an entitled brat.

At least, that's what my dad had told me Gemma's dad had once told him while in his cups and bemoaning life in a house full of, as he put it, *'Deranged women bent on making his life a living hell, before the stress eventually killed him and he went to actual hell for all the shit he'd done to keep them in pearls and diamonds.'*

Despite his best efforts, or perhaps the unfortunate side effects of shady dealings catching up with her dad, Gemma was a nightmare and always had been. She would never, I suspected, accept me.

Nor would she accept Michael spending time with me.

Fortunately, I didn't give a shit what she thought.

"Evening, Bane." An affable man nearing retirement and sporting a distinguished silvery beard greeted us. Introductions were made between his companions, Michael and myself. Conversations were struck. Jokes made and appreciated. We moved on, Michael's hand on the small of my back, sending heat dancing through me as he leant close and whispered a cheeky fact about the bearded gentleman who, as it turned out, was poised to retire and leave the company in the capable hands of his granddaughter, passing over his son for the position of CEO.

Quite the scandal, but undeniably the best business decision he could make.

"The business acumen skipped a generation," Michael confided, pulling me closer to him as we moved to avoid a passing waiter with a tray of drinks. He snatched a pair of champagne flutes as they passed and handed me one.

I sipped.

"Mikey!"

I actually laughed as one of the lads from our form at school greeted Michael, did a double take at the sight of me, and hesitantly asked, "Aimee?"

"Hey, Simmo."

A broad smile split his round face. "You remember me."

"And you recognise me." I grinned at him, then shot Michael a disparaging look. "Clearly I'm not unrecognisable after all."

Simmo blinked, glancing back and forth between us.

"Ah, what did you do?" he asked with a chuckle.

"A minor faux pas," Michael said. "In that, I started dating an absolute stunner and didn't quite realise we'd been to school with her."

Simmo snorted. "You fucking dolt."

I grinned.

"Easy." Michael rolled his shoulders and straightened his jacket. "I'm trying to make it up to her."

"Exactly how long did it take him to realise?" Simmo asked me, grinning from ear to ear.

"Two dates and Gemma pointing it out," I said.

Simmo's jaw dropped. He glanced over his shoulder to where Gemma could now be seen trying to schmooze a pair of older business types. She tugged on the arm of one, clearly trying to entice him into a more private conversation. He was dragged to a corner table, shooting an apologetic—or perhaps pleading?—look at his comrade, who shook his head and shrugged as if to say, 'Better you than me!'

"Well," Simmo huffed. "I bet she delighted in pointing that one out."

Michael growled.

"Oh, calm down, Bane," Simmo admonished. "A simple misunderstanding, I'm sure the lady will get over it in…what? Say"—he glanced at me, raising an eyebrow—"four or five more dates? In which you lavish her with praise, affection, and acknowledgement of the spectacular woman she's become?"

The grin returned to Simmo's face as Michael rolled his eyes and chuckled, "You'll bankrupt me with that talk, man!"

"Hardly," I said, narrowing my eyes at him. "We've been splitting every expense."

Simmo glanced at me with interest, then back at Michael. "You're on thin ice there, my friend."

"Tell me about it," Michael muttered, shuffling his feet. Fortuitously for him, someone called him over, and he excused himself to say hello, leaving us to chat.

Simmo had not been a friend of mine. He had not been one of the It crowd, but he had been adjacent to them through his childhood friendship with Michael and, as such, had still been outside my circle.

My circle had pretty much consisted of Suzie and a girl called Aria, who'd completely fallen off my radar when I'd left for uni. But I'd never had a problem with Simmo. Unlike Michael and his other cohorts, Simmo had always been nice to me.

To my shame, I realised I didn't actually remember his real name. Couldn't even recall where the nickname had come from. I'd have to ask Michael later.

"What're you doing with this hooligan?" Simmo chortled a grin.

"Right now, getting tipsy, but later, who knows." I grinned back.

He guffawed, glanced at Michael, who was chatting to a couple of men I presumed to be Simmo's colleagues, then leant into me. "No, seriously." He shook his head. "What's up?"

"We're dating." I frowned, confused. It seemed fairly clear since we'd literally just been discussing it.

Simmo stared at me. "Oh, come on."

I was game for a laugh, but this was a bit much. "Is it really so far-fetched?"

"Yes, actually." He frowned at me. "I thought you'd have more sense by now."

"What?" I stared at him, the breath abruptly knocked from me in shock.

He gestured from my feet all the way up to my head. "You're a catch, Thornbridge. Look at you. You're stunning. I've had at least three people telling me I simply *must* meet

Bane's new girl; she's got a brain, she's a looker with a brain, she's a looker, funny, *and* has a brain, who'd have thought he had it in him? And imagine my surprise...no, *shock*, to find it's you." He shook his head. "Not that I'm shocked you're funny, beautiful and brainy, we always knew that, but because you're with this jackass!" He flung a nod over his shoulder in Michael's direction. "You know him."

I blinked. And again. I was missing something here. "We both know him, Simmo. Known him for years."

"That's my point." He took me by the elbow and led me away slightly, keeping his voice low. "We've known him long enough. We've seen his temper. You remember that day he kicked the crap out of a kid for saying David Beckham couldn't shoot for shit?"

"I—" Yes, actually, now he mentioned it. I remembered. Although I hadn't thought about it for years.

"Or the time he was nearly expelled for chucking a computer through the window?"

The shattered glass had gone everywhere. We were on the second storey, and it hurtled into the playground outside. Could have killed someone, the teacher had said, lucky nobody was hurt, the head had reprimanded.

"Look, I know you always had a thing for him. You and, like, every other straight girl in our year. But just be careful, Aimee. I'd say that anytime, but with what's gone on this last week..."

Michael turned to tell me something, realised I no longer stood beside him, and bade farewell to his conversational companions before moving to rejoin me.

"Good to see you, Simmo," he said, smacking him on the shoulder in greeting.

Simmo smiled and returned the gesture, but not without a slight stiffness, a tension that belied his unease.

Oh my god.
He thinks Michael killed him.

Sensing the vibe lingering in our conversation, Michael tensed. Simmo noticed, made a lewd comment about what we might be getting up to later, laughed with Michael a moment longer, and then excused himself when he saw someone enter the room.

"What was all that about?" Michael asked, as Simmo's back retreated across the room.

Shit.

"Aimee?"

I shook myself. "Just remembering all the crazy antics from school." I smiled at him, and he visibly relaxed. "I didn't know you were still in touch?"

"Yeah, he married my cousin, so we see each other quite a bit."

Fuck.

"Which cousin? Emma?"

"No, Nigel."

"Oh… *Ohhh*. Well, that makes sense."

"Right? *Right?*" Michael grinned. "He's so much happier now he's just…him."

"I bet," I said, genuinely happy to hear Simmo was happy. But still…

He thinks Michael killed him.

"Rachael, how are you?" Michael greeted a stunning redhead, and the round of pleasantries began again, Michael radiating confidence and evident pride at having me on his arm. Occasionally, someone handed me a card or asked for one of mine. Once, someone saw me handing over one of my die-cut spaceships and demanded one of their own; business cards were always so *dull*, they'd never seen anything so cool *in their life*, I simply *had* to design something for them that was equally *quirky*.

Validating.

That was the only word I could find for the evening. Gemma might have been an icy harpy, but everyone else was surprisingly lovely. She was the only one who set my teeth on edge. Draped in a bold, sequined dress that screamed for attention, she held court among a few huddled figures. Her laughter, a bit too loud, punctuated the hum of conversations around her.

From snatched glances of her throughout the evening, something else became painfully clear; Gemma's social standing had diminished.

While she still had her cronies, the wider circle seemed to keep their distance, interacting with her only when necessary. It was apparent in their strained smiles and the way they excused themselves quickly from her presence. Those who flocked around here were, for the most part, familiar to me. I knew them from our school days. Only because I'd seen them around with Gemma, not because they were slumming it with us at state school. They were old friends of hers, from childhood, and while there was the odd one or two I didn't think she'd known back then, the dynamic there was a stark contrast to everywhere else in the room.

Elsewhere, people mingled. They'd arrived in pairs, small groups, or the occasional solo traveller. They were all here for a specific purpose; meet, greet, grow.

I had no idea why Gemma was here, but it wasn't for networking in a business sense. From snatches of overheard conversations, it seemed she was incapable of discussing anything beyond fashion and local gossip.

A part of me revelled in the sight of her dimmed queen-bee status. It was a petty part of me that I wasn't proud of, but it was undeniably gleeful to see her seeming so...pathetic.

As the night wore on, my initial schadenfreude faded into a sombre realisation. Gemma, for all her faults, was struggling to maintain her façade, and the effort seemed to cost her more than she was willing to admit. It was just...sad.

Endless greetings, introductions, and hushed words of sympathy, or support, or anger, or thinly veiled accusations took their toll on me, and Michael doubly.

An hour had turned to two.

"Come on," I said, "before we turn into pumpkins."

He glanced at me, at his watch, around the room, and I could almost hear his brain calculating how many remained he'd not spoken to yet.

"Fuck it," he said, and I giggled.

We retrieved our coats and strolled out into the night. "Okay," Michael breathed when we were well out of earshot of the manor. "Hit me."

I punched him in the arm. He captured my fist in his hands and tugged on it, pulling me into the circle of his arms and hugging me, laughing.

"I meant the truth," he murmured in my ear. "On a scale of one to fucked, how bad is it?"

I sobered. "Public opinion?"

He nodded.

I considered. "I'd say you're at a solid four. Not great. But nowhere near as bad as you think."

He shivered slightly at a gust of wind and pulled me closer to him, wrapping his arm tighter and rubbing up and down my back.

"Did they not seem…"

"Like they're all convinced you killed Hale and it's not really even a question. Like the only question is whether it was justified, and most think it was, but some are fence-sitting, and the odd few are ready to lynch you."

Michael huffed out a breath. "Yeah. That."

"Yeah. That."

His forehead dropped and pressed against the top of my head. "I didn't do it, Aimee," he said softly. "Please believe that."

Cold stole over me, raising the hairs on my skin and goosepimpling my arms. I didn't answer, too struck by the realisation that I *had* lied to Charlie after all.

I'd stand by him.

What that said about me, I wasn't sure, but it couldn't be anything good. Whatever his faults, I would not let this man rot in jail. Not for beating the crap out of a would-be child rapist.

Not, I realised, for killing one. I didn't believe for a second he had, but the realisation it wouldn't have made much difference was more than a little disturbing.

We drove home in silence. I realised too late that I'd never actually reassured him that I did, in fact, believe him. He must know that though? Surely? But when we reached my house, he didn't park but pulled up in front of the door and idled the engine. I paused, my hand halfway to the car door.

"Aren't you coming in?"

"Why?" His voice was flat.

The question caught me off guard. "Drink?"

"If I drink any more, I won't be able to drive home."

"So stay." The words escaped me before I could stop them.

A beat. He didn't answer. Just looked at me.

"Michael?" I dropped my hand from the door and reached the other out towards him.

"What are you playing at, Aimee?"

"What do you mean?"

"Did you forget the charade of the evening was just that? *Pretend?*"

I blinked.

Yes, actually.

"I thought—"

"What? That we're suddenly a couple for realsies?" He snorted. "Get a grip. And get out. I'm not coming in for a drink. I'm not staying the night. *Boundaries,* remember?"

I swallowed. "Right." Sliding from the car, I turned to say something else, but he leant across and pulled the passenger door shut with more force than needed.

The slam echoed through the night as he sped off down the driveway.

Fucking dick.

CHAPTER 10

Ducking myself and my umbrella out of the way of a passing couple, huddled under one of their own, I was eternally grateful Echo didn't need wrangling. Navigating the cobbled streets in the rain with a leash and an umbrella was problematic enough without throwing in a tugging hound.

"We should have driven," I told Echo.

She looked up at me with huge, wide, long-suffering eyes. I hated driving to the office. It was such a short distance it seemed ridiculously indulgent. Lazy. It was bad enough that I owned two cars, one for practical stuff and one for fun. But driving to the office was just obscene when I lived so close. Still, we'd already got soaked once on my run. Usually, I left Echo at home when it rained; running in the rain with her was a special kind of frustration and irritation. My morning runs were a time for calm, peace, soaking in the scenery.

Not that there had been much scenery to speak of today. I'd changed my route. A thing I never did. I was usually a creature of meticulous habit. But, today, I'd run the roads. Another thing I never did. Roads were ugly and hard. They reminded me too much of running in Manchester when I'd first started to realise I had monumentally fucked up. I'd settled. I was wasting away in a dead-end, thankless job and a perfect-on-paper-but-dull-as-dishwater relationship.

But the absolute last thing I wanted this morning was another encounter with Michael fucking Bane.

So, I'd avoided the park. I'd run the roads.

And it had rained.

Last time I'd gone running in the rain I'd wound up wrapped around Michael, back to a rough stone wall, his rock-hard cock sliding in and out of me, his lips hot on mine, my fingers tangled through his hair, my body aching for him, desperate for more, and Michael obliging. The memory of that orgasm had ricocheted through me as soon as the rain had started, leaving me taut with tension, need, and a desperate desire to have him in me again.

My phone rang.

Eurgh, now what?

I fished in my pocket for the hands-free, popped it on my ear, and picked up. "Hello?"

"Hey," Suzie's voice cracked down the line.

"Hey, sorry, I didn't get chance to call yesterday. It was manic from start to finish."

"Oh? Tell me."

I did, filling her in as briefly as possible as I dodged other pedestrians, eventually giving up and ducking under the awning of a cute café, and perching on a metal chair at a small table. Echo flopped on the floor beside me, grateful to be under an awning and out of the rain. She lifted a paw and waved it at me. Collapsing my umbrella and propping it against the table edge, I fished in my pocket and found her a treat to chomp on as I continued explaining yesterday to Suzie.

"So, he just dumped you at your door and left?"

"Yep." It still pissed me off thinking about it. "I just don't get it. We'd had a weird evening; there's no way that wasn't going to be weird with everything going on. But he'd been so attentive, so...handsy."

"Handsy?"

I could almost hear Suzie's eyebrows raise.

"Not like that!" I considered. "Although I wouldn't have said no."

"Aimee!"

"Well, I wouldn't!"

"I thought you were done with all that with him."

"So did I."

"Why the sudden change then?"

"He was… Well he was acting like…"

"Your boyfriend?" she finished for me.

"Yeah."

"The key word there is *acting*, Aimee. The whole point of going to that event was for people to see him, see you, and believe the whole spiel. That's not going to happen if you're bickering and insulting each other the whole time. Of course he acted like your boyfriend. That was literally why you were there."

I stared at the rain.

Shit.

"You believed it?" Suzie asked, and I hated the way her voice sounded piteous.

Silence was all the answer she needed.

"Come stay with me."

"What?"

"Just for a few days. Get out of town until this blows over. Take in the brisk, salty sea air of North Wales. It'll make you sleep for three days solid and do you the world of good."

"I can't."

"Why?"

"He needs my help. I can't just—"

"Yes, you *can*," she said firmly. "You've already helped him. You've done enough. Doing more is just going to hurt you."

"But—"

"Amelia," she said, a little more sharply. "This isn't the same for him as it is for you. He can maintain this pretence without any negative consequence. He doesn't have feelings for you. He's not going to get confused and go home crushed by the rejection. You are."

I didn't say anything. She was right. My feelings for Michael had always been a blazing fire that burned whenever I got too close to them. Years away had dulled them to a smouldering ember, but seeing him every day, even without speaking, had fanned those flames back to life.

Fucking him in the duck blind had left me sizzling in the face of them. All he had to do was look at me, touch my skin with his, and I was desperate for the taste of him.

I'd thought that was where last night had been heading.

I was so fucking wrong.

And it hurt.

"You really told him he's not the kind of man you want? Like, you actually said those specific words?"

I blinked. I'd been so lost in my own thoughts I'd almost forgotten Suzie was on the line.

"I did."

"Shit."

"What?"

"It's just... Damn, girl. You've not thrown shade that harsh since you told poor Billy Hardman you'd rather eat worms than suck his dick."

I snorted. "I'd forgotten about that."

"You even told him a worm would be a bigger mouthful."

"I stand by that conviction."

Suzie chuckled. "My point is, it's not like you. Even with Johnny, and all your frustration at how that ended up, you were never cruel."

"You think I was cruel?" Of all people, I'd have thought Suzie would have relished me knocking Michael Bane down a peg or three.

"This is a guy you slept with, went on two dates with, talked about taking things slow with—"

"He's the one that fucked that up, not me."

"Yes, he did. But did he really? Or did he just need a minute to process the fact this amazing new girl he was clearly smitten with was actually someone he'd known most of his life?"

"It's not my fault he didn't recognise me!" I snapped.

That still pissed me off.

"No, it's not. But you never brought it up, either. Why do you think that was?"

Echo's gargantuan paw landed on my leg. I glanced at her big dopey head, lolling on one side, tongue hanging out as she panted happily in her post-chew fugue. I petted her ears, and her eyes closed as she leant happily into the attention.

"You didn't want to remind him," Suzie said gently when I didn't answer. "You liked how he saw the new you."

Couldn't argue with that.

"Look, I'm the last person to encourage you to actually date the man. You know my opinion of him. All I'm saying is that you're sending very mixed messages here. Yesterday morning you basically told him he's a cretin unworthy of being scraped off your Jimmy Choos—"

"I did not!"

"You told him he's not enough of a man for you. Literally can't think of a more devastating thing to say to someone like Michael. And then you go to this party—"

"It was a networking event."

"—you're dressed to kill and flirting and heavy with the PDA, and in your head that means he's spending the night and everything's *back on*. But as far as he knows, the party was just you two faking it for public viewing, and really, you think he's a cretin you have zero desire to be with. Then you blindside him, asking him to stay the night; what's he supposed to think? You can't stand him, but you'll use him for sex?"

Well, fuck.

"You did that thing again, didn't you?"

I didn't answer. I really hated this lecture.

"You know, the thing where you get all in your head and have a whole elaborate fantasy about how things are going to go, and you forget to actually consider how the other people involved might really feel, in the real world. And then, you get pissed off with them for not living up to a fantasy and a set of expectations they never had a hope of meeting because they knew nothing about them."

Well, fuck.

"Shut up."

Suzie laughed. "You know I'm right."

I pondered. "Maybe."

"Did you mean it?"

Echo whined, and I patted my lap. She jumped up and settled her front half on my knees, stretching her muzzle up to lick my face. Wet paw prints soaked my coat, but I didn't care. "Mean what?"

"That he's not the man you want as an adult, womanly woman." The sarcasm was dripping.

"You should have heard how shocked people were that he'd brought a date to that ball," I said. "He's clearly a slut."

Suzie made a disgruntled noise. "What do you expect? This is Michael fucking Bane we're talking about. He always had women hanging off him like barnacles, and that was when he was a teenager, in high school, from the rough part of town."

I winced.

"Now he's handsome, successful, rich, coaches kids football; sure, he occasionally goes psycho and beats the shit out of people, but you can't expect a guy to have no faults."

"He's a slag."

"Really, Aimee? Slut shaming him? Come on, you're better than that."

"What kind of man goes about fucking women in parks without ever exchanging a word or having any idea who they are?"

"More than you would think, I imagine. And you're forgetting that you were right there, doing the nasty with him. What does that make *you*?"

"I was fulfilling a lifelong dream of getting together with a guy I've adored since I was eleven. He had no idea who I was and fucked me anyway."

A passing woman, startled at my words, gave me a strangled look and continued on her way.

Suzie sighed. "Look, even if he is a slut, and even if he intended to use you, even if that first dinner was just a way to try and show respect and salvage something of the situation so you *didn't* feel used...you can't deny taking you to that ball was out of character for him. He didn't have to do that to assuage his guilt. Dinner was enough. He didn't have to say everything he said at your place after dinner. He could have just thanked you for a lovely evening, said goodnight, promised to do it again sometime and then never bothered. Instead, he took you to a *ball*. He may not have known who you were, and finding out sure fucked things up. He got defensive thinking you lied to him, you got offended thinking he hated you—"

"He *does* hate me."

"If he really hated you that much, how come it was *you* he came to for help?" She paused, letting that thought sink in. "It was a shock. He handled it badly, and was a total dick about it but...wait... I'd forgotten that part. He was an utter twat about it, wasn't he?"

"Yep."

She huffed, derailed. Paused for a moment more. Rallied. "Are you really giving up on him completely?"

"Yep."

"Then how come you were ready to drop your knickers for him last night, and got so pissed off when he didn't let you?"

Well, fuck.

"He *hurt* me," I said.

"People hurt each other. Doesn't mean they can't still fall in love."

"Other people, maybe. I'm pretty sure he's just a dick."

"I'm not going to talk you into loving the guy. I've hated him for years. Recent events haven't improved my opinion, and I don't think you should be spending time with him right now. Not until his name is cleared and the real killer is caught. But I know you. At some point, you're going to calm down and realise you actually had a shot. A real shot. With *Michael, fucking, Bane.* If you blow it being a stubborn cow, you'll never forgive yourself."

I hugged Echo.

Fucking bloody shit.

"He hurt me. Again. And I am so past all this bullshit."

"Aimee," Suzie's voice softened. "I get it. If you convince yourself you don't want him, it won't hurt as much when you don't get him. I think it's part of why you ended up with Johnny to begin with; he was a safe bet. You knew you could have him, and there was no risk of rejection. You didn't think he could hurt you."

I snorted. "He did, though. Not intentionally. But being with him, staying with him so long. Hurt like hell."

"And leaving him was nearly as bad, I know. But you have said, many times, what hurt the most was waking up and realising you'd spent ten years of your life with someone who didn't make you feel all the things. Michael can be a dick. I'm not going to deny that. And maybe there is nothing in it. But you can't deny he makes you feel all the things."

"So what?" I snapped. "I should just throw myself at him and beg him to love me?"

"Girl—" Suzie took a breath. The kind of breath she usually took to stop herself yelling at her mother.

I winced.

"I'm saying," the word was elongated by her apparent frustration with me, "don't shut it down at the first hurdle. Give it a chance."

"It was a pretty fucking big hurdle."

"Was it? You lied to the police for him."

"I really didn't."

"Oh, come on!" she snapped. "This is me, please don't insult me by—"

"Oh, I lied to the police. But I didn't do it for him."

She snorted.

"Look, the world is fucked up. More so if you're a woman. Becca actually has a good man in her life. Why should she lose him, on top of everything she's been through, because he was protecting her?"

"That wasn't protection, Amelia. That was vengeance."

I didn't speak for a moment. "If someone did that to you, I'd have done the same damn thing. Consequences be damned. Maybe it's not the legal thing to do or even the moral thing to do, but on some level, it was the right thing to do. If Hale had stayed in jail, it would have been different, but back on the street, free to—"

"Do it to someone else."

"Exactly. I'm not protecting him because I have feelings for him." I sighed.

"But you do have feelings for him," Suzie said quietly. "If you didn't, you wouldn't be so shit scared of how much it will hurt if this doesn't turn into something real.

I hugged Echo harder.

"Look, I know he fucked up at the ball. He humiliated you. But we both know he's done worse before. And you swore you were done with him, then a few weeks later you were back to mooning over him again."

"I'm not a teenager anymore."

"No, now you're a woman. And you got a taste, however briefly, of actually *being* with him. As a woman. If he's willing to pursue that and you shut him down without trying, you'll have broken your own heart. *And*," she added in a far more playful tone, "I'm the one that will be stuck listening to all the woe and self-flagellation. And frankly I haven't the patience for it. So, pull your head out of your arse, and maybe avoid inflicting fatal verbal injuries on him for the time being."

I chewed on that. "Fine."

"Good girl," Suzie cooed. "Now, go get to work."

Eurgh.

It was going to be a long day.

Again.

❖

The front door to Kobayashi Maru decided we must do battle

as I struggled to get through with a dripping umbrella and a sodden dog. Someone grabbed the door, holding it open, took the soaked brolly from me and deftly shook it outside before closing the door behind me.

"Thanks," I said, breathless, then looked up and realised who it was.

Michael.

Well, fuck.

He was the last person I wanted to see at that moment. I'd forgotten we had arranged for him to be present for this meeting. And I couldn't exactly complain about him being here since it was literally all about him. But still, for the first time *ever*, I found myself walking into my own business and wishing I was elsewhere. Which was all on him.

And that really pissed me off.

Unclipping Echo's lead, I took the coffee Isla held out to me, grabbed her arm and pulled her to one side. "Right after this, we'll have our chat," I told her. "Just need to get everyone working first, okay?"

She nodded. Anxiety wormed in me as I noticed the bags under her eyes, which were slightly bloodshot, red, and so wide they seemed big enough to swallow me. The grey pallor of her skin wasn't right. It was also unusual for her; she was usually glowing with health, vitality, and whatever high-protein plant-based smoothie she'd had for breakfast.

I'd let her down, I realised, and mentally kicked myself. Whatever was wrong, she'd been trying to talk to me for days, and I'd always had something more important to do.

Unforgivable.

I sighed. Too late now, I'd have to get this over with and then I'd fix things with Isla.

"Alright," I raised my voice. "Campfire, people." I gestured for them all to gather, glancing about to check everyone was there. "Where's Rosalie?"

As I asked, the front door opened again and Rosalie pushed into the office, smoothing her damp, dirty blonde hair out of her face. She was in her mid-forties, tall and slender with—she regularly bemoaned—a slight plumpening around the waist and hips as a side-effect of having birthed three children.

"Thanks for coming in early," I said.

She smiled. "No problem at all." Given she worked a four-day workweek at most and came and went as she pleased to accommodate childcare, I knew she meant it. I'd never seen the point of holding people to a set nine to five or insisting they work all five days of the week. She had her job. She had her workload; as long as it got done to the standard I knew she was capable of, I couldn't care less how long it took her to do it or when she worked on it.

Rosalie was my campaign manager. I'd scurrilously poached her from another local agency who'd severely undervalued her talent, worked her to the bone, and were very reluctant to let her do things like the school run, and taking her kids to after-school activities, because it conflicted with their stringent nine-to-five grind.

Flexible working hours and a salary that was essentially double what she'd been on before, and she was even better at her job than she had been when I'd stolen her.

Astonishing what valuing people and trusting them to get stuff done could achieve.

Rosalie grabbed her desk chair and wheeled it over to join the rest of the team, who were lounging in various states of repose in their own wheeled office chairs with caffeinated or juiced and smoothied beverages. The exceptions were Michael, who stood a discreet distance away so we could work, and Melanie, one of my copywriters. Her wheelchair was parked at the end of the semi-circle of chairs they'd formed around a hexagonal table towards the back of the office. It had a glass top and the base was an aquarium that didn't currently have any fish in it because I'd spent the decorating budget for this year and decided fish would be purchased in the name of performance targets. The whole team, including myself, had targets to hit for either training or project milestones and when we hit them, we'd get to pick a pretty fish.

I was two weeks away from reviewing who'd managed what and actually getting something swimming in the tank. Until then, the water was still calming, and the plants and ornaments (which, naturally, recreated the Forest of Endor battle scene from *Star Wars*) were fun to look at. We used the spot as a breakout chat area when I needed everyone to see each other and speak.

We didn't have a meeting room or an imposing, expansive conference table.

"Okay, guys, for those of you who haven't met him yet, this is Michael—"

Bane raised a sheepish hand.

"—we went to school together. I've known him most of my life, and he's currently in a shitty situation. Anyone unaware of what's gone on?" I glanced about the group, nobody spoke. "Good, that saves a lot of explaining. I'm concerned about the media frenzy and public backlash that's developing. Michael's family have already been through—" My voice caught as an image of Becca rose in my mind. "—more than enough. He has a business that supports not just himself but also his sister and niece, and I will be damned if any of this fucks with them further by jeopardising that, or Michael's sterling reputation. Any questions so far?"

"A sensitive one, but I'd rather get it out of the way," Brennan said. He glanced at Michael. "I'm not suggesting they should be, but have the police spoken to you about Hale's murder?"

Michael didn't miss a beat. "Yes. The morning after, they came to see me to ascertain if I had an alibi, which I do."

"And that would be…" Brennan fished.

"He was with me. We attended a charity ball, then spent the night at my house."

"Ha!"

"Told you!"

"Knew it. Didn't I say?"

I chuckled. "Okay, enough. The point is, Michael's not

responsible for Hale's death."

"There's been no follow-up from them since?" Brennan asked.

"None," Michael said, "although with the way people are talking and the media I assume they will be back to ask more at some point."

Brennan nodded. "I suspect you're right about that, and we need to prepare for it."

"That's the plan," I said. "Now, this is sensitive, it's personal, and it's absolutely crucial we get it right. If any of you are uncomfortable working on this, for *any* reason, let me know later. I'd completely understand. You don't have to explain why. You say you're out; you're out. No issues. Okay, Brennan, you spoke first, let's start with PR. What's our initial approach?"

"We need to be focusing on Michael's character and contributions to the community." He glanced at Michael. "You coach the girl's football team, right?"

Michael nodded.

"And Rebecca is a member of that team?"

Another nod.

"Okay, we'll start by seeing what existing posts and content are out there from matches and coaching sessions. If we can get the media to pick them up and run with them, it should emphasise his positive impact and dedication."

"Great idea," I said. Relieved that he seemed to be on board. "Georgie, thoughts on social media?"

Georgie's head bobbed down, revealing the dark hair of an intricate undercut beneath the lavender locks on top. I wished I was brave enough for a cut like that. They consulted a notebook for a moment and considered the question. "I've been thinking we should encourage community stories, get people sharing their experiences with Michael and Rebecca, showing support." They glanced at Brennan. "We can encourage resharing old content for you, but I'd also like to see people directly showing their support."

"We can attend training sessions for the team and any

upcoming matches," Derek offered. "Get plenty of video footage, chat with the parents of the kids on the team, with the kids themselves if we're given permission."

Georgie nodded. "That should definitely work. But ideally we want to get friends, family, people that know Michael to share their own photos, videos, stories about him."

'You remember that day he kicked the crap out of a kid for saying David Beckham couldn't shoot for shit?'

I winced at the thought.

"What if people share negatives?" I asked. "Or start voicing their support for vigilante justice?"

Daiyu spoke up at that, "I'll start drafting some blog posts focusing on the legal and justice reform angles. Expert insights, case analysis, and how this situation reflects broader systemic issues. Try to keep the focus on facts, the actions of the police, and how catastrophically they've failed Rebecca, rather than speculation about who killed Hale."

"We can share key points from those on social," Georgie said. "If you're speaking to experts, maybe get them on the podcast?"

"I could have a chat with Claire over at Cheshire Sunrises," Melanie suggested. "See if she'd be willing to release something on the emotional toll of wrongful accusations on families, and support resources for those affected."

"Good. Just be delicate in how you ask. I don't want her feeling pressured." I frowned. "Actually, I'm really not sure about asking clients to get involved in this at all."

Melanie shook her head. "I don't think she'll mind. In fact, I think she'd relish the opportunity. She loves raising awareness of mental health issues. Since I started writing for her, she's been hellbent on picking controversial topics and making noise."

"Gets her good engagement," Georgie said. "Her LinkedIn comments are always fire. I read them for fun. And she's had a Reddit thread go viral off the back of that post you wrote her on the psychological effects of overheard adult conversations on children. She'll be well up for it."

I glanced at Tim. "Can you put a press pack together for them all to use? So, anyone posting or sharing anything has good photos of Michael, the football team, and his business? Make sure we're totally happy with *every* image, no room for misinterpretation or dumb comments."

"Yeah, remember that church picnic story at the start of the year?" Leah said. "And they posted a photo of the dad and his daughter, and it just made him look like a total paedo. He had his windows smashed and all sorts."

"'Don't *make Michael*'," Tim narrated as he jotted it down, "'*look like a nonce*'. Got it."

That gained a collected chuckle, until Brennan frowned, suddenly serious. "He's a bloke coaching young girls—even the most innocent of images is going to be trashed." He glanced at Michael. "That's no reflection on you. Just the sick trolls online."

"What if we stick to images of the girls, and images of Michael, but try to avoid photos that put them together?" Georgie suggested.

"Good idea," I said. "And let's double-check that we have parental consent from every parent of every child before anything goes out. I don't want Dad calling up pissed off because his ex-wife said it was okay, but he's fuming because nobody consulted him. Both parents, be sensitive while asking; there may be divorces, deaths, break-ups in progress. Children are a fricking minefield, guys, so tread carefully... Actually, let's get a legal consult on this before we do anything, make sure we've covered our bases." I paused a moment, considering what I was like at that age. "And ask the kids *themselves* if they're okay with their photos being used. And show them the *specific* photos we're talking about so they can check they're happy with them."

"No photoshopping," Rosalie said. "No matter how much they beg, 'Make me look thinner, make me look taller, take out my double chin, *argh*, my bum looks huge!' *No*. Find photos they're confident sharing, or don't share images of them at all. And Tim"—Roslie fixed him with a full-on Mum stare—

"remember these are *children*, they take offence easily, don't always understand we're joking, and can easily develop body image issues and complexes from a relatively good-looking guy making a glib remark he thinks is harmless."

Tim looked like the headlights had just found him and realised he was a bunny. "Maybe Georgie would be better speaking to them?"

"Why?" Georgie huffed. "Because I'm a *girl* like them?"

"No, I... Shit, I just meant cuz you're more sensitive than I am—"

Georgie was relentless. "From all the shit I've been through? Ooo, poor non-binary Georgie, didn't like being a girl so now she binds her boobs and uses weird pronouns. Obviously, *she's* going to know what to say to them."

"No, I wasn't thinking of that at all; you're just better with kids than me and—"

Georgie's composure cracked, and they laughed, playfully kicking Tim's chair with one heavy-duty goth boot. "Relax, dumbass, I'm just demonstrating Rosie's point."

Tim stared at them, then looked at me for help.

"Let's leave speaking to the girls and their families in the capable hands of Ros, shall we Tim?"

He nodded emphatically, his shoulders sagging and a relieved sigh escaping his lips as the tension drained from his expression.

"Okay, one more thing," I said. "We have a few heavy hitters at our disposal thanks to Michael's business connections and some of the parents he's done private football coaching for. I met Mason Wilder last night—"

There was an outpouring of ooos, aaas.

"—he had nothing but good things to say about Michael. Brennan, can you handle this?"

"Can I *handle* Mason Wilder?" Brennan looked like he'd woken up to discover it was Christmas, his birthday, and he'd won the lottery all in one morning. "Absolutely. I'll reach out directly. We're asking him to share stories, photos, or videos showcasing Michael's positive influence on his kids? Personal anecdotes, moments where Michael went above and beyond?"

"Exactly that." I smiled, then glanced at Michael. I'd been studiously avoiding eye contact with him this whole time, but I hadn't failed to notice his eyes hadn't left me since the conversation had started. He was watching me with an almost uncomfortable intensity, as if scrutinising my every word and action. "Anyone else you've got up your sleeve besides Mason Wilder?"

"Who's Mason Wilder?" Abbey asked.

"Plays for the Red Devils," Derek supplied.

"Is that a band?"

"No, genius, it's a football team. You really need to look up from your coding once in a while and enjoy the real world."

Abbey sniffed. "Could have just said he was a footballer."

I was still looking at Michael expectantly.

"You want other celebrities?" he said.

"If you have them?"

He thought about it. "Well, there's Sienna Blake, she's been down to support the team a few times since she left it."

"Wait, Sienna Blake, as in *Sienna and Paolo?*" Melanie said, her eyes wide with wonder.

"You know Sienna?" Leah said at almost the same time.

Michael's cheeks tinged pink, and he glanced down briefly. "Well, yeah. She's just Sienna to me though. She used to be on the team before she finished school."

"Wait." Georgie stood and trotted across the office, grabbed their tablet and returned. "I remember Sienna's intro segment. She talked about playing football for a local girls' team."

"Who the hell is Sienna?" Derek asked.

"Who's Paolo?" Daiyu seconded.

"They're from *Love Island*," Melanie filled in. "Basically, the new Tommy and Molly Mae."

"What's a Molly Mae?" Brennan asked.

Tim whipped his phone out, loaded Instagram, found her profile in record time and handed it to Brennan.

"Wow," he said. "You know this girl?" This was directed at Michael.

"No," Leah said impatiently, "he knows *SIenna*, the *new* Molly Mae."

I rolled my eyes.

"Yes, here it is!" Georgie handed their tablet over to Michael, playing a clip. "Is this you?"

Michael studied the video, then nodded.

"Yes, I remember this. She asked if it was okay to use the footage. All the girls went nuts; they were so excited to watch her on the show already, and this got them on it too."

"Wait"—Brennan reached for the tablet—"there was footage of you and the girls team shown on national TV?"

Michael nodded like it was nothing.

"Dude, you could have led with that!" Brennan shook his head with a laugh.

"I'd forgotten to be honest," Michael said, his eyes crinkling as he grimaced, hand reaching up to scratch the back of his neck.

"Okay." I wanted to wrap this up now. The thought of Michael being so friendly with Sienna of *the* Sienna and Paolo was giving me uncomfortable feelings. "Isla, can you go through Michael's contacts with him, see if there's anyone else he's forgotten about that might be able to help?"

Isla nodded. "Sure. So, contact details, a bit of context for how he knows each, and—" She paused, thinking. "Whether he wants to speak to them himself or if he's okay with Brennan or Rosalie getting in touch?"

I nodded. "Spot on. Right. We all know what we're doing?"

Collective nods.

"Great, let's get to it. And thanks, everyone. I see Angelfish in the future."

The group disbanded, nattering about Sienna and Mason Wilder and deciding we should definitely name the first two fish after them, which prompted Georgie to insist we'd need the fish sooner rather than later because if either celeb came into the office we couldn't miss the opportunity to get them to post a selfie with their namesake and tag us in. I watched them for a moment, happy to see them happy and fired up for work.

One thing I'd dreaded when I'd opened a bricks and mortar office was it turning into the same kind of toxic atmosphere I'd experienced elsewhere. But so far, so good.

I walked towards my office.

Michael followed.

I sighed. I'd had just about enough of him. Whatever Suzie said, he was an arse. Taking a deep breath, I took the proverbial bull by the horns and turned back to him. "I'll see you later," I said, standing up on the tiptoes of my Gucci boots and planting a swift kiss on his lips.

He froze, then played along, looping an arm around my waist and pulling me in for a longer smooch. I tried to pull away, and for half a second he kissed me harder, out of sheer spite, before releasing me. I eventually disentangled myself, and said, "Have a good day."

He had little choice but a graceful exit. "You too." He smiled, but his eyes told me he was pissed. Evidently, he'd wanted to speak to me.

Well, tough. I wanted to speak to you when you dropped me off last night, and you were having none of it.

Actually, I'd wanted to strip him of his suit, tie him to my bed, and ride him like a buckaroo for an hour, but semantics.

Clearly, every time I entertained the notion of that, he was going to smack me back down by reminding me how disgusted he was at the thought of spending time with me when it wasn't for public consumption.

I suppressed a shiver at the thought, once again feeling used. Turning, I walked towards my office. "Isla," I beckoned, "thanks for being so patient. Let's have that chat."

She took a deep breath, like she was steadying herself, and stood, passing Michael as he walked towards the door and heading over to me. The front door opened just before Michael reached it, and he stepped aside to let someone in before exiting.

I pushed my office door open, "Come on in," I said.

"Amelia."

I turned. Isla was just walking across the threshold and froze mid-step, sensing we weren't having our chat after all.

Charlie strode across the room towards me. "We need to talk."

I closed my eyes and sighed. "Just give me five minutes," I told Isla. "I'm so sorry. Come on in, Charlie." I ushered him through the door and let it close behind me, trying not to notice the woebegone look on poor Isla's face.

"At this rate, I'm going to have to give her a raise just to make up for how often I've given her the slip."

Charlie frowned, puzzled, glanced at the door, and realised I wasn't talking about what he'd rushed in to discuss. "I can come back?" he said.

"No, it's fine." I moved to the sofa and gestured for him to sit. "What's up?"

Charlie took a seat beside me and scratched Echo's head affectionately while he spoke. "I've been looking into your mystery investigator from yesterday. He was working for Hale. Or at least, *the Hales*."

Huh. "I guess that tracks, in a weird way. How do you know?"

"I showed the image you pulled from the CCTV of him to a few of the folks down at the police station. One of them recognised him. I thought they might; PIs often cross paths with actual coppers while they're working. Turns out this guy came to see Hale while he was in custody. He also spoke to Hale's lawyer at least once; my guy assumed the lawyer had retained him to find something that would help exonerate Hale." Charlie shook his head. "I've seen the footage they have on Hale. He should never have been released." His fists clenched, and he didn't speak for a second as he fought to keep his composure.

Echo whined, lifting her head and staring at him with huge, bottomless eyes.

"It was not easy viewing."

"I'm sorry," I said softly. "When I asked you to help, I didn't mean for—"

"I know you didn't." He sighed and patted my leg. "I'd assumed it was ambiguous since they released him, but my contact was so angry about the whole thing, I got curious and asked to see it." He shook his head again. "It's damning, Aimee. And there's nothing to refute it. Why he was ever let out... There's only one explanation."

Charlie stared morosely at the floor. It was an explanation he didn't want to face. Because then he'd be forced to do something about it. And that was complicated. I didn't push him. Eventually, he came to it. "Someone, somewhere, paid someone else to look the other way. And they took the money. And they let a man who tried to rape a child, and beat her half to death in the attempt, go free." His voice shook. "She fought *hard*. She made damn sure they were heard, that someone came, and he was forced to run. And they just let him..." He covered his hand with his mouth for a moment. "I gave nearly three decades of my life to the force. I've seen some shit on both sides. But when it comes to kids..." He shook his head again as if trying to dislodge the mental image of that footage and the weight of everything that came with it.

Someone knocked on my door. I glanced through the glass window beside it out into the main office and saw Isla loitering outside, nervously chewing on her fingernails. I frowned. Whatever was bugging her, it wasn't good.

Beside me, Charlie took a deep breath and huffed it out.

"Is it possible this PI *did* find something, and for some reason they're just not revealing it?" I tried. Seeing him like this wasn't easy. His disillusionment with the force had started well before we'd met, but I hated to add to it.

"It's possible, I guess." Charlie rubbed at the stubble along his jawline. "I can't think what it could be, though; there is no arguing he didn't do it, Aimee. It's plain as day in black and white. Unless there's evidence suggesting that he was acting under some form of automatism or mental disorder, which could indicate that he wasn't in control of his actions or aware of their wrongness at the time... But even then, he wouldn't just be released back onto the streets. He'd be placed in a secure medical facility for treatment to prevent any risk of him harming others."

Isla knocked on the door again.

"That girl," I breathed, suppressing a sigh. She was starting to annoy me.

"I'm looking into the lawyer as well as the PI," Charlie continued, though he glanced at the door and raised a questioning eyebrow at me for ignoring it. "Trying to see if they have a habit of springing people without due process. The lawyer's a stand-up guy from everything I can see. Your PI, on the other hand, is a blank slate. I've no idea who this guy is. The best I could dig up is the same name he gave you; Clark. No idea if that's first or last, may not even be his name. There's also no record of Hale paying him, or anyone other than the lawyer, and no record of the lawyer paying the PI or any other external investigator. At this point, I've no clue who he is or what he was doing with them, let alone why he'd be continuing to look into it now Hale is dead."

He paused a moment, his silence punctuated by Isla's frantic knocking. I glared at my door.

"Maybe it's personal for him," I offered.

"Maybe," Charlie said, "or maybe Hale didn't hire this Clark guy at all—"

The door burst open, and Isla scurried in, slamming it behind her. Echo jumped, saw who it was and relaxed slightly, shooting my assistant a baleful stare that clearly said she was about as impressed by the interruption as I was.

"It's not Clark," Isla said, slightly breathless, "it's *Clerk*. As in the unnoticed worker, silently carrying out transactions and ensuring everything runs smoothly. It's not his real name, just what he's called, and he's a scary bastard." Her eyes met mine, "He works for my father."

CHAPTER 11

Sunlight slanted in through the blinds at an odd angle, casting bars of light across Isla's face as she stood, rigid before me. "I recognised him when he came in yesterday. I've been trying to tell you," she stammered. "I was trying to tell you before that. Before all this—you remember? Please remember? I asked to talk? I was going to tell you then, explain why I lied, why I took the job here, who I am, but then it all kicked off, and you've been so busy, and if I'd had any idea any of this was going to happen and he'd be tangled up in it all, I'd have told you far sooner. I thought I had time. It hadn't affected anything yet and—"

"Isla." I raised my hand, palm out, and spoke with far more calm than I felt. "Take a breath."

She did.

"Good. Now another. That's it, keep breathing for a moment."

I watched her chest rise and fall, her face trembling, eyes brimming with tears. Slowly, she calmed. My skin felt hot. As if someone had lit a fire right at my back, and it was scorching every inch of me.

Breathe, I reminded myself. *Hear her out. Let her speak.*

But it was hard. So hard. I was remembering days in

school, thinking I had playmates at break time, only to go to the toilet and come back to find they'd run away at the first opportunity. Days the likes of Gemma had convinced me I could hang out with them, that I was one of them, only to trick me into lifting a box of Hint of a Tint from Boots and tell the security guard and get me in trouble. Come to think of it that might have actually *been* Gemma.

Years of childhood spent thinking I'd made a friend only to have it snatched away for one reason or another. They moved away, they made friends with the 'in' crowd and left me out, they were never sincere to begin with, it was all part of a bet to see who could get me or Suzie to give up our VCard first.

And here stood Isla, the first person I'd hired when I opened this place. My indispensable ally. My right hand. Of everyone here, she was the one tasked with keeping Kobayashi Maru functioning; her job, her purpose, was to help me steady the ship.

That was it.

She was my Scotty. Keeping us flying, effortlessly pulling off the seemingly impossible task of ensuring I maintained my sanity while juggling everything effectively.

I had a feeling it was about to turn out she'd been my Valeris all along.

"Better?" I asked.

She nodded.

"Good," I said. "Now, start at the beginning."

Charlie glanced at me, a look I didn't know creasing his face into a frown.

Isla took a deep breath. "My last name isn't Flemming. At least, not legally. I've gone by that since I was thirteen, but it's not my name."

The flames dancing over my skin turned to ice, which burned just as fiercely.

Who the hell is this girl?

"Flemming is my mother's name," Isla explained. "She and my father never married; I was…illegitimate. But he insisted I take his name." She snorted. "When I was young, I thought that meant he loved me. As I got older, I realised it was just his way of owning me. That's what he does, Aimee; he buys people."

"Who?"

"My real name is Isla Stanton." She straightened and met my eyes. "I'm Geoffrey Stanton's daughter."

I waited for the penny to drop.

Nothing happened.

"Stanton Media?" Isla said, looking from me to Charlie and back again.

"I feel like I'm missing something." I glanced at Charlie. He looked equally blank.

"The media mogul?" Charlie asked.

"Why would he hire a PI?" I asked.

"Why would he hire *that* PI?" Charlie countered.

Isla stared at us, then abruptly deflated. "I assumed you knew?"

"Assumption is…something to do with donkeys." I rubbed my eyes. I was way too tired for this. "Tell us like we're idiots who don't know anything?"

Because apparently, we are. Or I am, at least.

Isla appeared to wrestle with this notion for a moment, glancing back and forth between us with a doe-eyed frown. It occurred to me that whatever it was, the notion that everyone else didn't already carry the burden of this knowledge seemed foreign to her. My stomach churned uncomfortably. A bad feeling stirred in my gut.

"My father is Geoffrey Stanton. He owns and runs Stanton Media. Has numerous influential newspapers, TV stations, and online platforms under his control. He…*I,*" she corrected, "come from a family that has held considerable political power and wealth around here for generations. His rise to prominence and establishment of a media empire solidified it. He's…" She searched for words. "Not a good guy. I've no idea what the connection to Hale is, but if he had the Clerk working on Hale's case, there's probably a family connection somewhere. The Clerk sweeps in and tidies stuff up for anyone in the family and high up in the business."

"Hale was a trust-fund brat," Charlie said, "but his parents' money came from... Wait a second, I have it here..." He pulled out a Blackberry, of all things, and consulted some notes. "Here, oh." Charlie looked up at me. "Hale's father is a high-up in Stanton Media, CEO of one of their flagship newspapers. So..." He scratched at his chin, thinking. "Stanton likely wanted to avoid a scandal involving the son of one of his CEOs. It could have caused a major media frenzy, potentially embarrassing the company and damaging stock values significantly."

"Money," I said flatly. "This is all about *money*?"

"It's always about money," Isla snapped.

I looked at her. "You came in here acting like I'd be furious when I found out who you really are. Why?"

"I took the job here to... I didn't really want to be your assistant."

Yep, definitely Valeris.

Fuck.

My anger must have shown on my face because her hands flew to her mouth, then flapped about as she tried to explain. "No, please don't get me wrong. I *love it* now. Really, I do, I love working here. But my father made me apply. I refused to begin with, but then decided I would because of how you left Premier Media Solutions. How you stood up to them."

"I wouldn't say that, exactly." I frowned. That I hadn't taken Rich fucking Stanford to court ate at me some days. "I just left."

Isla shook her head. "I met Alice from PMS? Before she left?"

I nodded. I remembered Alice.

"We kept in touch on Facebook," Isla continued. "We'd always swap work horror stories and tell each other what was going on. She told me what happened, how you liberated her—"

"Really," I shifted from one foot to another, "I just

suggested she move in with her boyfriend for a fresh start."

"You got her the job in Scotland."

"I gave her a *reference*," I corrected.

Isla was shaking her head as if she refused to believe what transpired between Alice and me was anything less than the heroic emancipation of her friend on my part.

It really wasn't.

Charlie shifted closer to me a fraction of an inch. I wondered if he'd been about to put a comforting arm around me, or give me a hug, then had thought better of it.

My former employers were a sore topic, even now.

"But you set up on your own!" Isla exclaimed. Like this was some kind of revolution. "You exposed the toxic working environment at the company! They've never recovered."

I shrugged one shoulder. "Can't say I care, to be honest."

"Nor should you," Charlie muttered.

"I'd never seen anyone do that before," Isla said. "You hated how they ran the place, so you stook up to them. You walked away. I don't think it ever occurred to me that *I* could do that before Alice told me what you did."

"I really didn't—"

"My father has his finger in so many pies. Everyone, *everyone,* just does what he dictates. When I turned sixteen, he took me on as an apprentice, wanting me to work in the family business. Premier Media did some work for him on a project. I met Rick Sandford," she shuddered. "He was vile."

I frowned. "You were sixteen? Did he…?"

She shook her head. "He didn't touch me, but he was so sleazy. Kept suggesting I'd *'get ahead'*," she mimed air quote, "better if I *'gave a head'*." She looked like she was about to gag at the thought. I couldn't blame her. "I told my father, he just…laughed it off."

Charlie made a noise that sounded suspiciously like a growl. Guilt swirled within me. I could have taken that bastard to court, and I didn't.

I should have.

"Your father did nothing?" Charlie asked. I could only

imagine what he'd do if his daughter told him a thing like that.

"He said, '*Get used to it, kid. It's a man's world.*'" Isla's lip curled in disgust. "'*Not like you're all that bright,*' he told me. 'There's *only one way for a girl like you to get anywhere in life.*'"

I felt sick. "He actually said that?"

She turned away, cheeks flaming red. "I spoke to his wife too, thinking she'd be more sympathetic, maybe talk to him for me. But, turned out my being there at all was causing…issues. My stepmother hates me. So do my half-siblings. They made things…difficult. And I saw some stuff. Heard some stuff. Things I *really* didn't like. I started keeping track of every part of his business I knew about, hoping to find something I could use to shut him down. Or at least force him to go legit. There was a big fuss when you left Premier Media; Sandford was fuming about it. Came in and demanded Dad do something. Dad refused. And he was super pissed Rick had the gall to even ask." Isla shrugged. "Dad's been preparing for a run for office for years; he's got the political contacts and the social clout to do it, but he's impatient and moody and doesn't like to lose."

Charlie had been scrolling through notes on his Blackberry. "I thought there was a reason I recognised the name." He glanced up. "There was a rumour while I was still on the force in Manchester that Stanton Media were behind a scheme to discredit one political candidate and ensure another got in. But when their preferred candidate won, odd things started to happen. There were backhanders, questionable contracts awarded to certain companies without a transparent bidding process, and a few legal troubles that got brushed under the carpet because it was decided they wouldn't be pursued."

Charlie was frowning. "I don't remember all the specifics, but the gist was that the company was financially backing operations that skirted legal boundaries. No one could prove it outright, but the rumours pointed to a pattern of manipulating political outcomes to favour their business interests."

"That's just what made it into public perception; it runs a lot deeper than that," Isla said. "By the time I turned twenty-one, I knew enough to know I wanted nothing to do with them. I wasn't raised like them. It was just me and my mum and whatever handouts he remembered to send. At some point, someone told him it looked bad for him to have a daughter he didn't take care of, and suddenly, he was auditioning for Father of the Year. But it was all *fake*." Her voice caught in her throat, and her eyes scrunched up. When she opened them, she was fighting back tears. He'd hurt her with that deception. She'd thought her father loved her, and she'd found out he only cared to be *seen* to love her.

Unfortunately, I could relate. My mother often made me feel that way.

"I was a problem," Isla continued. "He just threw money and attention my way to make himself *look* better, and that's Stanton Media and the whole circus in a nutshell. He didn't make that company so successful by adhering to ethical standards; he did it by manipulating, threatening, and occasionally outright breaking the law. And try as he might to be a legitimate political figure now, he can't seem to dig himself out of the cesspit of deviants he stomped down on the way up.

"My stepmother and his *real* kids don't want me getting my hands on any of the money. They just wanted me to go away. And my father wanted Rick Sandford to go away, so he sent me here to try and get something on you—"

I stiffened and glanced at Charlie.

"—or from you, something he could use to get rid of him. Or at least shut him up. Never occurred to Daddy dearest that I might know who you are already. That I might be *inspired* by you. That being here might make me think I could actually do something to break away from him."

She glanced up, and as she caught sight of my face, she paled. "Oh god, I didn't tell him anything!"

I gave her a blank stare and concentrated on breathing.

"I wasn't going to apply for the job here at all. I didn't want to do his dirty work. But then I spoke to Alice, and she told me how you left PMS, so I thought I *would* come here, but not to help my fucking *father*," she spat the word. "I came to see if you could help me."

I took another deep breath, trying to keep my voice level. "Help you how?"

"Expose them!" she said. As if that should be obvious. "I've never been able to get proof or get anyone to take me seriously. I thought you would."

"Why?" I demanded.

Isla looked at me like I was stupid. "Well, you've seen it for yourself," she said. "I thought... You *left*. You must have something on them? On Premier Media, at least, if not my father. And if you could get enough on *them* to walk away and set up here without them fucking with you, I figured..." She glanced from me to Charlie, eyes widening as her voice rose. "You've got to have something!"

Charlie shot me a look: *Don't say anything just yet.*

When I didn't confirm her belief, Isla's eyes closed in disappointment. Somehow, I realised, without ever saying or doing anything, without even really having any fucking clue what was going on, I'd just let her down.

Badly.

"Isla." I took another nice, deep, steadying breath. "I'm not sure what you were hoping for by taking the job here, but I know nothing at all about your father's company. I've never had anything to do with him."

"But—"

"And even if I *could* help," I forged on as if she hadn't interrupted, "I really have my hands full at the moment trying to clear Michael's name." I swallowed the urge to tell her to pack her shit and leave. "Thank you for telling me the truth."

And fuck you for lying to me from the start.

"But—"

"Do you know any more about this Clerk?"

Isla's jaw clicked shut. She knew me well enough to know I

wasn't going to budge right now. She shook her head.

"Okay, well, we need to deal with this. When we're done, we can talk about your father and whatever it is you want to do there."

"Amelia," she said, one of the tears finally escaping and spilling down her cheek. "I'm *so* sorry."

I straightened. "For what? You were doing what your father told you to do."

"Aimee, I didn't—"

"If you remember anything else that might help, please let me know."

She stared at me. We were done, for now at least, and she knew it.

"I will." She turned and pushed out of the office.

"Christ," Charlie muttered. "When did you get that cold?" He glanced at me and sighed. "Ah, shit. She's really upset you." He paused, then huffed out a breath. "If it helps, I believe her. She may have been pushed to apply here, but I don't believe she's told your father anything that could be used against you."

"You've no way of knowing that."

Charlie shrugged. "Gut instinct."

I didn't answer. Instead, I stood and walked to my desk, buzzing through to Abbey on the intercom. "Abbs, there's a potential external threat that might target Isla. It's not her fault, but she's just informed me, and I need you to ensure all her devices and our data are secure."

"Sure, but everything's already—"

"Not enough," I interrupted. "The resources behind this could be significant. Check everything—make sure there have been no data breaches and strengthen our digital security wherever needed. Use whatever resources you need, and keep me updated."

"Got it," Abbey said. "Anything else?"

"Yes," I added, hesitating. "Make sure our devices are secure from any internal leaks, just to be safe."

Abby made an indiscernible noise. She didn't like it. Not

because she'd have to do it but because I felt it necessary to make sure nobody in the office was leaking information.

The thought clearly did not sit well with her.

It didn't sit well with me, either, but given the givens, I'd be an idiot not to check.

I thanked Abbey, and the intercom clicked off. I flopped into my desk chair and resisted the urge to dissolve in a puddle on my desk. I looked up at Charlie. "Can you double-check Isla's story? Figure out if she's actually on the level or if that whole spiel was just more bullshit?"

Charlie watched me for a moment. "I'll find out whatever I can about Geoffrey Stanton. I suspect that will answer your questions about Isla. Parents…they fuck you up."

"I've heard of Stanton Media," I said. "Everyone has, even if they don't realise it. They own a ton of smaller media concerns. But I need facts and some idea of what the hell they have to do with Eric Hale."

"Cleaning up the mess he made to avoid a scandal seems a likely scenario," Charlie said. "But then, why kill him? That attracts attention, and causes a whole other issue. It doesn't make sense."

He stood and moved towards the door. I went to get up, but he waved me back down. "No need. You look knackered. And you're different. Since we first met, you've changed."

"Not really." I shrugged one shoulder at him. "Better clothes, shinier hair, but otherwise the same."

He shook his head. "Amelia. You've wrapped yourself in armour thicker than dragon scales. You just hide it very well under soft designer clothes, floaty blonde hair, and a sweet demeanour."

I snorted. "It's not so sweet."

"It is when you want it to be," Charlie said. "But you're breathing fire whenever anyone comes near. Look at all you've achieved, what you've built here."

"All the good it does me," I snipped. "I hire fucking rats."

"Easy, Aimee." Charlie smiled sadly. "I get that you're mad at her. But she came in here and fessed up when she didn't have to. And even if she turns out to be a bad egg, it doesn't undo everything else. You don't have to keep the world at arm's length."

"She knew you were looking into it and would find out, so she preempted it to try and stay here."

"You don't know that." He crossed his arms, watching me intently. "She seemed genuine to me. Give the girl the benefit of the doubt."

"Why?"

"Because"—he pushed the door open—"there's little point building an empire just to sit it in, all alone on your throne."

The door swung shut behind him as he left.

Echo whined.

Now, why do I get the feeling that the last comment had nothing to do with Isla?

I couldn't argue with him. I'd been living in relative isolation since I'd returned to Ashfordby. I had work. I spoke to Suzie regularly. Occasionally, we went places and did stuff, but she'd been kept pretty busy herself, quitting her job, going back to uni, moving to a new city and somehow managing to keep up with all her online stuff. I interacted with clients on a daily basis. But socially…until Michael had started dragging me out, I'd done nothing since coming back here other than the odd dinner with my brother and sister-in-law and some of their friends.

And I'd been fine with that.

But Charlie was right.

At some point, the walls of this office and the home I was trying to make for myself would start ringing hollow if I didn't let other people in.

Still, nobody said it had to be Isla.

Or, for that matter, Michael fucking Bane.

CHAPTER 12

Elizabeth Infirmary loomed in the gathering dark like a great, hulking beast, its massive, shadowy form squatting in the gloom. A creature, biding its time. The dim, distant lights barely illuminated its cold, impersonal exterior, giving it the appearance of an ancient predator watching over the town, waiting. As if it knew that on any given day, a quota of those within would succumb to a dark, eternal sleep. The flicker of candlelight was already visible as we approached the front entrance from the car park. Hushed tones and whispered voices shared concerns, prayers, stories of the girl they were here to support or her family.

A collective solemnity had settled over the town as another day had passed, and Becca had still not woken. Shock over the murder of Hale had given way to fear that one of our daughters was lost, and we'd been so busy eating up the scandal surrounding the man who'd killed her that we'd forgotten to care.

It was Georgie's idea to arrange this. Around us, small groups gathered, their faces pale and waxen in the fey light of the candles, stark against the darkening sky. People held handmade signs with messages of support, while others simply stood silently, their presence a testament to the community's solidarity. A cluster of teenage girls and adults I took to be their parents stood to the side of the hospital's main entrance. They all wore identical football shirts. Several were crying and silently comforting each other.

Becca's team.

Michael's team.

Shit.

This was going to be tougher than I'd thought. The crowd extended beyond the main entrance, clustering around benches and along the walkways, each person contributing to the sea of flickering lights that spread warmth through the crisp evening air.

I'd hoped to park closer, sneak in the back and come out from within the building, but there were a lot more people here than I'd anticipated.

A lot more police, too.

Our social media campaign had taken off with a vengeance. The whole town was up in arms that a man caught beating a child on camera had merely been released under investigation. No charges. No bail conditions. Just allowed back out on the streets, where their own children played. The general consensus of public opinion seemed to be that Hale had paid someone off somewhere and, had he lived, their 'investigation' would have gone nowhere. Meanwhile, TikTok was flooded with clips of footie fans stitching a message of support posted by Mason Wilder.

It immediately went viral.

I'd watched Michael watch it all takeoff, a look of quiet bemusement and marvel on his face, and felt no small amount of smugness.

But *this*?

This was beyond me.

"Charlie?" My voice sounded small. The echo of someone else floating on the cool night air.

"Keep walking," Charlie said, so softly I barely heard him.

I'd been dead against coming to this. It felt...deceitful somehow, although I couldn't fathom that. Regardless of

Michael's actions, Becca's fight remained the same. Whatever I'd done in a misguided attempt to protect her uncle didn't change the horror of what had been done to her. What had been attempted.

Perhaps I'd simply wanted to avoid facing it again. Or perhaps I was feeling guilty for the gratitude and evident joy Michael's sister had taken in my presence the last time we'd been here. The thought that I might be, or at least become, her brother's girlfriend.

Despite the situation, she had been so happy for him.

And it made me feel wretched.

Fingers wrapped my own and squeezed. I almost pulled away, in no mood to put on another show of faux affection, only to have it thrown back in my face later. But something made me glance at Michael. He felt tense beside me, and when I looked at his face, I saw the closest thing to fear I'd ever witnessed in him. He'd always been fearless in school. What I'd seen of him so far as an adult had given the impression of a man who'd carried his indestructible teenage resilience into his full life. Who'd forged it into a rock-solid self-confidence. Recent events had shaken that. I'd seen it. But I hadn't realised how badly shaken his foundations were until now.

Squeezing his hand, I leant into his arm, resting my head on his shoulder slightly.

"They're here for Becca," I whispered softly, squeezing his hand tighter. "This is for her, not you." It was the only comfort I could offer, as it was the only thing comforting me.

He turned his head and looked down to meet my eyes. Our gazes locked and he took a deep breath, the look on his face shifting from fear to resolve.

He'd do anything for that girl, I realised. *Anything for the people he loves.*

I shivered, and Michael pulled me closer. I should probably have pulled away, but I didn't, selfishly leaning into the touch, the heat of him, and the thought of how astonishingly beautiful it would be to be counted among those loved ones. To be sheltered by that unquestioning impulse to do whatever it took to keep me safe.

Anything.

"Let's get this over with," he said, and led me across the car park towards the crowd.

Charlie fell in step beside us, glancing about in a superficially casual way that I wasn't buying for a second.

He was taking in every detail.

We passed faces that seemed familiar, a few I definitely knew. Uniformed officers peppered the crowd. Charlie had already warned us there would be more, in casual dress, mingling with the crowd to give them extra eyes on people without making the police presence seem overbearing. And to observe, without dealing with the odd changes in behaviour people often displayed when they knew a cop was watching.

Simmo raised a hand in silent greeting, slid through the crowd and gave Michael a more certain half hug and clap on the back than he'd managed the other day. Michael took it gratefully, yanking him into a full bear hug, and for a second, just a second, sagging against him. Simmo didn't miss a beat. He stood there and carried the weight of everything Michael had been burdened with for an instant, just an instant, giving him the slightest reprieve.

When they stepped back, Michael stood a little straighter.

"Thanks, mate," he whispered.

"Here if you need me." A pause, his eyes flickered away. "I should have said that sooner. I'm a shit."

Michael shook his head. "Not a bit."

"Nigel wanted to come, but one of us had to mind the baby."

A ghost of a smile crossed Michael's face. "How is Danny boy?"

Simmo grinned. "Everything."

Michael opened his mouth to say something more, and I was about to demand photos of the son nobody had bothered to tell me about when a shriek made us all jump.

"Coach Mike!" One of the team had spotted him. The girls swarmed, questions spewing from them in panicked, heartbroken pain.

"How's Becca?"

"Is she awake?"

"Can we see her?"

"That fucker deserved everything he got."

"Are you okay?"

I watched silently as he answered each question clearly, honestly, offered them comfort, and reassured them as best he could. I noticed how careful he was to give them friendly shoulder pats while smoothly avoiding any of their attempts to hug him. That wasn't for the benefit of the crowd; that was a practised boundary he'd clearly established and would maintain despite the girls' obvious distress. Their parents moved to offer their own words of support, make their own queries. Several shook his hand, a few offered hugs.

It was oddly marvellous, in a macabre and slightly horrific manner.

"How's he doing?"

I jumped, turning to find Brennan standing behind me. Further behind him, Derek ghosted the crowds, his camera caged in a gimbal and shooting footage. Rosalie waved to me from across the car park and mouthed, "Need me?"

I shook my head, and mouthed back, "Thank you."

She nodded and returned to a conversation she'd been having with a group of women who seemed familiar.

Silver hair curried into a stern bun clued me in; the bible bashers were out in force.

"He's bearing up," I told Brennan quietly. "This is phenomenal."

My mother caught sight of me, excused herself and came over, clasping me in a tight, slightly awkward hug.

I'd seen her only a couple of times since my return. Despite several invitations, she'd only been to the house once for a brief cup of tea. Dad had been over considerably more frequently and had fitted most of the kitchen for me, in fact, but Mother...well, she was always busy being a busybody.

Faith seemed to go hand-in-hand with an intense need to

spend a great deal of time caring for others while leaving your own to fend for themselves.

"Amelia"—she shook her head—"this is just terrible. I had no idea you knew the poor girl."

Maybe if you spoke to me occasionally, you would have.

I kept the thought to myself. "She's the niece of a friend from school, mum."

Mum nodded. "Yes, that boy you always liked."

I blinked, surprised she'd noticed, let alone remembered. "That poor boy. And his sister; she's younger than you two, isn't she?"

I nodded but neglected to mention Lexi's actual age. The last thing she, or Michael, or Becca for that matter, needed right now was anyone doing the maths on how old Lexi'd been when she had her daughter.

"Would you like me to lead everyone in a prayer?"

Breathe.

Stoically schooling my face to one of professional neutrality, I replied, "That's very thoughtful, thank you. I'm not sure how things will pan out. I'll let you know."

She nodded, patted my hand, then walked away. No need for further conversation or interaction. It was time to get back to her fellow thumpers and help them bang out the beat of their favourite mantras.

It's all part of God's plan.

Sufficient unto the day is the evil thereof.

Utter bollocks, in my opinion, but they seemed to draw a great deal of solace from such notions, and I didn't begrudge them that. My only objections arose when they tried to forcibly inflict them on others.

My own world view was distinctly lacking anything resembling religious belief. The closest I came to a doctrine was a simple phrase.

Faith manages.

And it wasn't born from religion but from *Babylon 5*—a belief that faith, whether in a higher power, the universe's equilibrium, or oneself, assures us that beneath the chaos of dark times, there lies an inherent order, a kind benevolence steering us forward, even when paths seem shrouded in uncertainty and despair.

I'd lacked faith of any kind for years, but slowly, I was coming to have faith in myself. It had left me more at peace with my mother's somewhat overbearing religion.

Yet somehow, it did nothing to dull the gut punch every time she abandoned me in favour of all the do-gooding she felt compelled to dedicate herself to so entirely.

I moved back towards Michael, who let out a breath and wrapped an arm around me, leaning in for a moment as if genuinely relieved I was back by his side. Then he introduced me to several parents and all the girls. We were mid-story about the time Becca had won a match by curving a free kick directly into the top corner from over thirty yards out. It was so super awesome because nobody had ever scored from that distance in the league before, and everyone said, even *Mason Wilder* couldn't have made that shot. Did I know that Michael knew *Mason Wilder*? He came to practise one time and ran drills with us, and even he said Becca was the best striker he'd ever seen. When we showed him the video, he agreed, he'd never have made that shot at Becca's age, maybe not even now—it was *phenomenal*.

"He was just being polite," a voice interrupted. "It's Mason Wilder, after all."

I glanced up to see Gemma pushing through the throngs. "Mike." She clasped him in a tight embrace.

I waited for her to break away and step back, but she didn't. Just kept clinging on in there.

Not awkward. Not awkward at all.

"Jeez, lady, paws off *Aimee's guy*."

"So cringe. Becca's not even met her yet, and you're already moving in on her man."

"Yeah, back off her bae, *Karen*."

I choked back a laugh. Michael extricated himself from the embrace, his face crimson and struggling to mask his annoyance.

He cleared his throat. "Don't worry, girls, Gemma's an old friend." He gave her a look so pointed it could have stabbed right through to her heart. "I'm sure she didn't mean anything by it."

"Don't worry, girls—"

I turned to the voice, and my brother stepped out of the crowd.

"—Gemma's never been very good at boundaries, but she's harmless. Like a declawed cat; a bit pathetic really."

"Who the fuck do you think you're talking to?" Gemma took a step towards my brother.

"Nobody of importance." Adrian moved past her like she was nothing and grabbed me for a quick, socially appropriate hug. "You okay, kid?"

I opened my mouth to speak, but no words came out.

"No. Dumb question." He turned to Michael. "Don't think we've met properly? Adrian." He extended a hand, which Michael shook. "Aimee's big brother." He kept hold of his hand a second, leant in, and said jokingly, "Don't worry, I'll forgo the obvious threats to dismember you if you hurt her." He winked and released his hand.

Michael chuckled. "I'd expect nothing less. I have a little sister."

The two men sized each other up, clearly coming to some form of unspoken understanding, nodded, then moved on to discuss the logistics of running a girls' footie team in a town where every school committee and parent association was filled with old school misogyny, patriarchal bullshit, and pearl clutchers pushing the trad wife life.

Gemma made a valiant effort to reinsert herself into the conversation, but was firmly rebuffed by the gaggle of girls who had clearly decided she was persona non grata and would not be tolerated. They made a very effective buffer, pushing her out and away from Michael who, they loudly informed her, wasn't interested in some *basic biatch*. And Becca was going to wake up real soon and she was, like, stoked to meet Aimee so Gemma needed to *wind her neck in*.

I was somewhat shook by the revelation that Michael had told Becca about me. Enough that she would have mentioned me to her friends and already wanted to meet me.

What the hell had he said to her about me? We'd been on one date before all this kicked off.

"*Auntie Aimeeeee!!*"

I turned just in time to catch the hyperactive ball of joy that was my nephew as he flung himself at me.

"Hey, buddy." I scooped the little guy up, smooshing him to me as his arms wrapped my neck, and for a second I understood the way Michael had sagged into Simmo's familiar embrace.

I wanted to fall down on the floor, curl up in a ball around Aaron and sob until the world made sense again.

"She needs to breathe, lad!" My dad chuckled and pried Aaron out of my arms.

Reluctantly, I relinquished him. "Hi, Daddy."

He replaced Aaron's arms with his own and seemed to understand. It was all getting a bit overwhelming, and I needed someone to hold me upright for a minute. It was all I could do to stop myself blurting the whole mess out to him and begging him to fix it.

He'd have tried.

So would Aiden.

But this was my mess; I wouldn't drag them into it. My brief reprieve was broken by a loud shout and the sounds of a scuffle.

"He's a murderer!" someone yelled, and my head whipped around so fast I'd be feeling it for a week.

"Why's he still walking the streets?" another yelled from the other side of the car park.

"Why aren't you arresting him?" someone else demanded of one of the nearby police officers.

I was moving, pushing through a human ocean to get to Michael, who had somehow been separated from me, despite the fact we'd been right next to each other moments ago. Charlie materialised by Michael's side and shouldered a couple of people out of the way as they made a beeline for him with a placard. I couldn't see what it read, but something was painted in angry letters on the other side; red paint dripped down the wooden batten it was mounted on. Michael was searching the crowd, and the look on his face was pure fury.

Shit.

If he goes off, this is going to get so much worse.

I watched him in slow motion as I struggled to reach him, his mouth opening to speak, his whole body tensing, muscles bunching beneath his shirt. I was still feet away. Someone slammed into me.

"Michael!" it wasn't a cry, or a shout, just enough to get his attention.

His eyes fell on me, and for a mercy, whatever he'd been about to say died on his lips. The crowd swelled around me as more shouts of "Murderer!" and "Arrest him!" echoed around us.

What the fuck is going on?

Someone else slammed into me, and I glanced over my shoulder, searching for my family. "Dad, get the kids out of here!"

"On it! What about you?"

"I'll be fine. Go, please!"

Peripherally I was aware of him scooping up Aaron and pushing his way to Aiden. Some words passed between them and my brother ruffled his son's hair in comfort, then both turned to help the gathered parents herd the girls away and back to their cars.

Teenage girls live on drama—I didn't envy them that task.

Stumbling, I finally managed to reach Michael, who wrapped a protective arm around me.

"Don't say anything," I whispered. "Don't respond at all. We're just going to walk inside. As calmly as we can, okay?"

"Aimee—"

"Michael." My voice was firm. I extricated myself from his arms, took his hand and led him quite purposefully through the throngs of suddenly angry people.

"This is mad, what the hell is going on?" Brennan met us on the way to the entrance.

"I've no idea, but we need to do damage control."

"Get inside. The less he's on camera with this, the better." Brennan nodded at a local news crew that was eating up every second of action and now had every camera pointing our way.

Shit.

I tugged on Michael's hand, pulling him a little faster. Charlie fell in behind him, shielding him from the view of the cameras as best he could. Something crashed into the ground just ahead of us, narrowly avoiding hitting me in the head and scarlet paint splattered the pavement, flying up and into my face.

"Faster, Aimee, just get inside," Charlie said behind me.

I stopped trying to be nonchalant and fast-walked the rest of the distance. Someone inside opened the doors as we approached and a nurse I recognised from our last visit ushered us through. We stumbled in.

"Get up to Becca," I told Michael. "Brennan, we need to get ahead of this. Whatever footage we got from before everything kicked off, get as much of it out there as we can. Make sure the reporters have it. And get out a press release. Address the incident directly, emphasise the purpose of the vigil, and make it clear that the gathering is meant to support Becca and her recovery. Highlight community solidarity and the positive outcomes of our awareness campaign." I thought for a minute. "This will go national now. Reach out to your contacts at the BBC and see if they're interested in a live interview; send them the footage; we just need to keep pushing the positives and focus on Becca."

"I'm on it," Brennan said, grabbing me as I moved to go back outside. "But you shouldn't go back out there."

"I'm not leaving you all to—"

"We know that," Brennan said. "And if this was a normal client, I wouldn't say a thing. But you're *in this*, Aimee. And you look like Carrie at the fucking prom."

I blinked, realised something wet was making my eyelashes

stick together, and reached a hand up to clear them. My fingers came away a gory red.

Shit.

"Okay, just…" I hated this. "Make sure everyone's okay? Nobody has to stay if they—"

"Christ, we're not leaving you," Brennan snapped. "Go sort yourselves out. I'll handle things here."

"I'll stay and help," Charlie said. "Go with Michael. Clean yourselves up."

I thanked them both, relieved I didn't have to go back out despite the worms of guilt squirming in my stomach. When I looked up, I caught sight of Michael. Despite my instructions to go to Becca, he was standing staring back at me. Red paint splattered his jacket, the shirt beneath, and his face, which wore an odd expression.

"Michael?" I stepped towards him, hesitant. He was bottled fury right now, and I had no intention of popping his cork. "Let's go see Becca, hmm?"

"They ruined your coat." He sounded genuinely furious at the insult to Burberry. "That's never coming out of wool."

I looked down and realised my trench coat was spattered with red, the checked collar having taken the brunt of it along with my face. For a second, I was back in the darkness of early morning, Michael covered in blood, shaken and dazed, mooning around while I'd burned his coat.

It was eerie.

Looking back up, our gazes locked, and I knew he was thinking exactly the same thing. Unbuttoning the coat, I turned it inside out, folded it deliberately and started towards the toilets.

"Aimee—"

"It's just a coat, Michael."

He trailed after me forlornly. We both scrubbed ourselves down as best we could. The nurse who let us in appeared as I came out of the bathroom and gave me a bag to put my coat in. Michael was right; there was no saving it. Probably wouldn't stop me trying, though.

Upstairs, we found Lexi pacing her daughter's room.

"Mike?" She rushed at him before he'd even made it through the door. "What the fuck happened? Are you okay?"

He hugged her fiercely and led her back to the bed so he could lean down and lay a gentle kiss on Becca's forehead.

The girl didn't stir.

For some reason, that shocked me.

Her bruises were turning to an ugly greenish-yellow, but at least the swelling had gone down since I'd last been here. She was looking a little more human.

Why won't you wake?

From what Michael had said, there was no reason she shouldn't. They'd sedated her heavily when she'd first come in, but she had woken briefly a couple of times since then before sinking into what now seemed like an endless slumber. She was no longer sedated. She could wake. She just hadn't. Her body was focused on healing itself and wasn't ready to face the world again yet.

Honestly, I couldn't blame her.

Perhaps it was for the best. Had she been awake, she'd have been in so much pain. There was no avoiding the inevitable psychological fallout from this, but as long as she *did* wake up, perhaps it was better it happened later, after the worst of the injuries were well on their way to healing.

"Just some idiots kicking off, Lex," Michael said. "How is she?"

"I wanted to come down, but I couldn't bring myself to leave her." Lexi plopped into a chair beside the bed. Her face was grey. Huge dark circles ringed her eyes, which had sunk into her drawn face. Wrinkles creased her brow where there had been none before.

She looked haggard.

"You still haven't been home?"

Lexi shook her head, her dirty blonde bob bouncing around her in lank clumps.

"Lex," Michael said softly, moving away from Becca and bending to take her hand. "We talked about this. Becca will need you to be firing on all cylinders when she wakes. You have to get some rest. At least get some fresh air and a shower."

"I can't leave her, Mike, what if she—"

"Not going to happen," Michael said firmly. "You heard what the doctor said; she's over the worst of it."

"But she's still not woken."

"I know." Michael looked back at Becca for a second, and I saw the doubt swimming in his eyes. The fear. None of it made it into his voice as he said, quite confidently, "She *will*."

We sat with them for a long stretch. Michael spoke softly for a while, catching Becca up on everything that had happened since he'd visited the previous evening. Even regaling her with the hilarity of Gemma getting knocked down a few pegs by a load of teens. He chuckled as he said it, and it made me smile.

Slowly, his chattering faded, he slumped in his chair, and he slept.

"He's out for the count," Lexi said, after ten minutes or so of watching him sleep. "You must be exhausted. Why don't you go home and get some rest?"

The polite part of me wanted to refuse and stay. But if I was honest, I was struggling after the shit show outside and craving the peace and solitude of my own home. Also, I was never sure when people said these things if it was for my benefit or theirs, and on the off-chance this was her polite way of saying, *"I don't really know you, please leave now before it gets any more awkward"* it seemed better to accept the offer graciously.

"Do you need anything before I go?" I asked quietly.

"No, thank you." She turned an exhausted face towards me and offered a half smile. "Really. *Thank you.* I'm not quite sure what he did to bewitch you into helping us, but I don't think he'd have survived the last few days without you. And I wouldn't have made it without him. We both owe you."

I shook my head. "You don't owe me a thing; it's the least I can do."

"He fucked up, didn't he?"

I blinked.

"That night he took you to the ball. He said things went sour, and he acted like a dick. He ruined it."

Well, shit.

Couldn't argue with that statement.

"I'd love to say it wasn't about you," Lexi said. "That it was *this* situation making him crazy. But I think we both know that's not true."

I shrugged. She sighed.

"Look, I don't know you. To be honest I don't even remember you from school; I was only there a year before you left, and you and Michael were never friends—" She winced. "Sorry, I didn't mean—"

"No, you're right. He hated me back then."

She gave me a quizzical look. "You didn't hate him?"

I snorted.

Understanding dawned. "Ah. Yes, well..." She ran a hand through her hair, staring out through the tiny window at the night for a moment, her mouth working as she fumbled about for the right words. "Look, our dad left when I was basically still a baby. Mike was only just in high school. Mum was a wreck after. She didn't raise me, *he* did." She took a breath, tears welling in her eyes. "He fed me. He clothed me. He made sure I got to school. He comforted me when I cried. Later, he provided for me. And when I fell pregnant at fifteen, he was everything. To me, to Becca, he was *everything*. Somehow, in all that, he put himself through uni, put me through my hairdressing qualifications, helped me get a great job, and encouraged me to push myself, all while making sure Becca wanted for nothing. That I wanted for nothing. And yeah, even our mum. She didn't deserve it, but he's taken care of her too. Not that she's grateful for it. He did everything we needed and nothing for himself. I'm betting he told you his footie career never happened because of an injury?"

I nodded.

"Utter BS. He could have gone pro. He was given a place

at Stockport County Academy just before Dad left, but he had to stop going. Mum wouldn't take him to all the training, and he had me to look after so he couldn't take himself. He would have done, even at the tender age of eleven. He'd have hopped a train, walked the rest, got himself there whenever needed. But he wouldn't leave me. And Mum just…" Her voice cut with years-old resentment. "He tried, even without the support of local clubs, but he was never going to get anywhere and he knew it. By the time he was looking at uni, his priority was going somewhere within commuting distance of home, to do something that would let him make enough money to take care of everyone."

She shook her head, took a breath. "Sorry, I'm babbling. What I'm trying to say is, his whole life, he's taken care of everyone else. And I've always thought the reason he never got anywhere dating women was because it just felt like more of the same to him. He'd go out on a couple of dates, but nothing ever clicked. It just felt like one more woman he'd be expected to take care of, and he just didn't have the energy for it. He was too busy working a full-time job, parenting a child that wasn't his and the child she'd had by accident. Running around coaching kids' football teams in his spare time. When he was younger, everyone wanted him because he was hot, popular, talented, and a badass…"

I blushed furiously, and she gave me a knowing shrug.

"These days everyone wants him because he's hot, popular, and loaded. They look at him and think, 'He'll provide for me. He'll love me. He'll make a good father.' They don't see *him*. They see what he can do for them. And he doesn't have it in him."

I glanced at the sleeping form of Michael Bane. His hair was tousled and fluffy on top from the quick wash he'd given it in the sink earlier. It had dried oddly and stuck out at weird angles.

It was strangely adorable.

I sighed. "I have no expectations of him."

"That's not what I meant."

I glanced back at Lexi.

"You're different. He came back from that first dinner date absolutely *buzzing*." She smiled. "He didn't shut up about you the whole night after he got back. Becca was begging to meet you, and he said, *'Soon, I'm sure.'* We have *never* met a girl he's dated before. He doesn't do long-term. He didn't believe it was right to subject me to a pussy parade when I was a teenager, and he's no different now with Becca. He rarely even mentions girls he's dating. But you, you he was happily telling us about. *You* he was thinking of bringing round for dinner."

Michael shifted in his sleep, and we both looked at him, panicked for a second that his burning ears would wake him. But he settled, his breathing deep and steady.

Lexi dropped her voice lower and continued, "I get that he screwed it up. He knows he did. And he's gutted about it, he really is. But…he deserves to be happy, Amelia. And for a second there, you made him happier than I've ever seen him." She fell silent.

"He didn't know who I was," I finally managed. "When he was gushing about me and getting all starry-eyed and hopeful. He hadn't recognised me."

"Does it matter?" Lexi shook her head. "He hadn't seen you for years; it's not like you were close friends—"

I held a hand up to stop her. "I get what you're saying. But it's more complicated than that. He hated everything about me for years. Now, suddenly, I've lost some weight, got some highlights, and have a bit of money; all is forgiven? I'm an acceptable choice now? I'm still me." I shook my head. "It was one thing to think he'd been pleasantly surprised by what he saw when we ran into each other again. But to know that he didn't realise who I was, and the instant he figured it out, he just…" I stopped myself. I was getting dangerously close to admitting he'd left that night.

"I never said he wasn't a dick about it," Lexi said. "He was. And I know you've stuck around to help 'cause of all this—" She glanced at Becca. "And maybe you'd never have spoken to him again if not. Maybe he'd never have talked you round, and that would have been the end of it. But my daughter idolises that man. And so do I. And if all this shit can give you two the time to figure things out...well, I guess that's some kind of balance to it."

"Lexi—"

"You don't get it," she snapped. "He'd never admit it, but he had hope. For a moment. That he wasn't going to be alone anymore. Finally, someone actually *saw him*. And then he realised who you were, and it all went away."

I frowned. "I don't know what you mean?"

"I told you"—the exhaustion seemed to be really making her snappish—"everyone fawned over him when he was a teen. They didn't really want *him*, they just wanted the fittest guy in school, and that happened to be him. When he realised you'd known him back then, and worse, you'd been one of those girls obsessing over him, he just... He thought he'd read you wrong. That you weren't interested in *him*, after all, and you were just another girl trying to find a guy you could hang off who would make you look better."

I stared at her.

"He realised how wrong he was pretty fucking fast, but the damage was done. You were pissed. I would have been, too, the way he acted. Just...all I'm saying is, there's another side to this. And he will never tell it to you himself, so I'm here, explaining, and *begging* you to try and get past it. Just...wait for all this to blow over. Go out to dinner again. Give him a chance. He doesn't know how to do all this." She gestured at me. "Really, he never has before. He's been parenting either me or my daughter since he was still a kid himself. He's a clueless fucking dope when it comes to emotions, and women in particular. Other women, I mean. Not us." She stretched a hand out and squeezed her daughter's arm. "It's not his fault."

We sat in silence for a time. I really didn't know what I was meant to say to all that.

Eventually, Lexi spoke again. "Just think about it. Please. If not for him, for Becca." The look on my face must have been one of shock because she actually laughed. "Yeah, I'm stooping *that* low. And playing *that* card. She was so excited to meet you. If she wakes up and it's all over she'll be devastated." She leant closer to me and made sure she was meeting my eyes. "And so will he."

I glanced at Michael's sleeping form. "He hasn't exactly seemed broken up over it."

Lexi snorted. "He's a man. You don't seriously expect them to actually say what they're thinking and explain how they're feeling? That one barely knows, let alone knows how to express it. Go on now. Home. And get some rest."

"I could say the same to you."

"You could, but it wouldn't do any good. She's my daughter. I won't *abandon* her."

The way she said that word, *abandon*, made me realise just how lucky I was to have two functional parents.

Even if one of them did kinda suck.

❖

I slipped from the room as silently as I could. Called an Uber. Loitered in the hospital corridors until it arrived, then slid out into the rain and dark and sprinted to the waiting vehicle. I dove into the back seat and shivered all the way home, clutching the bag containing my ruined Burberry.

Usually, I'd have a driver drop me at the driveway entrance to save them a little effort. Tonight I didn't bother, letting him chauffeur me all the way to my front door. I tipped him more than usual for the effort and ran in from the rain. My clothes were damp, and my whole body ached, but I was so wired I knew I wouldn't sleep. Halfway into the hall, I collided with the solid wall of an excitable Echo, who body slammed me and demanded cuddles and kisses and for me to marvel at how well she could chase her own tail.

After much fuss, I let her out into the back garden, closing out the freezing night before I kicked off my shoes and shrugged off my wet clothes while I waited. They went straight into the pile for dry-cleaning pickup.

My fluffy unicorn onesie, fresh out of the dryer and deliciously cosy, had never been so welcome. I pulled it on and dragged a thick blanket from a shelf, cocooning myself in it and shivering. Echo knocked to come in, and I braced myself, opening the door and closing it as fast as I could. The great black dog shook herself and trotted back into the house and towards the stairs. I followed but headed for the lounge. Echo huffed audibly and followed me, resigning herself to the fact we weren't going to bed after all.

My phone chirped from inside my purse, and I fished it from the hall table on the way past.

A text from Suzie: *Hello??????????? Did you die?*

The phone chirped again and a second message flashed up: *Poor choice of words, my bad!*

I chuckled. A third chirrup. *Call me when you can.*

We wandered into the lounge. I flicked a lamp on and thanked my forward thinking for setting the fire before I'd left. After a brief fumble with matches, I coaxed it to life, flopped on the sofa and stretched out my legs, wincing as my ankles protested at the lack of sleep over the last few days.

They were swollen and angry.

Great.

I dialled Suzie's number and scrolled back through the tsunami of messages she'd sent since I'd been in the hospital.

What the fuck happened? There's like a million stitched piss takes of Michael flooding TikTok.

I groaned.

This is so weird, I can't scroll without seeing 'Wolf In Coach's Kit'. Seriously, it's a hashtag. It's trending, along with that creepy whistle tune from Kill Bill! *What the fuck happened??*

She'd followed up with a flurry of shared TikToks.

"Finally!" Suzie's voice drifted from the speaker. "Where've you been? I've been messaging non-stop."

"Sorry, I was in the hospital. I just got home."

"What an absolute shit show!"

"Thanks. Just what I needed to hear."

"Sorry, I just mean…it was a vigil for a *child*. How can

people be like that?"

"Tell me about it." I flicked through the videos she'd shared with me. They all featured a very wholesome clip of Michael, shared by a parent of one of the kids he coached, abruptly transitioning into a sinister, photoshopped image of his beautiful face, overlaid on the body of a thug with a bloody knife. The image flickered; his face danced back and forth between a human and a snarling, feral wolf. All while Twisted Nerve whistled over it. The sounds and image combination set my teeth on edge and raised the hairs on my arms. Echo lifted her head, regarded the phone with disdain, and tilted her head back and forth to the whistling.

"You've seen them then," Suze said. "God, shut it off. I can't listen to it anymore!"

I muted TikTok but kept watching. The clip ended and some indignant yokel came on bitching about vigilante justice. I scrolled. Another, just the same, but this one stitched by a woman lamenting the fall of civilised society, and Michael Bane being the herald of an imminent doomsday. I kept scrolling. More. More. More.

Holy shit.

"Aimee, this isn't right." Suzie's voice crackled down the line.

"You're telling me. Christ, even if he had done it, it's not like he'd have murdered Florence Nightingale; the man's a paedophile." Even saying the words left a sour taste in my mouth.

"No, that's not what I meant—" She paused. "I mean, yeah, very valid point. But *this* isn't natural; people don't get angry with the guy who defends his family. And this started instantly. Like right when everything kicked off at the vigil. Like someone's running a *counter-campaign*."

"What?" I stared at the phone. "Why would anyone do that?"

"No clue. But that creepy wolf didn't come from nowhere, someone made it."

Cogs whirred in my brain. She was right. I hadn't even

considered it, but she was right. It was a lot of effort to go to, making a clip like that just for the sake of hating on a guy who hadn't even been arrested.

"Could it be one of the people who was there tonight?" Suzie asked.

"Maybe." I thought about it. "It was weird. Most of the people there were friends or family, people Michael and his sister know, school friends of Becca's, teachers, other locals from the council or school committee showing support."

"Why's that weird?"

"It's not, but every single one of the little protesters was…random. I asked Michael and Lexi after we'd gone up to Becca's room; neither of them knew who any of them were. Didn't even think the faces were familiar. I thought it was odd, so I asked Charlie to look into them. He left to do some digging and is still working, but so far, none seem to be from Ashfordby. They're not even from neighbouring towns. Most live in Manchester and work in or around the city."

"Why were they there then?"

"To make trouble," I said. "So odd. And it wasn't just them."

"Making trouble?"

"Yeah, we had the delights of Gemma to contend with too."

"Eurgh. How is dear Gemma?"

I snorted. "As vile as ever. 'Oh, let me help, Michael'. 'You must be so tired, Michael', 'I'll cook you dinner and massage your feet while telling you what a manly man you are, Michael'. Sycophant."

"You do a killer impression there," Suzie giggled. "But I take your point. She's clearly got some unrequited interest there." Suzie paused. "You know, thinking about it, she always kinda did."

"What?"

"Have a thing for Michael."

"Did she?" I frowned. "I don't remember them being a thing."

"Oh, they weren't. But she was obsessed with him in school, nearly as bad as you. Except she'd set her bitch pack on anyone who dared look at him."

I winced. "That part I remember."

"Some things never change."

"But everything's changed," I said. Gemma had wanted him too? Lexi's words echoed in my head. Maybe she had a point. I'd no idea what it was like to grow up with that kind of constant, slightly neurotic interest from every angle. "We're not kids anymore. And as far as Gemma knows, Michael and I are together. Common decency should stop her openly fawning all over him in front of me."

"Gemma may be common, but she's never been decent."

I considered that. Gemma's popularity hadn't come from looks but from the appearance of being fabulously wealthy. Whenever that wasn't enough, she would simply be loud and aggressive. She'd carved out her patch as queen bee from day one of year seven. She'd bullied those who were quieter or weaker, which was pretty much everyone. She'd make the boys laugh at the expense of the other girls, and pit those girls against each other, only granting reprieve to a favoured two or three. Those who were immune to her scathing tongue and occasional violent outbursts were just as popular as Gemma. But they held their own by being just as nasty.

"Are you okay?" Suzie asked.

"No," I said. "This is all getting so messy. I've no idea what I'm doing."

Suzie sighed. "Is it… Can you—"

"Get out of it?"

"Well, yeah."

My turn to sigh. "I don't see how."

"Just distance yourself from it all, from him. Take a step back. Walk back whatever you told the police."

Thin ice. "I can't."

"Of course you can, just say you got confused and—"

"But I didn't get confused."

"Aimee…I know you're trying to protect him. I even kinda

understand why, but…what if you're wrong? What if he…" She didn't need to say *killed him*. The question hung in the air like a guillotine.

I didn't answer.

"I'm worried about you," she continued.

"It'll blow over," I said quietly.

"I'm not so sure it will," she said. "Not quickly, anyway."

"It doesn't matter. I'm in it now." Silence stretched through the night and I shivered. "It's late. You should get some sleep."

"I will if you will," she said.

"Sure," I replied. We both knew I was lying.

"I'll call you in the morning. Try not to stay up all night watching pimple-popping videos."

"I need the dopamine," I argued. "Besides, you like ear-wax-pulling videos. How's that any less gross?"

"Fair enough. Night."

"Night."

Hanging up, I felt all the energy drain from me. A sudden abandonment. My fingers went lax, my phone slid from my grip and into my blanketed lap. It was probably for the best. Much more doom scrolling on social and I was going to completely lose it. Shivering, I shuffled across the cushions, closer to the fire, and leant over to snag some wood from the stack beside the sofa. After tossing it in, I sagged back, exhausted from the effort, and snuggled even deeper into the blankets.

Echo lifted her head from the hearth, sniffed at me, and stood. In an elegant leap, she landed nimbly at my feet, gently climbed up my legs, and flopped on top of them. Her great head landed on my stomach, and she yawned.

"You're a good girl," I told her. "And a good hot water bottle."

Echo turned her head and shifted so she was more comfortable, then promptly fell asleep. I wished I could fall asleep that easily.

Or at all.

The wood I'd tossed in the fire cracked, and I stared into the flames licking around them.

What if I'm wrong. The thought intruded, unbidden. *What if Michael killed him?*

I examined the thought. Turning it carefully in my mind, trying to make sense of it. Was it real? Was this actually a possibility? Or was it simply my anxiety getting the best of me and making me doubt my instinct?

Poking at the thought didn't change it. Real then. I quashed it. Then thought better of it and looked at it again. What if I *was* wrong? What if he *did* kill him?

An image of Becca, motionless, bruised and broken in a hospital bed flitted across my mind. If he had, I understood why. I wasn't sure that made it right, but it would at least be understandable. What was less comprehensible was my kamikaze mission to prove his innocence, based on…what, exactly? The fact he'd made me come harder than I had in years?

Given the sex life with Johnny Vanilla that had taken up most of those years, it wasn't a particularly impressive achievement.

But it was more than that. When he'd asked for my help, he had been sincere; he'd fucked up, he knew it, and he didn't know what to do about it. I'd seen no reason to let a good man's life go down the toilet because he'd lost control and become violent in the face of overwhelming violence inflicted on someone he loved.

If I was completely honest, I'd found it fucking sexy. Would he defend me like that, if someone hurt me?

I snorted a laugh at my own stupidity, and Echo started, lifting her head and regarding me with exasperation.

'Just go to sleep,' her eyes pleaded, *'the crazy always gets worse when you don't sleep.'*

Petting her head in apology, I prodded the thought some more. Aside from my apparent desire for a big, strong man to smash anything that hurt me, there had to be a reason I'd come this far. And after the conversation I'd just had with

Lexi, I wasn't at all sure it was reasonable or fair to expect him to protect me.

Who protected him?

Well, me, I guess.

But *should I*? That was the question.

He'd been honest with me when he'd turned up bloody and desperate. I'd no idea what made me so sure of it, but I was. Perhaps it was the fact he'd admitted his behaviour that night had nothing to do with the attack on Becca. It would have been easy, so very easy, for him to tell me he'd received a call or a message at the ball, that it had coincided with Gemma's meddling, that his reaction was to *that* news and not the revelation that I was a teenage geek in high school.

He could have pretended he was so shaken, he'd not known what to say or how to tell me. That he'd needed to go to Becca immediately. That we didn't know each other well enough for him to inflict that on me, so he'd said nothing and now regretted it.

Words.

That was all it would have taken. A few simple words. And instead of being hurt and furious with him, I'd have been sympathetic. Guilty even, for thinking so badly of him when he'd been trying to deal with so much crap.

But he hadn't. He'd told me the truth. Even though it had damned him. Despite it making me less likely to help him.

Why be honest about that and lie about the extent of the shit he was in? It made no sense.

Unless it was a double bluff. Tell the truth about something bad to hide the fact you're lying about something worse.

I glared at the fire. The thought that Michael might have lied to me, manipulated me, bothered me far more than the thought he'd beat the shit out of a guy. Maybe even more than the possibility that he'd killed Eric Hale.

Was it because Hale was a bad guy who'd got what was coming to him? Or was I just *that* blind when it came to Michael Bane?

If I was wrong, I'd just pissed away my reputation, my business, and everything I'd fought so hard to build. Worse, I'd dragged others into it, convinced them to endorse him, to support him, to protest his innocence when I knew damn well he was no fucking angel.

I didn't believe he'd murdered Hale. But I wasn't stupid enough to think it wasn't a possibility, or arrogant enough to assume my almighty gut was so infallible it couldn't turn out I was wrong.

But I didn't *believe* it.

And yet he *had* kicked the crap out of the guy. He'd lied about his alibi.

So had I.

At the time, it had seemed like the best thing to do. But at the time, I'd had no idea someone had come along and whacked Hale right after. If Michael was innocent, I might well have destroyed the evidence that proved it. His clothes would testify to the beating, sure, but they wouldn't show signs of whatever had killed him. Blood spatter?

Would that have exonerated him? Or would they just argue Michael hadn't been wearing the coat when he killed Hale?

Whoever had stabbed him would have got his blood on them, right? In a pattern. One that was markedly different to the pattern left by a beating?

I'd been so sure when I'd been babbling at Michael that the blood spatter told me he was innocent. But now…writing a character who was a forensics expert didn't actually *make* me one.

My fingers itched to Google it, but I was afraid of someone seeing my search history.

I didn't know. Maybe it would have exonerated him. Maybe it would just have proved he hurt Hale, and the police wouldn't have cared to look any further into it.

Maybe I'd have been better off staying out of the whole fucking thing and leaving him to sort out the mess he'd made. I had a sinking feeling that all I'd done for him was make it worse. If I'd known he'd left a murder scene, I wasn't sure I'd have made the same decision. Not because the guy was dead, but because of the scrutiny that came with murder. Some paedo getting his arse kicked wasn't going to have people scrabbling for justice. Michael was bound to have left evidence of his presence; shoe prints, fingerprints, DNA even. I had no idea if Hale had fought back. Something had made Michael's head bleed, someone had taken a good shot at his ribs. I had to assume that had been Hale—as far as I knew, he'd not seen anyone else. If Hale had touched him, scratched him, Michael's skin and maybe even his blood would be under Hale's fingernails, on his hands.

Alibi or no, the police might very well already know Michael was lying and had been there. And the fact he'd lied about it made it far harder for them to believe the line, *"Yes, officer, I beat him half to death, but I didn't stab him. That would be wrong."*

The extent to which I had screwed up was finally dawning on me.

"Fucking Michael Bane," I said aloud.

Echo huffed a sigh and gave me a scathing bombastic side eye as if to say, *'You wish you were.'*

"Quiet, you." I scowled at her, and I swear, she laughed.

CHAPTER 13

Morning came with a grey haze that seemed to wrap itself around the world, cocooning everything in a slightly ethereal mist. I watched dawn break through the lounge window, rolling in across the fields, as the sun struggled to rise and I attempted to muster some kind of enthusiasm for the day ahead. I forced myself up, into my comfiest joggers and hoodie, donned my running shoes and headed for the park, Echo in tow.

Someone once said that if you do the same thing often enough, it stops being a chore and becomes a habit. Sixty-six days doing the same task, and your brain gets so used to it that you'll do it without thinking. I'd been at uni when I'd started running. A suggestion from my counsellor to help me deal with my depression.

I put the theory to the test and ran every day. Sun, shine, snow, rain of toads, I ran. Until one day, I turned around and realised I'd run my way through a year and into a size eight.

The weight loss helped, but the mental clarity was liberating.

It's a habit I've maintained, come what way.

Deviating from my usual route hadn't worked out well, so we trudged down the familiar path, my breath misting in the cool air before me. Down to the water, along the bank, realising too late I should have taken another route. I came to the point a smaller path branched off and away, around the end of the mere. Pulling up short, my eyes followed the line of that little path. There was no rain today, nothing to compel me down there to seek refuge in the dilapidated hide I'd found myself in with Michael. No reason to venture down there at all, really. Yet my feet carried me forward, inexorably leading me back down that little path. Tall grass brushed against my legs. A flurry of ducks flew from the nearby bulrushes, startled by the sudden presence of Echo, as she padded down the path at my heel. She wasn't on a lead, but she knew better than to chase the wildlife. We rounded the corner, and there it was, as ramshackle as I recalled it.

Yet still just as charming.

Hesitantly, I stepped inside. For one deluded moment, I almost expected to find Michael in there, waiting for me, sprawled on a thick woollen blanket perhaps, scattered with cushions, on which he reclined in semi-nude splendour despite the chill air.

Ridiculous.

I stared around the empty shack. Echo sniffed about, lifted her head and gave me the side eye. As if sex scents from days ago still lingered, and she was silently judging me, like, '*Oh, now it all makes sense…you dumbass.*'

There was nothing for me here. Not now. I stumbled as I walked back out, caught myself on the door frame, and sighed. When I looked up, several stags wandered out from beneath the sprawling branches of towering trees. Bathed in the gentle glow of the morning mist, they stood in silhouette, perfectly framed by thick trunks and the lush canopy above. The soft haze of fog mingled with the earth, an otherworldly backdrop that seemed to blur the boundaries of reality. The quiet was profound, marked only by the distant sound of passing geese flying overhead, and the occasional rustle of leaves.

It was so beautiful here. I scanned the herd as more

appeared, looking for that brilliant white, majestic stag I'd seen when I was here with Michael. But Ashfordby's near-legendary White Hart wasn't there. I wasn't surprised. In all my years of coming here, that was the only time I'd ever caught sight of him. The snowy deer that lent the park its name were oft-mentioned but seldom actually seen. Local legend had it that the same great stag had walked these woods for hundreds of years. To see him was a blessing. And a rare one at that.

I doubted I'd see him again.

The thought made me sad, and I headed back towards the main path, Echo trotting along beside me. After a few minutes, I realised I wasn't even jogging anymore, just plodding along at a sedate walk. We rounded a bend, and the early morning sun spilt over the hill into a clearing, bathing it in golden sunlight that filtered through the trees, falling on a solitary deer. The soft, misty air around it was aglow, punctuated by beams of sunlight that pierced the dense canopy. The sunbeams seemed to set the very air ablaze, catching the doe in an almost divine spotlight. Its gentle presence momentarily suspended the reality of everything I had to face that day, and I took a mental photo, burning the scene into my brain to revisit later.

Echo waited patiently beside me for far longer than was reasonable until, eventually, she nudged my hand with her nose. I looked down, and she stared at me quizzically.

"You're right," I said. "No avoiding it." I sighed, picked up my feet, and ran home.

We found Michael sitting on the doorstep when we returned. He was freshly showered and in clean clothes so I assumed he'd been home. Echo bounded at him joyously, leaping about like she was still a small puppy and he was the most exciting thing to ever happen in her life, like, *ever*.

"Hey," he said. Wrestling Echo to some kind of calmness, he stood. "You're out early this morning."

"Couldn't sleep," I said simply. "How's Becca?"

He shook his head. "No change. But Lexi fell asleep about

three-ish and was still sleeping when I left, so that's something. She said you'd come home; why didn't you wake me?"

I shrugged. "You needed the rest."

He nodded, stepping aside so I could open the door. We walked in, and I headed to the kitchen to put the kettle on. I stood there staring at it dumbly, waiting for it to boil, just leaning on the counter, staring down at it. Like my brain had stalled and just didn't want to go anymore.

"Aimee?"

"Hmm?"

"Are you okay?"

I glanced back at him. He was leaning on the counter behind me, cutting a far too handsome figure in Armani jeans and a plum-coloured Boss shirt.

"I'm fine," I said. He'd said at some point he preferred tea to coffee, yet he always seemed to drink coffee with me. Despite desperately craving a cup of java, when the kettle whistled, I made tea in silence. We sipped it as the quiet continued to stretch between us. It wasn't uncomfortable. And actually something of a relief.

"Can I walk you to work?" he asked when we were done.

"Sure," I said. "I just need to grab a quick shower. There's bread and cereal if you're hungry." I pointed at the pantry, which was still something of a marvel to me.

"Thanks." He opened the door and stuck his head inside. "Niiiice."

Mother had thought I'd taken leave of my senses when she saw the plans for the kitchen. "Far too indulgent," she said. "Amelia, this will cost a fortune."

But it was exactly how I wanted it. And I'd saved a ton ordering everything individually from various places online, and fitting it myself. (Okay, so it was mainly my dad doing that part, but still.)

If Michael's reaction was anything to go by, Mother would eat her words when she eventually bothered to come and see it finished.

I trotted upstairs, blasted myself with a very quick, very hot shower, then pulled on my go-to *I really can't be arsed to dress today* outfit, which consisted of wide-leg trousers in a lovely blush shade of pink and a cosy, oversized jumper that looked very much like it could be cashmere but was actually mohair.

Much as I loved my designer gear, sometimes you could not beat ASOS.

We walked to work, a silent, slightly sombre trio. Occasionally, either he or I would make a valiant effort at conversation, but every attempt seemed to peter out. I spent most of the walk trying to figure out if he'd appeared to keep up appearances, or if he'd actually wanted to spend time with me. We got all the way into town without me reaching any kind of conclusion.

That was only the start of a day of frustration. I was hit by a barrage of drama the second Michael left me at the office door.

Last night had been an unmitigated disaster. Despite Brennan's best efforts at damage control—and he had managed a great interview on the BBC that morning—social channels were flooded with clips of the carnage. The trolls were dragging Michael through more mud than he'd ever seen playing football.

The natives were also getting restless. Hillary had called three times to complain about the effect my personal life was having on her launch, and "*Why haven't I sold a million products yet?*"

It was all I could do to stop myself from telling her the truth; she had a thing that many other people sold. They sold it at a considerably lower price point. And the only reason she had a brand and a USP *at all* was because of all my hard work creating it for her which, by the way, was above and beyond.

Generally speaking, you tell a marketing company what makes you different, and they use that. At the very least, you give them some idea of a USP, and they refine it for you. They don't usually have to think of an entirely different approach to doing what you're doing just so you have a hope in hell of actually selling any of the damn things.

By the time Charlie called to say he had something, I was done. I said we'd come to him, and texted Michael that we needed to road trip into Manchester. He was back at my office before I'd finished making sure the sky wouldn't fall in my absence. Slinking in through the front door, he nodded hellos at several of the team, then leant against the wall watching me bob back and forth between workstations, looking at something for Abbey, giving Rosalie final sign-off on a presentation, and feeding back on a video Derek had been editing.

What he was thinking, I had no idea, but it was an odd feeling to be so scrutinised. Even if the look on his face did give me the distinct impression he was appreciating the view. The intensity of his gaze as it followed my every move sent an unexpected shiver down my spine. A tingling warmth that spread through me, hardening my nipples and making me even more grateful for the heavy knit of my jumper.

The last thing I needed was Michael figuring out that, despite all logic, reason, and the fact he was clearly a twat, I was still silently panting over him.

Finally, I managed to escape, and he whisked me away in the sleek, sporty body of his Lotus Evora. It was a far newer model than my own Elise, which, honestly, I couldn't afford, but I also couldn't resist when I saw it parked outside one of the local dealerships.

Given how little I'd actually driven it, I really shouldn't have bought it.

But I love it.

Sitting next to Michael in his own Lexus was a special kind of torment. The low rumble of the engine matched the thrumming pulse that had been growing between my legs since I'd caught him watching me with such intensity. It did absolutely nothing to dull my frustration. As we sped towards Manchester, the smooth acceleration and the way my legs slid across the leather seat beneath me almost had me liberating Michael's cock from those Armani jeans, bending my head to his crotch and sucking the length of him into my mouth until he moaned and shuddered beneath me.

Instead, I sat on my hands and watched the countryside roll by, each bend in the road unwinding the tight coil of tension between us. We didn't talk much; the radio filled in the gaps, a low murmur of a morning show that neither of us seemed to pay much attention to.

Charlie's residence was a large, detached house, nestled in a secluded lane on the outskirts of Didsbury, framed by mature trees and an overgrown garden that gave it a slightly neglected, yet characterful appearance. Its brickwork, weathered but solid, hinted at decades of standing guard over its inhabitants.

"Brace yourself for this, kid," Charlie said, as we settled around his kitchen table. "I've been digging into the troublemakers who turned up last night and had Trev, my tech guy, looking at where those wolf videos originated. You were right, it's a deliberate smear campaign."

I glanced at Michael, who frowned and sagged a bit as the weight of yet more shit landed on his beautifully muscled shoulders.

I really need to focus.
But it's so hard....

Yeah. That thought was super helpful. I shook my head to dispel images of Michael's naked body and what I could do to it if I had five minutes and even a semblance of privacy.

"It's your old bosses at PMS. They're behind it."

It took my brain a minute to process what Charlie had said. "It's...what?"

"Premier Media Solutions," Charlie said patiently. "Isla mentioning a connection with her father made me think. Once Trev knew what he was looking for, tracing the social posts back to them was fairly simple. They've been actively trying to tank your campaign."

"Premier Media Solutions?" Michael said, staring from me to Charlie and back again. "Is that a joke?"

We both looked at him.

"That can't be a real company."

I sighed. "It is. I used to work for them."

"Seriously?" Michael snorted a laugh. "PMS?" He thought about it more and choked out a laugh that quickly descended into slightly hysterical laughter.

We gave him a minute.

For some reason, it made sense for him to be so overwhelmed by the mundane stupidity of the name that he didn't even care about the implications of what Charlie had just said.

It was a fucking stupid name.

"Why are they doing this?" I asked, when Michael had finally calmed down. "I mean, sure, they're petty wankers, but this feels excessive. It's a public spectacle at this point. They're risking their own reputations. Ashfordby isn't that far from Manchester, but where clients are concerned, it's a completely different world. We're not competing for business, we're not even in the same spheres; that's why I moved back home and didn't stay in the city."

Charlie shook his head. "I thought exactly the same. It can't simply be petty malice, although that's likely part of it. But they're businessmen, right? There's no profit in this for them; in fact, there's a huge risk."

"So, what's their angle?" I asked. The question dangled in the air like the tail of a snake trying very hard to disguise itself as a harmless vine.

Something told me I wouldn't like what happened if I tugged on it.

Charlie laid out some papers on the tabletop. "Here's where it gets interesting. Remember the Clerk?"

I frowned. "Our friendly neighbourhood PI."

"The guy that barged into your office the other day?" Michael asked. He was already pissed he'd not been there to fend him off. Thinking about it, that was probably why he'd wanted to walk me to work.

Charlie nodded. "Isla told us who he works for, and I've been looking into them and what motive they might have to get involved with Hale. We knew Hale Senior is a CEO at one of Stanton's newspapers. However, it turns out he's also one of the company's main shareholders. I also didn't realise until last night just how many pies Stanton Media has its paws in."

"Let me guess..."

Charlie slid a piece of paper across the table at me. "Do you recognise any of these?" He stood, crossing the room and turning his attention to his teapot, which he set on the table with a well-appointed tray of milk, lemon, honey and sugar. He poured us each a steaming cup. "They're Stanton's shell companies."

I scanned the list. "You've got to be shitting me."

Charlie handed me a highlighter. I took it and turned three names on the list a garish orange.

"They're all PMS clients—"

Michael hiccupped another laugh.

"This one"—I tapped the second one down—"is the biggest account they had when I left. They were always paranoid about losing it."

"Why so?" Michael asked.

I shrugged. "It would fuck them. They don't have enough clients to stay afloat without them."

Michael frowned. "That doesn't seem very sustainable."

"It really isn't," I agreed. "But they never had much business sense. And they were painfully complacent. One massive client comes in and ensures they've covered all their outgoings and their big fat salaries; suddenly, they have no interest in the smaller accounts, the *insignificant* ones. So, they lose them, ignore new leads, and fail to sign potential new clients. Instead of having a range of clients on the books, large and small, so the loss of one - even a huge one - doesn't threaten them, they face the very real possibility of the business going under if that one big fish is lost." I shook my head, exasperated at the memories of having to deal with their nonsense. "There were several times I had to step in to stop them losing clients big enough to cause them major issues, but this one"—I tapped the list—"I can't see how they'd even stay in business if they lost that one." I shrugged. "Assuming, of course, they haven't signed a ton of new clients since I left."

Charlie nodded, stirring a smidge of honey into his cup of tea. "They haven't. And spot on. From what I can tell, they only have a handful of clients left now, other than these guys; they've been haemorrhaging clients since you left—" Charlie consulted his notes. "Clover Fields Organics, TechFront Solutions, BlueWave, Canton and Sons, Hopstars and Stripes, and Silver Ravine Media have all gone. And as far as I can tell, they've signed no new ones."

"*All?*" I'd suspected they'd lose a couple when I left, and I'd known about Hopstars (who I may or may not have stolen without stealing them), but *all* of them?

"How many of those were your accounts before you left?" Michael asked, genuinely curious.

I was silent for a moment, then reluctantly admitted, "All of them." I shook my head. "Canton was pretty new, as well. They've managed to piss him off in record time."

"A couple seem to have ended their contracts on a particularly sour note, too," Charlie added. "Both are suing for breach of contract and loss of income."

"No wonder they were happy to trash my campaign. None of them have the self-awareness to realise they're reaping what they sowed here; they'll be blaming me."

Charlie nodded. "Looks like they've lost a lot of staff too."

"That's not unusual. The staff turnover there was obscene."

"Huh—" Michael had been perusing the list on the table in front of us. "That's one of mine." He glanced up at Charlie. "I had no idea." He frowned. That clearly didn't sit well with him. "We handle their investments, we should be aware of this, unless—"

"Unless they're purposefully trying to hide assets," Charlie finished.

Michael nodded, scanning the rest of the list.

I tapped another name on the list. "These guys approached me about doing some work for them a couple of months ago; I turned them down."

Michael raised an eyebrow. "The ick?

I nodded. "Didn't like their vibe."

"Solid call," Michael said. "Clearly we need to pay closer attention to our vetting process." His eyes landed on another name on the list. "Fairleigh and Finch," he said, "that's the solicitor's on Duke Street in town." He ran a finger down the rest of the names. "Christ, Foster Connections is on here too." He looked up at me.

"That's Gemma's dad's company, isn't it? It's a consulting firm?" I asked.

Michael nodded and jabbed a finger at another name on the list. "This is where Simmo works," he said, then stabbed at another, "and that's partly owned by one of the big wigs on the local council. Jesus."

"And this is just Ashfordby," Charlie said. "Isla wasn't kidding. Stanton's got ties up and down the country, but a lot more in Cheshire and Manchester than anyone else. Hale really made a public spectacle of himself. I'm speculating, but I'd guess they had no choice but to ensure his release, partly because it's bad press if he's found guilty, but also because he likely knew a lot."

"And wouldn't be above spilling Stanton's secrets if it shaved a few years off his sentence."

Charlie nodded. "Exactly."

My mind raced, connecting dots. "You're saying my public campaign to exonerate Michael was a threat to Stanton Media, because it was drawing attention to the fact they sprung that piece of shit from jail? So, they leveraged their connection to my old bosses to hit back at me?"

Charlie nodded. "I suspect they could have tapped any number of marketing people, but they chose them specifically because of their connection to you. Isla's story about spending time at PMS checks out, too. So, if Rick Sandford went to Stanton after you left, demanding his help, and he'd sent Isla to work for you–"

"When my name came up in connection to Michael, he knew exactly who to go to. Someone who already had a grudge against me and would be happy to do it."

"Exactly," Charlie said. "And if anyone ever finds out, it looks like PMS is just trying to get back at you for the way you left."

"How did you leave?" Michael asked.

"Loudly."

He grinned.

"And given how they've been haemorrhaging clients since you left, losing a major one like this really could put an end to them permanently." Charlie shrugged. "They're desperate, Amelia. Rick and his cronies are just pawns used to protect a more significant set of interests."

The revelation sank in slowly. "So, if Isla's family are willing to go to such lengths... It's not just about discrediting the campaign. There's something else here, isn't there?"

Charlie leaned back, his chair creaking slightly. "I think so. They may not have even told Sandford the full story. It was probably framed as *'Shut down the woman defending the murderer of our CEO's son'*. Clean, simple, effective."

"And you think there's more to the death itself?" I probed, not ready to accept the surface narrative. "Did Stanton have this guy killed?"

"Maybe, but it doesn't quite add up," Charlie said, tapping his fingers on the table. "Why go through all the trouble to clear Hale's charges, only to have him killed? If they wanted him dead, there are far less noisy ways to handle it."

"If the family has as much clout as Isla believes, wouldn't it have been easier to arrange his untimely demise in his cell?"

Charlie nodded. "Or an accident immediately after he had been released on bail. It would have been far cheaper than cleaning up this mess, and far less risky. Stanton's business savvy. From a purely business perspective, once they sprang Hale from jail, he was an investment, killing him, wasted that investment, and did so pretty much immediately after they made it. What would be the point? What does his death achieve?"

"Maybe they didn't want to be associated with him, but he

knew too much about Stanton's shady dealings to just let him be?" Michael said.

"Possibly." Charlie sipped his tea. "He was an ongoing troublemaker, and it wasn't the first time they'd had to clean up his mess. Yet he wasn't one of their own, just the son of a major shareholder. Protecting Hale protected his father which protected the business."

"Maybe they got sick of it," I said. "Like you said, he was an investment. If that's the case they'd surely be keeping an eye on him? Maybe they were surveilling him to make sure he didn't get in any more trouble, saw Michael kick the crap out of him, took it as an opportunity to be rid of him, and killed him. They knew Michael would be the obvious suspect."

Charlie paused, teacup halfway to his mouth, then set it back down. "That actually all stacks up," he said. "They couldn't possibly have predicted you giving him an alibi; discrediting your campaign doesn't just paint Michael as the villain, it also calls your own credibility into question, ensuring the scapegoat they planned to take the fall still takes it."

"Maybe," I said. "Still, it seems extreme." I dumped some honey into my mug, stirred it and sipped.

"It all seems…overly complicated," Michael said. "Or am I being naïve?"

"No, you're right…something doesn't quite track," Charlie said. He sighed. "I'll keep digging." He paused, thinking. "You really might be onto something with that surveillance. And if there's footage, we may be able to find it."

I had no idea how he'd go about doing that, but something told me it was better not to ask. I sipped my tea.

"If I haven't said it yet," Michael said, "thank you, Charlie." Michael dropped his gaze to the tabletop, rubbing his eyes. "I'm not blameless in this, and it's very good of you to help given…well, the truth of things."

Charlie stared at him for a long while. He didn't speak. At length, Michael looked up. Once he held his gaze, Charlie simply said, "You fucked up. And maybe somewhere down the line, you'll have to pay your dues for that. But this"—he waved at the paperwork—"is bigger than you. And to be blunt, I'm helping Amelia." He glanced at me and smiled. "She's a soft heart. I don't want to see it ruined." He gave Michael a pointed look.

Michael swallowed. Somehow, despite it being far less blatant, Charlie's words seemed like more of a threat than the actual—albeit good-humoured—threat my brother had made.

"By the way"—Charlie held Michael's gaze a moment longer, then looked at me—"Isla was telling the truth as far as I can tell; she's estranged from her family and has been for some time. There's nothing to suggest she's anything other than what she seems, and quite a bit to indicate she's been actively gathering information to use against her family."

"Yeah, well," I sighed, "I'm still pissed at her for lying to me."

"What did she really lie about?" Charlie asked. "She didn't tell you everything, she kept her personal life private until it actually affected you, at which point she came clean." He drained the last of his tea.

"She *was* trying to speak to you about something important," Michael chimed in. "For days, you said?"

"Sounds like she was already planning on telling you, even *before* it was impacting you directly." Charlie fixed me with one of those judgmental stares only a parent can muster.

I didn't answer, just finished my tea in silence. We left shortly after. I gave Charlie a quick hug on the way out, and we slid back into Michael's Lexus. I leant back into the seat, my head lolling to the side as I stared out of the window. Slowly, I felt my eyes closing, my mind drifting.

Sleep, finally, please...

"I have to say, I'm impressed," Michael said.

"Charlie's an impressive guy," I mumbled through a yawn.

"Not Charlie," he said. "I meant you. Your instant grasp of a complex situation, the way you navigated your way through it and thought of things even Charlie hadn't."

My eyes snapped fully open. I turned to look at him.

"And not just here, at the office too, you're

very...impressive." He smiled at me.

"So, what?" I said, unable to keep the derisive tone from my voice. "Because I'm a woman, it's somehow *impressive* that I understand how business works? Would you have said that to a man?"

"I... Well, no," he admitted. "I guess I wouldn't have."

I snorted and resumed my staring out of the window.

"I'd still be impressed," he clarified, "but wouldn't have felt the need to say anything about it." He paused, and I thought maybe he was done, but no, he just kept on digging. "It's odd isn't it, how we say things differently when speaking to women."

"I'm not sure what made you think I need flattering, Michael Bane." I closed my eyes again, thoroughly done with this day. "But that's not me."

"Christ! Can I say anything that doesn't piss you off?"

I huffed, sat up, and turned to look at him again, all thoughts of sleep abandoning me. He was right, I was pissed. But I wasn't quite sure why, not really. I took a deep breath. "I'm sorry," I said. "Think I was doing some hardcore projecting there. Talking about PMS brought up a lot of old resentment."

I waited for him to laugh, to make the obvious joke.

He didn't.

I sighed, folded my arms over my chest and hugged my fluffy jumper.

The drive back was going to be *fun*.

CHAPTER 14

"What did you forget?" I opened the door, expecting to see Michael standing there. He'd dropped me off about twenty minutes ago before heading back to the hospital.

"Amelia Thornbridge?" A tall police officer with clipped, russet hair greeted me with a raised, questioning eyebrow.

Behind him, a second, almost equally tall officer stood, head tilted to one side, blonde ponytail swishing in the breeze as she openly surveyed my house. She glanced at my empty ring finger and pursed her lips.

An odd buzzing sound filled my ears, like distant bees. It swelled, growing louder as the pitch sharpened. Before me, the police officer had been talking, probably offering introductions. I'd missed it completely.

Focus.

"We have a warrant under the Police and Criminal Evidence Act to search these premises for specific items related to an ongoing investigation. May we come in?"

I snatched the proffered piece of paper from the cop's grasp and scanned it. "His clothes?"

"Yes, ma'am. When questioned, he indicated they were here?"

"Questioned?" I stared at the man like an imbecile. "He just left, when have you questioned him?"

"My understanding is he's currently being questioned, ma'am, and when asked about his whereabouts that night, Mr Bane stated he was here. When asked about his clothes, he indicated they were also here."

I frowned, then stepped aside, waving them in.

Echo issued a low, barely audible rumble, and I petted her head to soothe her. "It's okay. They're the good guys," I murmured.

She eyed me sceptically, clearly unconvinced.

For a second, I found myself wondering why, if they truly were the good guys, I was about to lie my arse off.

And does that make Michael the bad guy?

The thought stopped me short, though not because I was shocked by the revelation but more because I found I genuinely didn't care.

It's Michael Bane.

I'll die on this hill if I have to.

Yeah... I probably needed therapy or something for that thought.

"What is it you're looking for?" I asked. "I'm fairly sure he took his clothes home." I paused, as if trying to remember. Even managed to glance up and to the left while I did it, instead of the right, the former supposedly being a subconscious indicator you're trying to recall something, the latter that you're lying through your stupid fucking teeth.

For all I knew, this was utter bullshit, but any port in a storm, right?

"They went to the dry cleaner the morning after the ball," I said, turning to walk into the utility room, both officers following in my wake. "They'd have come back the following day..." I flicked the light switch on and opened the cupboard, pulling out the rail and flipping through the hangers, pausing when I reached Michael's shirt. "Oh, no," I said, genuinely surprised they were still hanging there; I really had thought Michael would have taken them. "With everything going on, he must have forgotten." I pulled out several hangers and handed them over. "I'm not sure how much good they'll do you after the dry clean."

"Is it normal for you to immediately dry clean your clothes?" the female officer asked.

I shrugged. "I'm picky about my clothes. Unless it's underwear, PJs or workout gear, it all goes to the dry cleaners. I have a standing appointment every Wednesday and Saturday morning. Judy—that's the owner—or one of her daughters drops in to collect stuff and drop off what was collected the last time." I shrugged. "The ball was on a Friday. Saturday morning was a regular pick up. I just put his clothes in with my dress."

The woman raised an eyebrow, although whether it was at the revelation that I had all my clothes dry cleaned, or the fact I'd added the clothes of a guy I'd been on two dates with to the pick up, I didn't know.

Either way, I could feel her judging me, and it made me super uncomfortable. She glanced around my well-appointed utility room, and I bit down an urge to explain that, actually, I had a very limited wardrobe these days, opting for a few outfits that I really loved rather than a ton of cheaper stuff. To explain that, until very recently, I hadn't owned my own home. That I'd lived in a small, kinda shitty flat for years after uni. Then I'd had to sofa surf with Suzie for over a year while I'd started building up Kobayashi Maru, saved for a deposit, and had enough paperwork to prove to a bank that, yes, I really *do* have a salary this high and, yes, I really *do* make enough from the business to pay myself a hefty bonus and, yes, *of course,* I'll put down an astronomically high cash deposit to offset your risk.

To the point the actual mortgage I'd taken out was probably the same as I'd have needed for one of the two up, two down newbuilds in town.

"You don't owe her an explanation." I heard Suzie saying in my head. *"Nobody's fucking business."*

How many times had she said that after I'd blurted a

garbled excuse to someone or other about why I'd quit my job, why I'd left my seemingly perfect boyfriend, why I was essentially homeless and freeloading off my friend.

I hadn't been freeloading in the slightest; I'd paid my way while I'd stayed. Honesty, I think it'd helped Suzie as much to have someone there encouraging her, holding her accountable. Helping her figure out how to turn all her fabulous crazy enthusiasm for our fair green earth into something she could actually do full-time and earn a living from.

But that time had left me with a chip on my shoulder the size of Texas. I was aware it was there, my own sense of inadequacy. I was also aware it wasn't just about the fact everyone spent a couple of years convinced I was a complete fuck up, because they couldn't understand what I was doing.

No, it went right back to childhood and the many, many times I wasn't good enough then, either.

But none of that was relevant to the question of my drycleaning habits, and I'd be damned if I excused my existence to a complete stranger.

Said stranger was surveying the clothes in her hands. "There should also be a coat. Did that not go to the cleaners?"

Again, I looked up, left, wondered if I was actually just being really blatant in my attempt to appear nonchalant and struggled to remember how to speak.

"No..." I crossed the room to the coat rack, rummaged past a parka I wore when I walked Echo, the coat I'd been wearing earlier, and pulled out Michael's. "It didn't need it."

I handed it over, and they both looked at it.

Just for a second, I could see the cogs turning. As if they'd had a narrative constructed in their heads already that said I'd sent everything to the cleaners to destroy the evidence. Because I was an imbecile who didn't realise that wouldn't work.

But here was the coat he'd been wearing, which surely would have borne the brunt of any bloody incident, and I hadn't even bothered sending it.

They weren't to know it wasn't the same coat.

And they'd never find out either; I made a mental note to do something to thank Abbey for all the times she's babbled on about the dark web. I'd get her yet another Yunzii keyboard to add to the collection of kawaii cuteness that overran her whole workspace. Something with a cat. Hopefully, she'd never know I'd put all that info to use buying a replacement, ridiculously expensive designer coat so that nobody missed the one that was languishing in the bottom of my burn bin as literal ashes. To make sure there was nothing to trace the sale back to me.

Gotta love Bitcoin.

Was it bad that I was slightly impressed with myself that I'd actually managed to access the Tor browser and use a VPN?

It's not like I planned to do it regularly; it was an extreme situation.

"Shoes?" The blonde asked.

Shoes. Right.

Maybe you should focus on not getting arrested.

I looked through the shoe rack. "I don't see them—" I knew perfectly well where they were. "He must have worn them home."

The police officer consulted her notebook. "He indicated he left everything here, shoes included."

I frowned, and looked through the shoes again. Then went out into the hall and checked by the front door, under the stairs, the usual places one might put shoes. I paused, thinking. "We were in the garden," I said, as if I'd just remembered, moving back through the utility room to the back door and swung it open. Echo promptly bolted out through it and bounded joyously across the lawn.

Sure enough, there were his shoes, sat by the back step in the full glare of the sun, right where I'd left them. Honestly, I'd been hoping nobody would ever ask, and I could just quietly dispose of them at some future point when a reasonable amount of time had passed.

I reached for them but was stopped by a swift, "Please, let me."

Stepping aside, I watched the woman produce an evidence bag and hold it open as her partner retrieved the shoes and dropped them in it. He scrunched his nose at them. "Look a bit worse for wear."

I shrugged. "He was a bit worse for wear. The hospital was—" my voice genuinely caught at the memory, "—rough."

Not that he wore them to the hospital. But if you've even half a heart...

The blonde's face softened, her brow crinkling and her voice sounding considerably less pointed as she said, "I would imagine. Do you know Rebecca well?"

More than half a heart, then. Good for you,

I shook my head. "I hadn't even met her before....I knew her sister a little when we were kids, but there was a decent age gap, so..." I shrugged again.

The blonde nodded. "I think that's everything. We'll let you know if we need anything more."

And they left. Michael's clothes folded neatly in an evidence bag over the arm of one officer, bagged shoes clutched securely in the hands of the other.

I watched Echo play until they cleared the end of the drive and disappeared from view. Then I went back inside and threw up.

If they figured out what I'd done, we were both utterly fucked.

CHAPTER 15

The following day dawned to a drizzling rain that left me staring out of the window and seriously contemplating skipping my run. But, that way lay madness, and I was already teetering on the brink. So, I gamely donned my running gear and cajoled Echo into coming with me, despite the fact she wanted to go about as much as I did.

I'd braced myself for Michael to be sitting on the steps again when I returned, but he was conspicuously absent.

Disappointment crushed me.

Stupid, stupid girl.

I'd got a brief text message from him last night to explain he'd been 'invited' to answer some questions the second he'd got to the hospital. They'd taken him into a small room that he took to be the security office and had done it right there. No formality, no recording, just a chat asking him to confirm his alibi and provide the clothing he'd worn.

He'd said nothing beyond a clinical explanation of what had happened.

I told him they'd been, collected his clothes. I asked if he was okay.

He said yes, tired.

We said goodnight.

And I hadn't heard from him since.

Even now, the brevity of those messages nauseated me. No matter how many times I reassured myself he was just taking precautions in case anyone read his texts. I spent far too long in a ridiculously hot shower, struggling to get the worry from my mind, the morning chill from my bones, and yet again quashing the deluded notion there could ever be anything between us.

Shivering, I stropped about the house getting changed, then drank an angry cup of coffee while drumming my fingers on the island in my kitchen and willing my phone to ring.

Finally, I gave up and went to work.

I'd been in there all of five minutes when the door swung open, and Michael fucking Bane sauntered in, carrying two trays laden with Costa Coffee cups. Brennan darted over to relieve him of one before he spilt them.

"I wasn't sure what everyone liked," he said. "So I got a random mix." He offered an exhausted smile, and everyone flocked to see what he'd brought and stake their claim. He snatched one up before anyone could get to it. I assumed it was his own until he handed it over to me.

I took a slow slip and confirmed; cinnamon latte.

I glared at him.

"I know," he said. "I'm sorry I didn't call last night. The last few days were...a lot."

"Thanks for the coffee."

"Yeah, thanks!" Brennan echoed.

"I'll take whatever this is," Isla said, snagging the closest. She eyed mine, a wry smile on her face. "Is that cinnamon?" She smirked, knowing full well it was my favourite.

"Quiet, you," I said.

"Oooo a cortado," Daiyu purred, "that's mine!"

"Is there anything with caramel?" Melanie asked.

Michael peered at the cups, selected one and handed it over.

"Epic!" she grinned. "I'll save the cappuccino for Tim."

"What's this?" Derek picked a cup up and sniffed

tentatively.

"Erm"—Michael examined it—"mocha?"

Derek made a noise of low-key approval and took it.

"I'll take an Americano if there is one," Abbey said.

"With or without milk?" Michael asked.

"Cow juice me," she replied, and he handed one over. "Ta!"

The door went behind me, and I turned, expecting to see Rosalie. Instead, two police officers walked in, their expressions sombre. The taller of the two, a sandy-haired man in a neatly pressed uniform, glanced around the room before fixing his gaze on Michael.

"Michael Bane?" he asked, his voice formal and stiff.

"Yes?" Michael responded, stepping forward, the coffee abandoned on Isla's reception desk in the centre of the room.

"I'm Sergeant Harris, and this is PC Jenkins—" the officer introduced himself and his partner, the same blonde woman who'd visited me yesterday.

Her observant eyes missed nothing of the office's layout and the people in it.

"We need to speak with you in private, if that's possible," Sergeant Harris said.

"What's happened?" Michael stepped forward. "Is Becca—"

The sergeant's face softened. "No," he said quickly, "as far as I know, her condition is unchanged."

I turned to Michael, and he reached an arm out to me. I stepped into it without thinking, and he leant on me harder than I'd expected. I stood up straighter to take more of his weight.

"Whatever it is, just get it over with," he said. And something in his voice told me if this was it, if they were here to arrest him, it would almost be a relief.

I kinda knew how he felt. But then again, the thought of them taking him away made my throat close up painfully.

"Are you sure? It's—"

"I'm sure, please." He gestured for them to come further

in.

"This is regarding an ongoing investigation," Sergeant Harris continued. "Your cooperation is important." They crossed the room to us. "Can I ask where you were yesterday between six and eight pm?"

I blinked, glancing up at Michael in confusion. He frowned and looked down at me, equally perplexed. "Ah...I guess I was with you?"

I thought about it. "I think so," I said. Though I knew full well, he'd dropped me off at home just before seven. But I had no idea where this was going. If he needed another alibi...

"No, wait, I got to the hospital just as regular visiting hours were starting. That would have been around seven. So...six we'd have been driving back from Manchester?" He glanced at me, and the relief as I realised I could just tell the truth was palpable.

"Yes, that's right, wait—" I checked my phone. "I called a friend right after he dropped me off so I can tell you...six fifty-two," I said.

"You say you were driving. Where had you been?" Harris asked.

"We went into Manchester to see a...friend," Michael said.

"And you say you went to the hospital?" he pressed.

"To visit my niece. Your own officers can confirm that—they questioned me there."

The sergeant nodded as the PC continued to note everything down.

"Great, thanks." Harris moved as if he was going to just leave without explaining the point of this little conversation.

"What's this about?" I asked.

He adjusted his belt slightly, avoiding my gaze as he spoke. "I'm afraid there was another murder last night."

"Another..." Michael never finished the sentence. Though whether it was from shock or awe I wasn't sure. I knew what he was thinking. I was thinking the same; he quite definitely hadn't done this one.

If someone related to Hale was dead, surely that put Michael in the clear?

"Who?" I asked.

"A private detective," the blonde said, "he'd been investigating the death of Eric Hale."

Michael caught me as I sagged forward. "Charlie," I whispered.

"Oh god," Michael said. "We were just with him, that's who we went to see—" he kept talking, and one of the officers answered, but I couldn't hear a word. My head had filled with a loud ringing. I shivered violently, and Michael's arms pulled me closer to him, holding me up. He spoke to me, I didn't hear.

Isla appeared in front of me, bending down and saying something. I didn't hear her either. My throat closed completely; I couldn't breathe.

Charlie.

No, no, no, no, no. This is all my fault.

Isla grabbed me by the shoulders and shook me slightly. Her lips formed my name, but I still couldn't hear her. Frowning, she said something else, stepped aside and pointed behind her, forcibly turning me around to look. Vaguely, I saw the door opening and Charlie walking in, but it was too much to take in.

Charlie.

Tears fell hot down my face. Still, I couldn't breathe.

Wait, Charlie?

I blinked, clearing the tears from my eyes. And I saw Charlie, walking towards me, large as life.

I flung myself at him. He stumbled, taken aback by the sudden presence of me in his arms, but caught himself (and me), clearing his throat uncomfortably.

"Charlie?" I choked out.

"Yeah, kid," he said, and I finally sucked in a breath, clinging to him for a second. He let me, holding me for a moment. "The fuck is going on?" he finally demanded, setting me back on my feet and taking a slightly awkward step back.

He kept hold of my shoulders, though, keeping me steady.

"She thought it was you," Michael's voice said behind me. "They said a private detective was killed and—"

"Christ." Charlie's face went white. "Easy, Aimee. I'm fine. It's okay."

I gasped another breath. "I thought..." I shook my head.

Charlie turned on the police officers. "What the hell did you say to her?"

"Nothing, I..." Harris stuttered, sucked in a breath, and remembered he was a professional. "We were ascertaining Mr Bale's alibi as part of the ongoing Hale investigation."

"And you just nonchalantly mention that a private dick was murdered without specifying a name? Did it not occur to you that someone in this room might know the victim? Or, perhaps," he snarled, "know someone else who was a PI? Who the fuck trained you?"

"Easy, Charlie," Michael said, "it was a misunderstanding."

"If it wasn't Charlie," Isla said, "who died?"

Charlie looked at her, closed his eyes for a second as he realised just how badly they'd screwed this up, and took hold of her arm gently. "It was the Clerk—"

Isla gasped.

"—I'm sorry, Isla."

"Wait, *she* knows the *actual* vic?" the blonde asked. I'd forgotten her name.

Charlie muttered something about gods saving him from the incompetence of the young. "There's a reason I asked you to wait for me," he snapped.

"You're no longer on the force, *sir*," Sergeant Harris said firmly. "You have no reason to be here at all."

My breathing had finally levelled out, and my head had stopped spinning.

"*You* have no reason to be here at all," Charlie said pointedly. I wasn't quite sure that was right, but clearly, Charlie was done with whatever shit was going on with the local police, and he'd decided to vent on this poor soul.

"We needed to ascertain Mr Bane's whereabouts at the

time of the—"

"And now you have," Charlie said flatly, ushering them quite firmly towards the door. "You can leave. If you need more information, send someone with a little more competence."

"But—"

"Not interested, sergeant," Charlie said. "Come back with a DI or a warrant, or don't come back at all." He pretty much shoved them out of the door and closed it behind them.

I shivered, wrapping my arms around myself. When Charlie turned back to the room, he caught sight of me, then Isla, who had started crying. I shook my head and nodded in her direction.

He crossed the room back to where Brennan was guiding Isla into a chair.

"Easy," he said gently. "I know you didn't like the guy, but it's a shock. Give yourself a moment. You're going to feel it; that's okay."

Isla gasped. "He was an ass," she spat. "But what does this *mean*?" She looked up at Charlie, eyes like saucers; they were huge and drowning in unshed tears.

Charlie didn't answer. Michael was by my side again, taking my arm. "Are you okay?"

I nodded.

"She's not okay!" Isla hiccupped. "She's not slept or eaten in days, and she's stressed out of her wits. And you ask if she's okay?" Isla glared at him. "I've changed my mind about you. I'm no longer team Bane; you can fuck right off."

I laughed.

Couldn't help it; the laugh bubbled up my throat and escaped my mouth before I could stop it.

Michael just stared at her, dumbfounded.

"Dude," Abbey whispered. "Don't dis the guy who brings coffee."

Isla sniffed. Brennan handed her cup back to her, and she took a sip. "Okay," she said reluctantly. "The coffee is good. But you're on thin ice, Bane. Watch it."

Charlie laughed that time.

When Michael looked at him, shocked, Charlie shrugged and said, "You're not the only one who had a tough week." He glanced pointedly at me. "Let's go to your office, shall we?"

I nodded and led the way. Echo had been sleeping on my sofa throughout the ordeal.

Good thing I didn't get her to be a guard dog.

Echo lifted her head when I walked in and sat gratefully beside her. She cuddled into me, and my arms wrapped around her big neck and hugged her to me. Michael followed, holding the door open for Isla, who sat beside me on the sofa and petted Echo absently. Charlie brought up the rear and let the door swing shut behind him.

"My father did this," Isla said.

"We don't know that," Charlie replied softly.

"Who else could have? Or would have?" she demanded. "It must have been him."

Charlie shook his head. "It makes very little sense for your father to have his fixer killed. Far more likely, whoever is responsible for Hale's death killed Clerk because he was getting too close to the truth."

"Are the deaths similar?" Michael asked.

Charlie hesitated. "Both were stabbed, and stabbed in the same manner. They're waiting on confirmation it was the same knife, but it appears to have been. Hale, however, was severely beaten." He paused. "The Clerk was not. So it appears they don't have quite the same MO. If it turns out the knife wasn't the same, they're likely to pursue them as separate but related rather than the work of a single killer."

He let that sink in. The police being unaware of what Michael had done was screwing up their investigation.

We talked some more, but reached little in the way of a conclusion. I sent Isla home for the rest of the day. Charlie went with her; he wanted to install some security cameras to make sure she was safe. I just sat. I couldn't move from the sofa. I was so tired.

It was just me and Michael and Echo in the office, and he was prattling on about something but I wasn't even listening.

I was so done.

"Michael," I said, and something in my voice stopped him short. "Can you take me home, please?"

He frowned. "Of course."

I stood without another word and walked out, snapping my fingers for Echo to follow. She dutifully trotted at my heels. I didn't even bother speaking to anyone on the way out, just made a beeline for the front door, turned down the alley beside the building and found Michael's car parked up in my space. I rarely used it, home being so close, but for some reason, it irked me he'd chosen that spot and not another. There were several free.

The car beeped as Michael unlocked it, opened the passenger door, folded the seat forward and patted the back of it. "Come on, girl," he said to Echo.

She glanced at the cramped backseat sceptically but, with a little more encouragement, hopped in and settled down with a whining yawn. He clicked the seat back into place, and I slid into it.

We drove back to the house in silence. When I reached the front door, I hesitated. Honestly, I just wanted to walk in and shut it behind me. But that would be rude. Sighing, I found my keys, unlocked the door and shoved it open, stepping inside and leaning on the wall while I kicked my shoes off, abandoning them where they fell and padding through to the kitchen.

Michael followed me in and shut the door behind us.

So much for taking the hint.

I was so tired.

"Aimee?"

I ignored him.

"Amelia?!" Michael's tone sharpened. "Why are you ignoring me?"

"I'm tired," I mumbled.

Silence.

The glass cupboard seemed unreasonably far away. But it was closer than the kettle, so I guessed it would do. Opening the cupboard, I reached and picked up a glass, shivering. The glass slipped from my hand and smashed on the floor.

I stood there, staring down at the broken shards dumbly. Echo padded in and started sniffing around it.

Michael's footsteps ran down the hall. "No, girl, come here!" he called Echo away.

She obediently turned and wandered over to him.

"Stay," he said. "Aimee? What are you doing?"

"It fell," I said lamely.

He sighed in exasperation and started shuffling about the room. I bent down and started picking up shards of glass.

"Wait, you'll—"

A sharp shard bit through my palm, and I whimpered, dropping it back to the floor.

"—cut yourself." He made a disgusted noise and grabbed me around the waist, physically lifting me off the floor and sitting me on the breakfast island in the middle of the room. "Stay," he said. Exactly as he had to Echo a moment before, half teasing but clearly annoyed.

I sat there, staring at him dumbly, belatedly realising he'd found a dustpan and brush from somewhere and had been coming over to clean up before I'd decided fingers had been invented well before anything else and would do just fine.

When he was done sweeping up the debris, he cast about the room until he found the bin and deposited everything in it. Turning back to me, he made a face and snatched up a tea towel, grabbing my wrist and yanking it out to wrap the towel around my palm. Blood seeped into it. I watched the pattern of it expand, fascinated.

"What's going on with you?" he demanded, pulling the towel away and inspecting the cut. It seemed pretty determined to continue bleeding. "Do you have a first-aid kit?"

I didn't answer; my head was swimming.

"Amelia?" he snapped.

When I still didn't answer, he growled something unintelligible under his breath and started banging about the room. Echo came over, stood up on her hind legs, sniffed my palm tentatively and whined.

"Yes, girl," Michael said, "Mummy's an idiot."

Echo snorted and cast him a sidelong look that clearly said, "You're *the idiot.*" Jumping down, she trotted out of the room, and I heard her thwacking a cupboard door in the utility room.

To his credit, Michael did not ignore her; instead, he went to investigate and came back with the first aid kit. The same kit I'd used on him the night he'd turned up here bloody and confused and frightened.

God, was that really only a week ago?

He cleaned my hand, frowned over my plasters and finally cut some little strips to fake stitch it together, then bandaged it.

"Aimee?" he said softly. "Are you okay?"

I just stared at my hand.

Michael's palm touched my cheek. It was wonderfully cool, but he snatched it away, and I almost whimpered. It returned, this time on my forehead. "You have a fever!" he exclaimed.

I pulled away from him. "I'm fine."

"No, you're not. You're burning up." He drew back, assessing me, frowned, and looked at me closer. "When did you last sleep?"

I shrugged.

"Eat?"

I considered, and realised I couldn't remember.

"Christ!" Without another word, he scooped me up and carried me from the room.

"Put me down," I said.

"Hush," he replied, irritated.

Like he was scolding a foolish child.

My jaw clicked shut. Suddenly, I didn't have the energy to argue with him. My head lolled against the solid muscles of his chest, and he paused. "Huh," he said. As if he hadn't expected that to work. He shifted me gently in his arms, holding me closer, tighter, and kept walking.

Echo followed us from the room. I glanced down to find her trotting at his heel, bouncing slightly on her back legs as she walked so she was high enough to sniff at me.

Her concern made me feel better. So did the thick solidity of Michael's arms around me. One looped around my back and waist, the other held me under the knees, my legs dangling over one of his arms. He walked us up the stairs, hesitating a moment on the landing, uncertain, then forged on into the bathroom. One foot kicked the toilet seat closed, and he sat me gingerly on it. My intention was to stand up and march right back out, but instead, I found myself slumping against the wall and staring at his arse as he lent into the shower, turned on the water, and spent a moment fiddling with it, testing the temperature. When he re-emerged, the sleeve of his shirt was damp.

He didn't appear to care.

Bending, he pulled down the zips of my ankle boots, jugged them off and placed them on the floor, before gently taking my hands and pulling me up. He unbuttoned my trousers and let them puddle at my feet, wrapping an arm around me, taking most of my weight, and guiding me to the shower. Lifting my jumper up he slid it over my head.

"Hey—" I reached feebly after the cosy wool. "Careful, that's my favourite."

Michael huffed a laugh.

I was about to make a crack about the lengths he'd go to just to see me naked, but when I looked up at his face, he'd carefully turned it away, averting his gaze.

He wasn't even looking at me.

My body convulsed in a ferocious shiver, and my legs abruptly gave way. I'd have landed flat on my butt, but Michael was still holding me, had taken my full weight without blinking, and lifted me into the shower. The water hit me. It was cool, so soothing, but not cold. He stepped in behind me, oblivious to the water spraying all over him, and held me to him as he smoothed water over my face, my hair. My eyes closed. I forced them back open, but they fluttered shut again. Vaguely, I was aware of him slathering me with a soaped-up washcloth, turning me and repeating. Strong hands gently washed my hair, fingertips massaging my scalp.

My sense of him faded, and when it returned I was perched on the edge of my bed, wrapped in a fluffy dressing gown as he deftly removed my soaking underwear, being careful not to touch anything but fabric.

It was either incredibly chivalrous or seriously insulting, I couldn't decide.

I managed to get my eyes open long enough to see him tugging a lacy negligee from a drawer, holding it up, blushing, and stuffing it back in. He resumed his search and came up with a pair of pyjamas. Winnie the Pooh stared at him with a wide, ponderous grin. Beside the yellow bear read the words, *Let's begin by taking a smallish nap, or two.*

"Cute," Michael said, under his breath.

I closed my eyes before he turned back and caught me watching, feeling the pjs slide up my legs. I looked at him again as he lifted me to my feet, pulled them up, and carefully unwrapped me from the dressing gown, struggling to tug the shirt onto me and button it up while stoically refusing to look at me properly. His fingers grazed my breast and he froze, a tiny gasp escaping his lips. When I didn't move, he finished the last buttons, flung back the duvet, and scooped me up one more time so he could lie me down. Pillows were rearranged about me until he was satisfied I was well supported.

"Here, girl," he said softly, patting the bed beside me. Echo's solid weight landed at my side.

She stretched out down the length of me, her chin resting on my shoulder.

"Good girl," he whispered, and tucked us both in before silently exiting the room.

I slept.

A cool, soothing pressure covered my forehead.

I slept.

Shivers wracked me, jolting me awake. Beside me, Echo lifted her head and whined. I tried to soothe her, but couldn't make words happen. My body felt like a dead weight, jerking randomly in fits and starts. A soft blanket was drawn up to my chin. A body slid into the bed behind me, pressing into my back, one arm wrapping round my stomach and pulling me back into him. The shivering stilled, slowly, gradually.

I slept.

When I finally woke, I was alone in bed. I sat up, gingerly. Michael had towel dried my hair and it had gone to frizzy curls. Soft light filtered in through drawn curtains, falling in my face. It was warm, and bright, and the reality of the last few days finally hit me.

Drawing my knees up to my chest, I hugged them and sobbed. Great, big, ugly, gasping sobs.

When I was done, I stuffed my feet into my slippers and padded downstairs in search of my dog. The scent of fresh bread made my stomach do an impressive impression of an angry badger.

I was abruptly ravenous.

A low, excited bark sounded from the kitchen as my feet hit the stairs. Echo barrelled into me as I reached the bottom. She bounced up on her hind legs and lifted her face to mine, one paw resting on each shoulder.

"Hey, lady." I hugged her to me, releasing her slowly and followed the scent of food.

Michael stood in my kitchen. He wore CDLP boxers and yesterday's shirt, rumpled, the sleeves pushed up to the elbows. He bent to the oven as I watched, opened the door and pulled out a baking tray I didn't know I owned. It was occupied by two plump loaves of crusty, golden bread. He set the tray on the counter, closed the oven then deftly switched it off. As if he used such contraptions daily.

"Hey," he said without turning. "Your fever broke a few hours ago. I'm glad you slept. How are you feeling?" He pulled a bread knife from somewhere, sliced off some thick wedges of bread, slathered them with butter, and sat them on a pair of plates, each with a bowl sat atop it. He reached for a pan on the stove and turned the heat back on to warm it up. Once satisfied the contents were suitably hot, he poured a thick and delicious-smelling soup into each bowl and picked up both plates. Turning, he finally looked at me and was startled, as if he hadn't quite expected me to be there.

Blonde hair flopped into his face, the usually well-tamed waves curling over his eyes. He waved the plates at me, almost sheepishly.

"I made soup," he said.

"And bread," I replied.

He shrugged. "Can't beat fresh bread."

My eyes danced over a flour-strewn work surface and a large bowl with remnants of dough in the bottom.

"You made that *from scratch?*"

As he moved to set the plates on the island in the centre of the room, I snooped at the loaves remaining on the baking tray. The tops had been scored with a complicated pattern that looked like vines.

"You bake," I said stupidly. "Bread?"

He looked up at me. "Something wrong with that?"

I blinked. "No, it's just…unexpected."

Michael smiled, and the light in the room went up a few watts.

"Please"—he gestured at a bowl—"eat."

I slid onto a bar stool and picked up a spoon, ladling a good helping of thick, orange soup, and taking a tentative mouthful. Flavour exploded on my tongue. Butternut squash, ginger and apple. I closed my eyes, savouring it, before devouring another spoonful. The bread was warm, buttery, and so good.

Michael watched me carefully, a small smile lifting his lips. We ate in companionable silence. When my bowl was empty, he refilled it without a word, adding more bread to my plate. At some point, he brought over a fat teapot on a tray and set a steaming cup in front of me.

I sipped. Hot. Strong. Slightly spicy. The perfect amount

of milk.

It was actually better than the coffee I'd been about to make myself.

"You've been holding out on me," I finally said between mouthfuls.

He raised an eyebrow, questioning.

"The man can cook."

He nodded. "Is that so rare?"

"Yes. Actually."

"And here I thought you abhorred sexism."

I chuckled and pointed at my oven. "That thing," I told him, "never been used. I don't bake. I can't cook anything more complicated than chilli. Where did you even *find* flour?"

"I got a few bits." He nodded towards some half-empty bags cluttering up a corner of my worktop. "They deliver anything right to your door these days."

I stared at him. "So why not have them deliver bread?"

He shrugged. "I like to bake, I like to cook. It gives me time to slow down, focus on something simple, clear my head. And at the end of it, you get a good meal." He shrugged. "My parents weren't ones for cooking. Or shopping. Or…parenting, come to think of it. Lexi's quite a bit younger than me, and she was always hungry."

Lexi's words from the other night floated through my head. She hadn't been exaggerating. He'd basically raised her. "You learned to cook for your sister."

He nodded. "Just me, I'd have made do with cereal. But she was a scraggly child, malnourished, always screaming crying with hunger. When she was a baby, it was because there was never enough formula, and Mum refused to breastfeed her from the start." He shrugged. "I never understood that. Free milk right there, and you insist on making her have stuff we can't afford to pay for. Later, when I was older, I got it." He took a mouthful of soup. "She didn't want Lex drinking all the shit she took." Another mouthful. "I found a book on baby food at the library; it had all sorts in there about what kids need, what they can eat, at what age. I learned pretty quick. Used to steal cash from Dad's wallet every chance I got, then I got a paper route. That made things easier." He paused. "Until he left." He bit a piece of bread and chewed thoughtfully.

I didn't say anything, just let him ponder the thought for a while and ate my own bread. It was delicious, still warm from the oven. I'd been so focused on my soup that I hadn't fully appreciated the bread until now. I chewed it slowly, savouring every bite. He'd added pecans for a little crunch. Hints of cinnamon and nutmeg gave it a deliciously subtle flavour, and the carefully cut vines on the top had been glazed with something sweet; honey or maple syrup, I couldn't tell which.

Suddenly, I was remembering home ec lessons, and how focused Michael had always been compared to the riot he tended to create in everything else. How the teacher had once lectured him for bringing the wrong ingredients to bake scones, only to have Michael inform her that it wasn't wrong, just different, *the egg was essential*. By the end of the lesson that teacher had been chomping on hot buttered scones and eating her words.

She always taught scones with his recipe after that.

It had never occurred to me that interest might be his own. I'd assumed his mother had given him the recipe. From the sounds of it, she wouldn't even have bought the ingredients.

Fuck.

Funny how your perspective on people can change in an instant.

The cuckoo clock in the hall called out the time, making me jump. "It's ten?" I said, startled. "In the morning?" I'd slept all damn day and all through the night.

"Yeah, guess you were really wiped." He looked up at me. "I should never have put all this on you."

"Not like you planned to."

"Not the point." He turned away from me, staring out of the window. "I didn't even notice you were…" He trailed off. "I'm an arse."

I shrugged. "Yeah. But you're one hell of a chef."

He turned back to me, a broad grin splitting his face. God, he was gorgeous. Whoever had sculpted that jawline deserved a fucking Turner. When he smiled, he went from attractive to uncomfortably sexy. Suddenly, I remembered him pulling my clothes off the night before, his hands in my hair, washing my skin. Heat rose in my face, and a tight, aching throb beat between my legs.

He was right there. Inches away. Sitting in my kitchen of all things.

Michael Bane.

I was staring at him like a total dope. I cleared my throat, stood, and picked up the plates, moving to load them into the dishwasher. For a split second, I could swear disappointment flashed across that beautiful face. It was gone in an instant, but it deepened the ache inside me.

I wanted him.

So badly.

It almost hurt.

I wanted to go to him, wrap my arms around his neck, tangle my fingers through his hair. I wanted him to lift me right off my feet, set me on the counter and kiss me like he had after dinner the other night. I wanted his fingers unbuttoning me, stroking my breasts, stroking lower. I wanted his mouth on the hot, throbbing nub of my clit, to feel his tongue circle it and taste me and lick that throb to a blissful explosion. To thrust his fingers deep inside me and feel how wet I was for him, how much I wanted him.

The plates rattled onto the countertop, and I took a slightly unsteady breath.

Whatever I might want, I would not humiliate myself yet again by trying to have a man who was clearly not meant for me. I'd spent years in high school lusting after him, imagining in excruciating detail exactly what we'd do to each other when he finally realised I was the one for him.

He was the first boy I'd ever masturbated to, the first guy I'd ever had imaginary sex with, the only one I'd ever wanted to ask me to the dance, walk me home from school, go to the cinema with at weekends, make out with behind the old swimming pool building at the back of the school.

But he'd never done any of that. And not for lack of trying on my part. I wasn't subtle in my youth. I was vocal and crass in my obsession with him, and he was vicious and relentless in his rejection of me.

Yet none of it compared to the crushing sting of the look on his face when Gemma had told him who I was. When he'd realised what I was. The silence on that drive back home. The total shutdown of everything we'd been doing, everything we'd been feeling. The crushing realisation that I wasn't in the midst of some homecoming romance where the boy sees the girl all grown up and realises she was perfect for him the entire time; he was just too dumb to see it.

He hadn't known who I was. I'd just been a stranger in the park, good for a quick fuck. Maybe he'd toyed with the idea of letting me become more. But that was when he'd thought I was somebody else. Not the geeky nerd from school. Not the pariah, the embarrassment, the chubby, ugly, freak.

Specky-four-eyed weirdo.

I took a deep breath and let it out slowly. I might have outgrown the need for glasses (my dad realised how much it bothered me when the bullying started in Primary school and paid for private care throughout high school to correct my eyesight), but I'd never forgotten how sharply that barb stung.

"So," I said. "What have you been doing all this time while I was sleeping?" I glanced about. "Aside from making a mess in my kitchen?"

He didn't answer for a moment, and I looked back at him. He was watching me from the island, the smile gone from his face, something slightly sad, and cold replacing it.

"Browsing your library," he said. His voice had gone flat. "Do you know you don't have any cookbooks?"

I nodded. "Sounds about right."

"An alarming number of *Star Trek* novels, though. And *Buffy the Vampire Slayer*. I didn't even know there *were* novels for these things."

Here we go. Mock away.

"Also, cowboy romances? What's that about?"

"Cowboys, surprisingly."

He snorted a laugh. "I meant, why the hell do you read that kind of trash?"

I bristled. I mean, sure, they were unmitigated trash. That's why I liked them. But I didn't want him to think that.

"Escapology," I said.

Because letting on I'm mortified you saw them would only compound the humiliation.

"A lot of Terry Pratchett, too," he said, seemingly oblivious to my mortification.

Whatever lingering heat I'd been feeling froze. *Do not insult Pratchett in front of me, Michael Bane. Some things I simply won't stand for.*

"Yours are way nicer than mine. I didn't know they did leather-bound ones. My paperbacks are falling apart. I've read them so much."

I blinked.

"Have you read the collab he did with Stephen Baxter?"

I blinked again. Harder. *I'm hallucinating.* "*The Long Earth*?"

"Yes! Great books. I've not read the last one yet, I got side tracked, but I love this whole multiverse thing. Such a cool concept."

I was definitely hallucinating.

"Someone told me there's a film out about something similar; I can never remember what it is, though."

"*Doctor Strange*?"

"Is that it? Superheros or something?"

"Marvel."

Michael nodded. "Is it any good?"

"I enjoyed it." *What the hell is happening?*

"Well, I loved *The Long Earth*. I never realised that counted as sci-fi when I first started reading it. Lexi got me into Pratchett. I was trying to find good girl role models to read to her when we were kids and ended up with Tiffany Aching. Then *Equal Rites*, of course. That was years ago now. We're both still obsessed. So sad when he passed away. There'll never be another writer like him." Michael shook his head, looking genuinely mournful. "I picked up *The Long Earth* just because it was him, no idea what I was getting into. But it turned out to be one of my favourites."

He fell silent. Looked at me. Smiled, in a kind of hopeful, puppyish sort of way. When I didn't say anything, his face fell a little.

It reminded me of Echo when she charged at me with a ball, full of excitement and eager to play, only to have me pat her on the head and promise we'd play later when I was done working.

Was he actually serious?

An image played across my memory of him animatedly bouncing on the sofa, shouting at a Romulan on the TV the other day.

Could it be that the great Michael Bane was a closeted sci-fi guy?

Surely not?

"If you like the multiverse," I offered, "there are a few things we should watch."

The smile was back. Brighter. Dazzling.

He stood, trotted over to the bags on the counter and pulled out a selection of popcorn. "Toffee, salted, or sweet?"

I stared at him. The staring was becoming habitual. I really had to quit it and get a grip. He was just feeling shitty for all he'd put me through and trying to prove he wasn't a colossal dick.

Aaand I should not have thought the words *colossal dick* while looking at Michael Bane. It made me want things I couldn't have. Or rather, one specific thing. A rather large, specific thing.

"Toffee," I said. And padded out into the hall.

He followed with the popcorn and the tea tray.

"We'll start with *Yesterday's Enterprise,*" I said. More to have something to say that didn't end in me begging him to fuck me with his colossal dick. I didn't *actually* think he'd enjoy a

Star Trek marathon. "Although that's more alternate timeline than multiverse, but still, awesome episode," I told him, loading up *The Next Generation* on Netflix and flopping on the sofa. "We need *Parallels* for the multiverse." I was still thinking about things I shouldn't, like reaching up and grabbing a fistful of his shirt and dragging him down on top of me. But that would spill the tea. "And *Mirror, Mirror*, of course."

He sat next to me. Not on the opposite end of the sofa, but right next to me. After setting the tea tray down on the coffee table, he poured out some more and ripped open the bag of popcorn.

"That's *Star Trek*, right?"

I blinked. "Right."

The world's gone fucking mad.

CHAPTER 16

"So, this Wesley kid," Michael said, waving the popcorn bowl in my direction, "he just appeared out of nowhere *again*."

I took a handful of popcorn. "I told you, he used to be a regular member of the crew before he left for the academy. They brought him back whenever they had chance."

"So you say." Michael set the popcorn on the arm of the chair beside him and took a huge handful. "But maybe he's not. Maybe he's just like a"—he wafted his fist about, errant bits of kernels flying everywhere—"a nexus of weird shit."

I stared at him.

"You've shown me two episodes of this show," he said, "and in both, this kid just pops up out of nowhere when weird shit's going down." He shrugged, scratching Echo on the head as she hoovered up the fallen pieces of popcorn from the sofa. "Maybe that's not a coincidence." He hiked an eyebrow at me.

All thought had abandoned me completely by this point.

I had been willing to accept that Michael Bane might humour me and sit through a few hours of Trek as a one-off. A thank you. A gift to make up for the colossal shitstorm he'd driven straight through my life. But to realise that actually, upon viewing the show, he'd *liked it* and *wanted to watch more*.

That was all a bit much for me to bear.

And yet, here he was, gamely batting about theories on everyone's favourite insufferable Wunderkind Wesley, Wesley Crusher.

Who was, actually, one of my favourite characters and a huge childhood crush. Not that I'd ever admit it.

I still followed Wil Wheaton on Instagram.

"Also." Michael paused to chew and feed Echo some more popcorn. "*The Big Bang Theory* makes *so* much more sense now."

"You watch *Big Bang*?" My voice was a confounded whisper. At this rate, it was going to turn out he'd been a closet *Babylon 5* buff all these years and was actually a bigger geek than I was.

"I love *Big Bang*!" He chuckled, and the smile that split his face was like watching the aurora borealis spark across an arctic sky. The world around you might be a frozen wasteland, but you didn't care, because it was so fucking beautiful. "And *Young Sheldon*, me and Becca watch it every..." His voice trailed off.

His face fell.

He'd forgotten, just for a time, but it had all just come flooding back.

I couldn't stand the pain on his face. I wanted to see that smile again.

"You know, I think you're onto something with that Wesley theory," I said. "We'll have to watch *Journey's End* next. There's this whole thing about him being further along the evolutionary spectrum than the rest of us and capable of a load of weird shit."

"I knew it!" Michael gestured emphatically at the TV, dislodging Echo from his lap.

She whined, and he gave her a piece of popcorn by way of an apology.

"There's something dodgy about him."

"The dodgy part is more the time-travelling space alien

with an unhealthy fixation on a teenage boy, but yeah, Wesley's pretty dang weird."

"Time travelling...what?" He shook his head.

That's it. He's done. Back to normal now, and no more of this liking Star Trek *business.*

"Maybe we need to start at the beginning?" he said. "This is so much more complex than I ever realised."

I snorted. It was no use. I'd clearly fallen into a parallel universe myself, and this was mirror-Michael. Best to just go with it until he'd grown his moustache and everyone else realised.

"The Trek verse is one of the most detailed, well-rounded and extensive fandoms out there," I said. "It's predicted the future nearly as many times as *The Simpsons*. Even people who've never watched it understand Trek references; they're so ingrained in the collective consciousness."

He sat up. "What did it predict?"

"Well, mobile phones," I began, pointing at our own devices resting on the coffee table. "They're like the communicators in the original series. Then there's tablet computers—pretty much like the PADDs they used on the show."

He seemed genuinely surprised. "Really?"

"Yep," I continued, warming to the subject. "Automatic doors, which we totally take for granted now. Oh, and voice-activated computers—basically the precursor to Siri and Alexa."

Michael's eyebrows shot up. "That's...actually pretty cool."

"And don't get me started on virtual reality," I added. "The Holodeck might be the ultimate VR experience we're all still dreaming of, but VR headsets today are definitely a step in that direction. And then there's telepresence and video conferencing."

"I had no idea," he admitted, looking back at the screen with new respect. "*Star Trek* was really ahead of its time, huh?"

I laughed. "You could say that. It predicted AI and the complexity of the related ethics. There's an episode of DS9 that fully predicted the carnage that followed 9/11 and all the issues with civil liberties and security measures, how fear can be used to justify drastic actions and the erosion of freedoms. It aired years before the Twin Towers were hit, but it's eerie watching it back now. Then there's racial and gender equality, LGBTQ+ rights, refugee issues, the ethics of cloning and genetic engineering, environmental stewardship—"

"Okay, okay." Michael held both hands up, chuckling. "I get it! I'm sold! Can we find out if Worf asks Deanna out when he gets back to the right reality now?"

I snorted tea. "Sure."

"I'm right, aren't I?"

"We'll see."

"I mean, how can he not? She's gorgeous and clearly gets him, which can't be easy, what with him basically being a werewolf—"

There was a knock at the door, and I struggled to get up through my laughter to answer it. I was still chuckling as I padded down the hall and swung it open.

"Well"—Suzie crossed her arms and took a step back—"not the state I was expecting to find you in." She pushed past me and into the house. "Ah, baby girl!" Her arms opened expansively, and she braced herself for the full weight of echo barrelling into her chest. Suzie caught my hound in a bear hug, and half fell, half flopped to the floor, burying her face in Echo's ebony fur and planting kiss after kiss on her and making smooshy noises.

I shut the door.

"Were you being funny?" Suzie demanded of Echo. "Were you? Were you being a loon?"

I sighed, glancing up from the pile of my two best friends on the floor as Michael wandered out of the lounge. He frowned at the sight, or rather, at Suzie.

"I know you," he said, scrunching his face up, trying to place her.

Suzie's head snapped up at the sound of his voice. She was one of those people with features that radiate natural elegance.

Her face was framed by a cascade of voluminous, curly black hair, swept to one side above perfectly shaped eyebrows. Large, expressive eyes stared up from beneath the peak of one of her signature berets, and her full lips were subtly highlighted with a nude lipstick.

"Amelia," she said, "I don't mean to alarm you, but there's a *man* in your house."

"Yeah," I said. "Michael, you remember—"

"Don't tell me," he said. "I got this." He fixed Suzie with a penetrating stare, and I almost laughed again to see the blush that crept up her face, adding a rosy tint to her flawless cocoa skin.

She didn't like Michael, never had. But she'd also never disagreed; he was one of the best-looking blokes she'd ever clapped eyes on in real life.

Michael snapped his fingers. "Susan." He grinned broadly. "You were in our form, right?"

"Sure," Suzie said, her tone droll, "give the guy a medal. He remembered the only black girl in class."

Michael's face fell. "I'm sorry, I didn't mean to—"

"Easy, Suze," I said, "he was only trying to avoid a repeat of the whole 'didn't realise who I was' thing."

Michael rubbed the back of his neck and shifted his weight from one foot to the other, his eyes briefly meeting Suzie's before dropping to Echo, whose gaze was easier to hold.

"Come eat some popcorn," I said, "you'll feel better."

Suzie crinkled her nose in a decidedly Suze way. "Is it toffee?"

"Natch." I walked past them all and back into the lounge, settling myself on the sofa and patting the seat next to me.

Suzie wandered in, sat down, and took the offered popcorn. Her mouth opened to say something, but Michael walked back in. Catching sight of Worf pulling out Deanna's dining chair and ordering champagne from the replicator, Michael did a little leap, punching the air. "Yes, mate! Get in there!"

Suzie's mouth clicked shut. She watched, fascinated, as

Michael settled himself in the armchair and continued to stare at the TV, enraptured. The credits rolled on one episode, and he hurriedly jammed his finger into the remote to skip to the next.

"Ha, it's John Locke!" he said, pointing at the TV and addressing Echo as if she had watched *Lost* and had the faintest idea what he was talking about.

Suzie leant as far into me as she could and whispered, "What the fuck is happening?"

"Damned if I know," I said, "but he makes good soup."

She startled, turning to me and mouthing the words "*makes good soup*" as if they were a foreign language.

"Have you watched this?" he asked, looking at Suzie and pointing at the TV.

"I try not to." Suzie was looking from him to me and back, like it was Wimbledon and Paul Bettany had actually showed up to play.

"Oh, you should," he said, "bloody brilliant."

"Amelia." Suzie turned to look at me fully. "What kind of witchcraft have you pulled here?"

I shrugged.

"Come on?" She looked back at Michael. "You're seriously buying this?"

"What?" we both said in unison.

"You remember the time *he*"—she pointed at Michael—"humiliated you in front of the whole school when you turned up to the fancy-dress disco in a homemade Seven of Nine outfit. He pointed at you and shouted, 'Han Solo called; he wants his Millennium Falcon back'."

Cold rushed through me, and for a second, I thought I'd puke. I did remember. Vividly. It had taken me weeks to make that outfit. Seven's iconic skin-tight catsuit in shimmery silver fabric.

It had never occurred to me that such things only look good if you happen to have a figure like Jeri Ryan.

On an overweight kid who had yet to develop any kind of boobs, it was a train wreck. In hindsight, it was rather amazing nobody had commented before Michael had seen me. I'd caught a look or two walking in, but hadn't thought much of it. Everyone looked weird; it was fancy dress. And then I'd seen Michael, standing on the dance floor, exuding effortless cool in a white t-shirt and black leather jacket, his hair slicked back in a perfect imitation of the Danny Zuko quaff.

I wasn't thinking about what anyone else thought of me. I wasn't thinking about anything but how fit he looked.

And then he looked at me, and spoke, and said…that.

I might have been fat, but I managed to run out of there faster than the fricking Flash. I'd cried all the way home, tearing strips off my stupid costume as I went. By the time I made it back, I looked like I'd had an unfortunate encounter with Wolverine. And I didn't go back to school for a week after.

"Amelia—" Michael began, but I couldn't. The happy bubble of comfort had evaporated. Reality reigned once more. And reality sucked.

Men like Michael Bane were not meant for girls like me.

I stood up and walked out of the room.

"Aimee!" Suzie called after me. When I didn't reply and just kept walking to the back door, she followed me. "Aimee! Wait!" Jogging to catch up, she caught me as I shoved the door open, and Echo darted out. "I'm sorry. That was way over the line, it's just…surreal seeing you sitting in your lounge with him watching fucking *Star Trek*." She shook her head. "What's his game here?"

I stared at her and took a deep breath. "No game. He likes Trek." I shrugged. "I was equally baffled."

She blinked. "I don't get it."

I huffed out an exasperated breath. "Is it really so hard to believe that he'd enjoy something I like? Is it really so impossible to think someone could be hot and popular and also share an interest with me?" I was getting angry now, though, in fairness, it had more to do with the fact I was really struggling to believe it myself, and less that I thought Suzie believed that.

She frowned. "No," she said flatly. "In fact, Johnny was both hot and popular and liked several things you did. If that's really all you want in a man, you let go a fucking gem."

I turned and walked out of the back door, letting it slam behind me. I realised too late I was only in my slippers, but I'd be damned if I went back inside.

The back door was flung open and Suzie marched out, her emerald green, velvet cape wafting in the breeze. The cape, originally an outdated velvet curtain from a thrift store, had been expertly tailored to mimic a high-fashion runway piece, complete with a dramatically oversized hood and intricate gold thread embroidery along the hem, giving it an almost regal appearance.

It was ridiculously over the top, and so typically Suzie.

She planted her feet wide on the doorstep, her fist on her hips, and fixed me with a full-on hero pose resplendent with a withering glare.

"Would you take that giant chip on your shoulder and feed it to some pigeons or something?" she demanded. "You might be carrying a load of shit from childhood about not fitting in, and always being the weirdo freak, and nobody ever liking you for it. But the adult world does not see you like that, Amelia. We are not all judging people by high-school cafeteria standards anymore.

"Get over it! I'm sorry I dredged up a painful memory. But my point was not that you like fucking *Star Trek*. Seriously, who gives a shit? Smart is the new sexy. Geek chic is all the rage these days. You've built a killer fucking brand around your love of all things sci-fi and nerdy. Would you *please just bloody own it?* I wasn't saying you're weird and nobody likes you. I was pointing out you've hitched your cart to a dick of a fucking horse!"

"Oh, so I should go back to Johnny Vanilla, should I? Spend my life in a dreary job, never achieving anything, or being anything, just so I don't damage his fragile male ego, just so I don't threaten his poor sweet baby dreams? Get married, pop out a few children, and wait for the midlife crisis to hit before I can reasonably have decent sex again while banging the fucking PE teacher at my idiot kid's school?"

"Jesus Christ!" she exclaimed. "Johnny wasn't that bad!"

"You go fuck him then, see how you like it!" I screamed.

"There's more to life than decent sex!" Suzie crossed her arms defiantly. "What happened to keeping your distance until all this blows over?"

"That was your idea, not mine!"

"But that's *all* I'm suggesting. That's the *only* reason I'm pitching a fit at the sight of him in your house!"

"You know as well as I do he didn't do it."

"Thinking a thing, and knowing a thing, are not the *same thing*! You can't throw yourself into something just because some guy with a big cock and a ridiculously chiselled jaw makes you come a lot."

"Why not?" I demanded.

"That's not what healthy relationships are built on!"

"No? What are they built on?"

"Loyalty, love, respect, mutual shit, I don't fucking know. And no, Johnny wasn't right for you, but at least you shared common interests. He understood you, he liked doing stuff with you, he—"

"Belittled me every time I tried to have an original thought," I countered. "Ridiculed me if I bought the clothes I actually liked, just because it wasn't to his taste. Shamed me into wearing stuff I didn't even want. Was so insecure I had to pretend my salary was half what it actually was, even when I was in a job that didn't pay me anywhere near my worth. *Shrugged* when I told him I was getting *sexually harassed* at work and said it *must have been my fault for flirting with him*!"

Suzie paused, winced, and tilted her head to one side. "Okay, I'll give you that. But you're scaring the shit out of me here, girl. You've worked your arse off to build something different, something you can be proud of, and you've put it all on the line for the sake of an idiot pretty boy. I get that Johnny wasn't it for you. That he didn't…tick all the boxes. But you're deluding yourself if you think you've found a guy who can play at your level at work and also appreciates you as a person. For who you are."

"Why can't I have both?" I demanded. "Why must I choose between a person who shares my interests and someone who values and supports my ambitions? Why can't I have someone who sees me, all of me, and loves me for everything I am, for the whole person, not just the parts that fit the ideal they have for a woman? Why must I conform to everyone else's expectations of who I should be and what I should want in life? Why must I make myself small just to fit into someone else's box?"

"Well, I guess he fits perfectly into *your* box, or you wouldn't be so fired up!"

I stared at her.

She glared back.

We both dissolved into simultaneous fits of laughter.

When she could finally breathe, she stepped down into the garden to join me and wrapped me in a hug. "Look," she said into my hair, "I'm not saying you can't find someone who gives you both. I'm just saying…is that guy really *Michael Bane*? You went through so much getting out of a relationship that didn't give you what you needed. I just don't want to see you falling right into another. Especially not with *him*."

I drew back, shaking my head. "You've not seen the man in over fifteen years. Now who's judging on high-school standards?"

She chewed on her cheek for a bit. "Touché," she finally said. "Okay. So, maybe this time, the geek *shall* inherit the earth…and get the guy." She scrunched up her nose and ruined it by adding, "Even if the guy is a douche." Then turned to look over her shoulder and back into the house. "You can come out now, pretty boy."

Michael stepped out of the house, and I belatedly realised he must have heard that entire exchange. Heat flooded my face.

"I've never known anyone make that sound so insulting before; it's really quite a skill," Michael said, considering Suzie for a moment. "For the record, I have no intention of hurting her again. I didn't intend to hurt her the first time. Though, I realise, recent events *are* hurting her. And I'm very sorry for that."

They surveyed each other a while longer. "Okay then," Suzie said finally. "Benefit of the doubt granted. But if you fuck her over, Michael Bane, I know more pig farmers than any northern girl has a right to, and the only thing left of you would be your stupid designer shoes."

Michael shivered. Although whether that was from Suzie's words or the fact he was standing on the step in nothing but a shirt and boxers I wasn't sure.

"I'd expect nothing less," he said, his face solemn with absolute sincerity.

Suzie nodded as if that put the entire issue to bed. She turned back to me. "Look, I came to make sure you're okay." Her voice softened. "After everything at the hospital and with this..." She gestured vaguely at the air, probably indicating the general chaos of my life currently. "I thought your situation might benefit from a little positive social karma." She looked pointedly at Michael. "That is, if he has any clothes?" She tilted her head and considered his crotch. "Although my guess is we'll get more views if he stays like that."

Michael blanched. "I'll get dressed."

He disappeared back inside. Moments later, I heard the front door open, the beep of his car unlocking, the front door closing. He must have left the holdall full of clothes he'd been living out of all week in his boot.

"What fresh hell are you about to subject us to?" I asked.

"Virality, darling, nothing less."

I rolled my eyes, resigned myself to the inevitable, and went inside to get dressed. As I wandered up the stairs, she followed me back in from the garden and started pulling GoPros and tripods out of a bag I hadn't even noticed she'd been carrying when she'd arrived.

By the time we came back down, fully dressed, Suzie already had several cameras set up and rolling. As Michael and

I shuffled out uncertainly, she spread her hands wide across the expanse of the garden. "We're going to build a rainwater harvesting system," she declared. "It's simple, it's eco-friendly, and it's going to help cut down your water bill, Amelia."

Michael raised an eyebrow, clearly sceptical but playing along for my sake—or perhaps for the lack of a better option. "What do you need us to do?" he asked.

"First, we need to clear out the gutters and set up a way to channel the water into a storage unit. I found a couple of old barrels in that shed at the end of your drive."

I blinked. There was no shed at the end of my drive. Wait...

"You mean the shed on the derelict little lot on the way to the train station? The one you took one look at and declared must be full of treasure, just going to waste?"

Suzie waved her hand, undeterred. "Semantics," she said. "They're solid barrels. They'll work perfectly." She pointed at a pair of enormous blue plastic barrels that had magically materialised in my back garden.

"But how did you get them here?" I asked.

"A lovely chap in a disgracefully large pickup gave me a lift."

I shook my head. "Did he, by chance, see you attempting to roll the damn things down the road and swoop in to rescue you?"

Suzie made a *tssk* sound, as if that should have been obvious. Given strangers (usually men) regularly saw her in the middle of doing random things and stopped to help, it actually didn't surprise me. I'd have been more shocked if she'd made it all the way here from the train station *without* attracting at least one would-be hero.

She was already pulling on gloves, her beret firmly in place. Between that and the cape, she was quite the picture.

I couldn't help but smile a little. It was hard to stay mad when she was this fired up about something good. I grabbed a pair of gloves and handed some to Michael, who took them with a nod, a silent truce forming between him and my bestie as we all got to work.

As Michael climbed the ladder to inspect the gutters, Suzie leant hard into filming, narrating her actions for her followers. "Rainwater harvesting is not just an eco-friendly move—it's a statement. You're saying yes to sustainable living, right in your own backyard," she explained.

I busied myself with connecting pipes to the barrels, following Suzie's instructions. I'd long since given up asking how she knew to do these things. Ironically, she'd learned a lot of it by watching YouTube videos. I'd never plucked up the courage to point out the cyclical lunacy of that particular aspect of influencer life. Since her channel had taken off and she'd ditched her job designing boring fashion for equally dull women, she'd gone back to uni and started learning about it all in a more formal manner.

It hadn't dulled her sparkle, not one bit.

The physical work was grounding, the simplicity of the task soothing my frazzled nerves. Michael handed down leaves and debris, his earlier reluctance washed away by the rhythm of our work.

Suzie took her camera on a tour of the garden to show off the compost heap she'd helped me start on a previous visit. She checked the consistency, stirring the pile with a garden fork (I've no idea where she found one of those). "This is to aerate it", she explained to the camera. "By adding the mulch and leaves Michael cleared from the gutters, we're balancing our 'greens' and 'browns'. 'Greens' are your nitrogen-rich materials, like kitchen scraps, which Amelia has been adding for weeks, and 'browns' are your carbon-rich materials, like these leaves and mulch. This balance helps speed up the decomposition process," she explained, thrusting the fork into the heap and turning it over to demonstrate.

She scooped up a handful of partially decomposed material and let it crumble back into the heap. "This mixture will break down into nutrient-rich compost over the next few months. It's perfect for enriching garden soil, reducing the need for chemical fertilisers, and it's a fantastic way to recycle kitchen and garden waste." Suzie pointed her camera at the rich, dark soil at the bottom of the heap. "Look at this! It's already turning into beautiful compost. I'll come back in the spring and help Aimee plant some wildflower beds to attract bees and butterflies. We'll use all this compost then. And if you want to know how I got this one started, there's a step-by-step tutorial in my membership club. You can access all my tutorials on upcycling and eco-renovations for £9.99 a month. Don't worry; you can cancel anytime. It's all about making sustainable living easy and accessible for everyone."

Michael sidled over to me, standing right behind my shoulder and whispering in my ear, "She's become quite the force. Is this what she does for a living?"

"Uh-huh." I watched her flit about to another part of the garden and start talking animatedly about how we would be transforming it into a sacred space for wildlife. "She's also studying Wildlife Ecology and Conservation at uni."

"She's only just doing a degree?" He sounded surprised. "I thought you both went to uni together?"

"We did, this is her second. The one she actually wanted to do, before her parents talked her into something more practical and depressing."

"This whole area is going to be a vegetable patch," Suzie explained with zeal. "And there's an old greenhouse at the bottom down there I'm hoping we can patch up for growing orchids."

I honestly didn't much care what my garden looked like as long as it was pleasant to sit in and relax during the summer, ideally with some kind of fire pit, so I'd given her free reign. She was in her element here. As much as urban living had sparked her imagination, Suzie was a country girl at heart. Moving to Bangor, spending more time in nature, she was starting to remember that.

I was waiting for the day she came back here, realised how much she loved it, and never wanted to leave again.

"Phenomenal," Michael said, and I turned to look at him. He was watching Suzie go, an expression of genuine awe on his face. He caught me looking. "What?" he asked.

"You keep finding new ways of surprising me, Michael Bane."

He grinned. "Excellent."

I laughed and leaned back into his shoulder, tilting my head up to look into his face. "Alright, Mr Burns, steady on."

One of his arms slid around my waist. My breath caught in my throat.

"How have I surprised you now?" he asked.

I wasn't sure he'd even realised he'd wrapped his arm around me and was pulling me back into his chest.

I wasn't going to point it out, in case he stopped.

"Most people think Suzie's absolutely bat shit when they first meet her." I smiled wryly. "It takes a while of actually listening to her and being open to what she's saying before they realise that, actually, she's kind of a genius. It usually takes longer still before they appreciate the beauty in it. But you..." I shook my head and leant it against his collarbone. "You spend twenty minutes with her and just get it."

Michael's other arm wrapped around my waist. "Is that odd?"

I shrugged. "Maybe not if you know the right people"—I nodded Suzie's way—"but she's always struggled to find the right people." I paused, thinking on that for a minute. "I guess that's why we're such good friends."

Michael was silent for a moment, and we watched as Suzie energetically marched across the garden, Echo cantering along playfully at her heels. Belatedly, I realised Suzie had wrangled my hound into a GoPro harness and roped the pooch into getting puppy vision footage for her video.

"Maybe that's why I got it so fast," Michael said softly.

"Hmm?" I'd almost forgotten what we were talking about.

"I've never really found the right people either."

I turned to look at him.

"Oh, I've got plenty of *people*," he said. "But they've always somehow missed the point of me," he sighed. "They see the flash and the money and the face. They assume I'm something

I'm not. They remember the anger and the fights and the frustration of me when I was younger, and they assume I'm…"

A killer.

Neither of us needed to say it.

It had hung in the air, thick and cloying like mustard gas since the vigil. Actually, since that networking event, when one of his oldest friends had walked right up to me and told me to watch my back.

"It never occurs to them that I might have a soul."

My hands moved to his and I squeezed. But as I released him and stepped away, he grabbed me and pulled me closer, head dipping and blocking out the sun. My heart fluttered, as I belatedly realised he really was this close to me, and we weren't even out in public.

His grip on my waist tightened, and he squeezed me hard against his stomach, one hand slipping down slightly, cupping my butt, pressing me into him. I lifted one hand to his chest, laying my palm flat against him, and I could feel the hammering of his heart. He squeezed harder, his head dipping lower, and just as I thought he was about to kiss me, actually kiss me, Suzie came bounding back through the grass, Echo hot on her heels.

I dropped my hand, cleared my throat and stepped away.

We weren't alone. We were with Suzie. And her cameras. And all her 2.4 million YouTube followers. And he didn't mean that.

This was all just another show.

"Think of it, Amelia," Suzie said, "oh, you're not done. Here's"—she grabbed my arm, dragged me back to the new contraption forming in my garden, and helped me secure a filter made of sand and gravel at the mouth of the barrel. "Every drop of water we save here is one less strain on the town's system, one small step towards a greener planet."

She beamed at me, and I mentally shook myself, grinning back like nothing was wrong. Because it wasn't, not really. This was what I'd agreed to. The charade. It wasn't Michael's fault I was so dumb I kept half-believing it myself.

As I thought it, he came over to help her stabilise the barrel. When we finished, Suzie put down her camera and took off her beret, running a hand through the tangled curls of her hair. Her face flushed with exertion and satisfaction as she glanced at Michael, then me. "Okay," she conceded, nudging me playfully. "Not just a pretty face."

Michael chuckled, looking at our handiwork with a nod of approval. "I have to admit, it's impressive. And practical."

Suzie's smile was triumphant as she pulled us both into a muddy hug. "Teamwork, folks." She grabbed both our arms and dragged us back to the house. "Did you say something about soup? I'm starving."

"Wait till you taste the bread," I said. "He baked it from scratch."

As we walked in, I saw her silently mouthing the words to herself in bemused wonder. *"Baked it from scratch…"*

❖

The day waned into evening as we retreated into the house. Suzie devoured what was left of the soup, took her laptop and retreated to my office to edit all her footage together. Michael milled around, slightly forlornly, unsure what to do with himself, until I commented I was hungry and he immediately set about cooking. A quick search of Suzie's bag revealed the usual stash of fresh veggies.

"She seriously grew these in a flat in the city centre?"

I nodded. "You should see the balcony garden she's got going on in Manchester. The patio pots in Bangor pale in comparison."

Both Michael's eyebrows arched. His estimation of Suzie was going up a notch every hour.

I was glad. I just hoped whatever he cooked for dinner elevated him in her estimations to a similar level.

He routed around in the bag, pulling out freshly picked carrots, spinach, kale, peas, and three small pots containing still-growing parsley, basil and thyme. Suzie had stuck little lolly pop sticks with the names carefully scrawled on in Sharpie, so I didn't get confused.

"Nice," Michael said, opening my fridge and surveying a load of food that hadn't been in there when I'd fallen asleep yesterday and was, presumably, delivered along with the soup supplies. He started pulling stuff out, ransacking my cupboards, and before I knew it, he'd pulled more dough from somewhere (clearly made earlier) and started shaping it into a garlic flatbread.

The scent of garlic and fresh herbs soon filled the kitchen as Michael kneaded the dough, letting it rest while he prepared the vegetables. I watched him move around the kitchen with a natural ease, his earlier uncertainty replaced with confidence and purpose. It was clear he found solace in cooking. And I found solace in watching him.

Suzie wandered back in to show me her final edit and make sure I was happy before she posted it. She sniffed the air tentatively and followed the scent to the oven. "This thing actually works?" she glanced at me. "Who knew?"

I smirked. We tweaked her video, and by the time it had gone live, Michael was plating up a mouthwatering lasagna along with the flatbread, and pouring us each a bottle of Zombie Dust from my stash in the fridge.

He took a swig, did a double take, then picked up the bottle again for another look. "Damn, that's a nice beer!"

Suzie snorted. "Don't you start. She's *obsessed.*"

"I'm not obsessed," I protested.

"Girl, you ordered a crate of the stuff twice a week after you left PMS—"

Michael chortled

"—just to make sure that, when Rick the Dick inevitably fucked up, and the company sacked them, they knew where to find you."

"And?" I bristled. "They liked working with me. I made them a fortune. It's not my fault nobody at fucking PMS—"

Michael plain hooted that time.

"— could figure out how to put together a decent eCampaign, and their sales plummeted."

"No, but it is your fault you emailed them every time a crappy one came out just to '*make them aware*' of the issues with it."

Michael snorted the sip of beer he'd been taking. "You stole them?" He laughed again.

"I did not!" I was indignant now. "I merely ensured they were aware of how badly that place went to the dogs when I left. And that I remained front of mind so they immediately came to me when they finally tired of PMS."

"I hear the cramps are a bitch," Michael said.

Suzie snorted her own beer. And we all tucked into the food, chomping and chatting as companionably as Suzie and I would have, even if he'd not been there.

Like he just…fits.

"Wait, the guy's *dead*?" Suzie asked through mouthfuls as I caught her up on events. "Thank Christ it wasn't Charlie. Is he okay?"

I nodded. "Same old Charlie."

"Kicked the cops out for being young and imbecilic," Michael added.

Suzie huffed. "So he should."

The conversation wandered to speculation over who might have done it, and I felt more than saw Michael relax as he realised that, whatever Suzie's opinions of him as a potential love match for me, she didn't truly believe he was a killer any more than I did.

The evening darkened. We watched *The Martian*, which I'd been trying to convince Suzie to see since it had come out, to no avail. Her love of plants meant she loved stuff about botanists, and a botanist on Mars was just too good for her to miss. She'd always refused, on account of it being sci-fi, but apparently, the revelation that Michael Bane could enjoy *Star Trek* had convinced her to broaden her own horizons. And Mars seems about as broad as we could get. Plus, we both thought Matt Damon was fit. While Michael didn't quite appreciate that side of it, he certainly enjoyed the cinematic eye candy created by all the CGI—not to mention the clever problem-solving and scientific ingenuity.

When the credits rolled, Suzie excused herself to bed and showed herself to the guest room she always stayed in when she was here. Michael stood a little awkwardly.

"Well," he said, "I'd better be going."

I hesitated.

Don't say it.

"You can stay if you like?"

He looked at me.

Fucking idiot. Of course, he doesn't want to stay.

I shrugged. "I might get a fever and need more cuddling."

For a long moment, he stared at me, saying nothing.

Moron. See. Now he knows you're still pining for him, and he's going to think you're even more pathetic than ever.

But he grinned. "I wouldn't want to take advantage of you in your weakened state."

I feigned a yawn to cover my shock.

He's flirting with me. And there's really *nobody here to see it.*

"I said cuddle, mister, no funny business."

Michael's face quickly schooled itself into a serious expression, but his eyes still danced with amusement. "Perish the thought."

Echo executed an extended stretch and even bigger yawn, turned and trotted off to bed. I followed, wondering how to handle the logistics of a dog who was used to sleeping on the bed with me and a guy who would, presumably, not be okay with that. But Michael simply stripped to his boxers, climbed into bed, and arranged his long legs around the already sleeping form of Echo, stretched across the foot of the mattress.

I slid into the bathroom to put my PJs on and slipped into bed beside him. We both lay on our backs, staring at the ceiling.

"How's that fever?" he asked.

"Not sure, you should probably check."

He reached a hand over and laid it on my forehead. "Seems dodgy. I should definitely keep you warm."

"If you think that's necessary."

"Essential." He stretched his arm out so I could roll into his shoulder. I laid my head on his chest and my hand a little lower. He flinched when my freezing feet touched his legs.

"Christ," he said, and I tried to pull away. His arms pinned me in place. "Don't you dare."

I settled back down again, unsure what to say or do.

"Aimee?" he said sleepily.

"Yeah?"

"You really never believed I'd done it, did you?"

"No," I said, then thought about it. "I considered what would happen if it turned out I was wrong. But no, Michael, I never believed you did it."

"That's really quite remarkable." I could tell by his voice he was almost asleep. "Why?" he mumbled.

"Why what?"

"Why didn't you?" his voice faded.

Sleep took him, preventing me from having to answer, *"Because I love you."*

CHAPTER 17

"Do we really have to do this?" I asked Charlie on Monday morning. We stood at the edge of Hardman Square in Spinningfields, surrounded by the slick glass and towering, modern office buildings that defined Manchester's business district. It was uncomfortably familiar. I'd spent far too many mornings standing in exactly this spot, staring at exactly that building, wishing I didn't have to go in but knowing I did.

It had taken entirely too long to figure out that, actually, I didn't.

I hadn't returned since the day I'd literally fled the building, with Rick Sandford in pursuit, clutching his bloody nose.

But that wasn't the end of it.

Things had got messy, with my dickhead boss unsuccessfully attempting to sue me for breach of contract and theft of intellectual property. Even when I'd got that sorted out, the non-compete clause in my contract left me incapable of working at another agency anywhere close to the city.

Which was all fine with me, as it turned out. I was sick to death of the rat race anyway, and had zero inclination to work for someone else ever again. Kobayashi Maru was born in

Suzie's flat, over on Curry Mile, as a digital-only freelance business serving international clients. I'd avoided returning to this part of town ever since.

Now, here I stood, before my own personal purgatory, about to willingly walk back in.

I've lost my mind.

The building's glass façade reflected the clear blue sky and the neatly manicured greenery of the square. People bustled around us, heading to and from meetings, grabbing coffee from the nearby cafés, chatting on their phones. The area exuded a high-energy, professional vibe, and my anxiety was ratcheting up a notch with every passing yuppie.

Charlie adjusted his collar, gave me a reassuring smile, and said, "No. We don't have to do this. But you said you want answers, and these guys are the only avenue we currently have to get any. If you want to leave, we leave."

I sighed, looking up at the imposing structure. It was a far cry from my cosy little office on the cobbled streets of Ashfordby. The entrance, flanked by sleek, modern art installations and lush planters, was constantly in motion, with people flowing in and out through the revolving doors.

It made me dizzy.

"Fine," I muttered, taking a deep breath and stepping forward.

The pavement beneath my feet was pristine, a testament to the meticulous maintenance of this high-profile district. It often shocked me how many people came to the city and saw only this. Not the graffiti-marred streets littered with swathes of homeless, huddled in doorways, camped out in tents, sleeping their days away because it was the only safe time to get some shuteye. They knew they'd have to stay awake and moving come nightfall. Mostly to keep warm, since there were few places they could go after dark.

I'd once collected some visiting friends from Piccadilly, only for the first thing they saw on exiting the station and heading down towards Piccadilly Gardens to be an ageing man defecating into his own hand while squatting in a doorway and babbling unintelligibly. They were shocked. And I'd realised just how used to such hideous human deprivation I'd become since moving here, as it hadn't even struck me as odd.

Welcome to Manchester.

Somehow I doubted any of the higher ups in any of these offices had ever stopped to think about the plight of those living on the streets around them. They were too busy basking in their seven figure bonuses and planning their next holiday to Dubai, which would last several weeks and involve a business meeting or two so they could expense it and write the whole thing off against their tax bill.

Heaven forbid they contribute more to funds that could be used to get that homeless man the medical care he needed. Or build shelters with open access and food for all.

"You've gone to the dark place, haven't you?" Charlie said.

I glanced at him. "Is it that obvious?"

He gave a small smile. "Only because you've told me about it before. I know what the look means."

"I hate it here," I said.

He nodded. "I know. Honestly, having spent some time where you live now, I'm starting to hate it myself."

I snorted a laugh. "Sure, come live in murder village; it's so much more fun in the country."

"I always fancied living in Midsomer," he quipped.

"Well, there'd be no shortage of work for you," I said, "and you'd get to berate your sergeant as much as you wanted."

Charlie chuckled and patted me on the shoulder. "Aimee, you really don't have to do this. What he did to you... We can find another way."

"This way is quicker."

"Yes, but—"

"Let's just get it over with."

He frowned, shook his head slightly, and bowed to the inevitable.

We walked inside.

With every step, I wondered why I wasn't still holed up at home, as I had been all day yesterday, with Suzie on one side of me, Michael on the other, a hound over my feet, and a film marathon happening on the flatscreen.

My former bosses knew we were coming. Maybe the front desk had told them we were on the way up. Maybe they'd had some other, more nefarious way of being aware of it. I tried not to overthink. Either way, we were led into the big conference room, which was dominated by one of those excessively large tables specifically designed to intimidate people by the sheer expanse of posh, polished wood extending between them and the kings in their court.

By which, I mean the three horsemen of the apocalypse (I know, there should be four, but the ego on Rick Sandford was so colossal he used up the quota that could have been taken by a fourth). Rick was, by far, the worst of the three. The original founder of the company he'd partnered up with Craig a couple of years later, and they'd brought in Howard around the same time I'd started.

"Amelia." Howard rose from his chair to greet me.

The other two remained seated. Howard was a man of average height and average looks, with the kind of pot belly that came from too much beer and not enough exercise. Of the three, I knew him the least. He'd still been new when I'd been hired and in that awkward hazing phase where the other two were constantly winding him up with 'harmless' pranks and practical jokes.

He'd kept himself to himself, and I was fairly sure I'd never seen him crack a smile. The only time he'd spoken to me was to berate me for a lack of efficiency or inform me on the daily that I was late returning from lunch (I wasn't).

Seating himself, Howard glanced at Rick, who sat to his right in the centre seat. I supposed Rick must have been attractive when he was younger. His personality was so vile I struggled to see past it, but objectively speaking, he was well-proportioned and physically pretty fit. His hair had gone to the salt-and-pepper grey that led to several of the girls around the office referring to him as 'the silver fox'. Whether this was genuine or their way of staying in his good books, I could never tell.

He's an ass.

"Ross," Rick greeted Charlie, "I see you haven't improved the company you choose to keep."

Charlie smiled. "It's okay, I won't be here long."

Rick bristled but didn't respond.

"Let's get this over with," Craig said. "What do you want, Amelia?"

I grabbed a seat at the opposite end of the table and swivelled it over so it was directly opposite Rick before I sat down. He'd always been insistent on arranging them *just so*, to ensure nobody was equal to him. If the way his eyes narrowed was anything to go by, the move had the desired effect.

He's pissed.

Rick had ambitious dreams of running his own company, enjoying a lavish lifestyle, and spending freely. Unfortunately, he sucked at business management. And marketing. And being a decent fucking human being. When he hadn't been able to pay Craig (previously a small-scale web designer working remotely) significant sums for client projects, Rick had talked him into a partnership.

"You can start," I said, "by explaining how you were so moronic you ended up over a barrel with Geoffrey Stanton holding a gun to your heads."

Howard blanched. Even Craig looked nervous and fidgeted in his chair. Rick didn't even blink.

"You're assuming I didn't jump at the chance to just fuck up your shit," Rick said.

What a dick.

"You're right. I was assuming you can't possibly have been dumb enough to risk this just to take a swipe at me." Out of the corner of my eye, I saw Howard take a breath and look decidedly uncomfortable. Even Craig seemed uncertain.

Bemused by the pretty city office and the promise of a huge pay cheque while drastically reducing his workload, Craig had jumped at the partnership and waived the outstanding amount owed as his 'buy in' to the company.

Dumbass.

By all accounts, everything had gone well for a while after Craig had got involved. Until they'd once again hit a wall where income versus expenses were concerned, and pulled the same trick on Howard.

Fortunately, Howard was actually capable of lead generation and closing clients, so things had markedly improved since he'd started. Unfortunately, he was just as incapable of delivering on anything promised as the other two were, and that was where I'd come in.

"But then," I said, baiting my hook, "it seems you were dumb enough to fuck up every *client* I left. So maybe I'm wrong."

Rick snorted. "Small fry, Thornbridge. You never did grasp the importance of power. Stanton Media, that's power."

"Sure." I nodded. "Shame it's not yours."

He glared at me. "We've let go of the garbage you brought onboard."

I glanced at Howard. "Guess you had no part in that then."

That hit home. Howard straightened in his chair. They'd hired me as a writer. Soon realised I'd taught myself WordPress and could build a reasonably decent website, so had got me started doing web dev. Then, it was SEO. Then, it was just helping out with social media. Then, it was explaining to clients why they needed all of the above, and upselling them on as much as possible. Then, it was making sure everything we promised actually got done and delivered.

Before I realised it I was doing the job Rosalie now did for me, but without any support from them. While also doing the job of a full-time copywriter, a full-time web developer, plus a ton of other random deliverables, *and* managing everyone else. Projects were planned, executed, and delivered by me. All while I shouldered a lot of the creative output and made sure everyone else completed their parts on time, to brief, and to a high standard.

But I'd never been the one to generate new leads and bring new clients on board. That was all Howard.

They'd pissed away all his hard work as soon as I left, and they realised they didn't have a clue how to do it all without me.

Given how often Rick had tried to fuck me, despite repeated and insistent rebuffing, I couldn't say I was overly bothered at the thought my leaving had fucked them over.

Howard, on the other hand, seemed bothered.

"I'm surprised you were so willing to risk the backlash," I said nonchalantly. "Especially given how popular Michael is and..." I paused "...recent developments."

Howard and Craig both looked at Rick blankly.

They didn't know.

"I'd think you'd be more bothered by the fact the guy Stanton sent to give you your marching orders wound up dead."

"What?" Howard exploded.

"Clerk's *dead*?" Craig said dumbly.

Rick didn't bat an eyelid. He was well aware.

"I'm betting he got too close to the truth and was removed from the equation," Charlie said. "It does make one wonder, though, just how close you three are to that same truth. And how...problematic that might be."

"You really shouldn't try to make threats like that, Ross, you're too much of a pussy," Rick said.

"That was an observation, not a threat," Charlie said. "I wouldn't bother threatening you, Sandford. I'd just hand the file I have on you and your operations here over to the Serious Fraud Office and let them deal with you."

"Yeah?" Rick said. "Why haven't you then?"

Charlie chuckled. "What makes you think I haven't?"

"Okay, that's enough." Howard stood. "What do you want, Amelia?"

I gave him a level stare. "I want to know how deep in this you are."

Rick snorted. "I'm sure we've no idea what you're talking about."

"Give it up, Rick. We know you're behind the shitstorm on social media—"

He smirked.

I ignored him. "Frankly, I don't care about that. What I want to know is if you were involved before that?"

The grin vanished.

The fucking bastard, I'm right.

"I want to know if Stanton had imposed on your services as soon as he realised he had a problem in the hometown of one of your former employees," I said. "And he perhaps asked you to handle it by setting up cameras to keep an eye on that problem?"

Craig got a slightly panicked, deer-in-headlights look on his face. Howard planted both fists on the surface of the conference table and turned away. He didn't answer, but he also didn't meet my eye as Rick replied.

"We have no knowledge of any of this." Rick smiled. "But you've rather outstayed your welcome, Amelia. Time to leave. Unless of course"—he gestured at the table top—"you'd like to stick around for a one-on-one conversation...for old time's sake."

An image of his sweaty, gross, fat sausage fingers pushing me back onto this fucking table and fumbling at my dress as I struggled to get out from under him flashed through my mind.

I stood. Charlie followed suit.

"Don't worry, Rick"—I smiled sweetly—"I still have the video of our last little encounter. If I ever get nostalgic, I'll just rewatch it...with your *wife*." I turned on my heel and stalked out of the room.

As the door swung shut behind Charlie, I heard Howard's raised voice demanding, "What video? What the *fuck* did you do to her?"

We didn't speak until we'd cleared the lobby and were back out into the sweet Manchester air.

"That went well," Charlie said.

"We'll see," I said, casting one last look back over my shoulder at the glass prison it had taken so much effort to escape.

I was so done with this place.

CHAPTER 18

It didn't take long.

I'd been home all of an hour that evening when someone knocked at the door. Echo got there before I did, standing to her full height on her back legs and staring ominously out of the window. I knew whoever was out there was on the receiving end of a very intimidating look.

She'd frightened off at least one delivery driver with this shtick before, even without barking.

If she barked, I suspected I'd walk out to a steaming pile of human poop on my step and skid marks in my gravel from whatever vehicle had just speedily vacated the premises.

The door swung open to reveal a CitySprint courier and a sky-blue van parked up on the drive behind him. "Amelia Thornbridge?"

I nodded.

He handed me a small package. "Sign here, please?"

I took his tablet and scrawled on it with my fingernail, passing it back.

"I just need a quick photo." He took a snap of the package in my hands. "Cheers!"

"Thanks," I said, and closed the door.

Echo sniffed at the package suspiciously.

"Yeah... I'm half expecting it to explode, too," I said, padding back down the hall.

Michael had gone straight to the hospital after work to see Becca, and Suzie had reluctantly headed back to Bangor this morning. She had lectures and seminars and all that good learning stuff. She'd offered to skip, but I'd refused.

I was a big girl; I could handle my own shit.

Pushing open the door to my study, I settled myself cross-legged in my desk chair and booted up my laptop. Unlike the rest of the house, this was the room I hadn't really done properly yet. I'd shoved in a cheap desk, cheap chair, and cheap bookshelves that would have to suffice for now. It felt spartan.

Cold.

I didn't spend much time in here; it was mostly used for storing my books and fandom stuff until I could afford to do it how I actually wanted it. Most of my stuff was still carefully packed in boxes in one corner. I'd unpacked some of my books to make it feel more like mine, but it hadn't worked very well.

The laptop took an age to load; it was the ancient one I'd bought when I'd first been at uni. That it was still running was a testament to my ex's technical skills. Who, I had to concede, was always very good at fixing it when it broke.

Without Johnny's tender ministrations, it had slowed alarmingly over the last couple of years. The thing finally booted up. I ripped open the package and tipped out a pen drive, letting it fall on the desk in front of me. I'd been expecting it, but still, I was slightly shocked the whole ruse had actually worked.

There was no note with it, but it wasn't needed. I knew who'd sent it, and why.

Thank you, Howard.

Finally, he'd been pushed too far and done the right thing. I hoped it was enough for him to get out of the whole shit show. But that wasn't my problem now. This. This was my problem.

I plugged in the drive and had one heart-stopping moment of feeling like an utter imbecile as I waited for it to load, worrying I'd just willingly hooked up some kind of virus to my computer.

But no. It was exactly what I'd been expecting it to be; the security footage.

The video of whatever had happened to Eric Hale. The reason Stanton had known Michael was in the frame for the murder and tried to push it onto him. The reason, I suspected, the Clerk had also been killed.

A dark night filled the screen. They'd clearly been parked in a van across the street from Hale's house. Or maybe set the camera up in a tree or something and left it there? The footage was grainy, not great quality, perfectly typical for the kind of cost cutting I'd come to expect from PMS; why buy something that would do the job well when you could get something cheap and make one of your serfs work hours to try and salvage it?

Hale's car was visible in the drive. A timestamp in the bottom left corner of the screen clearly told me this was a few hours after Michael had unceremoniously dumped me back home and sped off in his taxi.

I now knew that, while I'd been on the phone to Suzie, trying to make sense of whatever the fuck had just happened, he'd stopped that taxi and got out. Started walking back to me, trying to calm down. Part way back, he got a call from Lexi telling him what had happened to Becca, and then…what? From the time that had elapsed, he hadn't charged over there instantly. Or maybe he had, and it had taken him that long to find out where Hale lived.

Either way, they'd sent me a clip that picked up in the Witching Hour. A man walked into shot. For a brief instance, his face was visible to the camera, and there was no mistaking the profile, even in the dim light.

Michael.

He paused, staring at the house, his expression thunderous and utterly terrifying. A moment ticked by, as if he was wrestling with what to do. For a second, it seemed he'd leave without doing anything, but the front door opened, and Hale walked out.

Michael tensed.

The man stumbled to the car, rummaging around in his backseat for something, and that was it. Michael was walking to the house. Up the drive. And before Hale had even turned to look at him, he'd pounded his fists into him one, twice, again. The man dropped to the ground, dazed, and tried to get back on his feet. Michael punched him back down. Hale kicked out wildly, catching Michael in the leg. He dropped, head bowed, and Hale's flailing kicks caught him again. In the head, in the ribs. As Michael caught his breath, Hale managed to get to his feet and tried to get in his car, presumably to drive away. But Michael recovered, stood, and rained fury on the man in the kind of frenzied violence I never thought I'd see in real life.

It was over in seconds.

You'd think it would take longer, but it really didn't.

Swaying slightly, Michael stumbled down the drive. He turned, staring back up at what he'd done, and looked rather like he might pass out. The bloodied form of Hale moved, crawling on all fours and managing to stand.

Michael walked away.

Hale remained, very much alive, struggling to get back up his drive to the house.

I watched him for long moments, wondering why I didn't feel relieved.

It had happened exactly as he'd told me. I no longer needed to wonder. To fear that Michael actually killed this man.

But I'd never been afraid of that. I'd truly never questioned that what he'd told me was true. I had been certain, right from the start, that if Michael was responsible for this man's death, he had been completely oblivious to it. Could injuries from his beating have killed him after the fact? Sure. But I knew he'd been stabbed. And I knew, beyond a doubt, that Michael had not done that.

I knew.

This video proved nothing to me where Michael's guilt or innocence was concerned.

It changed nothing.

But somehow, seeing it happen changed everything.

I wanted to say the man in this video was not the Michael I knew. But it was. He'd always had this in him. This rage. This fierce, insane drive to protect the people he loved.

And I didn't care.

Fuck me, I *liked* it.

It should have shocked me to my core. Sickened me. But it didn't.

I had no idea what that said about me, or my own psychology, or my own damage, but I knew what it said about him.

He was exactly what he had always appeared to be. Whatever other people might think of Michael Bane, I'd not read him wrong.

The only surprising things about him were the parts of him I'd never seen before. The caring, nurturing side that had learned to cook and raised his sister more like she was his daughter, even though he'd still been a kid at the time. The side that had hunted down books about strong women so he could show her that she didn't have to be like their mother. That she could be better, do better, have better. The side that hadn't hesitated when she'd fucked up and got herself pregnant so young. He'd just stepped up again. Helped her raise another girl to be fierce, and strong, and wilful, and wild.

And thank fucking god he had. She'd need every ounce of that strength to recover. But Becca would pull through; I knew she would.

Just like I'd known Michael might have beaten the shit out of the guy who'd done it to her, but there was no way in hell he'd murdered him.

The more disturbing thing about all this was that I still wasn't convinced I'd have cared, even if he had.

Something flickered on the screen, and another figure came into view. They were on the other side of the street, back to the camera, a long coat sweeping down almost to the floor... Wait, no...it was a short coat over a...ballgown?

"What the fuck?" I leant forward, pulling the laptop closer. "That's a woman."

She stalked up the driveway, seeming to glide through the night, an illusion caused by the length of her dress and the fact you couldn't see her feet, rather than any supernatural shit at play.

Probably.

Hale was still struggling to make it to his open front door. He hadn't cried out, I realised, which was odd. But maybe he was in shock. Maybe Michael had done enough damage that he couldn't. Or maybe he knew that nobody would come to help him because he was a piece of shit who deserved what he got.

The woman drew closer. Hale wobbled on his feet and turned, hearing her approach. He was braced for another blow but relaxed, presumably when he realised it was a woman. Doubtless, he thought, she'd seen he was hurt and had come to help.

How wrong he'd been.

Metal flashed in the night. A swift flash caught by the camera's night vision, and the woman raised her arm, plunging it down once, twice, again, then finally leaning forward and down as Hale fell back to the ground.

She dragged the blade across his throat, and a dark spurt of blood cascaded across the drive.

The night was silent save her footsteps as she walked back down the drive and off-screen.

"Jesus Christ." I was breathing hard.

I'd watched a lot of people die on TV and in films, and in some ways, this was just like that. A disembodied death on my laptop screen. But in other ways, my gut knew it wasn't.

My gut understood he had been a real person, and whatever he'd done, he'd just been brutally butchered before my eyes.

I managed to grab the bin beneath my desk before my lunch made it back up my throat, and I puked into it. It took me a minute to get my breath back and stop heaving. Acid burned my throat and mouth. After padding into the kitchen, I ran the tap until it was icy, filled a glass of water, rinsed my mouth out, and spat bile back out into the sink. Then I did it again and kept doing it until I didn't taste vomit.

I poured another glass of water, then returned to my laptop, braced myself, and rewound the video to just after she'd slit his throat. I played it from there, zoomed in, frame by frame.

Nothing.

You couldn't see her face, couldn't see any distinguishing characteristics about her other than the fact she wore a coat over a dress. They could have been any colour in the light; black, dark blue, maroon. There was no way to tell. They blended together in the dim light, making it impossible to discern any distinguishing features on either piece of clothing. Her hair colour was also hard to tell. It didn't seem dark enough to be black, but other than that, it could have been anything other than bleached blonde. It wasn't just the clothes and hair that screamed *female*; something about her bearing, the way she carried herself... Although I supposed, realistically, it *could* have been a man.

Somehow, I just knew it wasn't.

I rewound it again, watched it again, and again, until finally a flash of something caught my eye just before she went off camera.

I'd thought it was the knife glinting again the first few times. But I finally realised it wasn't the same hand the knife had been in.

What is that?

I zoomed in to the max and watched in slow motion as a gaudy bracelet came into focus.

Red.

The dress was red.

I recognised that bracelet.
"Holy fuck," I whispered.

CHAPTER 19

"Where are you?" I asked.
"Still at the hospital. Are you okay?"
Am I?
"Yes…No…maybe?"
"Well, that clears things up," Michael said dryly. "I'll be leaving soon; should I swing by the house?"
"What's the deal with Gemma?" I said.
Silence reigned on the other end of the phone for a second. "Eh?" Michael finally managed. "What does Gemma have to do with anything?"
"Exactly," I said. "Did you two date?"
Michael laughed. The sound was abrasive and set my teeth on edge. Although, maybe that had more to do with what I'd just watched than Michael.
"I'm serious," I snapped. "What's the deal with you two? Were you dating? Friends with benefits? What?"
"Just friends," he said, his tone sobering. "Wait, you're not jealous?" he teased. "Of Gemma? Come on, Thornbridge, she's—"
"Michael, I'm serious! Why is she so fixated on you?"
"She's not," he said, suddenly defensive. "I mean…she's weirdly clingy. But she's always been like that."

"But just with you, right?"

"No, she's...well, actually..." He paused. "Yeah, I guess more with me than anyone. But we're just friends; you've really nothing to worry about."

"Just friends?"

"Yeah. I have zero interest in that particular bag of crazy. She's never been my type, and even if she were, I don't do relationships, and I don't shit where I eat. Having a fling with Gemma would just get messy. I don't do drama. Or messy. So no, we didn't date. And no, I've never slept with her."

"You don't shit where you eat?" I said, incredulous.

"Yeah. She's always been part of my friend group. I think she flirted a bit when we were in school, but I was very clear. Not interested. She was well and truly friend-zoned years ago. Aimee, what's this about? This isn't like you to be—"

"I'm not jealous!" I snapped. "Get to the house. You need to see this to believe it."

All traces of humour vanished from his voice. "I'll be right there."

I hung up. Took a sip of water. Stared at the laptop, the screen paused on the closeup of Gemma's ugly, gaudy bracelet.

Michael found me there a while later. I hadn't moved, although the water in my glass had gone.

"Aimee?" he called from the front door, which, I realised belatedly, I hadn't locked.

I really need to start locking the doors.

A basic precaution, really, when your arch nemesis turns out to be an actual fucking psycho-killer.

I stared at the screen. "In here," I called.

He ran in. "Are you okay?" He dashed across the room and took in my appearance, frowning. "You been sick?"

I nodded.

"What happened?"

I pointed at the screen.

He frowned, peering at it. "I don't get it?"

I quickly saved down the enhanced screenshot of the

bracelet, and let him watch the video from the start, turning my face away. Suddenly the thought of watching it again was too much.

"Jesus," Michael said. "Aimee…I'm so sorry. I never wanted you to see me like this. I—"

"Just watch to the end," I said.

He did.

Then he sat on the floor.

"Well," he said. "At least now we can prove I didn't kill him."

I looked down at him. He turned and frowned up at me. "Can we do anything with it? Make it clearer who the guy is?"

"Woman."

"What?"

"It's a woman."

Michael frowned, got to his feet, rewound. Rewatched. "Fucking hell," he said. "You're right, she's wearing a dress. I was wondering what the outfit was. That's a long dress, isn't it, like a…" He hesitated. "…a gown."

His breath caught in his throat. He gasped a little, struggling to even his breathing. "Like a ballgown," he said.

I nodded.

"You asked about Gemma." He took a step back. "Amelia, I know you hate the woman, but you can't possibly think—"

"I didn't," I said. "Never occurred to me. Not until I saw this."

I pulled the screenshot up.

He stared at it for a long moment. Then sat back down on the floor. "Oh my god." He dropped his head in his hands. "I gave her that."

"What?"

"That bracelet. We did a Secret Santa years ago. I got her, and I gave her that. She wears it all the time. I figured she just really liked it—"

"You thought she really liked *that*?"

He glared at me.

"Sorry," I said. "Off-topic. But I'm not going mad, am I?

That is definitely her, isn't it?"

"That's her bracelet. Definitely. And I think she was wearing it at the ball that night. Did they post any photos of the event? Maybe we can check."

"No, she was definitely wearing it. I remember thinking how ugly it was."

His eyes widened slightly, and he looked down, a hint of discomfort flickering across his face.

"Sorry. It didn't match her dress; it stuck out."

We sat in silence for a time. Echo wandered in and flopped down between us. We both went to stroke her and our hands collided. I expected him to snatch his back, but instead he wrapped it around mind and squeezed. "What do we do now?" he asked.

"Fucked if I know." I sniffed, took another sip of water but ended up gulping air from the empty glass, and hiccupped. "I'll call Charlie," I said. "He'll know what to do."

"Thank fucking Christ for Charlie." Michael stood and left the room.

"Amen," I whispered and pulled out my phone, grateful when Michael returned with another glass of water.

CHAPTER 20

Charlie sat at the island in my kitchen and watched the video several times through. He studied the screenshot of the bracelet. He sipped his tea, and thought for a long while.

Michael and I sat on our own bar stools, silent, almost contrite. As if we were naughty school children he'd caught stealing White Lightning from the corner shop.

Eventually, he drained his teacup, replaced it on its saucer, and fixed Michael with a look I imagined used to be enough to break mafia types.

"What do you want to do with this, Michael?"

Michael sat up straighter. He swallowed hard and glanced at me. I said nothing. Just waited.

"I think," he said, looking back at Charlie, "it's time I had a chat with the local constabulary." He paused and dropped his head. "An honest chat."

Charlie nodded.

"You can't be serious?" I said. "Michael…you'll go to jail."

He lifted both hands in a 'so be it' gesture. "This is what I should have done to begin with, Aimee," he said. "I never should have dragged you into this. I adore you for everything you've done to protect me. But this is…far bigger than me."

I stared at him. "You'll go to jail," I repeated.

"Aimee—" Michael sighed. "Perhaps that's not the worst thing?" He reached over, hesitantly taking my hand and squeezing. "I know what I am," he said quietly. "I've known for years. But to see it, really see it like that..." He trailed off. "What that man did to Becca, what he tried to do..."

"You don't have to explain it, Michael, I get it."

"It doesn't make what I did right."

I watched him a moment. "I don't care," I said finally.

He lifted his face to mine, frowning. "How could you possibly not care? You watched that video, you saw me..."

I shrugged. "I've seen you like that before."

"No." He shook his head vehemently. "You've seen me lose it before. Everyone in class did. But not like that."

Silence fell in the kitchen. Echo, disliking the atmosphere, whined softly.

"You'll go to jail," I was a broken record. "I can't—" *lose you.*

"I may be able to help," Charlie said.

We both looked up at him.

"I'll come with you to the station, Michael. We can explain it together. We have leverage. Someone at that station took a bribe from Stanton. I'm fairly sure I know who it was. I can't *prove* it, but I have a damn good poker face. Stanton had people watching Hale; he had to know this video existed, but he chose not to share it. Instead, he set one of his goons to work, making it look like Michael killed him when they knew he hadn't. All to distract from what they'd done." He shrugged. "I'd wager that Gemma has some connection to them somewhere along the way, and they had a vested interest in keeping her name out of it. There's also the question of who killed Clerk"—Charlie shrugged—"that's a very long chain of events and two murders that wouldn't have happened if they hadn't released a paedophile back onto the streets. In the grand scheme of things, kicking the crap out of a guy who'd just done the same to a child might just get swept under the rug."

"Do you really think so?" I said.

Charlie nodded. "There's a chance. But I warn you, it is only a *chance*. I can't guarantee they won't press charges. On the plus side, with this"—he nodded at the video—"and the rock-solid alibi you have for the other murder, being as you were with the police at the time, there is no way they can pin any more on you than assault. You didn't use a weapon. With a decent lawyer, even if they don't make a deal, you have a good shot at minimal jail time."

"No," I said.

"Amelia, enough." Michael's voice faltered, his shoulders slumping as he rubbed his forehead with weary fingers. "Please. I did this. Gemma isn't a physically strong woman. Whatever her reason for doing what she did, she'd never have been able to do it if I hadn't kicked the shit out of him first."

"Well, what if they say that?" I demanded. "What if they decide you two were in it together, and you *both* killed him?"

The men looked at each other. Charlie sighed. "She has a point. I don't believe it for a second, but they could conceivably frame it like that."

Michael shook his head. "It doesn't matter. She killed a man, Aimee. Gemma. Gemma, who we went to school with, slit a guy's throat and walked away like it was *nothing*. Doesn't that bother you?"

"Honestly? It barely surprises me. She's always been a raging sociopath. There's a reason I've hated her my whole life, and it wasn't just because she was so close to you. It never occurred to me that she'd do something like this, and yes, it bothers me. Yes, she needs to answer for it. But the woman's always been unhinged."

"Really?" Michael seemed genuinely shocked. "I never saw it."

"Why would you? She was so busy fawning over you and feeding your ego you never bothered to see past her popularity."

Charlie shifted awkwardly on his stool. Echo whined again.

"I wish I could counter that," Michael sighed, "but you

may be right. It doesn't change anything, though. She killed this man. He was a bad man, but he was still a man. What about the Clerk? Was that her too?"

I looked at Charlie.

"I've no idea," he said. "Forensics say the knife wounds were similar, but they haven't been able to match the weapon." He tilted his head and waved a hand. "Of course, if they *had* a weapon, that would be considerably easier. She's still carrying it when she walks out of shot; she may well have kept it. They currently have zero reason to suspect this woman. None. If they know where to look they might find the knife. Having the knife in hand should tell them if it was used in both attacks. They can check her alibi. If nothing else, they can ascertain she *didn't* kill the Clerk, and that will help them figure out who *did*."

"We can't sit on this, Aimee," Michael said. "This isn't you burning my coat and replacing it with another one."

Charlie cleared his throat.

Michael winced. "He didn't know that part, did he?"

"I hadn't mentioned it," I said and shrugged an apology at Charlie. "Honestly, I forgot."

He laughed. Michael and I both startled at the sound.

"Only you could forget that. It's a problem, though. The new purchase could be—"

"Dark web," I said.

Charlie raised an eyebrow. "Payment?"

"Bitcoin…"

Both eyebrows went up. "Nice."

"The point is," Michael said, "Amelia knew I *hadn't* done this. We *know* Gemma did this. I have to come clean. I can't let her, and potentially whoever killed the Clerk—if it wasn't her—get away with it because I'm afraid to face the music."

Charlie was nodding. I sensed that his opinion of Michael had improved somewhat. I also had a sneaking suspicion that he'd have forced this regardless of Michael's wishes. Or even my wishes. He'd just given Michael the chance to prove he might be a bad boy in some people's book, but there were degrees.

There were lines.

There were limits.

I wondered how Charlie would feel if he knew I didn't give a flying fuck if Michael crossed them.

Still, he was right. "It's not just about you anymore," I conceded. "But this seems risky?" I looked to Charlie.

He sighed. "I'm not going to lie to either of you. It might not go how we want. Whichever course you take, there's a risk one or both of you is going to get screwed for this. This is the lesser of two evils; you're in a no-win scenario here."

I sat up straighter. A slow smile spread across Michael's face, and when he looked up at me, it became devilishly wicked. "We don't believe in no-win scenarios."

Fuck.

I should have known that would come back and bite me on the arse someday.

"Then it's settled," Charlie said, and stood. "We should go now. There's a record of the time that the courier arrived. The longer we wait, the harder it is to explain the time taken to turn this evidence over. The last thing we want is to implicate Amelia."

Michael went white. "She had nothing to do with this," he said. "As far as they're concerned, I slipped out of the house. I came back without her knowing. I cleaned my clothes. I burned my coat. I bought the replacement. Amelia's only involvement was trying to support me through it and going to see her old bosses when it became clear they were behind the smear campaign." Michael took a breath. "She just found out I lied to her when she saw this video."

Charlie was watching him carefully.

I sighed. "Michael—"

"No!" he shouted, and I withdrew. He winced and said more softly, "No, Aimee. I'm not budging on this. You and Charlie knew nothing until you saw this. When you did, I told you the truth and asked for help. Charlie agreed to come with me to the station. *That's it.*" He slid off his stool and pulled me to my feet, lifting my chin so I had to look up at him. "That's it," he said again. "Right?"

I dropped my gaze, and he sucked in a deep breath. "Please? I've fucked up literally everything with you, at every point I possibly could have. Please. Let me do one thing right?"

"But what if—" The words died on my lips as his locked onto mine. His hand slid around the back of my neck, his other arm wrapping my waist and pulling me into him.

I kissed him hard, pressing against him, both hands snaking up his shoulders, around his neck, and pulling him deeper into me. His tongue parted my lips, and for a second, I knew nothing but the taste of him.

Then he pulled away, leaving me breathless. "I'll come back," he said softly.

"When?" I whimpered. Michael glanced at Charlie, who was studiously looking at something fascinating outside the window.

"Soon," he promised.

CHAPTER 21

The phone stubbornly refused to ring. Except when Suzie called to check if there was news. Then I kept letting it ring out and texting her to stop. I needed to keep the line free. But she'd just call back half an hour later. After several hours of this, with the last of the day's light fading from the world and a bleakness settling over me that I was terrified to name, I finally answered her call and told her to, "Stop fucking calling, just text me!"

Okay, okay, she texted. Then, after a few minutes, *Sorry!*

She wanted reassurance. I knew that. She wanted to know I was okay, that I wasn't in trouble, and that she didn't need to call my lawyers, post my bail, and take to TikTok live to protest my innocence.

The video of Ashfordby's assumed vigilante murderer making a homemade rainwater system had already gone viral. Apparently, if Suzie was friends with him, he couldn't be evil because she was literally the embodiment of all things pure, good, and wholesome.

She was also incredibly impatient. But underneath it all, buried deep, I sensed she was also genuinely concerned about Michael.

Despite herself, she was starting to like him.

And all she wanted was reassurance.

But I didn't have it in me.

How long is soon? I wondered for the billionth time, as the long shadows stretched across the lounge walls. As I lay motionless and stared at them with unblinking eyes. Amber rolled towards the house from over the hedgerows at the bottom of the garden, bathing one triangle of the room in the soothing glow of the sun's dying rays.

Echo chased the puddle of sunlight across the rug for as long as it lasted, then leapt up onto the sofa and sandwiched herself between my back and the thick, plush cushions that padded it.

Darkness fell across us like a shroud. Exhaustion claimed me, and I slept, only to have nightmarish dreams of Gemma chasing me through the halls of our old high school, a knife in one hand and Michael's head in the other.

I woke with a start to the phone ringing and frantically answered it.

"Any news?" Suzie's voice said.

"*NO!*" I hung up on her and didn't even bother texting an explanation this time.

Sorry! Came the message almost instantly. *But you have to either answer the texts or answer the fucking phone.*

Fuck off!! I was sleeping.

Oh. There was a break of several minutes. *Sorry.*

Apologies mean nothing when you keep doing the same fucking thing.

I was being harsh, and I knew it, but right then, I didn't fucking care.

Desperation finally drove me to my feet and down the hall to the loo. I'd been stubbornly refusing to go because it meant getting up, and now my bladder had cramped painfully.

Since I was on my feet, I figured I might as well relocate, and after letting Echo out briefly to relieve herself went upstairs and ran a scalding hot bath.

Sliding into the bubbly water was the first relief I'd felt since Michael had left with Charlie. A cold had settled within me, bone-deep and bitter.

What had I been doing all this time? Fannying about punishing him for needing a moment to process the fact he'd not recognised me. Who cared? Seriously? Who actually gave a shit?

I'd thought I was done caring about what people thought of me, whether or not I fit in, who liked me, who didn't, if I was popular. But turned out I was just as shallow as I'd always derided Gemma for being.

It had hurt that after all these years, she hadn't even bothered to get to know who I was now. She'd made a snap judgement that I was still basically the same and treated me pretty much the same way she always had.

It hurt me more that, if I was honest, I'd done exactly the same thing to Michael.

I'm no better than Gemma.

I sent that thought winging its way out into the ether, and dumped my phone on the side, submerging myself beneath the surface, hoping the warmth would fully take hold of me and chase away this horrible chill.

When I surfaced, my phone was pinging.

Fuck Gemma, Suzie replied. *She's a fucking psycho.*

But I'm no better.

Bullshit. You'd never have assumed he was the same as high school if he hadn't shut down and fucked off on you when he found out who you were.

That was true. The thought hadn't occurred to me in any of our previous encounters up to that point.

Gemma judged you on the past without ever speaking to you. Michael fell in your estimations because he acted like it mattered. Because he did a shitty thing. It's not the same.

The water went cold as I tried to figure out if I believed her or not. Towelling off, I flopped onto my bed and half-heartedly pulled a blanket over myself. Getting under the duvet was just too much for me.

Sleep eluded me.

Hours ticked by as I stared at the ceiling and willed my phone to ring.

Periodically, I tried calling Charlie, but his phone went straight to voicemail every time.

Panic spiralled in me at the possibilities of what that meant.

My back cramped, and I rolled on my side, only to have a familiar scent fill my senses. It sent me bolt upright. "Michael?" But it was just his shirt, left from when he'd stayed the other night, lying on one of the pillows. I tugged it on and wrapped myself in the scent of him, curling up in a ball around Echo and sobbing.

Time passed. The phone never rang. But just as the morning sun began to claw her way back over the horizon and the blueish haze of dawn light softened the night, I heard wheels on gravel.

I was up, and down the stairs, and at the door before the car had even parked.

An Uber deposited a lone figure on the driveway and, naked save a hastily buttoned shirt, I opened the door wider just as he straightened and looked up at me, standing there in the doorway.

He looked like hell.

At the sight of me, relief flooded his face, and he cleared the driveway, took both the front steps in one stride, caught me round the waist and lifted me clean off my feet.

I buried myself in his shoulder, wrapping my legs around his waist and clinging to him, just as I had that morning in the rain, in the hut by the lake.

My fingers tangled through his hair, his arms locked around me, and I felt a shudder ripple through him as he walked us inside and kicked the door shut behind us. I expected him to put me down, to speak, to cry, something, but he didn't even pause, just walked upstairs with me still in his arms, his lips finding my collarbone as we went. He kissed all the way along it, into the base of my neck. I drew my head back, and his lips followed the line of my neck up until I broke away and found his mouth with my own. He moaned, reaching the landing and pushing me into the wall for a moment, the kiss deepening, frenzied. Then he was moving again, down the landing, into my room, where he threw me on the bed.

"Tell me to stop," he said.

"Never."

The smile that spread across his face was slow, predatory, curving one side of his mouth up higher as his eyes drank me in. It was a sexy, lopsided, smouldering look that froze me in place. I watched as he peeled off his clothes. The shirt was first, baring the broad expanse of his toned chest, the thick, corded muscles of his arms, and a subtle six-pack, fading into the neat, flat V of his stomach. Shoes, socks, jeans were discarded, and he stood there, staring at me, breathing like he'd been running, nothing but his boxers remaining. He rolled them down slowly, that grin slowly parting his lips as he kicked them off.

"Don't move," he breathed and disappeared into the en-suite.

Seconds later, the shower blasted water at the wall, and I remembered where he'd been all night. For an instant, it totally killed the mood. I started to move, to stand, to go to him and ask what had happened.

"Stay!" His voice barked through the open doorway.

I narrowed my eyes in his direction and writhed in place with frustration. Moments passed in agonising anticipation, until finally he emerged, steam billowing behind him, a towel still working the moisture off his skin. He returned to the spot he'd stripped in, dropped the towel, and leant down the bed, grabbing me by the ankles and sliding both palms up the back of my calves. My legs parted, heat flooding me at his touch. Fingers tightened around my legs and he pulled, dragging me down the bed, pushing my feet up until my ankles rested on his shoulders.

His lips pressed against the soft skin on the side of one of my knees, and he leant further into me, kissing down my thigh, parting my legs wider until I felt his breath, hot and ragged between my legs. His lips touched my clit as fingers glided inside me, tongue slowly circling the tight bud. I wriggled beneath him, caught between the need for more, and the infuriation at how slowly he was teasing me. Sensing my frustration, Michael's lips took me into his mouth and gently sucked as fingers swirled inside me, finding just the right spot, applying just the right pressure, rocking into me in just the right way.

I gasped, my hips rising to meet him and force him deeper inside me. Pleasure built within me, tightening everything until the pressure built to an almost unbearable heat. I gasped as his mouth suddenly sank lower, fingers switching places with his lips, and as his tongue sank inside me, he took my clit between two fingers and rocked it back and forth between them, rubbing the throbbing bud of tension to exquisite release. Ecstasy broke over me, wave after wave. Every time I thought I'd reached the end, I was hit by an even more intense pulse of pleasure. I cried out, my fingers clawing into the bed, every muscle in my body going rigid, and for a moment I couldn't move, couldn't breathe, couldn't do anything but bask in the ever-cresting waves.

Finally, the orgasm ebbed, receding from me and taking every inch of tension I'd been feeling with it. My body went limp, and I sank back into the bed, panting. Sweat slicked my forehead.

But Michael wasn't done. Fingers slowly unbuttoned the shirt I wore, gently lifting me off the bed and sliding it from my shoulders. My breasts were encircled by his hands, squeezing, thumbs finding the hard points of my nipples. He climbed up and onto the bed between my legs, the long, solid shaft of his cock gliding inside me. He moaned, bending over me, gripping me tighter, his mouth finding mine and kissing me hungrily, as my legs locked around his own and he rocked into me, deeper, deeper, pulling back and pushing in again.

Grabbing a fistful of his hair, I kissed him harder, planting both feet on the mattress and rising to meet him as he buried himself in me. The kiss deepened, his rhythm gaining pace. He broke away from my lips, his breath coming hard and fast.

Morning light played across his face as his eyes closed and his face tensed in concentration. He was close, and he didn't want it to end yet.

Gently, I pushed him off me and rolled him over so he sat on the bed, straddling him and crossing my legs behind his back. I leant back, bracing one arm behind me and guiding him inside with the other. His eyes snapped open as I slid down the length of him, taking him deeper inside me, sliding off and teasing the tip of him before slipping all the way back down. His hands caught my buttocks, guiding me, slowing me, his whole body shuddering with pleasure as his eyes once again closed for an instant, then opened again so he could watch me. So he could see every second of me riding him. Finally, he could stand it no longer, and he pulled me up, hugging me to him and kissing me again.

I shifted my legs, feet on either side of his hips, and rose up and down, gently, then faster. He gasped, fingers digging into flesh, pulling me down into him harder, and deeper, the length of him rubbing against my inner walls, fire spreading and cresting until I cried out again. He gasped, groaning out his pleasure as my pace quickened, then let out a hoarse cry, his arms reaching up and circling my back so he could thrust deeper inside me in the final moments of his release.

Spent, he sank back onto the pillows, and I gently lifted myself off him, discarding the condom I hadn't even noticed him putting on and flopping down beside him. My legs tangled through his, one arm splayed across his chest. He turned his face to me, traced his fingertips up my arm and to the back of my neck, and kissed me.

It was a long, languishing kiss that only ended because we both needed to breathe.

"What happened?" I finally asked.

"Fairly sure you fucked me into the bed," he chuckled.

I hid my face against his chest and mumbled, "Not what I meant."

He sobered. "We're okay," he said. "I'll explain, I promise. But can we just lie here a minute?"

I kissed his chest by way of answer, and snuggled closer to him. His arms wrapped me tighter, one hand lazily stroking up my leg and pulling me tighter to him.

We slept. I woke shivering, opening my eyes to see Echo, staring forlornly at me from the landing. Sliding from the bed, I tossed a blanket over Michael and left him sleeping. Pulling on joggers and a hoodie, I trotted downstairs and let Echo outside, putting the kettle on before joining her in the garden with a ball and watching her bound around exuberantly for a while. The morning was hazy, bright sunlight struggling to filter through lingering clouds, and the grass was glassy with dew.

Inside, I fed Echo, made coffee, and returned to bed.

Michael woke a few hours later, sitting up with a start and staring around in confusion, hands pawing at his face to clear the sleep from his eyes. His gaze lit on me, and he smiled sleepily, the tension easing from his shoulders. I'd stripped back down and got back in bed with him nude, my coffee long since drunk, a book resting on my drawn-up knees.

"What're you reading?" Michael asked, sleepily.

"*Neuromancer*," I said, flashing him a look at the neon pink and yellow cover. It sported a man's face encased in a high-tech visor, wires trailing from it, as a cigarette dangled from his lips.

Michael studied it curiously. "Any good?"

"So far, it's intense," I said. "Futuristic hackers and corporate espionage flavoured with a good helping of cyberpunk."

Michael smirked. "You not had enough corporate intrigue in the real world?"

I shrugged, not really in the mood for jokes. "Michael—"

"I know," he said. "And I will. But is there coffee first?"

I rolled my eyes. "First, he needs sex, then he needs sleep, now he needs coffee." I gave him a pointed stare. "For an independent man, you're incredibly needy."

"Fair point." He kissed my knee. "I'll make the coffee." And he slid from the bed, wandering off downstairs starkbollock naked.

He returned with two steaming mugs of coffee, and I set my book aside, taking mine and sipping it tentatively. Somehow, he'd managed to add the amount of milk I actually liked, so I could drink it straight away without it being too hot.

When exactly did you notice that particular habit?

I was coming to realise Michael had been paying much closer attention to me than I'd credited.

He slid back into bed, getting under the duvet this time and snuggling in, huffing a couple of breaths on his coffee. It still scalded him when he took an impatient sip, and he winced.

"Should've added more milk," I said.

He gave me a scathing look. "If I wanted a latte, I'd go to Starbucks."

I smirked. "Starbucks doesn't have naked women to play with when you're done."

That got his attention. "I get to play?"

"Depends," I said.

He raised an eyebrow, silently asking, '*On?*'

"What happened at the station."

The lust died in his eyes. "Okay," he sighed, taking another sip of coffee. "I'm not avoiding telling you anything. I just needed a brain break from it before I tried to explain."

He sipped his coffee some more. "Charlie is a fucking lifesaver, let's get that out there right off the bat. I'd have been railroaded without him." He took another sip of java. "He told me to let him do the talking, and I did. He laid it all out; his investigation to help clear my name, discovering the involvement of PMS in the social media campaign, enlisting your help to go quiz them on what they knew—" He paused, his brows furrowing and his mouth tightening as if tasting something bitter. "They were *not* happy about that."

"Eh," I said.

He nodded, clearly agreeing. "He then explained the video showing up, and that you called him and me immediately.

Before he let them watch the video, he said I had some things to tell them, and then he left me to explain what really happened that night."

I went cold.

"Of course"—he waved a hand, as if it went without saying—"I didn't mention your involvement. As far as they're concerned, I slipped out in the middle of the night, and you were none the wiser. It got a bit tricky when they started asking me about how I'd bought that bloody coat—"

I smiled despite myself.

"—but Charlie distracted them by outlining all he had on some guy I'd never even heard of, who apparently runs the whole station. He was right, they didn't want it getting out. And his poker face is sublime, don't ever play with him."

"Noted."

"They were sceptical at first," he continued. "I assume it sounded like I'd fucked up and was now trying to backtrack. They weren't interested, pointing out everything I'd told them just made it more likely I'd killed Hale." He closed his eyes for a second and took a deep breath.

It was weighing on him. The fact he'd left the man in such a state. The fact Gemma had got to him because of that. And, I would imagine, a gnawing uncertainty that had also been haunting me ever since I'd watched that footage; why *the hell had she done it?*

"At that point, Charlie gave them the video. He also showed them the screenshot you enhanced of the bracelet and several photos he'd dug up off Instagram from the ball, showing Gemma's outfit and clearly showing her wearing the bracelet. He then laid out multiple images going back years of her wearing the same bracelet." Michael shook his head. "I'd never even thought about how much she wears it. But apparently, she rarely takes it off."

I sipped my coffee and didn't voice the theory I had on why that might be.

"Honestly, after seeing that, I think they were happy to put the whole incident to bed and leave me out of it. *But*—" He took a deep breath. "There was one caveat." He looked up at me. "They need my help proving she did it."

"They have the video."

He shook his head. "It proves nothing. Charlie was right; they pointed out that all it proves is that someone killed Hale while wearing her bracelet, or one that looks just like it. There's apparently also a chain of custody issue with it because of how it came to you and the conflict of interest you have." He shook his head, and I could see the irritation. "I spoke to Charlie at length about this. Without my help, they're going to struggle to investigate her because they have no probable cause to search her house, request her clothes from that night, try to find the murder weapon..." He waved his hand in an *and all the rest of that* gesture.

"Well, what are you meant to do about it?"

He took a deep breath and huffed it out. "They want me to wear a wire and try to get a confession from her."

"You've got to be fucking joking."

He shook his head. "Aimee, if I do this, they get what they need to put her away. Or...get her the help she needs? I don't know, I can't help thinking she must be having some kind of psychotic break. Why else would she do this?"

I stared at him.

"What?"

"You really don't get it, do you?" I said.

He shook his head dumbly.

"Michael, she's in love with you."

He laughed, then sobered as he realised I was serious. "No."

"Yes."

"No!"

I picked up a pillow and whacked him with it playfully. "It's blindingly obvious."

He snatched the pillow from my hand and wrestled me down onto the bed demanding, "To who?"

"Literally anyone but you."

He sat back up, a flummoxed expression on his face that

made me giggle and said, "Well, shit."

And for some reason I was surprised that he'd actually taken me seriously, trusting my judgement, instead of requiring some kind of proof.

"But why kill Hale?" He rubbed at the stubble across his jaw, squinting one eye shut and tilting his head, as if that might help him see her reasons more clearly.

"The exact logic?" I said. "I've no idea. But I would guess she followed you that night, saw what you did, and thought…I don't know, maybe she'd finish what you started for you? That she was protecting you? I've no idea; I'm not saying she isn't batshit"—I shrugged—"but whatever the reason, in her head at least, she did it because she loves you."

"Who goes around killing people because they love someone?"

I waited, patiently.

"Though I guess… Well, fuck. I damn near killed the guy because I love Becca so fucking much."

And there it was.

I frowned. "You're right though. I mean…surely there must have been more to it than that?"

"I really hope so." Michael sighed. "I mean, why was she there to begin with?"

"She followed you?"

"The taxi? From the ball, to your house, to where it stopped, to me pacing around like a caged wolf trying to figure out what to do? I was wandering about for an age, Aimee, in a total daze. If she'd followed me right from the ball, she'd have caught up well before I got to Hale's."

I shrugged. "I've no idea. Maybe she was working up the courage to approach you and, when she saw what happened, thought it was a better way of gaining your affection?"

"Killing him?" Michael pulled away. "That would never make me—"

"I'm not saying it would." I laid my hand on his arm. "But if she *thought* it would?"

"I guess that could explain it," he conceded. "But why

would she have that knife on her? She didn't just find that in the street. She definitely didn't take it from Hale. So, she must have brought it with her?"

I chewed on that for a moment. "Could she have heard what happened to Becca, and—rather than follow you there—gone to take matters into her own hands? To impress you? Maybe she had no idea you'd be there and went independently."

His shoulders slumped. "I guess. Christ." He paled. "I hate the thought she did this out of some…misguided, what? Love?" He shook his head and scrubbed at his eyes, though whether he was trying to rub away exhaustion or dispel the mental image of what Gemma had done, I couldn't tell.

"Maybe this is good," he said after a moment. "Like, maybe I can use this? I couldn't figure out how the hell I was meant to get her to confess, but if she thinks I'm grateful to whoever did it?"

I thought about it. "She might 'fess up to impress you?"

"Yeah."

We sipped coffee and considered. "I guess it depends on just how unhinged she is," I said. "If she's delusional enough and wants to believe you'd want her enough…I guess it could work."

"She's never struck me as delusional. Narcissistic, sure." He sat up a bit straighter. "Although"—he drummed his fingers on his coffee cup—"now you've mentioned it, she has seemed a little…extra lately."

"Extra?"

He screwed his eyes up and pursed his lips. "I'm not sure. Desperate, maybe? I've caught her trying to flirt with some of the more eligible bachelors at those infernal networking events. She's always turned up at every charity ball I've ever been to, but she's never been one for the business side of things until a year or two ago."

I sipped my coffee, wrapping both hands around the cup to steal whatever warmth was left in it. "What changed?" I asked.

Michael scratched his chin. "Her father gave her a job."

I raised an eyebrow.

"Yeah, that was my response too. Honestly, I thought it was just to placate her. Give her something to do." He shrugged. "She's not exactly the career type."

"Maybe she took it seriously, though? Was making efforts to bring in new business."

"Possibly." Michael shrugged again. "It always felt like she was more interested in getting a ring on her finger than business in her daddy's bank."

Both my eyebrows went up that time.

"You've been gone a while." He shrugged one shoulder. "Gemma's…place in the world isn't the same as it was when we were teenagers."

"I noticed that." I thought back to the ball. "She's not the queen bee anymore, is she?"

Michael shook his head. "Not even close. She's…tolerated, I suppose would be the best word. I found it sad. That's why I always tried to be nice; I felt sorry for her. She knew nothing about her father's work. So, while people there were happy to have conversations about work, politics, marketing, or money, she had nothing to contribute. Except"—he waved his coffee cup—"thinly veiled attempts to ensnare someone who'd give her a better position socially."

I frowned. "You've lost me."

"Old school thinking isn't it? You marry well and gain the standing of your husband. Gemma's clearly not been satisfied with the station afforded by her birth."

I shivered as the chill morning air stole over my bare skin. Michael glanced about, spotted a blanket on the ottoman, stretched out to snag it, then slung it around my shoulders. I snuggled into it gratefully as he covered us both better with the duvet.

"Was she ever?" I asked.

He frowned. "What?"

"Happy. With the lot afforded her by birth."

Echo leapt onto the bed and flopped between us. Michael

scratched her ears in greeting and she lolled over onto one side, tail thumping the duvet, eyes sliding shut, delirious from his attention.

"It always seemed she felt we were beneath her. At school, I mean. She was friends with all the wealthy set from the posh school. Lorded her wealth over the rest of us. Like she was better than us, and only occupied the same space and deigned to breathe the same air because Daddy was labouring under some misguided delusion she needed to be humble." I snorted. "Not that she was ever humble."

"Christ, you really did hate her, didn't you?"

I shook my head. "Bane, most of the school despised Gemma and her cronies. They made our lives hell. Just because they had more money."

"But they didn't," Michael said, looking up from Echo. "Gemma's Dad's doing well these days, but he was in serious shit when we were at school. She didn't go to posh school because they couldn't afford it."

"I knew it!" I jigged so excitedly that I sloshed coffee on my poor, long-suffering hound. "I always knew she was full of shit."

"Yeah. He turned it around eventually, but it's only the last decade or so their family have actually had enough to play at the level she's always pretended to occupy." He shook his head, brow creasing in a frown. "I always thought it was kind of cute when we were at school. That she was so determined to be seen to be more than she was. Like she was striving for better." He tutted. "It was only when we left, and I was actually working my arse off to create something more for my family that I realised how full of shit she was." He shrugged. "She had no interest in putting the work in."

"She feels she's entitled to it. Why should she work for it like the rest of us?"

Michael nodded. "Exactly. Her father worked his arse off to turn things around but—"

I grabbed his arm. "Michael, that's it!"

"What?"

"You said her father's company was one of the ones on Charlie's list, right?"

Michael blinked. "Fuck." He whistled. "The list of companies Stanton Media has a stake in? Yes, it was."

"What if that's how he turned it around? What if Stanton bought into the company, and that money was how they stayed afloat?"

"And it didn't just stay afloat, it now makes a mint," Michael said. "If he bought shares when they were worth nothing, they're worth a shit ton now."

"And what would happen if Stanton sold those shares?"

Michael frowned. "Nothing."

I deflated.

"But..." Michael raised a hand, his eyes moving, roaming side to side, but unfocused, as if searching his thoughts. I gave him a minute. "A weird story came out while Hale was in custody. It popped up on my newsfeed that day, and I thought it was odd, but I was getting ready to collect you for the ball and with everything that happened that night, I'd totally forgotten. But think about it. Stanton Media is not just a conglomerate; they're a behemoth with media outlets at their disposal. What if that story was a warning shot to Gemma's dad? A sign Stanton Media could tank her father's company stock if they wanted to?"

I frowned. "How would they do that?"

"Market manipulation," Michael said, leaning in closer, a slow smile spreading across his face. Like he'd just figured out the final move to open a Japanese puzzle box. "Imagine this—" He set his empty coffee cup down with a thud, and spread both hands wide. "—Stanton Media starts circulating negative news, baseless scandals, and financial troubles about Foster Connections."

"That's Gemma's dad's company?" I asked.

Michael nodded. "Stanton Media has newspapers, channels, online platforms. If they wanted, they could flood them with negative stories about any company. Public perception shifts, investors get nervous, stock prices begin to plummet."

"But that would be illegal, right?" I remembered who we were talking about. "Not that Stanton seems to be above that kind of shit."

"Exactly," Michael said, "and proving it, especially when they control so much of the media, would be incredibly difficult. And while the stock is tumbling, Stanton could be short-selling. They profit from the decline they orchestrated. Once they cover their positions, they could offer to buy out the company at a fraction of its value or demand crippling concessions."

My jaw dropped. "Seriously? That's actually a thing people can just do?"

"It is." Michael nodded. "Well, not easily. You'd have to be in a position to do it. But Stanton certainly is. I'm not sure it makes much business sense, he'd be tanking his own investment. But he wouldn't actually have to *do it*. The threat could be enough."

"Is that it then?" I said.

He glanced at me. "It could be."

"We know they had PMS watching Hale. They forced them into that by threatening to withdraw their business and ruin them. Why not enlist someone else—"

"Someone with high stakes in the company but no real clue how anything works?" Michael said.

"Exactly. Tell Gemma she's going to lose everything, go back to being no better than the rest of us?"

"She might just do something extreme." Michael nodded.

"It's a bit far-fetched though, isn't it?" I tilted my head, thinking. "Why get some randomer to murder someone? If they're as shady as we think, wouldn't they have…I don't know, hitmen or something?" I blinked. "Even that sounds ridiculous."

Michael deflated. "You're right. It all seems absurd. Although, they had the Clerk poking about in things…maybe a hitman isn't so far beyond what we know they've been doing."

"But that's just it," I yawned. "Gemma's no hitman. Makes no sense for them to ask her to do it."

"Maybe they asked her dad and he asked her."

"But why ask her dad?" I frowned, dredging an image from my memory of Gemma's slightly pudgy, balding father. "He was no spring chicken when we were kids he's got to be...what, in his 70s now at least?"

Michael sighed. "I guess. But why else would she do it? If they didn't pressure her into it?

"I still think she did it for you," I said, wincing as the colour drained from Michael's face. "She must know what Becca means to you. Maybe she thought this was her shot."

"At what?"

"You." I shrugged. "She avenges Becca, you're overcome with gratitude and fall into her arms, grateful someone else shouldered the burden for a change."

Michael frowned. "As if that would work!"

I snorted. "Doesn't matter if it would or not. If she *thought* it would... Has she ever tried to be more than friends?" I asked. The thought made my guts squirm.

He thought about it. "Not really. But she's very clingy, always has been. And she'll hug me and hang off my arm if I let her. She's never pushed it beyond that, but there have been comments." He winced. "Quite a few, actually. It's a bit of a standing joke. I don't need to bring a date to events because I already have a 'wife' at them."

I made an ick face.

"Sorry," he said. "I never took it seriously. Just thought it was the lads ribbing me. A bit of banter."

"But she could have taken it seriously," I said. "She could have spent years thinking there's more there." I thought about it some more. "What happens if you try and get her to confess, and she realises what you're doing?"

He looked at me. "I wondered that. But...what choice do I have? It's this or jail. Charlie worked miracles, but they wouldn't budge on that point. If I don't get this confession, they're pressing charges."

"But the video can't be used as evidence," I said.

"But I confessed," he countered.

"Oh. Right." My coffee was gone. I stared morosely into the empty mug. "I want to help."

"Aimee—"

"Shut up." I put my mug down on the bedside table. "If this is going to work, she needs to be emotional enough to want to believe it. If I piss her off enough, that might just give you an opening."

He frowned. "How are you going to piss her off?"

I actually rolled my eyes at that one, then leant over and kissed him. Deeply. With tongue. He grabbed my waist and dragged me closer. When I broke away, he had a slightly dazed expression on his face, and his cock was rock hard and throbbing between us. I tingled at the thought of it, but I forced myself to wait.

"Trust me," I said, "I can piss her off."

He shook his head, trying to clear it and get back to the previous thought process. It was a struggle. All his blood had suddenly rushed elsewhere.

"Okay," he said, "we'll go together." He stroked my hair out of my face and kissed my forehead. "We do this," he said, "and we're free and clear."

"Oh? Clear to do what, exactly?"

He grinned. "Well, we've got a ton of Marvel films to watch. I really want to know what happens with that whole Dominion war thing..." He rolled me into the bed, grabbing my arse and settling himself between my legs. I could feel the tip of him teasing my entrance, and I wriggled, trying to push myself onto him.

"Plus," he said, holding himself back just far enough that I couldn't get my way, "there are a few other things I really need to do to you."

"Need?" I said.

"Need," he confirmed, "assuming, of course, you're okay with that?"

He leant forward and I kissed him again, slower this time.

He slid gently inside me, no preamble, no foreplay this time, the solid force of him filling me, taking it slowly, gradually building to a steady rhythm. I wrapped my legs around his own and kissed him, and kissed him. Breathless, I arched my back as the steady strokes within me built, and he thrust harder, deeper, taking my breast in his mouth and nipping at it gently, before sucking hard. I gasped, as electricity jolted down from his lips all the way to where his solid presence pounded into me, slick from my own wetness.

Rocking into him, I dragged his face back up to mine and kissed him, losing myself completely in the feel of his tongue in my mouth, his hands on my body, the length of him gliding into me, and out, slamming back in and making me buck, desperate for more, more, more, more.

He was happy to oblige, and thrust faster, harder, bracing himself on the bed and breaking away from my lips, ploughing into me until I was lost to the ecstasy, lost to the sounds of his own release.

Lost to him.

CHAPTER 22

Wine glasses clinked softly, punctuating the collective murmurs dissipating through the room. I say 'room', but 'space' would have been more accurate.

Bloody typical. I finally get to come to this place, and it's for a fucking sting.

"Stop scowling," Michael whispered, leaning down and into my hair. "We're supposed to be blissfully, irritatingly happy, remember."

"I really wanted to come here," I whispered back.

"And now you're here," he chuckled. "What's the problem?"

"I'm not *here*, here, I'm just here."

He pulled up short, took two glasses of prosecco from a passing waiter, and handed me one. The look on his face was a picture worthy of the walls; lips pursed, eyes slightly narrowed, a sidelong smoulder aimed my way. "Run that by me again?"

I sighed. "I'm not here for the experience," I whispered. "I can't enjoy it."

"Okay," Michael said, comprehending the problem. "How about this? We come back another day when all this is a distant memory. You can take your pick of anything in here, and I'll buy it for you."

I laughed, snorting prosecco.

"Dead serious." He held up his hand, little finger extended and crooked in invitation. "Pinky promise."

I considered him. "You understand how expensive the artwork here is?"

"Why yes, ma'am, I do."

I sipped my prosecco and surveyed the space. It had been a grand textile mill in a former life, its vast open floor plan and high ceilings now lending themselves perfectly to expansive art installations. The rustic industrial elements were preserved, blending beautifully with the contemporary art pieces, past and present, juxtaposed to stunning effect. Paintings dotted the walls and hung from custom-built installations throughout the room, but the space also housed statues, sculptures, even digital pieces with interactive elements.

"Fine." I hooked his finger with my own and shook. "And don't ever call me *ma'am* again."

Michael chuckled some more and held out his arm. I took it, and he led us on past a large red brick wall, built in the middle of nothing purely so a local graffiti artist could deface it with Banksy-style figures. Peering at them curiously, I concluded they were all the same character at different phases in life, standing with their backs to us and staring out towards an ever-changing horizon. A child faced the spring, a teen the summer, middle-age greeted the autumn, while an ageing man stared down a frigid winter.

I shivered, and we moved past it.

"Are we even sure she's here?" Michael said.

"According to her social media." I glanced at him, and he gestured very subtly to his ear.

He wasn't speaking to me. He was asking Charlie, who was currently sequestered in a surveillance van that sat just outside, giving every appearance it belonged to a local florist. With him was a DCI I'd forgotten the name of, who'd come down from Chester to take over the investigation. Charlie hadn't said anything, but I suspected he'd had a hand in that. He'd made no secret of the fact he was thoroughly disgusted with the local lot. Or at least, the ones who'd been part of letting Hale loose. I also suspected the new big cheese was the one who hired Charlie on a retainer to join the surveillance team, despite him no longer being on the force. Charlie had already put a ton of time into this case working for me, and he was quids in with the new boss.

Michael had an agreement, in writing and carefully checked by his attorney, stating no charges would be brought against him for the assault on Eric Hale. He'd also insisted they add that no repercussions would befall either Charlie or me for any help we had rendered during the whole affair.

It was carefully worded. Even if they did find out what I'd done and that Charlie was aware of it after the fact and complicit, legally, there wasn't a damn thing they could do about it.

At least, there wouldn't be once we got Gemma to spill her rotten guts.

"I heard someone say there are stunning paintings over towards the back of the room," Michael said unnaturally loudly.

"Smooth," I whispered.

"Yeah…I suck at this."

We meandered through the brightly coloured, shining pieces, Michael following whatever directions he was hearing while trying to look nonchalant. Our path took us round a large sculpture of what appeared to be metal statues of ten or twelve people (it was tough to tell where one ended and another began to get an accurate count). They were welded together in warped and imaginative ways.

"Are they making love or eating each other?" I asked Michael, tilting my head to one side as we skirted the edge of the piece.

"Both?" he ventured.

I was about to reply when I caught sight of a flash of pure, brilliant white. "*Oh*," I said, pulling up short.

Michael stumbled into me, and out of the corner of my eye, I saw him follow my gaze, his expression tense, expecting to see Gemma.

Instead, we were both greeted by a painting. The canvas was taller than me. A majestic stag of pure white with elaborate, towering antlers, set against the backdrop of a dense, misty forest. Flowers surrounded the stag, littering the forest floor, climbing the trees, twining through its mossy antlers. The soft hues of the flora lent pink, purple, and blue to the dark depths of green in the forest. Light seemed to radiate from the stag, casting a gentle glow through the trees and creating a dreamlike, ethereal air. The woods blurred out the closer they came to the edge of the canvas, a soft, serene frame. The entire composition was rendered in a kind of wash style that left the colours rippling down the canvas.

Beneath it, a simple plaque read, *The White Hart*.

"He's beautiful," I said, staring at the painting.

"Beautifully tacky," a voice behind us interjected.

My head whipped around to find Gemma lurking, like an embittered, demented cat, waiting to pounce.

"Honestly, Amelia, if you're going to persist in attending these events, you could at least pretend to have a modicum of taste."

Apparently, the claws are coming straight out.

"Says the woman wearing *that* bracelet," I said, eying the gaudy piece of costume jewellery that had given her away in the end.

Well, that neatly let Charlie know she was wearing it, at least. Even if she'd washed it since her attack on Hale, it would likely still contain remnants of blood.

Arterial spray went everywhere.

Gemma bristled. "It has sentimental value," she said, giving Michael a knowing smile.

He returned it, playing along.

What if he's not playing?
What if he's in on it?

I quashed the ridiculous notion.

Absurd.

"What do you think, babe?" I said, turning back to the painting. "Isn't it perfect for my office?"

Michael slung an arm casually over my shoulder and leant into me. "Work or home?" he asked.

"Home," I said.

He appeared to consider it, then nodded thoughtfully. "The room's certainly tall enough for it. We'd have to hang it on the north wall, though, or the sunlight could damage it."

Reaching up, I clasped the hand dangling over my shoulder and squeezed it. "Do you like it?"

"Isn't it more about if *you* like it?" he countered.

I was peripherally aware of Gemma glaring at our clasped hands. I leant back into him, resting my head on his chest and looking up at his face.

"But I want you to love everything in my space. I mean, you're practically living there now." I giggled in a manner so girlish even I found it annoying.

He wrapped his other arm around me, laying a protective hand flat on my belly and pressing me back into him.

"True," Michael conceded.

I swear I could hear Gemma grinding her teeth.

"Okay," he said, "let's get it."

I turned and flung my arms around his neck, squealing in an even more alarmingly girly fashion as he lifted me from the ground. My feet kicked up behind me. I planted a ridiculously overzealous kiss on his lips before he set me back down.

Back on solid ground, I continued to cling to him dramatically. Partly for effect but partly because I'd just given him a huge hard-on and assumed he didn't want the whole room to see it.

"Really, Mike," Gemma said, her lip curling. "In public?"

Michael laughed. It sounded forced, to me, at least. "Well, you know women and art." He shrugged and waved over a gallery attendant, who practically fell over themselves to get to him. "We'll take it." He nodded at the painting.

I squealed, kissing him again.

This time, I was forcibly pulled away from Michael's lips by a cold, vice grip locking around my arm and yanking me back.

Hard.

That actually hurt.

And for the first time since this whole charade began, I felt a whisper of fear.

I'd watched this woman murder a man in cold blood. She might not be holding a knife, but she despised me. A guy she hadn't even known had died gurgling; what the hell would she do to me?

"Let go of me," I said. I didn't have to feign the distress in my voice.

"You are making a spectacle of yourself," Gemma hissed.

"Who cares?" I said, shaking her off and sheltering in Michael's arms.

"*I* care," Gemma spat. "And *he* cares. Not that *you'd* know. Not that you know the *first thing* about him."

"I know him better than you," I shot back. "*Biblically*, one might say." I smiled sweetly.

Gemma rolled her eyes. "Please," she laughed. "Like that makes you special. He's fucked half the women in town, the attractive ones, at least. It escapes me how he ended up with the *fat, ugly geek* from high school." She sneered at me.

I slapped her.

It was unbelievably stupid.

And immensely satisfying.

The *crack* of my palm colliding with her shark-nosed, stuck-up face rattled through the room.

Around us, conversations stilled. People stared in shock.

Michael stared in shock, and he really wasn't faking it.

That wasn't exactly part of the plan.

"Fuck you, Gemma," I said. *In for a penny...* "Fuck you and your Regina George bullshit. High school is over. We are grown-arse women. And your jealousy is, frankly, *pathetic.*"

She lunged at me.

Michael blocked her, holding me at arm's length and

planting himself between us.

"*Enough*, Aimee!" he sounded furious. "What the hell do you think you're doing?"

He's faking, he's faking, don't freak out.

"Oh, wake *up*, Michael! You'll let her bully and belittle me, but somehow *I'm* the bad guy?"

"You hit her!" he yelled.

"She deserved it!" I shot back.

Our improv was exceptional. We hadn't practised that bit.

People were clustering now, curious to get a good look at the drama. Oddly, it made me feel safer.

"*She* has been my best friend for years," Michael said. "You think I'll just let you hurt her?"

"Excuse me, sir–" the gallery attendant was back. "Do you need any help?"

Michael ignored him.

Help really wasn't part of the script.

"You're seriously taking her side?" I shrieked. "After *everything* I've done for you?"

"God, I don't even care at this point!" he yelled. "I've had enough of you. And your"—he waved an arm at the painting—"weirdo bullshit!"

Ouch.

"Michael—"

"No, you heard him!" Gemma stepped up beside Michael and laid a hand on his arm. "I knew you had to have something over him to make him act this way. It ends *here*."

"Fine"—I pulled my phone out—"I'll just make a call, *shall I?*"

Michael hesitated, then turned to Gemma. "Please—" He held his hand up and dropped his voice to a whisper. "This is… I can't risk pissing her off."

"Don't worry, Michael." Gemma stepped between us.

Genuine panic skittered across his face, but I shook my head, ostensibly at the idiocy of Gemma. I actually wanted to let him know it was fine.

Let her fucking hang herself.

"You don't need her anymore." Gemma tilted her head, lips tightening in a smile that seemed to scream *pity*. "You never did. Make whatever calls you like. It won't matter." She spun on her heel and led Michael away. He followed like a stray puppy, holding his arm out to her. She hung off him like a fucking barnacle, leaning into him and whispering, giggling, as he deftly led her from the room and out into a courtyard flanked by trees, fairy lights twinkling through their bare boughs.

My stomach twisted. The sight of them walking off together was threatening to make me spew up my prosecco. Gemma glanced back over her shoulder at me, smirked, and cuddled into Michael, wrapping an arm around his waist. He draped his arm across her bare shoulders. As she turned away from me, a look flitted across her face, somewhere between determined and deranged. And my feet were moving.

I couldn't do it. Couldn't watch him leave with her.

A hand grabbed my arm, wheeled me around, and steered me into a corner.

"Breathe," Charlie said. "I know it looks like he's going off alone, but he's not." He slid his hand around my own for a moment, and when he pulled away, I realised he'd slipped me an earpiece. I stuffed it in place.

"I *do*," Gemma was saying softly. "That freak can say what she likes. We'll tell them you were with me that night. I mean"—she snorted—"that's far more believable anyway."

I fucking knew it!

I actually had to clamp my jaw shut to stop myself from shrieking out in the middle of the room.

"What do you mean?" I heard Michael ask softly.

"I know she lied for you," Gemma whispered.

I craned my neck to look out of the windows and could just make them out, standing alone by a huge fountain. She turned, leaning into him in a grossly sinuous way.

Like a succubus poised to strike.

Acid burned the back of my throat. I swallowed it, and the urge to run out there and smack her again.

There was a muffled sound, and through the window, I saw Michael perch on the edge of the fountain, gesturing for Gemma to join him.

She practically sat on his lap.

"Fucking skank!" I muttered, then clamped a hand over my ear and looked at Charlie in horror.

"They can't hear you," he said. "You might want to stop staring quite so obviously, though."

"She can't see me," I hissed.

"No." He smiled and gestured at a nearby statue as if we were discussing it. "But we don't know who else is watching."

That shut me up. I circled the statue so I could see them without having to turn and stare quite so obviously. It was no use; I couldn't see them well enough. Whipping my phone out, I opened my camera, zoomed in as far as I could, and tried to point it at them without being too brazen about it.

Michael was smiling at her like she was the answer to his fucking wet dreams. Gemma practically swooned across his lap.

"It wasn't your fault," she said softly. "It was such a shock what that man did. And you'd already had such a horrible shock that night. Finding out who *she* really was—"

Gemma put so much venom into the word *she*, I was worried I'd keel over, even at this distance.

"—but I was there for you. I've always been there for you. When that night turned...messy, I was there. I took care of it."

Michael leaned closer. "You were *there*?"

"Yes," she whispered. Glancing around before continuing. "He called just after you left the ball."

"Who did?" Michael sounded alarmingly nonchalant, given the circumstances.

"Daddy," Gemma replied. "I was so shocked to hear about Becca..." The catch in Gemma's voice actually sounded genuine. "I thought he was calling so I could find you and break the news gently, but then he started saying such horrible things." She shuddered. So hard I could see it, even on my phone. For a second, I actually felt sorry for her. "Oh, God, he was so angry. Raving about loyalty and family honour."

Michael was frowning but had clearly decided to let her rant.

"I would have hung up, but then he said the business was in trouble—"

I glanced at Charlie, who nodded in acknowledgement—we'd been spot on with that.

"He said I'd be out of a job. No more '*cushty salary for swanning about*', as if all my hard work at those fucking business events was meaningless." She whimpered slightly.

I could feel that pain, that frustration. I didn't want to empathise with her, but a rush of understanding flooded me. How hard would it be to have your own father tell you you're worthless? Maybe she didn't know what she was doing, but she'd clearly been trying. Instead of encouraging her, he'd mocked her efforts.

"Worse, *he* could lose his position. There might even be a hostile takeover." Gemm shook her head. "Can you believe the gall of that man?"

"Who?" Michael asked.

"Geoffrey Stanton," she hissed. "Apparently, Daddy didn't save the business all on his own. *Apparently,* some shit-head media guy swept in and saved it for him. Now he owns more of our company than we do!" She was seething; I could hear it in her voice. "All those years, all that time, all that...struggle. And now, he says, we could lose it all again over some...*paedophile*." She spat the word. "*Disgusting!*"

Michael made a sympathetic noise and patted her arm.

"I knew what I had to do." She looked up at him. "It was so obvious. But I wasn't sure, not at all. And then Daddy said how upset you'd be. How devastated. How unfair it was that poor Becca would never get justice. And I could see it all for a second. It all made sense. Still, I got there and couldn't make myself do it. But then I saw you. And I knew. It was the right thing, wasn't it?"

She grabbed Michael's arm, and he stiffened. An almost

imperceptible recoil that, mercifully, Gemma didn't seem to notice. "When he got back up," she was saying, "I made sure he wouldn't come after you."

Michael looped an arm around her and hugged her to him. "I can't believe you did that for me," he said. "Why didn't you tell me?"

"I would have"—she sounded irritated—"but you were gone. I thought after I saw you, once I knew we were both there to do the same thing. That *meant* something, didn't it?"

Michael made an encouraging noise but didn't speak.

"Yes! It did. I thought you'd finally see it, too. But by the time I caught you up, you'd gone to *her*." She laid her head on his chest, her fingers caressing it. "I waited all morning. But you never came out, and then I saw the police go in and…it was too late. She'd spun her *lies*. And there you were, forced to parade around with *her*."

"It's been hell," Michael admitted. He dropped his chin to his chest, raising a free hand to cover his eyes. I was fairly sure his lip wobbled.

Oh, come on now, that's a bit much.

Gemma made a sympathetic noise, and for an awful moment, I thought she'd kiss him.

I couldn't stand here and let her lips anywhere near him, deal be damned.

But she only stroked his face, her fingers brushing his stubbled jaw.

"I thought she'd help me," Michael said. "But she just made it worse. All those ridiculous videos on social media!"

A disgusted scoff sounded from Gemma. "They *said* she was bad at her job," Gemma said. "I didn't realise *how* bad."

"Who said?" Michael asked, very subtly shifting his body to angle her in a slightly different direction.

Behind her, out of her line of sight, Charlie stepped through the trees as others moved through the shadows around him. I blinked, glanced over my shoulder, and belatedly realised my PI was no longer with me.

"Her boss, from wherever she used to work," Gemma

said, almost idly. Her attention was fixed on Michael, and she was facing away from the approaching police officers. "They said she couldn't be trusted. I knew they were right. And then she set *him* on me." Gemma's eyes went distant. "I could barely believe it."

"Who?" Michael asked, one hand raising, almost imperceptibly, to halt the approaching police officers.

"That PI," Gemma said absently. "He had all sorts of questions. How did I know her? Why did I hate her? She set him on me like a *dog*."

"That must have been awful," Michael said quietly. "I'm so sorry she did that to you."

"Well"—Gemma straightened—"I soon dealt with *him*."

"Dealt with him?" Michael nuzzled her hair. I thought I might puke. "What do you mean?"

"I...you know."

He drew back, frowning and shaking his head. She didn't like him moving further away from her. As he stood and stepped back, she stood and stepped forward. "I killed him. I had to. Just like Hale. She thought a transparent lie would protect you?" Gemma laughed. "I'm the one who actually *dealt with it*."

Gemma tilted her head up, smiling up at him with a kind of awestruck, radiant expression on her face.

As if she were staring into the face of a god.

Charlie lifted a finger to his ear; I assumed, confirming with whoever was in that van that, yes, they'd got that. He nodded at another man about his age, less physically fit, balding, in a suit I suspected had once been tailored to him perfectly but had now gone a little snug.

"Gemma Foster?" he said formally.

Gemma turned to look at him, irritated by the interruption. "*What?*"

"You're under arrest for the murders of Eric Hale and Christopher Fieldhouse—"

So that was the Clerk's real name.

"—you do not have to say anything. However, it may harm

your defence if you do not mention something when questioned, which you later rely on in court. Anything you do say may be given in evidence."

Gemma laughed and turned back to Michael. "I guess they let *anyone* in here."

"I'm sorry, Gemma," he said, shaking his head and stepping back. Further back this time. Out of her reach.

She tilted her head, raising her eyebrows, then tried to step forward again. To be near him again. "For what?"

A police officer gently caught her arm with a firm grip, preventing her getting closer. She stared down at the hand restraining her, frowning, looking back towards Michael. "Mike?"

Oh god. She really has no idea what's happening.

"I'm sorry we didn't see this," he said softly. "I'm sorry we didn't get you help when you needed it." His head dropped. "I'm sorry for everything."

The police moved in, cuffing Gemma. Somewhere near the door, someone must have caught sight of the drama unfolding outside. It rippled through the room as guests turned, flocking to the windows with muttered questions, gasps, and pointing phones, filming everything as they watched an officer cuff Gemma's hands before her.

"Michael?"

They led her away. Another officer stepped forward, and gestured for Michael to follow him. He did, while Charlie trailed in their wake, as officers held back the throngs of nosy onlookers and kept them in the old mill. Shoving through them, I tried to get out, but was stopped by a tall, burly officer who wasn't interested in listening to my garbled explanation of being part of the sting.

Luckily, Charlie caught sight of me and waved to the officer to let me out, before I embarrassed myself any further with the use of the word 'sting'.

The crowd's murmurs grew louder as reality set in around us. Outside, I shivered. We watched them usher Michael away somewhere they could remove his wire, take his statement or whatever, and this would finally, *finally* be over.

Gemma, wide-eyed and stumbling, kept struggling to follow Michael, calling his name. She didn't scream or shout. Didn't even seem to notice the cuffs on her wrists or the officer who was pointedly removing a large, ornate dagger from her purse and placing it in an evidence bag.

She just had that in her purse?

Christ.

Despite the PCs' best efforts to gently cajole her into a patrol car, Gemma kept jerking away from their grip, eyes locked desperately on Michael as if hoping he'd change his mind. The look she shot at the cops every time they stopped her seemed more confused than angry. And when reality finally dawned, and her face scrunched up as tears flooded her eyes and spilt down the front of her dress, I got the distinct impression she was not crying because she had been caught.

She was crying because Michael had walked away and left her.

"There but for the grace of god," I muttered.

"No, Amelia. You're nothing like her." Charlie stepped closer as three officers finally managed to wrangle a now-sobbing Gemma to a police car.

A female police officer I thought was the one who had come to my house guided her in, one hand protectively guarding the immaculately slicked-back crown of the crying woman's head.

"You could never be *that*," Charlie said. "But I'm curious; how did you know she wouldn't suspect he was trying to trick her into confessing?"

"He smiled at her."

"And?"

He didn't get it. I couldn't blame him.

"He gave her hope," I said. "He dangled in front of her the one thing she'd desired more than anything else, pretty much her whole life. He let her believe it might actually happen. The potential of that thought, that you might *actually get* the thing that was always *impossible*. Something always just out of reach, that made you ache inside for years, die a little every time you thought about it, because you knew you could *never* have it, but you could also *never* stop picturing it, longing for it. Playing it out in your mind in excruciating detail. Over and over. Because you were addicted to it, and the exquisite pain that came with it... A person sees the slightest hope that thing might become real? They'll do anything. Say anything. They just *need it*."

Charlie considered me for a long moment, eyes searching my own. And I knew that he knew. That everything I had done for this man had been fuelled by a similarly blind, utterly unhinged desperation to have that thing I'd wanted for so long. The thing that had eluded me most of my life, yet now somehow seemed to be my life. Like it had just been waiting for me, somewhere out there in the ether.

Like it was meant to be.

And I'd known it all along. But the world kept telling me, *'No, this isn't meant for you.'*

But then I'd seen him that first morning running in the park. And he'd smiled at me. And I'd thought, *But what if it is?*

And down the rabbit hole I'd fallen. Through the looking glass I'd wandered. Into the mirror universe I'd run.

Charlie frowned. "He managed to convey all that hope with a smile?" Charlie asked. He raised an eyebrow as if he couldn't quite credit it. Or perhaps he was a little jealous.

It's a strange thing to realise anyone could wield such an effect on another, with seemingly zero effort, and little (if any) self-awareness.

"Yep," I said.

"But how?" Charlie's frown deepened.

"Because," I said, with a bittersweet smile, "he's Michael Bane."

EPILOGUE

"Well," Suzie said, craning her neck to see all the way up the canvas. "It's very...*big*."

We both took a step back, sitting on the lip of my desk to consider the painting.

"It is, isn't it," I said.

"Yes." Suzie paused, considering it. "And this room...is rather *small*."

"I never used to think so."

"No."

"But I see it now."

"Yes."

The White Hart stared out at us from the wall. Regal, ethereal, utterly perfect.

"I *love it*!" Suzie squealed. "It's like it's *become* the room."

"Right?" I said. "*Right??*"

"Of course, your mother will think it's witchcraft."

"Pfft, she still thinks that about the tea Daiyu gave her when she came to the office."

Suzie considered that. "It *is* very tasty tea. Are we sure it's *not* magic in some way? Maybe it grants wishes."

"Not possible," I said, leaning over and nudging her shoulder with my own. "Mother didn't choke on it."

We collapsed in giggles for a while. Echo padded in to see what all the fuss was about, eyed my new painting suspiciously, and retreated into the hallway.

She was not fond of the delivery men who'd brought the painting. They hadn't taken the time to fuss over her and tell her what a beautiful girl she was and make the obligatory, *"You don't have to worry about people breaking in at night!"* joke.

She'd been even less fond of the box while it waited in the hall. Considerably more concerned about the sight of me up a ladder, holding a power tool, and trying to make sure the screws needed to affix it to the wall were level.

But that was *nothing* compared to her reaction when it had actually been unpacked and hung in place.

She took one look at it, glared at me as if to say, '*Why do you hate me?' a*nd fled.

"However much did it cost?" Suzie asked.

"Not as much as it should have," I said. "Apparently, the gallery owners were appreciative of all the free publicity they got as a result of our little sting—"

"Yeah, that video of you bitch-slapping Gemma and her getting hauled off in handcuffs has like *a billion* views." Suzie picked up one of the frappuccinos she'd grabbed on the way in, stuck the (metal, reusable, because we love turtles) straw in her mouth, and sucked on it thoughtfully.

"They offered it to me at a discount. I practically bit their hand off."

A few days had passed since Gemma's arrest. News had been slow at first. Evidently, there were some complications in questioning her due to concerns over her mental health. Eventually, however, armed with the recording of her conversation with Michael, the police got a full confession.

Suzie had arrived that morning, tired of trying to convince me to answer my damn phone, and too confused by the process of trying to piece together exactly what had happened via text.

I felt bad, but I'd been so exhausted the last few days, I just hadn't had it in me to go over it and over it anymore.

Especially not on the phone. For some reason that always confuses things.

"So," Suzie said. "Gemma purposefully dropped a bomb on your budding relationship at the ball, having heard on the grapevine Michael was out on a cosy dinner date?"

Apparently, I didn't get the choice of not rehashing this at least once more. I guess I owed her that much, at least. "Yep. Apparently, that's not the norm; his flings get drinks in bars and the occasional movie, but *dinner* is a special thing."

Suzie chewed on that information for a while. "Is this a guy thing? Or a Bane thing?"

"Definitely a Bane thing."

"Huh." She sipped her drink and walked around the room, staring at the painting as she went. "Everywhere I go, it's like its eyes keep following me."

"Creepy, isn't it?"

"Yes! It's *fabulous*."

I laughed, picked up my own drink, and took a sip. "The current theory is that Gemma had been coping all these years with the comfort that the women in Michael's life were fleeting, flings, meaningless. Evidently, she was told Michael had been out to dinner with an unknown woman, stopped by his house, and overheard him chatting with Becca while they kicked a ball around in the garden. I've no idea what he said, but it was enough to convince Gemma that he might be entertaining something serious with the mystery dinner date." I sighed. "Then she goes to the ball the next night and sees that the woman in question is *me*. Lowly little me. So she was already on tenterhooks before she got a call from her father, blaming her for the imminent loss of the family business, all their wealth, and telling her she had to go fix it, or they'd lose everything."

"Christ," Suzie muttered. "And we thought your mother was difficult."

I shook my head. "He never should have put that on her. Michael spoke to Nikki, Miranda and Jessie. Apparently, Gemma was in hospital a couple of years ago after a breakdown of some kind. When she got out of the Priory, she asked her father for the job to give her some kind of purpose, something to do. Something to be proud of. Worse"—I winced—"something that had nothing to do with Michael."

"Oh god. So she was trying to move on from it all?"

I nodded, rubbing at my eyes to stop them from welling up.

"Honestly, it's kind of fucking tragic. She expected to inherit the business eventually. So, she thought she should know how it all worked." I huffed out a breath. "You should have seen how people treated her, though. So dismissive, almost rude. Like they didn't want to be seen speaking to her. Nobody took her seriously. Had she not hung on to her little inner circle from high school all these years, she'd have been completely alone."

"Serves her fucking right," Suzie said.

I winced. "You know, despite everything, I feel sorry for her. The thought of her pining away in the wings all those years, never dating anyone, never leaving town. You know she did the same degree course as him?"

Suzie shook her head. "I didn't know what happened to her after we left."

I nodded. "I hadn't a clue. Michael hadn't mentioned it. I'm actually fairly sure he'd forgotten about it until the police asked. But yeah, she did. And commuted with him every day. Train rides and walks through town, seminars and lectures, and studying together. All that, all those years, just waiting for him to notice her..."

"And I thought you had it bad," she quipped. At the look on my face, she winced. "Don't start thinking that. You're nothing like her. You moved away, got your degree, dated a ton of guys—"

"Easy..."

"—dated a handful of guys. Had a serious relationship that we all thought was going to lead to marriage. Said fuck you to your boss, fuck you to your boyfriend, and built yourself a business from scratch. Yeah, you ended up back here, but you're a badass boss bitch these days. And she's...just been stuck here this whole time." Suzie huffed out a sigh. "It's depressing to think about."

"That's what I mean... I want to hate her. I mean, I did hate her. But mostly, I just pity her."

"Don't get too nice," Suzie warned. "She would have come for your next, I'm sure of it."

I thought about that. "Maybe," I conceded. "Isla did say she'd come in the morning after the ball. Isla was pleased; she'd heard of Foster Connections and knew they were local, she thought we had a potentially big fish interested in us taking over their marketing and chatted to Gemma for quite a while. But apparently Gemma just asked a load of questions that, in hindsight, were rather odd."

"Shut the fuck up!"

"Yep." I sipped my frappe. "Whatever her father said to her that night tipped her over the edge. She went to Hale's to kill him. Couldn't bring herself to do it. Then she saw Michael and..."

"Christ," Suzie muttered. "You have to wonder—"

"Don't!" I warned. "He's driving himself nuts with guilt, wondering if she'd ever have done it if he hadn't turned up when he did. Or if she'd have bottled it, gone home, and left her father to handle it."

Suzie scoffed. "But he can't blame himself for that! Clearly, she was unhinged to be there with a knife to hand in the first place?"

"Exactly," I said. "She seems to have suffered some kind of break from reality. Everything her father said, everything she was seeing, all merged into one weird narrative in her head, and she thought she was doing the right thing." I swallowed. "What bothers me..." I hesitated before admitting it. "...is that I'm not entirely sure she wasn't."

"Aimee!" Suzie stood, gawping at me, then thought about it for a minute. "You mean because of who Hale was?"

I nodded.

"And what he did?"

Another nod.

She pursed her lips. "He wasn't the only person she killed, though."

"True."

"And if she was poking around at your office, she really might have been coming for you next."

I blew out a long breath. "I'm not sure she knew what she was doing by then."

"Did Isla say what she was asking?"

I shook my head. "No. News broke about Hale, and she was so worried about her father's involvement that she forgot to tell me. She only realised when she saw the footage from the art gallery on social media and recognised Gemma. Then she freaked out."

"How's she doing now?"

I shrugged. "I've no idea. She seems okay, all things considered. But given everything she's found out about her father, she has to be in pieces."

Suzie wrinkled her nose. "He's always been a dick, though, and she knew that, right?"

"Yes. But there are degrees. Whatever Stanton's personal involvement in all this, the upshot is that a paedophile walked free because of a payoff her father made, and two people died as a result. That can't be easy to live with, even if you assume he wasn't directly pulling the strings. And he was definitely pulling strings."

Suzie was frowning, and I was touched at her concern for Isla. I shared it. We all did. The team had closed ranks round her in the midst of all the media attention. Rosalie was like a mamma bear defending her cub. Brennan didn't let her out of his line of sight when they were in the office, unless she was going to the bathroom.

"We'll look after her," I said, more to reassure myself than Suzie. "At least as much as we can. We've been trying to keep things as normal as possible for her. Not sure how we can help with the psychological fallout. Especially if her father's prosecuted."

Suzie's eyebrows went up. "Is that likely? I thought he was above such things? Fancy lawyers and all."

I shrugged. "They've arrested Gemma's dad for...coercion, I think Charlie said. So far, they've not touched Stanton."

"But he knew Gemma had killed Hale and tried to frame Michael!" Suzie cried. And again, I was touched by the indignation in her voice where Michael was concerned.

Apparently, he was growing on her.

"*Technically*, it was Rick Sandford who knew what Gemma had done, and it was Rick running the smear campaign against Micheal. Sandford has admitted that the Clerk got them to run the social campaign and set up surveillance on Hale. But Rick never spoke to Stanton directly or anyone else at the company. He was fine doing the social stuff as it meant dicking with me."

Suzie made a noise disturbingly like a growl. I patted her arm.

"But—" I continued, "—he swears blind he refused to do the surveillance at first. They're not PIs, and Stanton has....*had*—" I corrected myself, "—a perfectly good private dick. But the threat of losing Stanton's business was enough to convince Rick he had to do it. Trouble is, Stanton's lawyers are arguing the Clerk was told to contain the situation through any legal means necessary. Anything he did beyond that was of his own volition and not by Stanton's order."

Suzie snorted.

"Exactly. But how do you prove otherwise? Charlie's still trying to put enough together to prosecute."

"So, how did the other guy end up dead?" Suzie asked.

"Apparently, the Clerk was trying to get Gemma to tie up their loose ends by planting the murder weapon on Michael." I shook my head. The thought still made me furious. "I assume that once she'd killed Hale, they figured they might as well take advantage of the situation. And I would imagine they were also trying to cover their own backs and distance Hale, and by extension Stanton Media, from the whole thing. But they underestimated Gemma's feelings for Michael."

"It was the one thing she'd never do," Suzie said.

I nodded. "Suggesting it got the Clerk killed. Although, in all honesty, I'm not sure anyone at Stanton Media ever thought Gemma or her father would *kill* anyone. From what Charlie said, Stanton put pressure on Gemma's dad to hire Hale for a role at a new office they had just opened in Dubai. Get him out of the country, out of the way. Mr Foster felt backed into a corner, knowing how ruthless Stanton can be, and concluded the same thing Michael had; that Stanton could tank his whole company fairly easily if he wanted to."

"So he didn't actually threaten that?"

I shrugged. "Maybe. Maybe not. Either way, Gemma's dad called her in a rage, telling her to take care of it. He got her so riled up, blaming her for everything and making her feel like shit that she got completely the wrong end of the stick."

Suzie's jaw dangled, and her eyes went wide. "You've got to be kidding me?"

I shook my head. "Nope. We always thought it was a massive overreaction on Stanton's part. Turns out it wasn't *his* overreaction. Gemma acted on her own delusional thinking or a misunderstanding of what her father said. Her dad made the whole situation sound dire, freaking out over what they could potentially do. He either didn't explain properly, or she heard 'take care of it' and leapt to her own conclusions. She thought she was doing the right thing, saving the company, saving Michael. Her dad thought she was just going over there to pack Hale's bags, drive him to the airport, and put him on a plane."

"That's so sad."

I frowned. "Don't feel bad for Hale, Suze–"

"For Gemma!" Suzie exclaimed. "She'd ruined her life. And all over a misunderstanding."

I chewed on my straw and tilted my head at the stag, suddenly worried it wasn't hanging perfectly straight after all. "People don't jump to murder as the solution unless there's already something seriously broken inside," I said after a moment.

"True," Suzie conceded. "But her dad was clearly aware she had issues, put huge pressure on her, and sent her off to deal with a *paedophile* in the middle of the night, *alone*?" She made a noise of pure disgust. "Is it any wonder she broke?"

"Maybe not." I sighed.

Suzie sipped her frappuccino. "I wonder what Gemma's mother thinks of all this."

"She's paid for a stampede of lawyers, I know that."

"Doesn't mean much," Suzie said. "She'd do that to protect her precious reputation no matter what she thought of her daughter."

"Maybe. But she's leaving her husband to rot."

"Huh." Suzie sipped her drink. "Maybe there's hope for her yet."

"I guess," I said. "Either way, it seems Gemma's lawyers are trying to gloss over a few unfortunate details in order to shore up their arguments for keeping her out of jail and sending her to a nice cosy facility somewhere instead."

Echo whined from the hall, and I absently patted my leg. She padded over reluctantly, jumping up for a reassuring hug. I petted her.

"Charlie says forensics confirmed the same knife was used for both murders. The blood of both victims is on Gemma's ugly bracelet. They'd found the clothes she'd been wearing both times, also covered in blood. Apparently, she tried to get the blood out with *Vanish*."

Suzie rolled her eyes. "Amateurs."

"Right?"

"I guess we'll never really understand it." Suzie turned to check out the painting from yet another angle. "Maybe that's a good thing. Like, if it made sense to us, wouldn't that mean we're as mad as she is?"

I shrugged. "Probably. Although...given how much I just spent on this painting, an argument *could* be made."

Suzie gave me a sidelong look. "What happened to Michael buying it for you?"

"I can buy my own ridiculously large, far-too-big-for-the-room, stunning white stag paintings, thank you."

Suzie waved her frappe at me. "And flowers, too."

"Woman, if you start singing Miley Cyrus, we're going to have issues."

She cackled. I left her pottering about the garden, camera in hand, and headed to the office. I'd been there far too infrequently lately, and the work was piling up to an overwhelming point.

Isla handed me a coffee as I walked through the door. I was about to ask her to start calling all the people waiting for me to ring them back when the front door swung open again behind me. Echo barked her happy yips and launched herself at the man walking in through it.

Michael Bane.

"Hey," he said.

"Hi." I took two swigs of my coffee, pretending I wasn't nervous at the sight of him. "How's Becca?"

A grin split his face, and my nerves vanished. "So good," he said, "she walked three full laps of the ward while I was there."

"Three?" I gasped. "That's *amazing*! Has her eye opened yet?"

"She can see shadows." He grinned proudly. "The doctors think she should recover her sight. She might need glasses and possibly corrective surgery to see perfectly, and she has some scarring around the eye that she *hates*, but"—he choked a little—"she'll see."

I hugged him, almost tipping my coffee all over him in the process.

"We're all so glad to hear it, Michael," Isla said, taking my coffee cup from me with a pointed look and retreating to a safe distance.

"Thanks," he said. Then louder, "Really, guys. Thank you all so much. You've been amazing."

There were murmured words, nods, well wishes. Quietly, I was relieved the police had kept Michael's misadventure with Hale out of things. As far as the world was concerned, he'd been exactly where he'd said he was that night; with me. It wouldn't have changed how I felt about him, even if it had come out or did come out in the future. But it might have changed how my team saw him, and I'd have hated that.

He'd have hated that.

I shuffled on my feet, wishing I'd worn higher heels. "Have they said when she can go home?" I asked when everyone else had run out of pleasantries.

"Early next week, hopefully," he said.

"That's great!"

We stared at each other.

"Well," I said.

"So," he said at the same time.

I dropped my voice to a whisper. "I guess there's no need for us to 'date' anymore, huh."

He nodded. "Nope."

Ouch.

Oh, come on, what did you expect?

"Well," I said, "see you around then."

"I'm sure I'll see you in the park."

I nodded. "Of course."

He said goodbye to everyone and walked out of the door.

Echo whined.

I knew exactly how she felt.

"Some good news, boss."

I turned to look at Rosalie.

"Caster Libre signed this morning."

"That's fantastic, Ros. Well done."

"New lionfish called Nala level of well done?" She winked at me.

"Naturally."

She inclined her head. "It was mostly you, to be fair. We've been getting floods of interest since the story broke." She shrugged. "The trick is filtering out the time wasters."

"Well, in that case, it will have to be a pair of lionfish. But you're still a marvel," I said, and meant it. "Isla, can you make a start on my callback sheet, please? Let's see how fast I can get through them. Who's first?"

"Hillary."

I dropped my head. "Of course."

The front door swung open, and Michael strode back in, fixing me with a determined gaze. His steps were quick, closing the distance between us so rapidly that I didn't have a chance to react. Then his arm caught me round the waist, and in a single, swift, graceful move, he dipped me down towards the floor, his lips sealing on mine.

Slowly, he stood us back upright and released me. A wolfish grin split his face.

I cleared my throat. "You look mightily pleased with yourself."

"Why wouldn't I? I just bagged the best girlfriend in Cheshire."

I raised an eyebrow. "Presumptuous."

"Accurate."

I huffed. He took that as acceptance. "Dinner later?" he asked.

"Are you cooking?" I returned.

"Not tonight. Tonight, I want to show you off."

"Why?"

"Because," he said, with a bright smile, "you're Amelia fucking Thornbridge."

For those who like a good local legend, here is The Legend of the White Hart, and a bit of old-school Ashfordby folklore. In case it isn't obvious, this is entirely fictional, and not a real local legend! Enjoy…

THE LEGEND OF THE WHITE HART

Legend tells of the White Hart, a mystical creature that roams Cheshire's green fields and rolling hillsides. A great stag. Seldom glimpsed, yet unforgettable. His shining coat is as white as the purest snow. Atop his wise head, colossal antlers rise like the boughs of some ancient, mossy tree.

The tale goes that the White Hart appears only to those who find themselves at one of life's crossroads. To see the stag is both a blessing and a challenge. An elusive quarry for hunters, those who pursue the White Hart are led down unexpected paths. Through shaded woods and hidden glens, this beautiful creature reveals those places within us we never dared explore.

To pursue the White Hart is to seek your truest character and deepest desires.

Centuries ago, when winter's grip had finally faded and bluebells carpeted the earth, a young and gallant knight hunted the great woods of Cheshire. After hours roaming the trees, he spied the magnificent White Hart. Enchanted, the knight (whose name is lost to history) chased the Hart deep into the forests of Alderley, across the sandstone of the Edge itself, where the elderflowers were tangled through the hedgerows and lavender was just starting to bloom in the thickets.

Long rode the knight, spurred by the thrill of the chase and occasional glimpses of the Hart's glowing, ethereal coat, dancing in the brush ahead. He charged through Delamere and the great expanse of the forest there, where the trees were cloaked in a perpetual mist and echoed with the calls of hidden creatures. In a labyrinth of ancient trees and shadowy paths, the White Hart seemed to dance just beyond reach, weaving through the thickets and twining vines of honeysuckle, always just out of the knight's reach.

Days stretched into nights that became longer days. The knight rode on, finding himself in the shadow of the great castle at Beaston. Weary from the pursuit, he paused to rest within the cool stone walls and gazed out across the Cheshire plains from atop the rocky crag. Just as he thought he might give up the chase and remain, a flash of white amidst blue and violet spikes of wild clary drove the knight back to his horse, and on he rode, descending into the valley and following the River Bollin as it wound its way through fields of meadowsweet, past a small, hidden fall of water that whispered secrets of old, and into the foothills of high peaks.

All through the fields and forests, they roamed until finally, the knight drew into a clearing thick with briar roses and the golden glow of dappled sunlight. Here, he waited, gathering roses in armfuls and laying them on a great stone at the centre of the clearing. Tethering his horse to a nearby tree, the knight waited, and as twilight rolled through the trees, and the moon bathed him with her silver kisses, the great White Hart appeared.

Silent as the gathering darkness, the knight raised his bow, poised to strike as the great stag approached the altar of roses. But as his arm drew back to fire, the knight was captivated by the creature's otherworldly beauty and lowered the bow to the earth. The stag's ears twitched, and his head turned to regard the knight for a long moment. Their eyes met, and a sense of deep and abiding peace swept through the young man, stealing the breath from his lungs.

He closed his eyes for a long moment, and when he opened them, the great White Hart was gone. Dazed, the knight stumbled and tripped through the clearing to where the stag had stood. There, in the soft earth, amidst the sunken prints of the magnificent beast's hoofs, briar roses bloomed anew. The snap of a twig startled the knight from his reverie, and he turned to see a beautiful young maiden step from the trees. Moonlight shone from her white blonde hair, and her feet were muddy and bare to the earth. He supposed she had once worn a fine gown, but branches and thorns had taken their toll, and it was tattered about her shoulders.

"Did you see it?" she asked softly, eyes bright with the magic of the Hart as she shivered in the fickle light of the moon. The knight nodded, removing his long woollen cloak and holding it out to her. She took it, whispering her thanks, and bent to marvel at the roses blooming in ever-thickening abundance all about their feet. She slumped, exhausted, on the great slab of stone and lay down to sleep. The knight tucked his cloak about her to keep away the chill and sat watch all through the night. At dawn, he drew the axe he carried strapped to his horse and raised it, not in battle, but in determination. He set to the trees surrounding the clearing and, before long, had raised a modest hut amidst the delicate blooms and thorns of roses.

There he remained, with his fair-haired maiden, abandoning his title and lands to become a guardian of the forest. It is said that sometimes, in the quiet of the evening, the knight can still be seen walking the woods, hand in hand with his love and joined, on occasion, by the great White Hart, who greets them both as old and dear friends.

To this day, the White Hart remains a symbol of the journey to self-discovery and the unexpected paths we tread. Those who claim to have seen the White Hart speak of how they were irrevocably transformed, of profound revelation, loves found and lost, and truths too poignant to ignore. To see the White Hart is a rare gift and a sign of great and marvellous things to come. For young lovers to glimpse the pearlescent glow of the beast is said to be an omen of great passion, abiding love, of a long future lying ahead, just around the next tree, in a clearing in the forest where the briar roses bloom.

ABOUT THE AUTHOR

Briar has been a professional copywriter for many years (far more than she cares to admit). She began her career working for large companies and agencies before realising she could do it all for herself. Now, she happily writes for businesses and entrepreneurs she's passionate about and dreams of the day her fiction becomes popular enough for her to retreat into fictional worlds full-time. Growing up in Cheshire and falling in love with its countryside, small towns, and villages, she's enjoyed creating a fictional world that reflects her own.

For updates on Briar's latest work, book reviews, and other musings, visit her website at **BriarBlack.com**, or follow her on Instagram, TikTok, and Facebook **@BriarBlackBooks**.